The Sowers Trilogy

HARVEST OF TRUTH

D0628124

Books in the Sowers Trilogy series:

Where Freedom Grows
In Fields of Freedom
Harvest of Truth

The Sowers Trilogy

HARVEST OF TRUTH

BONNIE LEON

BROADMAN
&HOLMAN
PUBLISHERS

Nashville, Tennessee

© 2000
by Bonnie Leon
All rights reserved
Printed in the United States of America

0-8054-1274-3

Published by Broadman & Holman Publishers, Nashville, Tennessee
Editorial Team: Vicki Crumpton, Janis Whipple, Kim Overcash
Page Design: Anderson Thomas Design, Nashville, Tennessee
Page Composition: Leslie Joslin
Cover Design: Steve Diggs & Friends, Nashville, Tennessee
Cover Illustration: Janice Leotti, Artworks, New York

Dewey Decimal Classification: 813
Subject Heading: FICTION
Library of Congress Card Catalog Number: 99-045733

Library of Congress Cataloging-in-Publication Data
Leon, Bonnie.
Harvest of truth / Bonnie Leon.
    p.   cm. — (The Sowers Trilogy, bk. / 3)
ISBN 0-8054-1274-3 (pbk.)
1. Russian Americans—Fiction. I. Title.
PS3562.E533H37   2000
813'.54—dc21

99-045733
CIP

1 2 3 4 5   04 03 02 01 00

ACKNOWLEDGMENTS

I wish to thank the Russian and American people who made this journey. If not for their courage and endurance, there would be no story.

And I praise God whose limitless love and constant presence produces strength out of weakness. For it is He who enables us to take up the Sword of Truth and face the enemy.

GLOSSARY

Balalaika: A three-stringed Russian musical instrument with a triangular body.

Balanda: Trash soup with a wretched odor. It was made with fish, including the bones, and sometimes contained grains. Leaves were often found floating in it.

Dochka: Little daughter.

Draniki: Grated potato pancakes.

Isolator: An open dugout used to punish prisoners in work camps. During the winter months, prisoners often froze in the isolator. Death was hastened by guards who poured water onto the prisoners. During the summer months, lime was sometimes dumped on the enslaved.

Man trip: An open train of cars used to transport miners in and out of mines.

Mamochka: Mama

Matroshka dolls: Also known as "nesting dolls" they are made of wood and hand painted. A set includes five dolls nestled inside one another, each being slightly larger than the one before.

NKVD: People's Commissariat of Internal Affairs— administered police organizations in Russia from 1917–1946.

Pashka: A rich and tasty mixture of sweetened cheese curds, butter, and raisins.

Rope rider: A man who brings the cars up and down in the mines.

Stolypin wagon: Prison wagons used to transport prisoners on the railroad.

Trip: Anytime a car went into or out of the mine, it was called a trip. The cars carried coal, tools, and men.

Zek: Prisoners

CHAPTER 1

Yuri forced himself to keep putting one foot in front of the other. It wouldn't be long now. He didn't know exactly how far he and Alexander had come, but it had to be nearly a couple thousand kilometers. Since fleeing the train wreck, they'd walked, hitched rides on wagons, and hopped trains while dodging railroad officials. Now he was almost home. They'd spent days and nights hiding in wheat fields and deserted barns, gladly accepting offers of work and food. When there were no offers, berries and plants helped ward off hunger, and small rodents and rabbits provided meager meals. The journey had been long, but now their destination was at hand.

Empty fields faded into a line of distant trees. Yuri peered down the road, hoping to catch a glimpse of his parents' farm. His heart told him to run, to hurry home, but his long legs had no strength to obey. Brushing dirty, brown hair off his face, he wiped his forehead with the back of his hand and glanced at the sun. Its heat pressed down, and he longed for an August rain shower. Wind picked up dust from the road and swirled it across the barren pastures.

Yuri's mouth felt as parched as the land, and he longed for a drink of water.

"How close are we to your family's farm?" Alexander asked.

"Very. It's just around that bend, beyond that grove of trees." His stomach knotted. If only they would be there. *You're being foolish,* Yuri told himself. *They're dead.* But as he drew closer, he continued to hope. He wanted to believe.

They followed the road past the trees. In the old days, his father would be standing waist-deep in golden grass swinging his scythe. He searched the field, but it was empty. He had known it would be.

His mother had always planted a large vegetable garden between the house and road. As he walked up the drive, he wanted to see her there. But the garden plot was empty. A broad band of clumpy dirt with sections of scraggly grass stood where the lush vegetable patch had once been. He stopped and stared at the small farm. A sharp breeze bent the birches growing along the road, the rustling of leaves sounding hollow in the peculiar quiet.

No chickens scratched in the yard, and no horses or cows grazed in the fields. Fences were more down than up, and weeds had overgrown much of the yard. A glass window in the front of the house was shattered, its wooden shutter hanging at an angle. Tufts of grass grew from the roof.

Yuri's chest ached and his throat tightened.

Nearly half a head taller than Yuri, Alexander silently stood beside his friend.

"I couldn't help hoping . . . my parents would be here—that it would be as it once was." Shielding his eyes from the sun, he continued, "I knew I was being foolish, but . . ."

CHAPTER 1

"Hope is never foolish." Alexander laid his hand on Yuri's shoulder and squeezed gently. "Do you want to go into the house?"

Yuri looked into Alexander's deep-set eyes and nodded. The two men walked side-by-side toward the rutted, overgrown driveway and, without hesitation, turned into the lane. Memories tumbled through Yuri's mind. He remembered how as a boy, he'd clung to the back of his young gelding, leaping fences and racing across the fields, his sandy hair swept back by the wind.

He could almost see his father standing atop a great mound of hay on the back of their wagon while Yuri handed up pitchforks full of golden grass. Yuri could almost smell the fragrance of fresh-cut hay. His mother used to bring cold water from the well, and Yuri and his father would guzzle it, then chat a while. Sometimes his sister Tatyana joined them, and often she collected wildflowers to take back to the house. But when the soldiers came and took his parents, all that had ended. And since sending Tatyana to America, he was all alone. Now there were only memories

His grief fresh, Yuri stepped up to the door. He stood with his hand on the weathered wood but didn't enter.

"Are you sure you want to go in? You don't have to."

"I do have to." Taking a deep breath, Yuri pushed the door open and stepped inside. Immediately he was enveloped by darkness and the musty smell of disuse. He waited for his eyes to adjust then took another step. Little was left of what he'd once known. A wooden chair with a missing leg and a busted back lay on its side beneath the front window, and a broken-down sofa stood against the opposite wall. Dust layered the few furnishings. Cobwebs like ancient lace encased the single light hanging from the ceiling, stretched to the corners of the room, and framed the windows.

Yuri picked up a torn book page from the floor. He read it, then tucked the paper into his pocket.

"What is that?" Alexander asked.

"A poem, a page from one of Pasternak's books. He was one of Tatyana's favorite poets," Yuri said sadly. Stepping into the kitchen and opening a cupboard, he found a single cracked plate. Taking the earthen dish from the shelf, he recalled how his mother had cherished the set of glassware she'd inherited from her mother. "Every evening Mama would set these out, and sometimes she'd tell us stories about her days as a young girl," Yuri said. He ran his hand over the plate, and without warning it broke in half. One section clattered to the floor. Stunned, he stared at the broken pieces and then carefully set the unbroken portion back in the cupboard.

A gunnysack hung from the edge of the counter. Yuri casually examined it and let it drop. As he wandered through the house, he tried to recapture the laughter and music that had once been part of his life. He closed his eyes and thought about the way Tatyana used to dance around the front room, her arms gracefully outstretched and her long blonde hair cascading over her shoulders. Like an unapproachable shadow, the memory flickered through his mind and was too quickly gone.

He walked into the tiny room where he'd slept, dreamt, and studied. He didn't remember it being so small. His bed was gone and so were the photographs of horses and palatial homes he'd cut from newspapers and magazines and hung on his walls. He smiled as he remembered how he'd longed to become a part of the aristocracy. *How foolish I was then,* he thought.

He stood at the window. Like the others, the glass was gone. He gazed at the distant trees bordering the fields. As a boy, he'd often leave his books to spend time at this window, either daydreaming about what life held for him or wishing he could be astride his horse, charging through the woods or open fields.

A breeze carried the smell of distant rain and warm hay. Yuri studied gathering clouds and remembered the days when he and his family raced to beat the rain as they gathered hay into the barns. Sometimes they prevailed, and sometimes they found themselves soaked by a downpour. He smiled and realized how much he actually loved farming. *Father, will I ever be able to return to it?* he asked, hoping one day it would be his work.

"It looks like rain," Alexander said. "We could use it."

"Yes. It would feel good. And since there is no haying to be done, I would welcome a shower."

"How long has it been since you've seen your parents?" Alexander asked.

Unexpectedly Yuri's mind filled with the image of his parents standing in the back of a government transport truck, his father's arm wrapped protectively about his mother's shoulders. Tears burned Yuri's eyes. His father's last words were, "We will live." He'd waved at his children as the truck pulled away.

Still seeing his parents, Yuri quietly said, "The soldiers came September 1930. It's been five years." He let his breath out slowly. "No one has heard from them. They were either executed or sent to prison and then to a work camp." His eyes roamed over the room. "I miss them." Yuri squared his shoulders. "I want to see if Aunt Irina is still on her farm. She hasn't seen me or Uncle Alexander since we were arrested. She knows nothing about how her husband died. I need to tell her. And it would be good to see my cousins." He looked at Alexander. "Is that all right with you? Is there anyone you need to see?"

"No. The only place I ever knew before my arrest was Kazan. And I have no family left." He hesitated, then with a half smile, said, "I'm happy to visit your aunt and then go on to Moscow."

The two left the house. Yuri stopped for a moment and looked back at the cottage. "I had a good life here." He turned and walked toward the road.

✻ ✻ ✻ ✻ ✻

Irina's farm was deserted, the house in disrepair. Clearly it had been empty for many months. In the barn, the ladder he'd used to climb into the loft and hide food still rested against the upper level.

Smiling, he folded his arms and gazed at the large room. He could still hear the tune of the balalaika, mandolin, and tambourine and feel the floor pulsate as friends danced in celebration. "The last night I was here, we had a party. It was my cousin's wedding." He leaned against the ladder and placed the heel of his boot on a rung. "The next day my uncle and I were arrested for stockpiling food. They found me hiding leftovers from the night before, up there." He pointed to the upper loft. "And they also discovered grain we'd hidden beneath the hay stacks. That was the last time I saw this place."

"Remembering is sometimes painful," Alexander said.

"Yes and sometimes good. I'm glad for the beautiful memories." Yuri plucked a piece of hay from a bale remnant and chewed on the end of it. "So, what do you think we should do now? Stay here or go to Moscow? Danger waits for us in both places."

Alexander walked to the door and looked out. "Some decisions are difficult to make. My father once said, 'When there seems no clear answer, search your heart. It will guide you.'" He turned back to Yuri. "What is your heart telling you?"

Yuri joined Alexander at the door and leaned against the frame. "I don't know. I knew it was foolish hoping to find my family, but I couldn't help myself. I didn't think much beyond that. We need a plan. I have friends in Moscow, if they're still there. Before I was imprisoned, we worked together in the underground. I told you about Daniel and Tanya? And Elena," he added, his heart quickening at the possibility of seeing her again.

"Uh huh."

"They will help and may be able to get us identification papers." He hesitated. "They might even help me get to America." He studied Alexander closely. "Have you ever considered leaving Russia?"

CHAPTER 1

Alexander shook his head slowly. "I have thought on it. But I belong here. I cannot leave."

"I feel the same but sometimes wonder if there is anything I can do here that would make a difference. And my sister . . . it would be good to see her again." He tossed the piece of straw to the ground. "I don't know what I will do."

"I understand your need to leave Russia, but I cannot. This is my home, and God is my family."

"I don't *know* if I'll go. I've just been thinking about it. My family is gone. The only one left is Tatyana. When I sent her away, I told her I would follow her one day." He folded his arms and studied the farm. "It's probably impossible. I don't know why I'm even talking about it." He pushed one side of the double doors open a little further. "I say we go on to Moscow. There's nothing for us here."

"What about the police? Security will be tighter in the city."

"Yes, but if we settle here someone might turn us in. The NKVD is everywhere. We need new identification papers."

"And work papers," Alexander said as he took a step into the yard. "What kind of work is there in Moscow?"

"When I lived in Moscow, Stalin had implemented many new programs. They were building new roads and constructing an underground rail system. And there is always factory work."

"You know, if we're caught we'll be executed."

Without looking at him, Yuri said, "There are worse things."

Alexander chuckled. "Yes. We've experienced some of them."

Yuri straightened and moved into the shadows. "Someone is coming," he whispered.

Alexander stepped backwards into the barn.

A man hobbled toward them. Yuri studied him. "That looks like Velodya Amalchenko," he whispered.

"Do you know him?"

"He was one of our neighbors."

The stooped man continued walking toward the barn. He was bent so far over that he looked at the ground, the top of his balding head preceding him.

The old man stopped and slowly lifted his head. He stared at the barn. Blinking hard several times, he peered at the shadowed place just inside the door where Yuri stood. "Is someone there? Who's there?"

Hesitantly, Yuri stepped into the light.

Wrinkling his grizzled face and scrunching up his eyes, the man gazed at Yuri. "Who are you?" His eyes widened and his mouth opened. "Yuri? Is that you, Yuri Letinov?"

"It is." Yuri took another step forward. "Mr. Amalchenko?"

A grin brightened his lined face. "My Lord! Ivan's boy!" He limped forward and held out a shaking hand. "Yes, it's me. I'm still here." He gripped Yuri's hand and held it. "It's good to see you. Everyone thought you dead. After the soldiers came, the whole village went into mourning. I never believed I'd see you again."

The old man felt like family, and Yuri could feel joy well up. "I made it with God's help," Yuri said, smiling broadly. Still hanging onto the old man's hand, he added, "It is so good to see you again."

Velodya glanced at Alexander. "And who is this with you?"

"Alexander Zharova—a friend."

Alexander stepped forward and shook the old man's hand. "I am honored to meet you, Mr. Amalchenko."

The man squinted at the tall stranger. He seemed to be determining whether or not he could trust Alexander. Finally, he said, "I am glad to meet you." He looked past Yuri and Alexander into the barn. "Yuri, I think the last time I saw you was at Lev's wedding. That was quite a party." His eyes sparkled at the memory.

"It was," Yuri agreed. "Now so many are gone. Why are you still here? The nearby farms look deserted."

"I'm too old for the collectives, so the government left me alone. There are a few of us elderly folks scattered around but not many. We help each other as much as we can. I don't have much, but I manage to eat and keep my house heated through the winters."

"What happened to my aunt Irina and cousins Serge and Anna, and Lev and Olya?"

Tears sprang into the old man's eyes. Taking a handkerchief out of his back pocket, he wiped his eyes and nose. "They tried to stay. But the soldiers came back again and again, taking what little food they had. They were starving. Your young cousins and Lev and Olya's baby needed to eat. They would have died. Your aunt Irina decided they had to go to a collective." Snuffling into his handkerchief, he continued, "Sometimes living is the most difficult thing to do." He looked squarely at Yuri. "She did the right thing."

Yuri nodded slowly. "You said Lev had a child?"

"Oh, yes. He and Olya have a little girl. Such a sweetheart she was. I will miss watching her grow up."

"Never give up. Hope for reunions," Alexander said kindly.

The old man studied Alexander and smiled. "I think I would like to know you better." Looking at Yuri, he asked, "Will you stay?"

"No. We're going to Moscow. Hopefully we can find jobs."

"The government projects continue, new bridges, dams, and buildings, but they're created at the cost of Russian lives. Maybe it would be good if you stayed here and farmed."

Yuri looked out over the land. "I wish I could." He pulled the door closed and secured it. "And how is your family?"

"They're gone. All dead. But they believed they had no reason to live." Shaking his head and looking at the ground, he said, "It would have been better if I had gone with them."

"I'm sorry, Mr. Amalchenko. I . . ."

The old man raised his hand. "Don't be sorry. I'll join them soon." He forced a smile. "Would you like to share a meal with me?"

"Yes. We've been traveling and would like that very much."

Mr. Amalchenko looked the men up and down. "You're barely more than skin and bones. Have you been in a work camp?"

Alexander met Mr. Amalchenko's gaze. "Yes."

"Many disappear, and almost none return. Why have you?"

"With God's help, we lived through months at the work camp. We escaped when our train derailed."

Mr. Amalchenko smiled. "I'm glad you're free. I will tell no one." He hobbled toward his farm, motioning for Alexander and Yuri to follow.

Thunder echoed and rumbled across the flatlands as a raindrop fell.

CHAPTER 2

STANDING ON A HILLSIDE WITH HIS arms folded over his chest, Yuri studied Moscow. Its hulking buildings of brick and granite stared back indifferently. A cathedral's onion dome rose above the other structures. Yuri remembered the church. It was beautiful. Sorrow filled him as he realized it now stood empty. Since the state determined God didn't exist and worshiping him was illegal, many church buildings were vacant. However, God's church still flourished, if only in the underground.

"It's impressive," Alexander said.

"Have you been to Moscow before?" Yuri asked.

"No. Never."

"It is a city like many others. It almost feels like home. I spent many months here with my friends Daniel and Tanya Broido."

"They are the ones who took you and Elena in after you were nearly executed?" Alexander asked.

"Yes. I was working with them in the underground when I was arrested the second time." A cool breeze blew Yuri's hair into a tangle. "I hope we did the right thing coming here."

"Only God knows," Alexander said as he glanced around. "Maybe we can find something to eat before going into the city." Smiling, he added, "We'll have a feast."

The two hungry travelers scavenged the forest for berries and mushrooms. Finally, with pockets stuffed with fungi and hands mounded with wild fruit, they settled in the shade of a large spruce. Yuri leaned against the rough bark and set the berries on his lap. He ate one, then after brushing away bits of dirt, bit into a large mushroom. "I always liked these better cooked. My mother used to fry them with vegetables and sometimes added pork." He popped the rest of the earthy-tasting fungi into his mouth. "After winter sets in, there won't be any more scavenging." He grinned ruefully at Alexander. "Except for rats, of course."

"I'd like to put my rat-trapping days behind me. I hope we'll be working." Alexander chewed a mouthful of berries.

"When I worked on Moscow's underground rail, we had quotas. Sometimes it was hard to meet them, and our food coupons would be cut. I was hungry, but not like I am now. I would love to have food rations again."

Alexander tossed a few plump berries into his mouth. "To have enough to eat sounds like a dream." He closed his eyes and chewed contentedly. "I must say, though, I do not remember any berries tasting so sweet." He sat up straight, and holding out a berry, added, "God provides better than any government."

Yuri finished the last of his berries. Dark juice stained his lips. "These are good, but sometimes I dream of beef stew and bread. I can barely remember what beef tastes like."

Alexander ate a mushroom. "My aunt Anya used to make roasted goose. She would fix it with baby onions and carrots. Just thinking of it makes my mouth water."

Yuri looked toward the city. "Maybe Tanya will have fresh bread. She is a good cook." He took a deep breath. "I pray she and her family are all right—and Elena." Remembering that he might see Elena very soon, the rhythm of Yuri's heart picked up. For so long he'd yearned to hold her, to kiss her, and to tell her of his love. If only she still lived.

A soft breeze touched Yuri's face, and a thrush landed on a nearby bush. It cocked its head, fluffed its feathers, then darted away. "I love the summer." He plucked a white flower with a yellow center and twirled it between his fingers. *Maybe I can pick a bouquet for Elena,* he thought, but quickly dismissed the idea as being foolish. He wasn't even certain she still lived in Moscow.

"I'm excited to discover God's plans for us," Alexander said confidently as he stood. "He has already done so much." Then he looked over the city. "Future plans will have to wait. Now we need to make it into the city before dark. It will be easier to find your friends."

As Yuri pushed himself to his feet, he watched a hawk gliding on the air currents. "If only we were like the birds. Their perspective of the world must be so different from ours, more beautiful I think." He ran his hands through his hair. "We would be free to soar from one place to another, unencumbered."

"Where would you go?"

"Home." Yuri watched the bird a moment longer. "Wherever that is."

✳ ✳ ✳ ✳ ✳

The city had changed little since Yuri's arrest. Crumbling streets were crowded with gaunt, anxious-looking citizens, and men in uniform were on nearly every corner. Electric buses and horse-drawn carts vied for space in the streets. The driver of a cart loaded with produce whipped and yelled at his horse as a bus headed toward them. He barely managed to move out of the transport's path to avoid being struck. A van moved past, just like the one that had picked up Yuri months before. It trumpeted its horn at a man hobbling across the street, and Yuri jumped. Keeping his eyes on the pavement, he continued walking.

"They're only driving by," Alexander said, resting his hand on Yuri's back. "They're not going to arrest you."

Frustrated at his response, Yuri stopped and watched the van disappear around the corner. "How is it that when facing execution, I feel God's peace? And when he leads me thousands of kilometers cross country, I feel his strength? But when a van drives by, I feel fear leaping in my chest?" He balled his hands into fists. "I'm still weak, so weak."

"We all are sometimes. It's not a sign of failure, Yuri, just humanness."

Yuri nodded. Swallowing hard, he merged into the crowds of people and continued toward Daniel's apartment house. It had been a long time since he'd walked these streets, and he could feel the familiar sense of danger and exhilaration that he'd known while working with the underground. He'd always felt good about doing God's work. His faith was stronger, and he wondered how it might be different now to work with Daniel.

Passersby suspiciously eyed the haggard men in threadbare, over-sized clothing and gave them a wide berth. Yuri straightened his spine, threw his shoulders back, and willed his legs to take strong, steady steps. He hadn't seen himself in a mirror for a very long time, but he knew he must look bad.

Although the weather was warm, Yuri wore his coat. A part of his mind still believed he was in prison, and he feared the coat would be stolen if he didn't keep it on. As he crossed the street, another van slowed. Yuri glanced at the driver who stared back at him. Yuri hurried his steps.

"No one knows who we are," Alexander said. "They're not going to arrest us."

Yuri kept up his quick pace. Under his breath, he said, "You don't know this city. The police need no reason to arrest someone." As the van continued on, Yuri stopped. Looking Alexander up and down, then glancing at his own well-used and soiled clothing, he said, "We look like escapees and don't fit in. I'm surprised they didn't stop us." He stared at the back of the van as it disappeared down the roadway. "We need to get off the street."

"God has brought us all this way, Yuri. In prison and at the labor camp, he protected us. We could have died in the train accident, but instead we are free. He has a plan and will take care of us. We don't have to be afraid."

Yuri smiled. "I know, but he doesn't want us to act foolishly either." He looked down the street and pointed to a nearby intersection. "We take the next left."

At the river, they crossed a bridge and turned right onto the road running beside the bank. Daniel's apartment building still looked shabby and dingy. It seemed strange that nothing had changed. So much had happened to Yuri in the last twenty months; how could the world remain the same? Taking a deep breath, he nodded toward the block building. "That's Daniel and Tanya's place." Uncertainty welled up. "And if they're not here?"

Alexander said nothing.

Yuri's stomach quaked. Across all the miles, he'd dreamed of being here, thought about what this reunion would be like, and now, he couldn't make himself move. What if his friends had been arrested? Or what if Elena found him repulsive like the people on the street had?

Alexander walked toward the apartment building. "Which one is it?"

Pushing aside his apprehension, Yuri fell into step beside his friend. His thoughts moved from himself to his loved ones. *Please be here. Please be alive,* he thought as he stepped up to the door. No sound came from inside. "She must still be living here. I can smell fresh-baked bread." He knocked and waited. There was no reply.

"Knock again," Alexander said.

This time Yuri pounded on the door.

"Who is it?" a soft voice asked from inside.

"It is Yuri Letinov."

The door opened just a crack, and pale blue eyes filled with confusion peered out, then they opened wide with surprise and pleasure. "Yuri?"

"Yes," Yuri croaked, his throat tight. "Tanya?"

The plain-looking woman whom he'd loved as a sister threw open the door and covered her mouth with her hands. "Oh, Lord! Yuri! Praise you, Lord!" Silent for a moment, she stared at the unexpected visitor. "It's you! Yuri!" She reached out and pulled him into a tight embrace. "Oh, Yuri, Yuri," she repeated as she held him.

Tears wet the young man's face. "Tanya, I . . . I didn't know if you would even live here any more."

Tanya stepped back, took his hand, and pulled him inside. "Come in! Come in!"

"Mama, who is it?" a small voice asked. Sasha, the oldest daughter, stood in the middle of the living room. Hands behind her back, eyes narrowed in suspicion, she studied the strangers.

Yuri grinned. She looked so much older and taller. Hadn't she been only seven when he'd last seen her? Now she must be nearly nine. "Hello, Sasha."

The little girl backed up a step. Her mother placed her arm around the child's shoulders. "Sasha, this is Yuri. Do you remember our friend Yuri?"

The little girl shook her head. "No. He is not Yuri."

Tanya gave Yuri an apologetic look.

"I've been traveling many, many days, and I know I look awful, but it is me," Yuri said. He looked at Alexander. "And this is my friend, Alexander Zharova."

Sasha continued to stare.

Tanya shook Alexander's hand. "We are glad to have you here." She turned a pained look on Yuri. "We thought you were in prison or dead."

"I was in prison, and God spared my life."

"You must be hungry and thirsty. Please sit. I will get you something." Tanya walked into the kitchen and ran water into a kettle. She filled a silver ball with tea and dropped it in the pot. "It will only take a few minutes."

Yuri scanned the apartment. It looked much the same. Brightly colored throw rugs and quilts draped worn furniture. Knickknacks cluttered a small wooden shelf, and Tanya's exquisite paintings still decorated the walls. He sat on the sofa, and Alexander sat beside him. "Is Daniel all right?"

"Yes. He's out, but he will be back soon."

"And Elena?" he asked, steeling himself against the worst.

Sasha answered. "She is at Mrs. Kerensky's house playing the piano. That is where we have our church meetings. Elena plays beautiful music for us. She will be very happy when she sees you."

Joy swept over Yuri. Elena was safe! She was alive!

"I made bread today," Tanya said.

"I know. I can smell it. I've been dreaming about your bread."

"He often told me about your baking," Alexander said with a smile. "Then I would dream of it also."

Tanya cut four slices of bread from a loaf and gave each man two. "It is not my best bread. Good flour is hard to find. But it will fill your stomachs."

"This looks wonderful," Yuri said, taking a bite and forcing himself not to devour it all at once.

"Thank you," Alexander said. After offering a silent word of thanks, he ate one slice in three bites.

Tanya dragged a chair from the table and sat across from the men. Compassion in her eyes, she watched them eat. "We prayed for you every day. I know it must have been awful."

Yuri and Alexander both stopped eating. "It was," Yuri said. "But God never left us, and I'm stronger now."

Sasha approached Yuri cautiously, her dark eyes studying his face. "It really is you." Placing her hands on his shoulders, she kissed his cheek. "I'm glad you are here." Glancing at Alexander, she said, "And you also."

Yuri took the youngster's hand, and after kissing it, pressed it against his cheek. "I missed you."

The little girl's eyes brimmed with tears. "We thought you were dead. When you didn't come home, I cried. Everyone cried. Elena especially."

Tanya returned to the kitchen and filled two chipped mugs with hot tea. She handed one to each man, filled one for herself, and sat down.

"How is Daniel?" Yuri asked.

"He is well. And Valya too. She is with her father."

"Is he still working in the underground?"

"Yes. There is such a need for God's word—now more than ever." Tanya sipped her tea. "You have been traveling far?"

"Yes, many days," Alexander answered.

"You look weary. Would you like to bathe and rest?"

"A bath sounds like heaven," Yuri answered. "We've been bathing in cold rivers and streams." He looked down at himself and held out his arms. "A kind woman in Siberia gave us these clothes, and we're grateful, but they need washing and repair."

"I'm sure I have something you can wear. I have a trunk full of clothes that people have donated for those who might need them." Tanya stood and set her cup on the table. "Please, come with me. They're in my room."

Yuri and Alexander followed her to the back of the apartment. "After you have bathed and dressed, you're welcome to sleep here in our bed," Tanya said as she opened a chest packed with clothing. She sorted through the garments, taking out underclothes, pants, shirts, and socks. She handed a stack to each man. "These should fit." Going to a small closet, she pulled out a box filled with shoes. "Go through these. I hope you find something your size."

Yuri hugged the clothing against his chest. It had been so long since he'd been mothered. It felt like food for his soul. "You are a good friend. Thank you."

Tanya's eyes glistened, and she reached out and touched Yuri's arm. "It's hard to believe you're alive. For so long we prayed for your return. When you didn't, we thought you were gone forever. I thank God you are here."

🐞 🐞 🐞 🐞 🐞

Yuri heard muffled voices and rolled onto his side. Opening his eyes, he stared at dingy wallpaper and tried to remember where he was. *Daniel and Tanya's! I'm at the Belov's!* He closed his eyes and whispered, "Thank you, Lord."

Alexander was still sleeping, so Yuri moved slowly and quietly. Dropping his legs over the side of the bed, he sat up and stretched, feeling more refreshed than he had in many months. He stood, listening to the animated voices on the other side of the door. Was Elena here? His heart hammered at the thought of seeing her again; then he caught sight of his image in the mirror. All he could see were sunken cheeks, hollow eyes, and bony shoulders. The Yuri he'd once been was gone. He looked old. Would the handsome young man he'd known ever return? *What will Elena think of me?* he wondered. *She might not even recognize me.*

"I can do nothing about how I look," he said softly, combing his hair smooth with his fingers and squaring his shoulders.

Taking a deep breath and walking to the door, he turned the knob and opened the door a crack. Above the clink of dishes in the washtub, Elena asked, "So, how is he, really?"

Tanya answered, her voice somber, "He is much changed."

Yuri started to close the door and retreat to the safety of the darkened room. *No. This is something you've been dreaming about for months.* Opening the door, he stepped into the room and forced a smile. "Hello," he said quietly, pulling the door closed behind him.

Elena, Tanya, Daniel, and the girls all looked at him. He sought Elena and watched as the petite woman's dark eyes filled with pain and pity. Then Yuri thought he saw revulsion. *I repulse her,* he thought, relinquishing all plans to take Elena in his arms and profess his love.

"Yuri! Yuri!" Daniel exclaimed as he strode across the room and pulled his friend into a fragile embrace. Kissing him twice on each cheek, Daniel held Yuri at arms length and studied him. "My friend, you're a miracle!" He hugged him again, still being careful not to squeeze too hard, as if Yuri might break. "Please, come and sit. Tanya has made cabbage soup, and there is a little fish in it." He guided Yuri to the table.

Elena hurried to Yuri, and for a moment he thought she might embrace him. Instead, she took his hands. Her eyes brimming with tears, she said, "I thought I would never see you again. When you didn't come home, we thought . . ." Tears spilled onto her cheeks, and she hugged him quickly and gently.

She doesn't love me, he thought. *My dreams have been a fantasy.* He let go of her hands, although he longed to pull her into his arms. He couldn't erase the look of revulsion he was certain he'd seen in her eyes. He glanced at Daniel and then at the others. "When I was in prison I hoped that one day I would be here with you all again, but it was difficult to believe it would ever happen." Then he smiled. "Now it has come true."

Daniel sat down, and Yuri sat across from him. Brushing away a lock of black hair from his forehead, Daniel leaned forward on his arms. "It is good to have you at our table again. We have missed you."

Tanya placed the bread and a steaming pot on the table. "Is your friend still sleeping?"

"Yes."

"We will save some for him." Tanya sat beside Daniel. The older of their two daughters, Sasha, stood beside her father, and the younger, Valya, stayed close to her mother, her large, dark eyes fixed on Yuri. Dipping out a full ladle of soup, Tanya filled a bowl for each of the girls, and they took their meal to the sofa.

Daniel said quietly, "Let us thank the Lord for our blessings." He bowed his head, and so did the others. "Father in heaven, our hearts are full. You have returned our good friend to us. We praise you and thank you. You are a good God." His voice broke and he hesitated. "I am forever amazed at your love and your power. We praise you for all you do for us. Thank you for this food, and bless the one who prepared it. Amen."

He looked up and studied Yuri. "It is good to have you home."

Barely able to speak past the lump in his throat, Yuri said, "It is good to be here." He glanced at Elena, and her eyes warmed as she smiled at him. Maybe he didn't repulse her.

Daniel accepted a bowl of soup from Tanya. "Tell us; what happened to you, Yuri?"

Yuri didn't want to speak about it, but he knew the truth needed to be shared. Gripping the arms of the chair, he looked at the faces around the table. He would tell only what they needed to know, no more.

"How did you end up in prison?" Daniel pressed.

Taking a deep breath, Yuri said, "A man I'd met over a game of cards turned me in to the police. I'd told him about God, and I guess he thought if he turned in a believer things would be easier for him. He was wrong. He died in the same work camp I was in. Anyway, the NKVD arrested me. I went to Butyrka prison here in Moscow." Yuri glanced at the girls and lowered his voice. "In prison I was interrogated; then I was locked in a small cell with several other men. For months there were many interrogations and beatings." He stopped and studied his hands. "When I couldn't stand it any longer, I signed a false confession. After that, I was sent to a work camp in Siberia. I met Alexander on the train, and he and I lived in the same barracks."

"Siberia? I've heard of the camps," Daniel said. "The reports are vague. Not many come back."

"The ones who disappear face a hideous destiny. We must pray for all those who have vanished from our streets and homes."

Tanya placed a bowl of soup in front of Yuri. "Is it hopeless? Is there anything we can do?"

"Nothing is ever hopeless. We fight a spiritual battle and must use God's weapons. Nothing else is sufficient." Yuri ate a spoonful of soup, then looked squarely at Daniel. "I'm thankful for my time there. Only in adversity did I truly allow God to become my strength. Until then I didn't understand his constant, devoted presence—and his endless mercy."

Yuri dipped his bread in his broth and took a bite. "After nearly a year in the camp, Alexander and I were sent to an extermination camp further east. The train crashed, and God provided a way for us to escape. With his help we made it here."

"How did you get here?"

"We walked, rode on the wagons of kindly farmers, and rode freight cars when we could. It's not easy to avoid the railroad officials."

Daniel reached across the table and placed his hand on Yuri's forearm. "And it is good you are here, comrade."

"It is like a dream."

CHAPTER 2

Sasha returned to the table, carrying her empty bowl. "You are very brave, Yuri."

Yuri put his arm around the little girl. "Sometimes, and sometimes not." He straightened and looked at Daniel. "Are things as difficult as they were?"

"Worse. Scrutiny by the police is more intense. We must watch for them always. People are more frightened and are turning on each other in an effort to protect themselves. Even Stalin has become paranoid and is charging his top officials with treason. Many have been tried and executed. Some of his men have taken their own lives rather than be humiliated and put to death. Even our beloved poets and musicians are being arrested. Some of them have also killed themselves rather than be imprisoned.

"Although no one has attempted assassination yet, many would like to see Stalin dead. He has reason to be afraid. The truth is, if man doesn't deal with him, God will."

"What do you plan to do now?" Elena asked.

Yuri met her dark eyes. "I don't know. I need to work, but I don't have identification or work papers."

"I can help you with that," Daniel said.

Yuri took a drink of water and carefully set his cup down. Keeping his eyes on the mug, he said, "I am thinking of going to America." He looked at Daniel. "Can you help me?"

"Yes, but it will take time," Daniel answered solemnly. "We would hate to see you go."

"You have only just returned. How can you speak about leaving us and going so far away?" Elena asked.

"I have no family here. And I have an address for my sister. There was a man on the train who had helped her when she was in Leningrad. He had a letter from her with her address on it. When he showed it to me, I could hardly believe it." Tears filled Yuri's eyes as he spoke. "Even now I do not fathom God's love."

"Yuri, I could use your help here," Daniel said.

"I've thought of that, but my sister Tatyana lives in America. And I have been thinking that is where I should be. But I will pray and let God show me what is best."

CHAPTER 3

TATYANA STEPPED OUT OF THE church foyer and onto the front porch. The morning sun already felt hot. It was a good day for a church picnic. Inhaling deeply, she gazed out over the neatly mowed lawn bordered by roses. She could smell the flowers' sweet fragrance.

"It's another hot one," Dimitri said. Baby Yuri whimpered, and Dimitri transferred him to his other arm.

Tatyana smiled and caressed her son's cheek. "Do you want me to take him?"

"No. I'll keep him a few more minutes. Soon enough he'll be wanting you. It sounds like his hunger alarm is about to go off."

Josephine stepped onto the porch, and tipping her face up to the sun, said, "What a perfect day for a baptism." Smiling at Dimitri, she added, "And what a blessing you are." She turned spirited gray eyes on Tatyana. "I knew he was a fine man the first time I met him in the cafe at Snoqualmie, and with the Lord's love alight in him, I believe we'll see great things from Dimitri."

Wrapping an arm around her husband's waist, Tatyana said, "He's already a blessing to me."

Susie and Carl joined their friends on the porch. Still fanning herself with the church bulletin, Susie said in a teasing tone, "Move on, you're blocking the steps. And I need shade." Glancing at the brilliant blue sky and cradling Evelyn against her chest, she squeezed past her friends and walked down the steps. The others followed.

A dark-haired woman with a wary expression stepped out of the church.

"Oh, I forgot, there's someone I want you to meet," Susie said, pointing to the stranger and grabbing Tatyana's hand. "I met her this morning. She's just over from Russia, and I thought you two would have something in common." She dragged Tatyana back to the stairway and waited for the newcomer. "Good morning, again," Susie said. "This is my friend, Tatyana. She is from Russia too."

The woman looked at Tatyana. "I not speak good English. You from Russia?"

Tatyana felt excitement rise. Someone from her homeland! She reached out and took the woman's hand. "My name is Tatyana Letinov. I am very glad to meet you," she said in Russian.

The woman's face brightened, and she smiled. "I am Janna Kamenev." She glanced over her shoulder at a young man with dark hair and a stern expression. "That is my husband, Antar. I would introduce you, but he is talking with the minister. It is so good to have someone here from Russia."

"Have you been in America long?" Tatyana asked.

"No. We sailed from Leningrad in February. It was very cold, but I was so happy to come to America! What a wonderful country!"

Chapter 3

"You don't miss Russia?" Tatyana asked, surprised at the woman's exuberance.

"Oh, no. Well, yes, maybe a little. But I have no one there any more, and this is such a beautiful land with so many wonderful things, and it is good to be free. I look forward to every day."

"I left Russia nearly two years ago, but I still miss it. It feels so good to speak in Russian and to meet someone from my homeland."

"I know," Janna said, "but life is hard there. So many people are hungry, and there are soldiers everywhere. Citizens do not know if they will be arrested. Antar and I decided it would not be a good place to raise children. What would become of them?" She scanned the green lawn and flowers and watched a passing car. "Here we have so much to be thankful for."

"Where is your home?" Tatyana asked.

"We are from Minsk. And you?"

"I lived on a farm outside Moscow. We did not live so far from each other."

"You two are just jabbering away," Susie said. "I can't understand a word of it, but I love to listen to you. Russian sounds so mysterious." She looked at Tatyana. "Ask her if she would like to come to the baptism and picnic."

"Janna, there is going to be a baptism ceremony and a church picnic at a nearby lake. Would you and your husband like to join us?"

"It sounds wonderful, but Antar and I must go to Seattle. My aunt and uncle are expecting us."

Tatyana was disappointed. She wanted so much to talk about home. "Maybe we can visit soon? Do you live close by?"

"Oh, yes. We do not live far from here." Janna pointed toward Morganville. "We live in a little house on the other side of town. Just past the wide curve. It is the small white house."

"Would you mind if I came for a visit?" Tatyana asked.

"I would welcome it."

"Then I will come," Tatyana said with a smile.

Janna's husband joined her.

"Antar, I would like you to meet my new friend, Tatyana. She is from Russia also."

Antar shook Tatyana's hand. "It is good to meet you. We have met very few Russians here."

"You are the first I've met," Tatyana said.

"We must go. It was good to meet you," he said and escorted Janna down the path.

Janna waved and smiled.

Tatyana watched until they walked out of sight and wondered if tomorrow would be too soon for a visit.

"It was so hot with all of us crowded into the sanctuary," Susie said. "I had difficulty concentrating on the sermon." Looking at the pastor standing on the steps, she added, "Not that your insights about Jonah weren't inspiring, but all I could think of was swimming this afternoon."

"You'd better watch out for whales," Carl teased.

"There are no whales in Lake Twelve, but if there were, I'd go for a swim anyway."

While greeting parishioners as they moved past him, the pastor managed to say, "I think even Jonah would enjoy a dip on a day like today."

"And what do you think a whale would do if he encountered me?" Susie teased, brushing a strand of damp, strawberry blonde hair off her face.

"I don't believe God will have to use a whale to reach you, Susie," the minister said with a smile. Then he turned to greet people before they moved down the stairway.

With her husband Carl at her elbow, Susie strolled down the graveled drive. "What do you think he meant by that?"

"I'd say he knows you well enough to understand you're strong but not too rebellious."

"I am not rebellious," Susie said indignantly.

"Oh?" Carl asked, lifting one eyebrow. Placing his arm around his spunky wife, he guided her toward the car. "It's a great day for a picnic."

"It is so hot. I hope there will be shade," Tatyana said.

"Oh, there are lots of trees," Susie explained. Eyeing Dimitri, she added, "But Dimitri won't need it. He'll be soaked."

Tatyana looked at her husband and smiled. Today he would be baptized. Although her love for her husband had grown steadily since their marriage, she'd often worried about his faith. Although he'd been loving, supportive, and hard-working, his Christianity had seemed flat and lifeless. Going to church had been a chore to him, and he rarely read his Bible. Although he'd try to listen to Tatyana's spiritual insights or questions, he'd never seemed interested. Sometimes she'd worried that he might not believe at all. Now she had no doubts about his salvation. He'd changed since surviving the cave-in. He was still the good, solid man she'd always known, but now there was another dimension to him. The spiritual part of Dimitri glowed with life, and he hungered for God's Word.

Yuri let out a squall, and Dimitri shifted his son onto his shoulder. Gently patting his back, he said, "I think he's hungry."

"I'll take him into the nursery and feed him before we go," Tatyana said and gently transferred the little boy into her arms. "So, you want to eat. Do not fret. Mama will feed you." At the feel of his mother, the infant turned to her breast. "I will not be long," Tatyana said as she walked back to the church.

🐾 🐾 🐾 🐾 🐾

At the lake, Carl pulled the car to the road's edge. Families from the church already crowded the beach. Some sat at picnic tables, and others rested on blankets. Leisurely they watched children splashing in the shallows and the better swimmers beyond the log barrier.

Susie climbed out. "There's a good spot right over there." She pointed at a shady place beneath a pine tree.

"Here, give me the blankets," Dimitri said. "I'll grab it." He hurried toward the lake.

Pushing the pram, Susie followed Dimitri. Standing beneath the pine, she said, "This will be perfect," then stooped and picked up two pine cones, tossing them into the bushes. Taking a blanket from Dimitri, she spread it out. "There's plenty of shade and a good view of the lake."

Dimitri laid out their blanket beside Susie and Carl's. Glancing at Tatyana as she rejoined the group, he grinned and said, "I know I'm going to get wet today. How about you?"

"Maybe," Tatyana said curtly. She placed the baby on his back and sat beside him. She'd let Susie talk her into buying a bathing suit, but now that the time to actually wear it in public was here, she didn't think she could do it. She glanced at Susie and said quietly, "I have been thinking; it does not seem decent for a woman to wear a swimming suit and expose so much of her body."

"It really is OK nowadays. Everyone does it."

"I do not know."

"Lots of American women wear swimming suits. I think it's fine," Dimitri said.

"And she looks really good in hers," Susie added.

Tatyana gazed at the water. "There were no lakes near my home in Russia, and the streams were cold. I do not know how to swim."

"Then we'll stay in the shallows and just get wet," Susie said. "But if you want to learn, I'm a pretty good swimmer. I could teach you."

Inwardly, Tatyana squirmed. There would be no graceful way to avoid putting on that suit. No one understood her embarrassment. Not wanting to appear foolish, she finally said with a sigh, "All right, I will swim."

"Everyone, please gather round," the pastor said as he walked to the water's edge. "Today is a special day. One of our own is going to be baptized." He waited while families gathered their frolicking children and then assembled along the shoreline.

With Yuri cradled on her shoulder, Tatyana clasped Dimitri's hand, and the two walked to the beach.

Margaret, a skinny woman with short wiry hair, stood beside the minister. She always led the choir at church, and as people crowded the water's edge, she raised her hands to lead a song. In a clear high voice, she sang, "Shall We Gather at the River." Everyone joined in.

Tatyana watched proudly as Dimitri and Carl joined the pastor. Dimitri's blonde hair hung characteristically onto his forehead, and he nervously brushed it away with one quick swipe.

As the singing quieted, the pastor said, "The Lord Jesus gave us only two ordinances. One is communion, and the other is baptism. And today, as a public profession of his faith and a symbol of the washing away of sins, Dimitri Broido will be baptized, just as our Lord Jesus was." He looked at Carl. "And Carl has agreed to help. Since Dimitri is such a big fella, I was afraid I might drop him," he jested.

Opening a worn black Bible, he read the verses describing how Jesus went to John the Baptist and asked the prophet to baptize him, closing with, "And suddenly a voice came from heaven, saying, 'This is My beloved Son, in whom I am well pleased.'" The minister closed his Bible and handed it to Margaret. "As Jesus did, we must do also." He, Carl, and Dimitri waded waist-deep into the water.

Dimitri stood in the middle as the three men faced the people. "A few weeks ago Dimitri came to me and told me he thought he should be baptized, and I asked him why." The pastor smiled at the big man beside him. "His answer was perfect, and he's agreed to share it with you."

Dimitri's warm eyes met Tatyana's and then roamed over the crowd. He wet his lips. "My parents have always been strong believers, and Christ was the center of our home. He was always very real to my parents, but until a few weeks ago I never truly understood their faith. I believed in God and in his Son, but didn't understand the difference between outward religious practices and inner faith." He glanced at Tatyana.

Her throat tightened, and she could feel tears burn her eyes.

"I watched my parents, my wife, and my friends walk with God. I knew they had something I didn't, but I couldn't understand what it was—not until Carl and I were trapped in the mine." He looked at his friend. "Carl never gave up hope. He kept talking to his friend Jesus and reassuring me we weren't alone. And I finally saw what I was missing. I didn't have a personal relationship with Christ. I didn't know him.

"I made it home that day and watched my son come into the world." His voice caught as he struggled to continue. "When I held Yuri in my arms, I knew God was real and powerful. I wanted to know him. And that day God held me in his arms."

Gently the minister placed his arm across Dimitri's back and gripped his forearm, and Carl did the same. "Dimitri Broido, you have accepted Jesus Christ as your personal Lord and Savior. Do you desire to be baptized in obedience to Christ?"

"Yes."

"And is it your desire to follow Christ?"

"Yes." His eyes teared. "Jesus gave everything for me. From this day forward, I will do my best to live for him."

"Then I baptize you in the name of the Father, the Son, and the Holy Spirit." He tipped Dimitri backwards, submerging his entire body, then pulled him upright. With a smile, he clasped the big man's hand and shook it. "Welcome to the family of God, son."

Dimitri wiped water from his face and smiled. "Thank you."

CHAPTER 3

Tears blurring her vision, Tatyana met her husband's loving gaze.

Carl pulled his friend into a bear hug and patted his back soundly. "Congratulations! I love you, brother."

As the men waded toward shore, Margaret began singing, "Washed in the Blood," and everyone joined in.

Dimitri headed straight for Tatyana. Ignoring his wet clothing, she stepped into his arms. Holding his wife and son, Dimitri kissed them both. "I love you."

"And I you," Tatyana murmured. She kissed him again. Taking a step back, but keeping her hand on his arm, she said. "Now we will serve him together."

"I knew it was only a matter of time," Carl said.

"So, what took me so long?" Dimitri asked.

"You're stubborn." Susie smiled and kissed his cheek.

"You're right, I am."

"Praise God," Josephine said as she stepped up to Dimitri. Pressing his large hands between her tiny ones, she said, "I am so proud of you."

"Thank you, but I did nothing."

"Oh yes, you did. You listened to the voice of the Lord." Her face crinkled into hundreds of tiny wrinkles as she smiled.

* * * * *

After a lunch of egg salad sandwiches, potato salad, pickles, fresh fruit, and cake, the men headed toward the forested side of the lake where cattails and lily pads crowded the lakeshore, fishing poles resting on their shoulders.

With her legs straight out in front of her, Tatyana leaned back on her hands and watched the men. She smiled. "They look happy." A cooling breeze touched her skin, and she closed her eyes for a moment. Opening them, she gazed at the blue sky. "I'll never forget this day."

Susie plucked a blade of grass.

"I wish we would come out here more often. It's always lovely."

"Why do they call this Lake Twelve? It seems a strange name for such a beautiful place."

"When they sectioned off the land, this was section twelve, so the name, Lake Twelve. I wish they would change it." She stripped off a ribbon of grass. "I doubt we'll ever convince the old-timers to do that though. They pretty much like things the way they are."

Tatyana lay beside a sleeping Yuri. As she closed her eyes and bathed in the cooling breeze and contentment, she listened to his steady breathing. The next thing she heard was Dimitri's voice.

"So, you're napping while the men are out foraging for food."

Tatyana forced her eyes open and looked up at her husband.

Wearing a broad smile, he held out a long string of trout. "They're really biting today."

Pushing herself up on one elbow, Tatyana tried to focus on the fish.

"They'll make a fine meal."

Tatyana yawned. "You caught all of those?"

Dimitri nodded yes.

Susie sat up. "Did you catch any, Carl?"

He held up one large fish. "Just one, but he's at least five pounds."

"He's beautiful." Susie stood and hefted the trout.

"It's your turn now, ladies. We'll stay with the babies while you swim."

"They'll need to be changed and fed first," Susie said, picking up Evelyn.

Tatyana's stomach churned as she lifted Yuri. She could think of no excuse not to go swimming. She would have to put on her bathing suit.

CHAPTER 3

❦ ❦ ❦ ❦ ❦

After the babies were fed, changed, and contentedly in their father's arms, Susie dug into her bag and pulled out a black, one-piece swimming suit. She looked at Tatyana. "You did say you brought yours, didn't you?"

With a sigh, Tatyana answered, "Yes. It is right here." Self-consciously, she held up her suit.

"Great!" Susie said and hurried toward the bath house. Tatyana followed reluctantly.

After changing into her suit, Tatyana wrapped a towel around herself and stepped outside. Embarrassed, she pressed her back against the bath house wall. "I do not feel good about this."

Susie touched Tatyana's hand. "It's all right, really. No one thinks a thing about a woman in a bathing suit." She folded her arms over her chest and said, "Let me see."

Glancing around to make certain no one was looking, Tatyana opened her towel. "So much of me is showing."

"I know you feel uncomfortable, but you'll get used to it, and you do look beautiful." Susie smiled. "I wish I looked so good. Compared to you, I'm short and stocky."

"You are not stocky." Tatyana looked down at herself and shook her head slowly back and forth. "In Russia I would never dare do such a thing."

Her freckled face crinkling into a smile, Susie took her friend's hand and walked toward the lake. "Well, you're not in Russia. This is America, and women can wear bathing suits."

Still clutching her towel around her, Tatyana waded into the cold water. "Oh, this is too cold," she said and started to retreat.

Susie stopped. "You'll get used to it." Hands on her hips, she smiled. "You'll have to get rid of the towel." She held out her hand. "Here, give it to me."

Tatyana hesitated a moment before she finally gave up the towel.

Susie flung it to the beach and headed away from shore. "Come on! It feels good!" She dunked herself, squealing as the cold water hit her skin. Splashing into deeper water, she laughed and motioned for Tatyana to follow.

Keeping her arms folded and tucked close to her body, Tatyana edged her way out, thinking, *At least the water will hide me.* Waist deep, she held her arms up. "It is freezing."

"Dunk yourself." Susie laughed. "It feels wonderful!"

Tatyana shivered.

"Come on. It will be easier to teach you to swim if we're in deeper water." They took another couple steps, stopping when the water washed over their shoulders.

"Dip your head in," Susie said as she disappeared beneath the surface. A moment later she reappeared and brushed dripping hair off her face.

Tatyana squeezed her eyes closed and dunked. When she came back up, water flowed down her face. She wiped it and blinked hard until her vision cleared. The water didn't feel as cold, and Tatyana had to admit she felt refreshed.

By afternoon's end, Tatyana had learned to swim a little. When she left the water, she was exhausted but delighted she'd tried. "I love swimming. When can we come again?"

"Soon, I hope," Susie said.

After replacing her wet bathing suit with dry clothing, Tatyana went to check on Yuri. He sat contentedly in Josephine's arms. "You will spoil him."

"No, you can't spoil these little ones," Josephine said as she smiled at the baby. "You can never give them too much love."

"I have a surprise for you," Dimitri told Tatyana.

"What?"

"I'm not saying. Just take off your shoes," Dimitri said as he rolled his pant legs up.

Her curiosity piqued, Tatyana stepped out of her shoes.

"Josephine said she'd watch Yuri." Dimitri steered his wife toward the lake. He pulled a canoe from the rushes, waded into the water, and floated it. "Climb in."

"Where did you get that?"

"Milton Drexler let me borrow it."

With Dimitri holding the canoe steady, Tatyana placed one foot on the bottom, then grabbing the side for balance, she lifted her other leg over and sat on the small bench in the middle. "Do you know how to do this?"

"I've seen it done. It doesn't look hard," Dimitri said, settling himself in the back and grabbing a paddle. Pressing the end of it against the lake bottom, he pushed the boat free. He dipped into the water on one side of the canoe and then the other.

As they left the beach, the landscape changed. The green of the trees seemed deeper, the colors more diverse. Hills invisible from the shore emerged from behind the forest. Watching the interaction between families, Tatyana had the strange sensation of watching a movie. Even the sounds were different; the children's voices echoed over the water.

Tatyana leaned back and let her hand hang in the water. It felt cool as the lake eddied around it. The sound of water lapping against the hull of the boat and the sway beneath calmed her. "I like this. Does a boat cost a lot of money?"

"More than we have." He eyed her hand. "Better watch out or a hungry fish might find your fingers a tempting morsel."

"A fish would not do that." She lifted her hand out of the water. "Would it?"

Dimitri laughed. "No, I don't think there are any man-eaters in Lake Twelve."

"Sometimes you are such a tease."

"I'm sorry, I couldn't help it."

For a while they were quiet as Dimitri paddled toward a small inlet congested with half-sunken logs, moss, and lily pads.

A heron standing in tall weeds opened its wings and lifted into the air. With a whoosh, he soared gracefully over the lake.

"He is beautiful," Tatyana said, her voice hushed.

"That's something you'll never see in New York City." Dimitri placed the flat side of the paddle against the water and slowed the boat. "I'm glad I took the job here instead of the Midwest. I love this area."

He leaned forward slightly. "Ever since the cave-in, it's as if I'm seeing through new eyes." He gazed at the trees and underbrush along the shore and studied their reflection on the still water. "I feel like I've been wearing dark glasses and haven't been able to see clearly. Now everything's sharper, more distinct." He pressed the paddle against a submerged log and pushed off. As they glided backwards out of the inlet, he said, "I don't ever want to leave the Northwest. I want to raise our children here."

Sadness swept over Tatyana at the thought of never returning to Russia. Her children would know nothing of the motherland.

She thought back to her meeting with Janna, and the joy of having a Russian friend washed over her again. It would be wonderful to return home. She looked at her husband. He didn't understand. He was an American, just as if he'd been born here. She said nothing of her sorrow and instead said softly, "Where you are is where I will be."

CHAPTER 4

WITH YURI ASLEEP ON HER lap, Tatyana leaned against Dimitri. It had been a lovely but long day, and she was tired. Wind rushed through the car window, blowing her long hair into a tangle. Her eyes closed, she said sleepily, "We will have to go back to Lake Twelve soon."

Dimitri hugged her with one arm. "We'll go as often as we can." He kissed the top of Tatyana's head, and she snuggled closer.

From the front seat, Carl said, "I read in the *Herald* this morning that another man jumped off the Aurora Bridge. The reporter said he'd left a note about his debt and not being able to take care of his family." Slowly he shook his head back and forth. "I understand about worrying over the lack of money. I do it. But I can't imagine killing myself because of it."

"The poor man," Susie said. "And what about his family? What will happen to them?" She glanced at the setting sun as they crested the top of Lawson Hill. "We're very lucky here in Black Diamond. The mine takes good care of us. We don't have a lot, but we don't really suffer. It's hard to understand the kind of despair that would drive someone to kill himself. I wonder if he knew the Lord." She leaned forward and stared down at the town of Black Diamond. "Is that smoke?" Clapping her hand over her mouth, she said, "Oh, Lord! It looks like it's near our house!"

Tatyana peered out her window. "Do you think it is on our street?"

Carl pressed harder on the accelerator. "Can't tell from here. We better get down there."

🐝 🐝 🐝 🐝 🐝

One street over from the Broido's and the Anderson's, Carl pulled the car to the side of the road. With her stomach churning, Tatyana stared at a small company house. Smoke was seeping from the front door and belching out the front window. Flames reached out the window and licked across the roof. Tatyana stepped out of the car. She could smell the smoke and hear the crackle of burning wood.

Neighbors stood in small groups in the yard. Two women clung to each other. One, her face wet with tears and her eyes filled with horror and panic, wailed, "My little boy! Tony! Please, someone help him!" Wrenching herself free of the other woman's arms, she ran toward the house.

A man charged after her. "No!" he yelled and caught her as she stepped onto the front porch. Wrapping his arms around her, he held her tightly while she struggled against him. "It's too late! There's nothing you can do! He's in God's hands now."

"Oh, please! God!" the woman screamed. "Maybe there is a way to get in through the back. Please! Try!" Suddenly the strength drained from her, and she crumpled against the man.

He cradled the woman but said firmly, "There is no way." Her shoulders shuddered with sobs.

Tatyana wept, her fist pressed against her mouth. "Father, help them." She squeezed her eyes closed. "Please save her son."

"We have to do something!" Dimitri said, running to the tortured woman. He talked with her a moment and ran to the house.

"Don't be a fool! Stay back!" someone shouted.

Others watched in horrified silence.

As Tatyana realized Dimitri's intent, she screamed, "Dimitri, no!" He acted as if he didn't hear, and she watched in terror as he grabbed the front door handle. He quickly let loose, glanced at his hand, then taking a step back, kicked the door in. Thick, black smoke rolled out and Dimitri jumped back, coughing and choking on the heated fumes.

"Dimitri! Come back!" Turning to Carl, Tatyana said, "Stop him! Make him stop!"

"Once Dimitri has his mind set, there's no changing it," Carl called back, shaking his head and running after his friend.

Dimitri circled around to the side of the house and peered through a window.

Without taking her eyes off her husband, Tatyana asked, "Please don't be foolish, Dimitri. Please. Remember Yuri and me." She looked at Susie. "If he goes in that house, he'll die."

Susie gripped Tatyana's hand and pulled her friend close to her side. "Father, please keep Dimitri safe," she prayed.

Clutching a crying Yuri tightly against her breast, Tatyana walked toward the house.

"Come on, Dimitri! It's no use!" Carl grabbed his friend's arm.

"There's a little boy in there!" Dimitri jerked his arm away and ran around to the back. "I can't just let him die."

"It's too late!" Carl said and grabbed Dimitri again.

With unexpected ferocity, Dimitri yanked his arm out of Carl's hand. "There's a little boy inside! And I'm going to help

41

him!" He felt the back kitchen door. It wasn't too hot. He pushed Carl aside, opened the door, and stepped inside.

Dimitri could see an orange glow in the living area. There was no fire in the kitchen, but the smoke was thick and suffocating. *Most of these houses are the same,* Dimitri thought. *She said her son was in the back bedroom. I'll have to go through the living room to get to him.* Taking a painful breath, he coughed, his lungs and throat burning. He pulled a handkerchief out of his pocket, covered his mouth, and stepped into the living room. Immediately the heat intensified, and the smoke thickened into a black wall. He almost retreated but couldn't bring himself to abandon the boy. Dropping to hands and knees, he felt his way across the floor. He could see the glow of fire along the walls and hear its roar. Thinking the bedrooms would be to his left, he prayed and moved in that direction. His eyes burning and tearing, his lungs strangling on smoke, he prayed, *"Father, show me where he is. Help me."*

When he reached a wall, his fingers felt along blistered wallpaper until they found what felt like a wooden door frame. *If he's in the back bedroom, I'll have to go down the hallway.* Intense heat bore down on him as he crawled forward. Something flaming fell beside him, but he kept moving. The crackling of wood, the popping of broken glassware, and what sounded like gun shots filled the air. *Ammo,* Dimitri thought and crouched lower. An explosion of splintering glass reverberated through the house as the front window blew out. *I was foolish. I can't do this,* he decided. Again he considered retreating, but as he turned he heard a fiery blast and felt the heat of torching behind him. He was cut off! *Lord, I need a miracle,* he prayed as he groped his way to where he thought the bedroom would be.

Crying came from somewhere ahead of him. Edging forward, he stared into the dense smoke but could see nothing. He tried to call out, but the words strangled in his parched and burned throat. He swallowed several times, trying to wet his vocal chords. He couldn't get his breath and coughed hard, trying to clear his seared lungs. In a hoarse whisper, he asked, "Are you there? Tony, are you there?" The only answer was the hiss of burning plaster and the pop of burning wood.

Flaming debris swirled around him, and his shirt sleeve ignited. He slapped at the shirt, extinguishing the burning material, and kept moving. *The boy must be dead,* he thought. *Father, if he's still alive, help me find him.*

Feeling his way, he touched what felt like a door frame. The door was open, and he crawled through, finding some relief from the intense heat. "Tony! Tony!" he croaked.

Muffled crying answered.

"I'm coming," Dimitri answered in a whisper, his throat raw. *Where is he?* he thought, heading toward the whimpering and knowing he had only seconds to find the child. "Tony, where are you?" he repeated.

He bumped into what he thought was a wall. Running his hands over it, he found a knob and yanked open a door. He caught a momentary glimpse of a small closet and a young boy huddled against the back of it before smoke blotted out his vision. "Tony!" He felt for the boy and quickly scooped the child into his arms. "We're going to be all right."

With the boy clinging to him, Dimitri felt his way along the wall, careful to keep his hand at what he thought would be window level so not to miss their only escape. The sizzle of burning wallpaper intensified, and he hurried, longing for blessed air.

✳ ✳ ✳ ✳ ✳

Staring through tears at the burning house, Tatyana asked, "Why did he do it? What about me and Yuri?"

Susie said nothing but gave Tatyana's hand a squeeze.

Carl moved around the house, peering in windows and shouting, "Dimitri! Dimitri!" Increasing heat forced him back.

Towing a wagon loaded with a large tank of water, hoses, and picks, the volunteer fire department finally arrived. One man shouted orders. "You two check the entrances! You men get some water on that fire!"

The crew acted quickly. Two men inspected the house, another cranked the hose out, and another made certain it didn't tangle. Two other firefighters stood at the front of the hose, one holding the heavy tubing and the other working the nozzle as water poured out. A steady hissing filled the air and steam surged.

"Is there anyone inside?" the captain asked.

"My friend," Carl said. "And a boy." He looked back at the burning structure. "You've got to get them out!"

"We've got people inside!" the captain shouted. "Keep hosing it down!" Pointing at a hot spot, he added, "Get some water over there!"

Still clutching Yuri, who now cried ferociously, Tatyana pleaded with God for her husband's life, knowing it would take a miracle. *"Please let him live. Please."*

Staring at the burning house, Carl said, "I told him not to go in, but he wouldn't listen to me. All he could say was, 'What about the boy? I can't leave him.'"

Despite the firemen's efforts, smoke and flames continued to devour the home. "We're too late. It's lost," the captain said, his shoulders drooping. "I don't want any of you men going in," he shouted at his crew. "There's nothing we can do." Under his breath he said to a nearby firefighter, "I'm afraid we'll have to do a body search when it burns itself out."

Clutching little Yuri more tightly, Tatyana closed her eyes. *"Dear God, please, no."*

✻ ✻ ✻ ✻ ✻

With the boy in his arms, Dimitri dove out the window, tumbling across the yard. He didn't move but lay huddled and shivering on the cool grass.

"He's alive!" someone shouted.

Immediately a firefighter ran to Dimitri and Tony. "Doc, we need you over here."

Doctor Logan knelt beside Dimitri and the boy. Gently rolling the coughing child onto his back, he said, "Try to relax, Tony." The boy shook uncontrollably. "Take slow, even breaths." He felt the child's skin. "He's going into shock." He stripped off his coat and laid it over the boy. "We need to get him to the Renton hospital," he told the nearest fireman.

"Oh, Tony, my Tony!" the boy's mother said. "Is he all right, doctor?"

"I think he'll be fine, but he needs to go to the hospital."

The mother knelt beside her son and held him, rocking back and forth.

"Dimitri! Dimitri!" Tatyana said, dropping to the ground beside her husband. She cried as she studied him. His face, hands, and clothing were black, and some of his clothing was burned. She wanted to hold him, but afraid of hurting him, she simply caressed his hair. "Praise the Lord. You are alive!"

Dimitri opened his eyes and looked at Tatyana. His breathing was raspy and shallow, and he coughed repeatedly.

The doctor felt his face and carefully examined his hands. "He's still pretty hot, and his hands are burned. You need to get him to the hospital."

"I've got my car. I'll take him," Carl said.

"He's also inhaled a lot of smoke. It will take a few days for his lungs to clear."

"But he is going to be all right?" Tatyana asked.

"Yes. I think so, but it will take a few weeks for his burns to heal, and his lungs are going to hurt for a while. He's a brave man."

Tatyana felt momentary relief, then anger. She rocked back, taking her hand from his head. "How could you?! You could have died! You did not even think of Yuri and me."

Dimitri tried to push himself up but coughing forced him back.

Susie placed an arm around Tatyana. "Now is not a good time, Tatyana. Calm down."

"No!" Tatyana broke free of her friend and stood. Still cradling Yuri in her arms, she paced. Tears wet her face. "I watched him go into that house," she said as she glanced at the burning structure. "And I didn't know if he would make it out alive. I prayed and cried. . . ." She wiped her eyes and nose. "I held his son. But did he think of us? Did he think of his own son? What if he had died?"

Carl stepped in. "But he didn't." He rested his hand on Tatyana's shoulder. "I understand your anger, but it's over now. We need to be thankful Dimitri's alive. He's a hero. Without him that boy would have died."

Tatyana whirled on Carl. "And what about his own son? If he died in that fire, who would be here to take care of Yuri?" She turned her back on Carl, and great sobs shook her.

"Please, do not be angry with him," a woman said.

Tatyana turned and looked at the boy's mother. She held Tony in her arms. "Do not be angry. Your husband was sent by God. He saved my son." She hugged the child tighter and kissed the boy's cheek. "If not for this man," she held an arm out toward Dimitri, "Tony would be dead. Your husband is very brave. You should praise him."

Tatyana looked at the child and wiped her tears. She tried to think of how she would feel if the boy had been Yuri. She could barely stand the thought and quickly pushed it away.

The woman took a step closer to Tatyana, and holding out her boy a little, said, "Tony is going to be all right." Then she smiled and looked at Dimitri. "Thank you. Thank you. May the Lord bless you."

Tatyana looked at her husband. He tried to smile at her, but it came out looking more like a grimace. "I just do not understand how you could not think of us," she said sadly.

CHAPTER 4

Dr. Logan stood. "Sometimes people react without thinking." He glanced at Dimitri. "But you can sort all that out later. Right now we need to get him to the hospital."

Tatyana knelt beside Dimitri and gently kissed his forehead. "I am thankful you are safe. I was scared. What would I do without you?"

CHAPTER 5

FALL WAS QUICKLY APPROACHING, and Tatyana shivered slightly in the morning chill. She pulled the laces tight on her boots. "I am not used to these. I hope I do not get a blister." A horn blasted from out front. After quickly tying the laces, she walked to the window and pulled the shades back. "She is here." Turning to Dimitri, she asked, "Could you get the buckets? I will bring the food and water." Opening the door, she waved to Josephine and Miranda. Smiling, they waved back. She hurried into the kitchen and grabbed the water jug and food basket from the table.

Balancing buckets and metal pots, Dimitri followed her to the truck. Glancing at the clear blue sky, he said, "It's a perfect day for berry picking."

"It's certainly that," Josephine said.

"Good morning," Tatyana said as she set the basket and water in the back of the truck.

Opening the door, Miranda said, "Good morning to you. What a lovely day. Where is the baby?"

"Susie is taking care of him for us."

"What a dear she is," Miranda said. "I thought it might be a little hard on you to take the baby."

Dimitri deposited the assortment of buckets and containers into the pickup bed. "You can ride up front with the ladies, and I'll ride in back."

Smiling, Miranda scooted closer to her sister and patted the seat beside her.

Tatyana glanced at Dimitri in the back of the pickup. Then she looked at Miranda and said, "Thank you, but I will ride in back."

Miranda pushed her heavy glasses higher onto her nose. "Are you sure? It's very bumpy and dusty back there. You're likely to get cold."

"I will be fine. And if I get cold, I can snuggle next to Dimitri. Besides, I am wearing a sweater," she added, glancing at the deep blue cardigan.

"I don't know," Dimitri said. "Miranda's right, it's rough riding."

Tatyana lifted her chin and set her jaw. "You forget I grew up in Russia, and I am used to such things. At home we had only horse-drawn carts. We were not so spoiled." She knew her tone was sharp, but Dimitri's patronizing attitude grated on her. *He's forgotten his boyhood,* she thought sadly.

"I didn't mean . . ."

"I will ride in back with you." She softened her tone and added, "It will be fun."

"Suit yourself," Josephine said. "Just get in. We can't spend the day arguing over where you're going to sit. There are berries to be picked." She turned the ignition, and the engine sputtered to life. "We've got a long drive ahead, and the day is getting away from us."

Tatyana quickly walked around to the back of the pickup. Taking Dimitri's hand, she stepped onto the bumper and over the tailgate, then sat on an empty gunny sack. "I have never ridden in the back of a pickup before."

Climbing in, Dimitri said snidely, "There's probably good reason." He sat beside her, folding his legs Indian style.

She looked at Mount Rainier. "Will we be going all the way to the mountain?"

"I don't think so."

Leaning out the front window, Josephine called, "You all set back there?"

"We're ready," Dimitri answered.

"All right then." She shifted into gear, and throwing a stern look at her sister, said, "Shut the door."

Miranda pulled the door closed and settled back in her seat.

Gripping the steering wheel, Josephine pulled onto the road, bumping through a pothole. The truck jerked as she worked through the gears; then it smoothed out. They picked up speed and headed down the gravel road toward Enumclaw and the mountains beyond.

Tatyana rested her back against the truck cab. Houses, trees, livestock, and cars whizzed past. Sitting backwards, the world looked different, but Tatyana liked the sensation. She closed her eyes, relishing the rush of wind and fresh morning air. Her hair flew wildly around her head, and she tried to capture it but finally gave up. Leaning against Dimitri, she said, "I like this."

Dimitri circled his arm around her shoulders and pulled her close. "It feels kind of strange not having Yuri with us."

"My arms do feel empty without him, but it is nice to just be with you." Tatyana took Dimitri's hand in hers and ran her fingers over the smooth, pinkish skin still healing from his burns. She kissed his palm. "Ever since the fire, I worry about Yuri. Even now, knowing he is with Susie, I am a little afraid."

"I didn't know it still bothered you."

"Sometimes I think about how helpless that boy was. . . ." She shuddered inwardly at the idea of her own son being in such danger. Tatyana's mind returned to the day of the fire. Dimitri had nearly died saving Tony. She and Yuri could have been left alone. She still didn't understand Dimitri's willingness to put his life in jeopardy for someone he didn't know. She let go of his hand and watched the blur of green flash by.

*　*　*　*　*

Forests closed in on them, forming a green wall along the road and shutting out the sun. Tatyana shivered and wished she'd worn her coat.

"You're cold," Dimitri said, stripping off his jacket and placing it over Tatyana's shoulders.

"No. You need your coat. I am fine."

"I am not cold. My wool shirt is enough."

Glad for the extra warmth, Tatyana said, "Thank you," and pushed her arms into the sleeves. She studied the trees. Already some of the leaves were changing color. "Do you think winter will come early?"

"It's hard to say. Some of the old-timers think so, but others say no. I guess we'll just have to wait and see." Dimitri studied thin wisps of clouds stretching across the sky. "The sky reminds me of home."

"Home? You mean Russia?"

"No. New York."

"Oh," Tatyana said. *Of course. Russia isn't home to you,* she thought sadly.

"In New York, some fall days are just like this—pale blue skies with clouds that look like cotton candy."

Tatyana smiled sadly. "I have seen this same sky in Russia also."

CHAPTER 5

"Are you still cold?"

"No. I am fine."

Dimitri took a deep breath. "Can you smell the pine? It's wonderful. If we were riding up front, we would miss it."

They made a sharp turn, and the road now paralleled a frothy white river.

"When I came to Seattle on the train, I saw this river," Tatyana said. "It is very unusual. The man on the train said it is white because of the minerals washed into it from a glacier."

"I've never seen anything like it." Dimitri turned and knocked on the back window of the cab. Josephine glanced at him over her shoulder. He yelled, "Can we stop?"

Josephine slowed and pulled to the edge of the road.

Dimitri jumped out of the truck, then held Tatyana's hand as she climbed down.

"What's the matter?" Josephine asked as she stepped out.

"I just wanted to look at the river. I've never seen one this color. Do you know what it's called?"

"They call it the White River," Josephine explained.

Dimitri walked along a path leading to the stream's edge.

Tatyana, Josephine, and Miranda followed.

Sitting on a log, Josephine said, "I suppose this is a good place for a break. It's only a few miles to the turnoff. Then the road gets real narrow and bumpy. And there's no stopping." With a mischievous grin, she added, "There are some steep drop-offs. If I recall, you were pretty much white-knuckled the last time you traveled along a cliff road."

Dimitri blushed. "I was a city boy then." He bent and picked up a rock and tossed it into the rushing water. "Mountain roads don't bother me any more. Except, of course, if the person driving is reckless, then I might feel a little insecure."

"If you're trying to say I'm a bad driver . . ."

Dimitri held up his hand. "I'm not, but you were pounding on those brakes pretty hard."

"I beg your pardon. There was nothing wrong with the way I used my brakes."

Miranda headed toward the woods on the opposite side of the road. "Nature calls," she said.

Her face in a pout, Josephine placed one foot on the log and rested her arm over her bent leg. She watched until Miranda disappeared into the heavy underbrush. Chewing on a stalk of dry grass, she said, "About my driving . . ."

"Stop bickering," Tatyana said. "Sometimes you two are like children."

Examining the straw, Josephine grinned. "Well, I guess I can't argue with that one." She looked down the highway, then sat on the log. "I've heard the berry picking is best past Twin Camps. I figured that's where we ought to go. It's beautiful up there." She looked at Tatyana. "You'll love it, dear."

"How high is it?" Dimitri asked.

"Well, pretty high, but I don't know exactly what the altitude is." Josephine studied the trees; some leaves were already turning red and yellow. "Looks like winter isn't too far off," she said smiling softly. "My husband Harry and I always loved to camp up here and wait for the first snowfall. There was nothing like it. The air felt crisper than at any other time and the snow was such a bright white. It always seemed extraordinary." A distant look settled over her face. "Those were good days."

Miranda crashed through the brush and stepped onto the road. "I'm ready to head up the mountain. How about you?"

Josephine stood and brushed dirt from the seat of her pants. "It's time we got going. Huckleberries aren't nearly as large as blackberries, and it takes a long while to fill a bucket. We're going to need all the picking time we can get. I plan to bring home several gallons." She climbed back into the truck and started the engine. Miranda slid onto the seat beside her while Dimitri and Tatyana clambered into the back.

A short time later, Josephine turned the truck onto a narrow dirt road. They bounced through potholes and dodged downed limbs. The buckets and pots clattered back and forth across the truck bed. Dimitri finally shoved the berry picking equipment into the front corner and kept it in place by bracing it with his foot.

Tatyana's seat felt bruised, and her back ached. She wished she'd ridden in front. As they followed the road up the side of the mountain, the right bank fell away sharply. Soon, even treetops were below them. Gripping the top edge of the truck bed, Tatyana gazed down at a sea of evergreens.

The road narrowed, and Tatyana fought fear. Any error could send them over the edge. She pressed her back against the cab and pulled her knees close to her chest. "Do you think it is much further?"

"No." Dimitri studied the road ahead. "It looks like we're nearly to the top. I hope so, anyway."

"Good," Tatyana said, taking a slow, deep breath.

The truck lurched abruptly and slid to a stop. Tatyana's stomach pitched. "What is happening?"

Dimitri peered around the truck. "What is it, Josephine?" He stood and looked over the cab. "It's a deer."

Tatyana stood.

"See, right there."

Tatyana saw only the flick of a black tail as the animal disappeared into heavy brush on the bank above them.

"Sorry about that," Josephine called out the window. "Hope I didn't scare ya, but I didn't want to hit it. They're beautiful creatures." Coaxing the truck into gear, she edged forward and settled back into a slow, steady pace.

Another thirty minutes passed before they entered a wide open area where Josephine stopped and turned off the engine. Her arm hanging out the window, she slapped the outside of the door with the flat of her hand. "This is it."

As Dimitri climbed down, he said, "I was beginning to think the road would never end. It just kept winding up and up."

Josephine climbed out and closed the door. She wiped her face with a handkerchief. "I'd forgotten how bad the road is. And how long."

Miranda stood beside her sister. "It's a bad one all right. There have been plenty of accidents over the years."

"You just have to drive carefully," Josephine said, tucking her handkerchief into a back pocket. She studied the hillsides and meadows covered with berry bushes. "It's worth our trouble though." She took a deep breath. "Can you smell that?"

Tatyana sniffed the air. It was filled with an unusual but pleasant aroma. "What is it?"

"Berries. Huckleberries warm from the sun and ready to be picked." Stretching her arm toward the nearby bushes, she said, "There are acres and acres just waiting for us."

Miranda folded her arms under her bosom. "I can almost taste huckleberry pie."

Josephine laid her hand on Miranda's shoulder. "Have either of you ever tasted Miranda's huckleberry pie?"

"No," Dimitri answered for both of them.

"Well, you will this week. It's wonderful. She always wins first place at the county fair."

Miranda blushed slightly and smiled. "I use an old family recipe."

"Let's stop talking about berries and start picking," Josephine said. Climbing into the back of the truck, she handed down buckets and pots. "What you want to do is to loop your belt through the bucket handle and fasten it. That way, you'll have both hands free to pick." Then, with a lard bucket dangling from her belt, she climbed down from the truck and walked to the nearest bushes. Miranda joined her.

Dimitri cinched his belt and scanned a nearby hillside. "How about over there? Seems to be a lot of berries."

"It looks like a good spot." Tatyana hiked up her oversized denim jeans and hooked her belt. "If these blue jeans fit, I think I would like wearing them." She smiled. "My mother would be shocked to see me in pants. In Russia, women always wear dresses. Well, most of them. Once when I was in Moscow, I saw a woman wearing overalls."

"Why don't you order a pair from the Sears, Roebuck and Company catalog? That way you can get some that fit."

"Maybe." Then, with a decisive nod, she added, "I will."

"Good. Now, let's get started," Dimitri said, striding toward the hillside. Tatyana had to run to catch him. "I'll start here, and you can work toward me," he said.

Tatyana walked several paces from Dimitri and began picking. The small, deep blue berries felt warm and firm between her fingers and fell easily into her hand. Unable to resist, she ate one. Its strong, tart flavor filled her mouth, and she quickly ate another.

"Stop eating them," Dimitri said with a grin.

"I only had two. You should try one. They are very good." A small brown bird with a yellow throat flitted past and landed on a nearby branch. Its tail twitched as the limb swayed back and forth. With a flutter of wings, it darted away. Tatyana picked a handful of berries and dropped them into her bucket. She glanced up just in time to see a small brown squirrel sprint across the ground and disappear beneath a log. Smiling, she returned to picking and eating.

Tatyana worked steadily. The sun felt hot without shade. Finally, she stripped off her sweater and tied it around her waist.

His bucket full, Dimitri joined Tatyana and peeked inside her bucket. "Looks like you've been eating a lot of berries."

"I believe a person should enjoy working," she said with a smile. Plucking a tiny purple berry, she held it up to the sun and popped it into her mouth.

"Don't complain if you get a stomachache," Dimitri said with a wry grin. "I'm going to dump mine. Then we can have lunch. I'm hungry."

Tatyana glanced at the truck. Miranda and Josephine were pouring berries into a large pot. "I want to keep picking."

Dimitri walked back toward the truck.

"Are you coming, Tatyana?" Miranda hollered.

"Soon. I want to pick a few more," she called back.

"What?" Josephine yelled.

"I will be there soon," Tatyana shouted.

The women nodded, and Tatyana returned to picking. Smiling, she thought about how good the berries would taste during the cold of winter. She would make pies and jam and be reminded of her day in the mountains.

Suddenly, the bushes to her right shook. Startled, Tatyana stepped back as a small bear cub scrambled out of the brush. He pounced on something and licked it up. Chewing, he sat back on his haunches and scratched his neck with his back foot. Seeing Tatyana, he scrambled to his feet, took several steps backward, then stopped and stared at the intruder, his black nose twitching as he tried to decide if she was dangerous or not.

How cute, Tatyana thought, wanting to reach out and touch the cub's black coat. "Have you been eating huckleberries too?" she asked softly.

The cub tilted his head and continued to stare at her.

Without warning, a large sow broke through the bushes. Tatyana held completely still. Sleek and fat, the bear's black coat gleamed in the sunlight. She studied Tatyana warily, then with a growl, swatted her youngster and sent him scurrying back into the bushes. Then she swung around and faced the intruder. Rising on her back legs, she sniffed the air, her small black eyes glaring at Tatyana.

Tatyana could see large menacing teeth. Her heart pounded so hard it felt as if it might explode. She didn't breathe. Should she run? Or would it be better to back away? What would happen if she stood still? Tatyana looked at the long claws on the bear's front feet. One swipe could kill her. She took a step backward.

The sow dropped to the ground, swung her head side to side, then stepped toward Tatyana.

CHAPTER 5

The frightened woman glanced at her husband and friends. They were busy sorting berries and didn't see what was happening. Should she call to them? As she took another step backward, the bear gave a threatening growl and moved closer.

"Father, help me," Tatyana prayed, pushing down her fear and taking another step back.

"Haahh!!" Dimitri shouted, and Tatyana jumped.

The bear swung around and stared at the big man running at her, waving his hands over his head.

"Haahh! Go on! Get!" Dimitri shouted.

Standing on hind legs, the sow pawed the air, but Dimitri kept coming. Finally, with a grunt, she dropped to her feet and fled.

Dimitri quickly closed the distance between himself and Tatyana. Grateful, she fell into his arms. "I was so scared! I did not know what to do." Dimitri held Tatyana tightly as her body shook from fear.

"Well, if that wasn't the most foolish thing I've ever seen," Josephine said sharply as she strode up to the couple. "You're lucky that bear didn't take you up on your challenge. Black bears don't generally bother people. You've just got to give them space. Tatyana was doing exactly the right thing."

"She had a cub. Did you see it?" Tatyana asked.

Concern flashed in Josephine's eyes. "I didn't see anything but the bear. If there's a cub involved, a mama bear can be real contentious." Glancing in the direction the bear had gone, she added, "You were both lucky."

Feeling as if her legs might buckle, Tatyana said, "I need to sit down." Dimitri helped her to a nearby boulder. Glancing around, she asked, "Do you think the bear will come back?"

"No. She hightailed it. Most likely she's moving her baby as far away from us as she can." Josephine glanced at the sun. "It's getting close to lunch. How about we hike on up to the beginning of the Naches Trail. It's not far. The view is spectacular. Plus, the last time I was here, there were still some relics scattered in the meadow from the pioneers who crossed these mountains."

Tatyana wasn't listening. All she could think about was what had just taken place. She took a steadying breath and closed.her eyes. She wished she were home, safely tucked away indoors.

"What's the Naches Trail?" Dimitri asked.

"Originally it was used by the Indians to get over the mountains. Later, settlers brought wagons over."

"I'd like to see it," he said.

"See what?" Tatyana asked, trying to focus on what was being said.

"Are you all right, dear?" Josephine asked.

"Yes, I think so," Tatyana said, standing.

"We can go back to the truck if you like," Miranda said.

"No, I am fine." Tatyana didn't want to appear childish.

🐜 🐜 🐜 🐜 🐜

Walking through knee-deep grass, Tatyana scanned forested ridges and deep valleys that stretched out for miles and miles. Beyond, jagged snow-covered peaks reached toward the pale blue sky. Tatyana stooped and plucked a fall daisy. Its bright yellow center had faded, but it was still lovely. Bright red blossoms dotted the meadow. Josephine had explained the vivid flowers were called paintbrush before she and Miranda had wandered off in search of artifacts.

A wagon wheel lay partially hidden within the grass, and Tatyana touched the rough, weather-worn wood. "I wonder what the people were like. They must have been very brave. I would have hated being a pioneer."

"I don't know. It sounds exciting to me," Dimitri said. "And I don't think they would have come so far if they didn't want to."

"That is not always true. I do not understand why people want to leave their homes."

CHAPTER 5

"I suppose they want something better." He stretched out his arm and turned in a half circle. "Look around. Wouldn't anyone want to settle here?"

"Being beautiful does not make a place home," Tatyana said, the familiar ache for her homeland welling up. "Sometimes it is difficult to find happiness in a new place. It is not always easy to be content."

"Are you talking about yourself?" Dimitri asked.

Tatyana plucked a white petal from the daisy.

"I thought we talked all this out. You said you were happy to live here."

With a heavy sigh, Tatyana said, "I have tried. But after Yuri . . ." She threw the flower to the ground. "I get angry with myself and wonder why I am not content. It is beautiful here, and most of the people are kind." Then she looked at Dimitri. "And I have a good husband whom I love. But . . . still it is not home. After Yuri was born, the old feelings came back, and I have longed even more to return to Russia. Yuri needs to know where he is from."

Dimitri clenched his teeth, and a muscle in his jaw twitched. "Russia is not his homeland. He is an American. This is his home."

"How can you forget so easily where you came from?" Tatyana demanded.

"It's Janna, isn't it?" Dimitri accused. "Ever since you've been spending time with her, I've noticed a difference. She's been talking to you about Russia, hasn't she?"

"It is not Janna." Tatyana hesitated. "We do talk of Russia, and it feels good to retell stories of my childhood and to hear Janna's stories. But even without that, I know I belong there."

"Tatyana, there is no way you can go back. All you will find there is death."

"You do not know that is true."

Setting his jaw, he said, "You are my wife, and you belong with me. This is our home, and this is where we will raise our children. And that is all I'm going to say about it." His expression hard, Dimitri turned and walked away.

CHAPTER 6

E LENA SAT ON THE BENCH BESIDE
Tanya. Her hands were pressed between her knees, and she
watched her friend paint. Each stroke of the brush added rich-
ness to the scene on her canvas. "I always wished I could create
something beautiful like that."

Tanya stopped and looked at Elena. "What about your
music? It's wonderful."

"That's different. Someone else wrote it. I only play the
notes."

"You're not just copying notes. You bring part of yourself to
the songs. You give them life, and your playing has a unique
energy. I can feel your spirit in the music as you play. It blesses
everyone who listens." She returned to her palette, dipping her
brush into spicy brown and then into burnt orange.

Elena studied the deserted park. A fine layer of frost covered yellowing grass, and naked trees reached toward a dark sky. Orange, yellow, and red leaves littered the ground and danced in the breeze. "Do you think it will snow?"

"Maybe. It's getting cold. Almost too cold for my paints."

Elena leaned back, enjoying the quiet. Longing for serenity, she closed her eyes and tried to soak in the tranquility around her. Even here, she couldn't put aside the city's confusion. Troubled citizens crowded buses, police vans cruised the streets, and the ever-present soldiers scrutinized it all. She needed more than a moment of calm; she needed peace that dwells within. She felt like a drowning victim, only it wasn't water she battled, but oppressive fear from persecution.

Since Yuri's return, her turmoil had increased. He seemed distant. The closeness they'd once known had slipped away. He'd changed. Although stronger and kinder in many ways, he withheld a part of himself, and Elena felt closed off.

During the months Yuri had been gone, she'd spent hours thinking of him and longing for a reunion. Although afraid to believe it would ever happen, she had hoped. When he did return, she was not prepared for his changed appearance and was shocked, although she now had a better understanding of how horrible his ordeal must have been. Gaunt and frail, he barely resembled the young man she'd known. He never told her about his months in captivity. He'd been friendly but detached, and fearing his rejection, she remained aloof.

If he cared, he would have told me what happened, Elena thought. *I don't deserve him anyway.*

A sparrow landed on a fragile birch branch. The limb swayed slightly as he tucked his wings against his sides. He cocked his head and studied his surroundings, then fluffed his feathers and carefully groomed himself.

"Little bird, why have you not flown south?" Elena asked. "If you stay here, you'll die. Your feathers will not protect you when it turns bitter cold." She swept her arm through the air. "Shoo. Fly south and you will live."

He flitted into the air but settled in a nearby tree.

Tanya quit painting and looked at the bird. "I'm always sad when I see how many sparrows stay. One winter when I was young, I found a tiny frozen bird outside our house. I took it to my father and asked if he could make it well again. Papa was so kind. He cradled it in his large hand and smoothed its feathers, but the bird was dead. His heart had stopped, frozen right through his feathers. Each year I find others."

"Why is it some do not know when it's time to fly south?"

Tanya thought a moment. "I don't know. Maybe they like where they are and don't want to move on. Or maybe they just don't listen to the inner voice God gave them." She placed the tip of her brush on the canvas but made no stroke. "It's like people. Sometimes they also forget to listen."

Elena puzzled over Tanya's words. What were people supposed to hear? She knew that some Christians believed they heard God's voice, but he'd never talked to her.

An elderly, bent woman shuffled toward a bench in the center of the park. Huddling deep into a threadbare wool coat, she slowly sat, panting as she tried to catch her breath. With a trembling hand, she reached into her pocket and pulled out a paper bag. Taking out a piece of hard bread, she took a bite and chewed slowly. Then she broke off a small chunk and tossed it to a sparrow on the ground. The bird ate it and hopped closer. After taking another bite, the woman tore off another piece and threw it just in front of her. The bird who'd landed in the tree joined the first and quickly ate the crumb. The woman's eyes glowed with delight as she watched the two sparrows. They fluttered closer, and the old woman offered more scraps. Immediately the birds snatched them up.

Tanya picked up her pad and pencil and began sketching the woman. First the lined face and wounded eyes still lit with hope emerged on the page. Then came the frayed babushka, the overlarge coat hanging over slumped shoulders, and finally, the long skirt and laced boots.

"Why are you drawing her?" Elena asked.

"She will be perfect for my painting. I will place her on the bench in the center of the picture."

Unaware of Tanya and Elena's scrutiny, the woman continued to share her bread with her feathered friends. The first slice gone, she started on another. She looked up and caught Elena's eyes and smiled.

Elena smiled back and then looked away.

The woman turned her attention on Tanya and watched the artist for a moment before refocusing on the birds.

Elena glanced back at the old woman. "I don't understand her," she said quietly. "Obviously she's poor. Why would she give away what little she has, especially to the birds?" She swung her right leg over the left and folded her arms across her chest. "I would never do such a thing."

"I think she must be a very kind person," Tanya said, continuing to draw.

The woman tossed out her last crumb and then folded the bag and returned it to her pocket. After she watched the birds for a moment, she took a piece of paper from her other pocket. Gently she unfolded it and began to read. Her expression softened with pleasure.

"That looks like the same paper we print Scripture verses on," Elena whispered.

Tanya looked more closely. "It does." She continued to paint. "If she's reading Scripture, she's not really poor."

"She's foolish for reading that in public. She could be arrested." Elena stood. "Maybe I should see if that's what she has and warn her."

"I'm certain she knows the law. Leave her. She must make her own decisions."

At that moment, three soldiers approached the old woman. The tallest of the three stood in front of her. He had a heavy black mustache and black curly hair that escaped from beneath his cap. His voice was loud and harsh as he demanded, "What is it you're reading?"

The woman let her hands and the paper rest on her lap. "Words of comfort," she said.

"Let me see it." He held out his hand.

Calmly the woman handed him the paper.

The soldier grabbed the document and scanned it. Then he bent over until his face was only inches from hers. "So, you find comfort in this?" He straightened and crumpled the paper. "It's rubbish. And you're breaking the law."

The woman met his eyes. "The Word of God is the law."

The soldier threw the paper to the ground and yelled, "I could arrest you for such defiant behavior. But you're an old woman and will die soon anyway. Leave this park." He glared at her. "And know this, old woman, there will be no second chances."

She pushed herself to her feet. Her eyes sparkled with tears as she briefly touched his hand. "I pray one day you will know the love of God."

The man glanced at his hand. Then he watched the woman as she hobbled away. Turning to Elena and Tanya, he said, "What are you staring at?" Then he marched toward them.

Elena's instincts told her to run, but looking at the two younger men, she knew it would do no good.

The soldier strode up to the women, and with his hands clasped behind his back, planted himself in front of Tanya. Dark blue eyes stared at her. "What are you doing?" His voice was cold and reserved.

"Painting. This is a lovely place, and I come here often," Tanya said calmly.

The man stepped behind her and studied the picture. "You are very good. I think I would like to buy this painting, but first tell me, what is this you are adding?" He pointed to the beginning features of the old woman.

"It is the woman you just ordered out of the park."

"Why put such an ugly old lady in this picture? I say, leave her out."

"She belongs there."

The soldier lifted his foot onto the bench and leaned an arm on his bent leg. "This is my painting now, and I don't want her in it. I will hang this in my home, and when visitors come, what would I say about a shriveled old hag? She is not a good example of a Russian citizen."

Careful to keep her voice calm, Tanya said, "Sir, I do not mean to be disrespectful, but she belongs in this painting. She is a reminder of our humanity. Each of us will be old one day, and I pray we will have the inner beauty this woman has." She set her brush aside. "Maybe I could paint you another picture? A portrait perhaps?"

Ignoring her offer, he spat, "Beauty? There's nothing beautiful about her." He straightened and tugged at the bottom of his uniform jacket. "I want this painting but without her."

"I'm sorry, sir, but I cannot. In her I see the face of Russia—sorrow that has not abandoned hope."

"You insolent woman."

"I'm sorry, I don't mean to be. But I would bring dishonor on myself if I were not truthful." Tanya looked out over the park, then back at the soldier. "I'm an artist. And I see truth in the faces of Russia's citizens as well as the beauty of God's creation. These are what I paint."

Balling his hands into fists, he shouted, "I don't care about the truth you think you see. You will do as I say!"

"Tanya," Elena said quietly, "you can paint her into another picture."

The soldier grinned cynically. "Listen to your friend. She is not such a fool."

Meeting the soldier's eyes, Tanya said, "When I sit down to paint, I pray, and God shows me what is to be on my canvas. I can't ignore his direction."

"Another Christian," one of the others muttered. "Arrest her."

The older officer held up his hand to quiet the soldier. A question crossed his eyes. Staring at Tanya, he said, "You talk as if God is real. Do you not know the government has determined he doesn't exist?"

"The government is wrong, for he is real and alive today."

The officer's face reddened. "I will not listen to your superstition."

"Then I will say no more," Tanya said softly, picking up her paintbrush and returning to her painting.

"That's enough!" The soldier grabbed the palette from Tanya and heaved it into the grass. Paints scattered. Next, he snatched the pencil sketch, tore it in half, and threw it to the ground.

Elena thought she might be sick. She grabbed her friend's arm and hissed, "Don't be foolish. Do as he says. Do you want to get us both arrested or killed? What about your children?"

Tanya faced the soldier. "I didn't mean to insult you. That was never my intention. I will be very happy to paint another picture for you." She picked up the two halves of her sketch and looked at them. "But I would like to remember the poor woman who fed the birds."

The soldier didn't respond, but again a questioning flicker crossed his face. He quickly hid it and muttered half-heartedly, "Keep your art work." Standing very close to Tanya, he said, "I don't want to find you painting here again." With a contemptuous look at both women, he marched toward the park gates, the other two soldiers following.

Elena bent and began gathering the scattered paints. "Why are you so stubborn? You could have gotten both of us arrested. All you had to do was make the changes he asked for. Why risk your life over a painting? You can always make another."

Tanya looked at Elena sadly. "It wasn't the painting but our freedom I battled for. We must take a stand against tyranny. If we don't, there will be nothing left to us. And the enemy will have won."

"But this seems like such a little thing."

"The gifts I possess were given by God, and they are precious to me. Should I relinquish them to Stalin?"

Exasperated, Elena said, "I agree with you in principle, but you don't make sense. First of all, what difference can one person make? And did you think about what would happen if you were arrested? What about Valya and Sasha? Who would take care of them?"

Tanya bent and picked up a broken paint vial. "If we don't stand up to the enemy, our children will have nothing. They will be nothing more than slaves to their government. And yes, I am only one, but there are others, and together we are many. I will do all I can." She looked at Elena. "What about your music? How would you feel if you were not allowed to play?"

"If it was music or my life, I would choose life. Music is not that important." Elena stuffed her hands into her pockets and stared at the ground. Even though Tanya had been foolish, she couldn't help but admire her courage. She looked at her friend. "Tanya, all I could think of was running. I'm a coward. I've always been a coward."

"That's not true. I've watched you for months. I've seen you stand up to oppression, and even though you don't embrace our beliefs, you help take care of the children so I can work on the Scriptures. And at church, you play the piano for us. If we were arrested, you would be also." She took Elena's hand. "You are good and strong."

Tears brimmed in Elena's eyes. Tanya didn't know how she'd hidden while her family was being arrested. She didn't know that fear had kept her from helping them. Softly Elena said, "I'm not the person you think I am." Looking into Tanya's eyes of love, she was tempted to tell the truth, but unable to bear her friend's loathing, she kept quiet.

Her voice barely more than a whisper, Elena said, "I have been thinking that if Yuri goes to America I will ask him to take me. I'm afraid all the time. I can't live like this any more. Each new story of Stalin's atrocities only makes me more fearful. Yesterday I was told that he watches the trials and sentencing through an opening above the court chambers. It is said he grins as the execution orders are read." Elena closed her eyes. "I am sick even thinking of it."

Tanya laid her hand on Elena's arm. "We don't need to be afraid. God will take care of us. He is our Shepherd and will show us the way." She glanced in the direction the soldiers had gone and then looked directly at Elena. "I understand your fear. I feel it too."

"You? I have never seen you afraid."

Tanya smiled softly. "Every Russian has known terror." She tightened her hold on Elena's arm. "If you believe God is asking you to leave, then you must go, but do not let fear or anger drive you from your home. You cannot run from your emotions, Elena. They will go with you. Someday you will be forced to face them."

"I wish I could be strong like you, but I can't any more. And I don't want to be like the sparrows who don't know when to fly away and then die during winter's cold. If I stay, I will be like them. I know I will die."

CHAPTER 7

PULLING THE APARTMENT DOOR
closed, Yuri followed Daniel and Alexander into the frigid
November morning. The illumination of fresh snow brightened
the faint dawn light. Icy powder crunched beneath Yuri's boots
as he stepped onto the street. "It's colder than I thought," he
said, bundling deeper into his coat.

Alexander took a deep breath and let it out slowly, fogging
the air. "I've been waiting for today. I have to admit, when we
wandered in here three months ago, I wasn't certain we'd live."
He stretched, reaching his arms over his head. "Ah, to be back
among the world again and strong enough to work feels good."

"The sun will warm the day," Daniel said, gazing at a hint
of blue behind pink clouds. He placed an arm over Yuri's shoulders and headed down the street. "I'm reminded of the days

before you were arrested, and it feels good having you beside me once more, comrade."

Yuri smiled. "I was away so long. There were times at the work camp when I thought I'd never see you again." He smiled at his friend. "And now, here we are, serving God together. You and Tanya have been good to Alexander and me. There is no way to thank you." Drawing cold air into his lungs, he added, "I am stronger."

"And you look much better." Daniel slowly shook his head. "When I first saw both of you I wondered if you'd recover. You were in bad shape."

"I'll admit to being shocked when I first looked in the mirror. I didn't look like me. But thanks to Tanya and Elena's cooking and mothering, I think one day soon I'll be my old self. But staying indoors so long and hiding while recovering has been difficult. It's good to have identification papers again and to be working."

Alexander smiled. "While in camp, I dreamed of good hot food and a warm bed. And then I came here and my dream came true." His expression serious, he looked at Daniel. "Now it is time to go back to work, and it wouldn't be possible if not for your generosity. God will bless you for sharing what little you have."

"We are pleased to give what we can. God has been good to us. He has always provided. Many times Tanya has told me that he shows her where to find food. When she sees people waiting in a line, she joins it, knowing there will be something we need. We also have good friends who give generously."

"I've seen God provide so many times, but I'm still stunned by his merciful power," Yuri said. "Although, sometimes, he's very creative." He chuckled.

Daniel stopped at a cross street, removed his hat, smoothed back his black hair, and replaced the cap. "This is where we go our separate ways. Alexander, you can join me. Since you're unfamiliar with the city, I can teach you the route and introduce you to some of the people we help. Yuri, you still remember your way around Moscow?"

"It's been a long while, but I'm certain I can find the addresses."

"Good. Then you'll be on your own." Daniel hesitated and then added, "Are you sure you're ready?"

"I'm ready. I've been waiting for weeks to get out here." With a wave, he headed down the street. "I'll see you at home."

☙ ☙ ☙ ☙ ☙

As Yuri trudged through snow and ice, the city awoke. At nearly every corner, a soldier or NKVD officer suspiciously eyed passersby. Yuri did his best to look like he belonged. When a police van roared past, fear swept over him as his mind was thrown back to the day he'd been arrested. He could still see the dark green van and smell the sweat and urine of the locker he'd been imprisoned in. *"Father, please not that,"* he prayed, dragging his thoughts back to the present. He tried to relax tight muscles. *I thought I was ready for this.* Anxiously, he glanced up and down the street.

He spotted a soldier harassing a man. He tipped the citizen's chin up with the tip of his rifle barrel and reached into the man's front pocket. Taking out identification papers, he studied them while keeping the gun pressed against his victim's face. Compassion for the victim as well as anger surged within Yuri, and he balled his hands into fists. He could see the man's legs quaking. *"Father, help him."* Wishing there were something he could do and knowing there wasn't, Yuri forced himself to continue.

The city's energy was infectious, and feeling stronger, Yuri picked up his pace. A small group of students laughed and shoved as they walked past. Once Yuri had dreamed of going to school in the city. As he considered the unexpected course his life had taken, sadness settled over him, but before it could take root, he cast it away. *Don't be foolish,* he told himself. *God's call is always honorable and better than personal desires. He knows the beginning and the end. There is no better place than within his will.*

He stopped in front of an apartment building that looked like most apartments in Moscow with its rows and rows of windows set in old concrete block. He opened a scarred door and stepped into a dimly lit hallway, then he hurried up two flights of stairs and down another corridor. When he found the correct apartment, he knocked and waited.

A small woman with gray hair and deep-set eyes, opened the door. Immediately her face broke into a smile. "Oh, Yuri, how good to see you! I was told you would be helping Daniel and Tanya again."

"Good morning," Yuri said, stepping inside. The apartment was small and bare, furnished only with essentials—a mattress on the floor for sleeping, two chairs, and an old wooden table. "It is a blessing to see you again too, Mrs. Belinsky." Reaching under his coat, he removed a bundle of rolled papers tied with string. He carefully untied the package. "These are for you," he said, holding out several sheets of paper.

"Thank you. Thank you." The old woman pressed the pages against her chest. "I don't know what Isaev and I would do without the Word of God. We will share these with our family and friends." She took Yuri's hand in hers. "May the Lord bless you. We will keep you in our prayers."

"Thank you. I am glad to work in the Lord's service." With a small bow and a smile, Yuri hurried back to the street. He caught sight of a soldier quickly stepping into an alley. Uneasy, he watched the alley for a moment, wondering why the man would abruptly duck out of sight. He heard and saw nothing and told himself, *You're being paranoid. Something is going on there, and it has nothing to do with you. It's not your worry.* After checking his list of addresses, he strode down the street.

CHAPTER 7

Leaving the busy part of the city behind, he turned onto an empty, quiet lane. Thoughts of Elena filled his mind. She was beautiful, her brown eyes alight with spirit. *If only she loved me,* he thought, remembering their meeting his first day back in Moscow. That day, all hopes of proclaiming his love to her had perished. He'd seen the revulsion and pity in her eyes. Since then, she'd seemed distant and sometimes aloof. The relationship they had shared before his arrest no longer existed. Although they'd never talked of love, he'd hoped there had been something special between them. Now it was clear he'd been wrong. *She never loved me,* he thought. *It was only the musings of a love-starved prisoner.* For so long he'd dreamed of a life with her, and now his heart ached at the knowledge that there would be no future for them together.

As he crossed the street, he caught sight of another soldier stepping into a darkened doorway. *Is that the same man I saw before?* he wondered, trying not to stare. *It couldn't be. There is no reason for anyone to follow me. No one even knows I'm in Moscow.* He took a deep breath. *Relax. You're being overly suspicious.*

When he reached Mr. Moiseyev's apartment, the big man pulled him into a tight hug. "Praise God! Praise God!" he repeated over and over. When he finally stepped back and studied Yuri, he said with a grin, "You're a living miracle."

"I am," Yuri agreed and handed the man several pages of verses.

Still grinning, Mr. Moiseyev said, "We are forever grateful to you and Daniel. Please tell him we are praying."

"I will," Yuri said and turned to leave.

"Wait. Wait. I have something for you." He disappeared for a moment and returned with a small package. Handing it to Yuri, he said, "It is not much. Just a piece of sausage, but give it to Tanya. She will make a meal of it."

"You're very kind. Thank you vey much. God will bless your generosity."

"Oh, it is nothing. So little for someone who makes such a difference in our lives. I'm glad to give it." Abruptly, he placed his hands on Yuri's shoulders and planted a kiss on each cheek. "The Lord bless you. And take care as you go."

Yuri nodded. "God will take care of me," he assured the man. Then he headed out of the building. Once on the street again, he scanned the area, searching for the soldier he'd seen earlier, but there was no sign of him. Breathing a sigh of relief, he proceeded to his next address.

Although he'd made two more deliveries and still hadn't seen the soldier, apprehension knotted in the pit of his stomach. No matter how hard he tried to dislodge it, it persisted. With only one more stop left, he considered returning home. *There are people waiting for these verses,* he told himself. *And you are frightened about nothing. Where is your faith?*

He hurried on. When Yuri saw the soldier again, his heart leapt in his throat, and he nearly stopped. Instead, he quickly stepped into a bakery and waited to see if the soldier would walk by. He didn't.

Acting as nonchalantly as he could, Yuri opened the door and walked out. With a quick glance down the street, he saw the soldier leaning against a building and acting as if he was disinterested in Yuri. *He's following me! What do I do now?*

He crossed the roadway, and the officer followed. His heart pounding, Yuri acted as if he didn't see him but hastened his steps. He turned onto the next street, and glancing over his shoulder, discovered the soldier was still behind him. His stomach churned. *"Father, I need your protection. I've only just begun serving you here. Please don't allow me to be arrested."*

Yuri searched his mind for a way of escape. He couldn't return home. That would endanger his friends. He couldn't outrun a fit officer of the Soviet army. If he confronted the man, the Scripture verses he still had hidden would be discovered. *"Father, tell me what to do,"* he prayed. The word *stop* came to mind, but that made no sense, so he kept walking. *"Stop. Wait for him,"* he heard again.

Taking a deep breath, Yuri turned into an alley, but it was a dead end. Fighting panic, he pressed his back against a building and waited in the shadows. The soldier stepped into the alley, and Yuri tried to slow his breathing. It was time to face his pursuer. He stepped away from the wall. The officer stopped, and the two faced each other. Neither spoke for a long while.

Finally, Yuri said, "You're following me. Why?" He sounded surprisingly calm.

The man studied Yuri but didn't speak. His dark blue eyes held a peculiar look. Yuri could see anger in them, but there was something else. The soldier smoothed his heavy, black mustache. "I will ask the questions," he said coldly. "Your identification papers, show them to me."

Yuri dug into his coat pocket and withdrew the false documents. His hand shook slightly as he gave them to the soldier. Yuri hoped he didn't notice and prayed the papers were in order.

The officer looked them over for a very long time, then finally seeming satisfied, returned the documents. "Why are you visiting so many different homes? You have made several stops."

Yuri searched for a reasonable explanation. "I've been sick, and now that I'm feeling better I wanted to see my friends."

"It seems strange that you would call on so many and for such a short time. Sometimes you didn't even go inside. And I saw you give away papers. I would like to see those." He held out his hand and waited.

"I have none."

The officer narrowed his eyes. "You're lying." Shoving Yuri roughly against the building, he snarled, "Put your hands on your head and face the wall."

He'd been found out. Yuri knew better than to resist. "All right, I have some, but they're only songs." He reached into his inside coat pocket and removed one sheet.

The soldier snatched it from Yuri's hand. Psalm 40 was written across the top. Yuri's persecutor silently scanned the page and looked at his captive. "This is not a song. There are no notes."

"It is." Yuri began to recite the Scripture passage. "I waited patiently for the LORD; and he inclined unto me, and heard my cry. He brought me up also out of a horrible pit, out of the miry clay, and set my feet upon a rock, and established my steps. He has put a new song in my mouth—"

"Stop! I will hear no more!" The young man pointed his rifle directly at Yuri's chest.

"That song was written hundreds of years ago by a man named David and recorded in the Book of Psalms."

"You are a *Christian,* aren't you?" He didn't wait for Yuri to respond. "What is it about you *Christians?*" He spat the word. "This superstition of yours has robbed you of reason. I've seen it again and again. Everywhere I find Christians shamelessly reading and quoting from their Bibles. Why do you disregard the law? Don't you care about your life?"

Yuri didn't think he actually wanted a response, so he said nothing.

"I asked you a question."

"I love life, but it is only a temporary state. What matters is my eternity with the Lord."

"You'll spend the rest of your miserable life in prison." He glanced down again at the verses, then shaking his head slowly back and forth, he said, "I have no wish to arrest a fool." Glaring at Yuri, he crumpled the paper. "Give me the rest of your subversive material, and renounce your faith, and I will let you go."

Yuri stared at his oppressor. "I cannot."

The man cocked his rifle and fixed it against Yuri's coat. "I have the authority to shoot you. Tell me the truth. There is no God."

Yuri felt a surge of faith and power flood him. "I cannot. God is truth. I love him, and he loves me. I will not turn from him."

The man jammed the rifle hard against Yuri's chest.

Staring into hardened eyes, Yuri was aware only of profound peace.

For a long moment, the officer kept his gun pressed against Yuri. Gradually the anger and challenge left his eyes, and he slowly lowered the rifle. "I don't understand you Christians. What kind of faith makes a man unafraid to die?"

"Faith in the living God."

A puzzled expression crossed the man's face.

Yuri held out his hand. "I am Yuri Letinov."

Lowering his rifle, the soldier looked at Yuri's outstretched hand and tentatively took it. "Tupolev Chernov."

Yuri smiled. "I'm glad to meet you. Will you let me tell you more about God?"

"Keep it to yourself. I don't want to know."

"I will not force it on you. But there is so much God wants you to know."

At first Chernov said nothing, then looking back toward the street, he asked, "What does this God want me to know?"

"First, that he loves you."

"Love? If there is a God, he's cruel and vengeful. He doesn't love. You've been deceived and are a greater fool than I thought."

Keeping a steady gaze on the soldier's eyes, Yuri said, "No. It is you who have been deceived." Tupolev clenched his jaw, and Yuri thought he saw a momentary chink in the man's armor. "God walks with me, and each day I know his love."

"You are wrong. There is no God. Stalin has said this, and he is our leader and protector." He looked at the street again. "I don't know why I'm even talking to you." He moved as if to leave.

"What if God has something to say to you and you do not listen? Is Joseph Stalin more powerful than God? Can he protect you if you ignore God?"

Tupolev said nothing, but stared at Yuri. "You may go."

Yuri took the remaining verses from his pocket. "Please, take these."

Tupolev stared at the pages, as if afraid to touch them.

"Please," Yuri repeated.

The soldier finally grabbed them and stuffed them into his jacket pocket.

"They are yours. Read them. I will look for you. Maybe we can talk again?"

"I will find you if I have more questions," the soldier said and walked away.

❧ ❧ ❧ ❧ ❧

Late that afternoon Yuri was still overwhelmed by how God had rescued him. Excitedly, he told the Belovs and Elena about his encounter with Tupolev Chernov and prayed there would be an opportunity for him to share his faith with the soldier.

"You had a close call," Daniel said, raising a questioning eyebrow. "I'm not sure you did a wise thing, giving him the Scriptures. What if he regrets letting you go? Now he has evidence to arrest you."

"I know it was a risk, but I did the right thing. God's Word is powerful, and if he reads the verses, they may change his life forever."

"I hope you're right."

Alexander clapped a hand on Yuri's shoulder. "It's just as I said. God will use us no matter where we are. In prison camp or on the outside. You did the right thing, comrade."

A loud rap at the door startled everyone. "Are you expecting anyone, Tanya?" Daniel asked.

"No. No one."

Squaring his shoulders, Daniel went to the door and opened it.

"I am looking for Yuri Letinov," a man said.

Yuri stood. "It's him, the soldier," he whispered.

"What do you want with him?" Daniel asked.

"Tell him Tupolev Chernov is here."

Yuri nearly sprinted to the door. "Tupolev Chernov, it is good to see you."

His face a mask, the soldier said, "I have questions."

"How did you find me?"

Unable to withhold a small grin, he said, "I am trained to follow people, remember."

Yuri glanced out onto the street.

"I am alone and wish you no harm." He peered into the dim apartment. "May I come in?"

Yuri looked to Daniel who swung the door wide. "Yes. Please come in. Welcome."

Tupolev stepped inside. Standing very erect and rigid, he looked at Tanya, Elena, and Alexander.

"Dear Lord," Elena said, clapping a hand over her mouth.

"What is it?" Daniel asked.

Tanya joined her husband and smiled kindly at the soldier. "We have met before."

Tupolev's eyes widened.

"I'm glad you're here. Would you like some tea?" Tanya asked.

Yuri glanced from Tupolev to Tanya. "You know each other?"

"We met in the park a few weeks ago." Tanya nodded toward the picture of the old woman sitting on the park bench feeding birds. She'd hung it on the front room wall. "I was painting this."

Tupolev's eyes followed Tanya's. "The painting. You finished it." He crossed the room as if drawn to the picture and stood in front of it. "You kept her in." He touched the old woman's face and looked at Tanya. "It is fine work. Is it for sale?"

"Maybe. Are you interested?"

Tupolev turned and looked at Yuri. "I read the papers you gave me. I do not understand what is happening, but I want to know more about God." He looked back at the painting. "She no longer looks ugly to me. What is it I see?"

"Maybe God is giving you new eyes." Tanya took the painting from the wall and handed it to the visitor. "Here. It belongs to you."

CHAPTER 8

SASHA RAN AHEAD. "COME ON. Hurry."

"I can't. I'll spill the soup," Elena said, switching the cast-iron kettle to her right hand.

"My turn," Yuri said, taking the pot from Elena.

"Sasha, walk with us," Tanya said, glancing up and down the street.

Sasha ran back to her mother and fell into step beside her. Breathlessly, she said, "It's a wonderful idea to visit Mr. and Mrs. Tereschenko. Do you think they'll be surprised?"

Daniel shifted Valya on his shoulders. "Probably."

"Jesus was born on Christmas," Valya said.

"Yes, he was, and we celebrate the birth of our Savior every year," Daniel said.

Alexander peeked inside his coat at the loaf of warm bread tucked against his chest. "I don't know if I can wait much longer to eat. This bread smells so good."

"You will wait," Tanya said sternly, though she was smiling.

Trying to avoid a deep drift of snow, Yuri slipped and bumped against Elena. "I'm sorry." He took a side step away from her but wished he could pull her close to him with his free arm. This would be his last Christmas with her, but he'd told no one of his decision. He glanced at Elena's gloved hand and fought the impulse to clasp it within his own.

Sasha bounded into a pile of deep snow. "Do you think St. Nicholas will visit tonight?"

Tanya looked at her daughter. "This is a time to think of Jesus, not gifts."

Sasha's shoulders drooped. "I know, I was just hoping."

"Soldier," Daniel whispered.

The group quieted.

"Will he arrest us for celebrating Christmas?" Sasha asked.

"Shh." Tanya grabbed her daughter's hand and kept walking.

Smoking a cigarette, the soldier leaned against a street light and watched the approaching citizens. Taking one last drag off the cigarette, he tossed it into the snow and stepped into the group's path. "What are you doing out?"

Forced to stop, Daniel said, "We're going to see friends."

The soldier's eyes moved from Daniel to Tanya, Elena, then Sasha, who huddled against her mother. He shifted his gaze to Yuri and the stew pot. "What is that?"

"Only soup. We're going to share it with our friends," Yuri explained.

The man walked up to Yuri, lifted the lid, and peered inside. The aroma of vegetables and sausage filled the air. He studied the contents a moment, then dropped the lid back, nearly dumping the pot. "All right. Go ahead."

✳ ✳ ✳ ✳ ✳

At the apartment building, Daniel opened the outside door and stepped into a dark hallway lit by a single naked bulb. After everyone was inside, he led the way up one flight of stairs and down another dimly lit corridor. "Room 212," he said, stopping in front of a splintered door. He knocked.

"Yes, who is it?" came an elderly voice from the other side.

"It's Daniel."

The knob turned and the door opened. A small, bent woman with wiry, white hair framing her face, peered out. Blue eyes nearly buried in wrinkles lit up, and a smile creased her face. "Daniel. Tanya. How nice to see you." She looked into the hallway. "You're all here. How wonderful!" She stepped back and opened the door wide. "Please, come in. What a special treat to have our friends visit on Christmas." She glanced at a nearly bald, heavyset man lounging in a threadbare overstuffed chair. "Velodya, we have company." She motioned for him to rise.

Smiling from beneath heavy brows, Mr. Tereschenko heaved himself out of the chair. "Welcome, welcome," he said, leaning heavily on a cane and clumping across the room. He greeted Tanya with a kiss on each cheek and did the same with the other guests.

Olya also greeted her guests with kisses. After everyone had been properly welcomed, she asked, "Would you like some tea?"

"That sounds wonderful. It is very cold." Tanya rubbed the palms of her gloved hands together for emphasis. "And tea will go very well with dinner."

Yuri held up the pot of soup, and Alexander removed the bread from beneath his coat.

"My goodness. Yes," Olya said. "Please, set them right there on the table." She shuffled into the kitchen, took a kettle from the stove, filled it with water, and returned it to the burner.

Mr. Tereschenko sat back down, and Valya crawled into his lap. "Did you know it's Christmas, and St. Nicholas will come to visit tonight?" she asked.

Hugging the little girl, Velodya said, "Yes. What a wonder is Christmas."

"Jesus was born on Christmas," Valya said, snuggling close. "Mama and Papa said he is the Messiah and that he loves me."

"And he does." Velodya chuckled. "He loves all children but especially three- and nine-year-old girls."

"I'm four," Valya said defensively.

"My mistake. I'm very sorry."

Olya lifted the lid on the pot. "Oh, how wonderful." Closing her eyes, she inhaled deeply. "Sausage. I can't remember the last time we had such a treat."

"We have a friend who gives us some now and then. It makes wonderful soup," Elena said.

Olya took Elena's face in her gnarled hands. Her eyes brimming with tears, she said, "You tell your friend thank you. He has reminded me of my childhood." A faraway expression filled Olya's face. "Before Lenin, when I was a girl, Christmas was always a grand celebration. We'd roast a pig, and many of the people of the village came to our house. After we had eaten, we joined our guests and walked from house to house. Someone would carry a tall pole topped with a star, and we'd sing Christmas hymns as we walked. The priest always lead the procession. We stopped at each home and had something special to eat, and sometimes we played games." She wiped tears from her eyes. "Those were wonderful days."

Mr. Tereschenko gently slid Valya from his lap and joined his wife. Placing an arm around her shoulders, he kissed her cheek. "And this is a wonderful day also. Our friends have come to visit and share a Christmas meal with us."

"Yes. God is good," Olya said. "And now we should eat. I will get the dishes."

Alexander asked, "Can I cut the bread? I've been smelling it all the way from home, and my mouth hasn't stopped watering."

Olya reached into a drawer and taking out a knife, handed it to him.

CHAPTER 8

While Alexander went to work on the bread, Tanya and Elena set out spoons, bowls, and cups.

"Butter would taste so good on the bread," Olya said. Her eyes sparkling, she continued, "But I used all I had on something special. I've been saving butter and sugar just for this day. I had some fall apples left, so I made strudel. I'm sure it isn't as good as I used to make because flour is so deplorable these days. Still, it will taste good."

"Strudel! I love strudel," Sasha exclaimed.

Yuri smiled but couldn't dislodge the ache he felt at this bittersweet time. This was his last Christmas in Russia and with these people. *Maybe I should stay,* he thought. *Maybe I heard God wrong.* But even as he considered staying, the peace he'd felt since making his decision wavered. He knew he must go to America.

"Gather around, everyone," Velodya said. "We'll thank the Lord and enjoy this meal which was prepared with such love." Everyone stood around the table and joined hands. Mr. Tereschenko bowed his head. "Our heavenly father, we are filled with joy on this special day. We're grateful to be able to gather in your presence, and we thank you for the gift of your son, Jesus. Olya and I praise you for our wonderful friends who remembered us on this holy night. May you shower them with your blessings. Amen." Wearing a broad smile, he looked up. "Sit. Sit. We will eat."

They ate, and the room resonated with the sounds of warm conversation, laughter, and the clink of silverware against ceramic bowls. When the soup and most of the bread were gone, the women cleared away the dishes, and Olya proudly presented her apple strudel. "It's not like my mama used to make. If only I had a little more sugar . . ."

"Stop," her husband said, raising his hand. "It will be wonderful."

Olya nodded slightly and set the dessert in the center of the table. Both young girls pressed in close and watched as she

89

divided the pastry into nine small pieces. Their eyes glistened in anticipation as they took their portions and sat on the couch to eat them.

As Yuri bit into the sweet flaky dessert, the flavor of apples and sugar filled his mouth. "This is delicious. I can't imagine it being better."

Olya blushed slightly. "Thank you."

"What a treat," Tanya said. "Thank you so much."

After everyone had finished eating, Velodya stood, and leaning on his cane, walked to a cabinet in the living room. "When I was a boy, we always celebrated Christmas with a special toast." He took two tapered candles and two crystal candleholders down, limped back to the table, and placed them in the center; then he lit them. Hobbling back to the cabinet, he opened the top door, reached to the very back of the shelf, and took out a bottle of wine. "I've been saving this for a special occasion." He blew dust off the bottle. "What is more special than celebrating the birth of Christ?" Using a corkscrew, he removed the cork and placed the bottle on the table. "We will need glasses. Yuri, could you get the crystal from the cupboard? I don't think I can make another trip across the room."

Yuri jumped up and crossed to the sideboard.

"They're on the second shelf," Velodya instructed.

Yuri quickly retrieved seven glasses. "These are beautiful."

"They belonged to my mother," Olya said.

Velodya poured wine into all the glasses. "Jesus Christ gave all he had to give." Velodya held up his glass. "A toast to his sacrifice."

Raising their glasses and nodding, the adults drank the precious wine. Velodya looked at his wife and took her hand. "Every day I am aware of his presence. He walks beside me, comforting me. I can see him in the love of my wife and friends, I hear him as he speaks to me through his Word. I have felt his presence in my darkest hours."

Eyes brimming with tears, Olya squeezed her husband's hand. "And I thank the Lord for providing me with a husband like you. We have been married fifty-eight years, and I've never regretted the vows I made to you."

Daniel looked at those around the table. "We also have seen dark days, but sharing the burdens with my family and friends has lightened my load. I see Christ in those around me, especially in my wife. She is always beside me." Taking Tanya's hand, he pressed it to his lips.

Tanya tried to blink back tears, but they trickled down her cheeks anyway. "I remember the day I met Jesus Christ as my Savior. I vowed to serve him. I have often fallen short, but he has never turned from me. And many times when I've failed, he's used my husband and friends to encourage me and help me continue. I praise Jesus for being my friend and always showing me unconditional love." She cuddled little Valya closer and kissed the top of the youngster's head.

Alexander stared at the table, then allowed his eyes to move from one face to the next until he'd touched each with a warm look. "I have known you a short time, but I feel you are my family and a gift from God. When I was growing up, I had a wonderful family, and it is because of their faith and strength that I know Christ. After I lost them, *he* filled the hollow place left in my soul." His eyes teared. "Even in times of despair, he's never deserted me."

Yuri's heart was full. "I remember a time not long ago when I believed God had forsaken me. A friend," he looked at Alexander, "reminded me that God never forsakes his children. And on a lonely . . ." his voice broke, ". . . Christmas morning, he brought the light of Christ back into my life." Tears flowing, he said, "Thank you, friend."

Sasha offered a shy smile and said sweetly, "I want to thank Jesus for loving me. He is kind and gentle. Sometimes when I'm afraid, I feel him near, and I'm not so scared anymore."

Elena shifted uneasily in her chair. Everyone had prayed except her. She stared hard at the table.

Finally, Velodya broke the silence. "On a night like this, our Lord was born." He closed his eyes. "Thank you, Father, for loving us so much you came to earth as an infant and lived among us." He looked up, and with his voice quaking and slightly off key, he began to sing, "Today the Virgin gives birth to him who is above all beings. . . ." The others joined in, and the candles flickered as their breath touched the flames. Joy radiated from the faces around the table. After singing the last line, "For unto us is born a young Child, the pre-eternal God," Velodya said, "Amen." For a moment all was quiet, then Sasha asked, "Is St. Nicholas going to come now?"

"Sasha," Daniel said gently, "we already have the greatest gift of all, the Son of God. How can we ask for more?"

Sasha frowned.

"Oh, yes, Jesus' birth is a wonderful gift," Velodya said, "but I do have something for you from St. Nicholas. He told me he thought the two Belov girls were very special and deserved something wonderful. He left your gifts with me, and I promised to give them to you."

Sasha and Valya's eyes lit up. "Really? He was here?" Sasha asked.

"Yes, of course," Velodya said, pushing against the table as he stood. Leaning on his cane, he walked again to the cupboard and reached into the bottom shelf. When he straightened, he held up two exquisite porcelain dolls.

The girls' eyes widened, but neither said a word as Velodya walked back to the table. One had thick, blonde hair and was dressed in an elegant white fur cape with a wide hood. Her face looked pink and fresh. He handed it to Valya who gazed at it as she gently cradled it against her. The other doll had long black hair plaited into a thick braid that hung down her back. She looked refined in a red fur coat. The old man's hand shook slightly as he gave the beautiful gift to Sasha.

"It is for me, truly?" she asked.

"Yes. That is what St. Nicholas told me."

"Oh, Velodya, they are too much," Tanya said.

"No. Not too much," Olya corrected. "They are just right for such precious children." She smiled, took her husband's hand, and pressed it against her cheek.

"But, where . . . ?"

"They have been here, waiting for the girls," Velodya said.

"Mama, isn't she beautiful?" Sasha asked, holding out her doll.

"Yes, very beautiful."

Olya pushed herself to her feet. "When I was a girl, my grandmother always told me a special story on Christmas. Would you like to hear the tale of the Snow Maiden?"

"Yes! Yes!" both girls cried.

"Then you must sit over here beside me," Olya said as she shuffled to the worn davenport and sat in the middle. She cuddled Valya on one side and Sasha on the other. "Long, long ago, in the far northern, coldest part of old Russia, a woodcutter lived with his daughter, Sonya. Her mother died when Sonya was very young, and the little girl was left all alone in their tiny hut for days on end while her father cut wood in the forest." As Olya told the story, Sasha and Valya kept their eyes fixed on the kind, old woman.

Yuri's mind strayed, and he studied his friends, wondering how they would accept the news of his leaving. He looked at Elena. Her skin glowed in the soft candlelight. *She is so beautiful. I will never stop loving her. How can I leave her?* His throat contracted, and his chest ached at the thought. He knew that once he crossed the ocean he would never return. *If only she would come with me.* He considered what it would be like to have her at his side in America but dismissed the notion as foolishness. She wouldn't leave Russia to go with him.

Trying to concentrate on something else, he thought about what he'd heard of America. It was a big country although not as large as the Soviet Union. It might be difficult to find Tatyana. *No, I have her address,* he quickly reassured himself. He'd heard that everyone had enough to eat and the people lived in absolute freedom. Could it be true? He could barely imagine what it would be like to live without persecution.

Yuri glanced at Elena. She was staring at him. For a long moment they gazed at each other, then they both looked toward Olya. Yuri struggled to listen to the story.

"And with a final hug, the Snow Maiden walked into the forest," Olya finished. She kissed the top of Sasha's head and peered down at a sleeping Valya.

"Another one, please," Sasha begged.

"No. That is all for tonight," Daniel said. "Your sister is already asleep. It is time to go home."

"But I'm not a baby like Valya. I'm not sleepy at all." With pleading eyes, she said, "Please."

"I do not mind," Olya said. "If it is all right, I can tell her one more story. It's not a long one."

Daniel shot a questioning glance at Tanya who nodded her approval. "All right, then," he said. "One more."

"This is the story of the 'Babushka's Christmas,'" Olya began.

Yuri leaned his elbows on the table and sipped his tea.

"You look sad," Elena said quietly. "Is something wrong?"

"No. I'm just tired." He sat straighter in his chair.

Daniel eyed his friend. "I think it's more than that. I've seen a shadow in your eyes all evening. Sharing our burdens lightens them."

Yuri hadn't intended to tell his friends just yet, especially not on Christmas. Setting his cup on the table, he looked at Daniel. "This is not the right time."

"Why? This is the best of all nights. And we want to help."

Yuri studied his friends. He folded his hands on the table in front of him and took a deep breath. "You know I have been considering going to America. I have made a decision."

"You're leaving us, aren't you?" Elena said.

Olya stopped speaking and looked at Yuri.

Meeting Elena's eyes, Yuri answered, "Yes. I must find my sister."

Daniel said nothing.

Alexander leaned forward on his elbows. "I have been praying you would stay. I can't believe this is the right decision. I know you have prayed, but have you listened for the voice of God?"

"Yes. Of course."

"Is it possible you misunderstood?"

"I have thought and thought. And I have prayed and prayed. It is what I'm supposed to do."

"But, you have just started back to work with the underground," Alexander pressed. "What about people like Tupolev?"

"God will accomplish his work here no matter what I do. There are others who are willing to help. I believe he has something else for me."

Alexander pushed his chair back and walked to the window. He stared out into the dark night. Keeping his back to the room, he said, "I . . . we need you here." He turned and stared at Yuri. "What if we all decided to leave? What would happen to those searching for the light of Christ?"

"Alexander, I don't take God's call on my life lightly. You know that. I believe he's asking me to go to America. Christ is needed even in a land of freedom. Believe me, I have reconsidered many times but find peace only in my decision to leave."

Silently, Alexander stared at Yuri. Then he abruptly swept his arm out toward the window and said, "There is a city filled with hurting people. This is a land shrouded in darkness. And you believe you are needed more in a country where abundance is known by all and Christian oppression is unknown?" Shaking his head, he said, "I fear you have been deceived."

Yuri leaned forward and covered his face with his hands. When he looked up, he said solemnly, "I don't always understand the workings of God, but he's asked us to go into all the world. I had hoped that my friends would give me support, not persecution, especially you, Alexander."

Alexander looked bereft. "My wish is not to inflict pain. We are brothers. I am only saying what is in my heart." He turned and looked outside. His voice grieved, he said, "I cannot hold you here, comrade. I will miss having you at my side."

Daniel placed his hand on Yuri's forearm. "All of us will miss you, Yuri, but you must do what you believe is right. We will pray for you."

"Thank you."

"You will be greatly missed," Velodya said somberly.

The room was dead quiet.

"Yuri," Elena began, her voice soft. "I have been thinking." She glanced at Tanya. "I have been thinking I would like to go to America. I do not belong here anymore. My family is gone, and I want a chance for a new beginning." She met Yuri's eyes. "Is it possible. . . would you consider taking me with you?"

Yuri's heart soared. It was what he had dreamed of!

Sasha ran to Elena and wrapped her arms around her friend. "No. Please don't go. I couldn't bear it if you left." She turned tear-filled eyes on Yuri. "Please don't take her away."

Yuri reached out and caressed Sasha's dark hair, then looked at Elena. "There is no one in America for you. Why should you leave your home?"

"I have nothing here." She glanced at Daniel and Tanya. "You have been wonderful to me, but. . . I can't bear to watch you destroyed when the soldiers come. They will come. They always do. I've seen it. My own family. . ." She couldn't finish and allowed her eyes to stray over the table. "I don't want to hide anymore."

"Getting out of the Soviet Union will be dangerous. You'll have even more to be afraid of," Yuri explained.

"Yes, but if we make it out, it will be worth it."

CHAPTER 8

Yuri wanted to say yes. Should he take her? Traveling with him would place Elena in danger. He'd be responsible for her safety. And what was God's will for her? Taking a deep breath, he looked at the special woman. "I don't know. I don't want you hurt."

"We have traveled together before, remember? You know I can take care of myself," Elena said, fire returning to her eyes.

His mind flashed back to the first time he'd seen Elena. She'd been standing proud and unafraid in the military truck that carried them to their execution. Even facing a firing squad, she'd been brave. But since then, the weight of living under tyranny had nearly extinguished the boldness in the young woman. What would become of her?

Meeting her eyes, Yuri knew what was right. "Yes," he said. "You may join me."

CHAPTER 9

TATYANA SAT ON THE SOFA AND slipped her feet into dress shoes. "Do you think the inn will be crowded?"

Dimitri peeked out the window at the white landscape. "Hard to say. It's Friday and payday, but the roads are slick."

"I hope there are lots of people. It is more fun that way." Tatyana stepped into her husband's arms, and together they took a couple of dance steps. "I love to dance." She kissed him and then asked more seriously, "Do you think Carl and Susie will mind if Antar and Janna came with us?"

"I thought it was just going to be the four of us."

"It was, but I talked to Janna today, and I think she is lonely. It has not been easy for her and her husband to make friends. I remember when I first came here—I felt lonely and out of place. Sometimes I still do. Anyway, I asked her to come with us."

"You should have asked Carl first."

"I know, but I felt sorry for her and did not think he would mind."

"Well, from what I know of Carl, he won't mind. But Antar's not very friendly. At work he keeps to himself, and I don't know anyone who's been able to get close to him." Dimitri buttoned his cuffs. "Since his first day at the mine, I've made sure to say hello whenever I see him, and I've even sat with him during lunch a few times, but he never has much to say. He acts like he doesn't like anyone."

"I know it seems that way, but I think it is something else. Maybe he is afraid because of something that happened in Russia. Janna said he keeps much of himself locked up, even from her."

"I doubt Antar will have a good time with us. He's not sociable, and I bet he doesn't enjoy dancing." Dimitri sat on the sofa beside Tatyana. "I've been wanting to talk to you about Janna. I don't think it's a good idea for you to spend so much time with her. The more you see her, the more downhearted you seem about living here. I don't think she's good for you."

Tatyana took a step back. "Janna and I are friends. She needs me, and I need her."

"What about Susie? She's your friend."

"Yes, but she is an American and does not understand about being Russian."

"I know you struggle living here away from your home, but I still don't understand why it is so important that you have a Russian friend."

Tatyana thought, searching for a comparison Dimitri would understand. "You and the other miners feel close. You share your work, and you know what it means to be a miner. I cannot because I am not a miner. It is the same with Janna and me." She fiddled with the earrings Susie had convinced her to wear.

"I know that sometimes when I visit Janna I feel sad and homesick. When we are together, we talk about Russia and what our lives were like there, and I miss it. But our visits also give me something I long for—a connection with my homeland."

Dimitri pulled Tatyana close and kissed her forehead. "I think I understand. But do you think you could find a way to be happier after seeing her?"

"I will try."

A knock sounded at the front door. "That must be Elise Johnson," Dimitri said as he headed for the door.

"I thought Josephine was going to stay with Yuri."

"She couldn't make it, so I asked Elise. She's a nice girl." He opened the door, and a pretty blonde teenager stood at the door shivering. "You look like you're freezing. Come in," Dimitri said.

Elise hurried inside. "Oh, thank you. It's bitter out. Daddy says it's going to get real cold tonight and freeze up solid."

Dimitri closed the door. "I hope not. The roads are already bad enough."

Elise shed her wool hat and coat and hung them up.

"Thank you for staying with Yuri," Tatyana said.

"Thank you for asking me. He's such a precious little boy."

"Well, we need a night out and are grateful that you've come over on such short notice." Dimitri took his coat and Tatyana's out of the closet and held Tatyana's while she slipped her arms into the sleeves. He put on his, buttoned it, then pulled on his gloves.

"He is sleeping now but will wake up soon," Tatyana said, wiggling her fingers into her gloves. "There is a bottle in the refrigerator."

Dimitri placed his hat on his head. "We'll be at the Green River Gorge Inn. And we won't be late."

"Stay as long as you like. Tomorrow's Saturday, and there's no school."

A horn sounded out front. "That must be Carl." Dimitri opened the door for Tatyana, and a blast of cold air swept into the room.

"Have fun," Elise said as Dimitri and Tatyana stepped outside.

* * * * *

Dimitri opened the car door and stuck his head inside. "Evening."

"Good to see you," Carl said.

Stepping aside so Tatyana could get in, Dimitri said, "Hurry up. It's freezing out here." Once Tatyana was seated, he slid in beside her.

"Hi, Susie," Tatyana said.

Susie turned and smiled at her friend. "So, you ready to dance?"

"Yes. I am excited." She leaned forward and placed her hand on the seat beside Carl's shoulder. "Carl, I did something without asking you, and I am sorry. I asked Janna and Antar if they would like to come with us."

Glancing over his shoulder, Carl smiled and said, "Sure. They can come along. That's one thing nice about this old Plymouth, there's plenty of room." He shifted into first and eased onto the snow-covered road. "They're living down on Roberts Road, aren't they?"

"Yes," Tatyana said.

Carl headed west. "I'm surprised Antar would want to go to the inn. He doesn't seem the type to enjoy dancing."

"That's what I told Tatyana," Dimitri said.

"It's Janna who wants to go," Tatyana explained.

As they approached the sweeping curve at the bottom of the hill, Carl slowed the car.

"It is the first house on the right," Tatyana said.

As Carl let off the gas and braked, the car slid toward the ditch.

CHAPTER 9

Tatyana gripped the seat, and Susie gasped.

He turned into the slide, and the car straightened. Slowing, he said, "That was almost the end of our evening celebration." He pulled into the driveway and honked. Immediately the front door opened, and Janna, bundled in an oversized wool coat, stepped onto the porch. Her dark-haired husband followed. In the dim porch light, Tatyana could see his jaw was squared and his mouth set in a hard line as he headed for the car.

"I'll ride up front," Dimitri said and climbed out. "Janna, why don't you sit next to Tatyana." He stepped aside and shook hands with Antar. "Good to see you."

Antar nodded and mumbled something indistinguishable.

Janna slid in next to Tatyana. "Thank you . . . for letting us . . ." She thought a moment, then said, ". . . come with you? Is that right?"

"Yes," Tatyana said, scooting closer to the door.

Antar sat beside his wife and pulled the door closed.

Carl glanced over his shoulder. "I'm glad you could make it."

"We are happy to be here," Antar said stiffly.

"Hello," Susie said. "Have you been to the Green River Gorge Inn before?"

"No. Never," Janna answered, her dark brown eyes alight with excitement. "We not know American dances, but I like to . . . learn."

Antar said nothing.

✳ ✳ ✳ ✳ ✳

Icy snow sparkled beneath the car lights as they climbed Lawson Hill. Carl glanced back at Antar. "Good thing you're here. We might need the three of us if I slide into the ditch. The road's pretty slick."

"Oh, we'll be fine," Susie said. "You're a good driver." She kissed her husband's cheek.

103

Carl gripped the steering wheel and kept his foot on the accelerator. They made steady progress, but two-thirds of the way up, the rear end of the car slid across the center of the road.

"Don't let us down now," Dimitri said. "I planned on dancing tonight."

Carl fought the skid, and for a moment they returned to the right side of the road, but the car slid too far. "I've got to stay out of the ruts," he said and steered toward the edge, putting his passenger-side tires on the side of the road. They spun, then bit into the deeper rock buried beneath snow, and the car continued to climb.

When they crested the hill, a sigh went out from the car's occupants.

"Good job," Dimitri said. "For a while I was afraid our evening out was going to be short-lived."

"I started praying at the bottom of the hill," Tatyana said.

As they crossed the bridge spanning the Green River Gorge, Tatyana strained to see over the railing and down into the bottom of the deep ravine.

Just on the other side, Carl pulled into the small parking lot in front of the inn.

"There aren't many people here."

"It's early. Give them time."

Dimitri stepped out and opened the car door for Susie, while Carl and Antar did the same for Tatyana and Janna. Music drifted out into the cold night air as Janna studied the inn. Its peaked roof sheltered a long front porch, and windows across the front were aglow. "It is bigger than I thought."

"I don't know how many are foolish enough to venture out in this weather," Susie said. "It's worse than I thought. I wasn't sure we'd make it up Lawson hill."

"Folks from Enumclaw can make it out," Carl said.

Susie shivered and pulled her coat tighter. "I'm cold. Let's go in."

CHAPTER 9

Tatyana walked back toward the bridge. "I want to look at the river first. It is so beautiful."

"It's dark, and the road's slippery. Be careful. It's a long way down," Susie said, studying the bridge warily "I don't like heights. Looking that far down gives me the willies."

Tatyana kept her hand on the railing as she walked to the middle of the bridge. Then she stopped and gazed down into the deep gorge. Far below, the Green River reflected the moonlight like glass, and snow clinging to steep hillsides cast back its brightness. The river rippled over shallows, wound its way around boulders, and swept into frothy white water as it danced over rocks. Massive cedar and fir trees grew along the river bank, stretching upwards toward the bridge. Over the years the roots of some had loosened, and now the forest giants grew at an angle, above the flowing water. Others had toppled and now lay in the cold wetness.

Dimitri rested his gloved hand over Tatyana's. "It's beautiful."

Tatyana took a deep breath. "I love the smell of cedar trees and the sound of a rushing river." Then she looked at Dimitri and said, "One day, maybe we can live along a river?"

"Maybe."

Janna walked slowly to Tatyana, then with her hands gripping the top railing, she looked down. Immediately she stepped back. "Oh, it is so far." Edging back to the rail, she looked again, and this time she didn't retreat. "It is . . . very pretty. I . . . remember a place like this . . . near my home in Russia." She looked back at her husband. "Antar, come, look."

"I have already seen," he said sullenly as he joined his wife. Resting an arm around her shoulders, he said, "It is cold. We should go in."

"Come on. You're making me nervous," Susie said. "I don't like that bridge. Let's go in. I want to dance."

The catchy beat of "In the Mood" drifted from inside, and Tatyana said, "I feel like dancing."

"Now you're talking." Susie said as she danced toward the inn door.

Tatyana took Dimitri's hand, and the two walked toward the inn with Janna and Antar following.

When they opened the door, a loud blast of music greeted them. Five musicians stood on a small stage, one on trumpet, another playing the clarinet, a third blowing into a saxophone, and one man puffing on a trombone. The last of the musicians stood strumming a bass, his eyes closed.

"They sound good," Susie shouted. "I want to get the full effect. Let's sit up close."

"I'd rather sit toward the back so we can visit," Carl yelled.

Susie shrugged and led the way to a back table. After they were all seated, a pretty, blonde waitress wearing a tight-fitting, belted dress and bright red lipstick approached their table. Smiling prettily, she asked, "Hi, Carl. It's been a while since you were here."

"How are you, Sally?"

"Good, all except for my aching feet. I've been on them all day. Ellen didn't make it in again. Her kids are sick. Did you hear they've got diphtheria?"

"Diphtheria!" Susie said. "Have there been any other cases?"

"Not so far, but you know how it can be. First, just a couple of kids get sick, and the next thing you know, the whole town is down with it."

"Are the children going to be all right?" Tatyana asked.

"Don't know yet. They're pretty bad."

"How awful," Janna said.

Carl leaned forward on his elbows. "Tell Ellen we'll be praying for her and the kids."

"I'll tell her. Now, what can I get you?" Her order pad in one hand and a pencil in the other, Sally waited patiently.

"I'd like a Coca-Cola," Susie said.

Tatyana brushed her hair off her shoulder. "I would like one too."

Smiling at Carl, Sally asked, "And you? Are you going to have a cola too, or maybe something a little stronger?"

"No. A cola's fine with me."

She looked at Dimitri. "So, handsome, what would you like?"

"Just a cola," Dimitri said.

Sally looked at Janna and waited.

"I like to try a Coca-Cola."

She winked at Antar. "And you?"

Antar looked at the table. "Vodka."

"Vodka it is."

As Sally walked away, Susie said, "Grrr, she's such a flirt." She looked at her husband. "Do you have to be so friendly?"

Carl grinned. "You wouldn't want me to be unfriendly, would you?"

"She's a floozy, Carl."

"You don't know that." Carl wrapped an arm around Susie's shoulders and pulled her close. "You have nothing to worry about. She doesn't hold a candle to you." He kissed his wife's cheek. "Besides, you're being judgmental. I don't think God would approve."

Susie leaned against him and smiled as the band began to play "Moonlight Serenade." "Oh, I love this song," she said and stood. "Come on." She pulled her husband to his feet and led him onto the dance floor.

"You want to dance?" Dimitri asked.

Tatyana eagerly stood and took his hand, but when she looked at Janna, the pain she saw on her friend's face made her wonder if she'd made a mistake in bringing her along. "We will be right back," she said and walked with Dimitri to the dance floor. Once in her husband's arms, she watched as Antar downed his drink. Janna looked like she might cry. She leaned against

Dimitri. "I feel bad for Janna. Maybe you should ask her to dance."

"She's married to another man. I can't ask her. I barely know them." He tightened his arm around Tatyana's waist. "Right now, I just want to think about us."

He made a quick twirl, and Tatyana laughed, following his steps as he swept her around the dance floor. She liked the way her skirt swished against her calves with each turn. By the time the next song began, she'd forgotten about Janna and Antar. She closed her eyes and rested her cheek against her husband's shoulder, allowing herself to be lost in the sweet melody of a waltz and her husband's arms.

The song ended far too soon. She looked at Antar who was still scowling. "Has Antar said why he is so unhappy?"

"No. He says as little as possible."

"We need to pray for him," she said as Dimitri led her back to their table.

Dimitri drained his glass of cola. "I worked up a thirst." He scanned the room for a waitress. Raising his hand in the air, he caught Sally's attention, and she immediately walked to the table. Dimitri lifted his empty glass. "Can I have another?"

"Certainly," Sally said and walked away, rolling her hips provocatively.

Dimitri looked at Antar. "So, how do you like living in America?"

"I like it fine," Antar said as he watched the dancers.

"Do you like to dance?" Tatyana asked.

"No. . . ." he started to say as he looked at Tatyana. "Well, not like this. In Russia I danced, real dancing."

Tatyana set her drink on the table and leaned forward on her elbows. "I remember too. We had wonderful parties. My uncle had a big barn, and neighbors from all around gathered there. We listened to the balalaika and mandolin." Her voice softened as she said, "Sometimes my brother would sing. And we would dance so hard the floor would shake."

Antar's eyes brightened. "Yes." He lapsed into Russian. "That is what I remember. We would celebrate and dance, sometimes until morning. Not this childish prancing, but the kind that takes real strength and endurance. It was nothing like this." Abruptly he stopped and regained his reserve. "That is the kind of dancing I like," he said more quietly.

Tatyana could see pain behind his eyes and understood. Life was good here, but it wasn't home. The familiar longing for her homeland welled up. Hoping to ease his pain, Tatyana said, "I miss it too. Maybe one day it will be better. We can pray."

Antar looked at her, and his expression softened slightly. "Now we live in America," he said in English. "In Soviet Union our lives were different. I will adjust to life here." Then he stood and looked directly at Tatyana. "I must learn these American dances. First you will teach me, and then I will teach Janna." He looked at Dimitri and asked, "If it is all right with you?"

Dimitri said nothing for a moment. Then he gave him a quick nod.

Antar flashed what could almost be called a smile at his wife and then held out his hand to Tatyana.

Tatyana didn't move at first. She looked at Dimitri who held his mouth in a tight line. "Are you sure?"

Dimitri nodded again. "Go. He wants you to teach him." She glanced at Janna.

"Yes. Please teach. I will watch," Janna said.

Tatyana allowed Antar to lead her to the center of the dance floor. Placing her left hand on his shoulder, she put his right hand on her waist and held the other in her right hand. "Follow my lead," she said, stepping backwards. His body rigid, Antar stumbled as he struggled to follow Tatyana around the dance floor.

Dimitri sat, with his arms folded across his chest, his face stony. Tatyana smiled at him, but he didn't smile back. *He's angry,* she thought. *He ought to understand. I am only helping Antar.* Then she looked at her partner and said, "You are doing very well."

"This is easy. Not a challenge like in Russia."

Tatyana smiled and continued to move to the rhythm of the music, careful to keep a respectable distance between herself and her student. Gradually he relaxed and moved more easily. When the song ended, she said, "Now you can teach your wife."

Antar bowed slightly. "Yes. Thank you." He walked back to the table and stood before Janna. "Would you like to dance?"

A smile brightened Janna's face. "Oh, yes," she said and stood.

"Your husband learns fast," Tatyana said as she sat.

Still sullen, Dimitri said nothing.

The front door burst open, and four men who were hanging onto each other and laughing stumbled inside. They lurched to the bar, obviously intoxicated, and ordered drinks. A blond-haired man stared at Antar. He nudged the man beside him. "Hey, isn't that the guy who left the sulfur ball in the coal? He could have killed us."

"Yeah, that's him," a redheaded man replied.

The blond man walked across the dance floor toward Antar. His friends followed. He stopped in front of Antar. "What do you think you're doing here? You think this place is open to anybody, even Commies? Didn't anybody tell you you're not welcome?"

His hands balled into fists, Antar glared at him. Janna laid a hand on her husband's arm and said in Russian, "Please, Antar. No fighting."

"You belong back where you came from. You don't even speak the language. None of you immigrants knows how to do a decent job. You could have gotten all of us killed."

"I do good job. And I will stay in America." Antar eyed his adversary. "You have too much to drink."

"I haven't had enough," the man bellowed.

Carl and Dimitri approached the group. "John, you're tanked. Why don't you go on home and sleep it off."

CHAPTER 9

John poked his finger against Carl's chest. "You go home. I'm staying." He staggered toward Antar. "They ought to fire you. But they won't." He looked at his buddies. "We'll have to do what the company won't."

Carl stepped between the two men. "Look guys, we don't want any trouble. Antar made a mistake. He's not the first one. And no one was hurt." He placed a hand on John's shoulder. "Just do like I said and go home."

John slapped Carl's hand away, and puffing himself up, stood chest to chest with him. "No one tells me what to do." He pointed at Antar. "He's gonna pay for his mistake." He shoved past Carl and bristled up to Antar. "I don't like you. Nobody does." He looked at his redheaded friend. "Ain't that right, Kyle?"

Kyle nodded. "Yep. Nobody."

"You're a freak and you don't belong on our crew. Find some other place to live."

"Antar, please, let's go home," Janna said.

Without looking at his wife, Antar gently pushed her behind him. Glaring at John, he said, "This is my home. I will stay. This is free country. I have a right to be here."

"That's what you think, but I'm here to tell you you're wrong." John pulled back his arm and swung, but Antar side-stepped the punch and watched as John swiped at the air and stumbled, nearly falling.

Righting himself, John turned and glared at Antar. "Get him!" he shouted to his friends.

Kyle jumped Antar, swinging and landing a blow to his chin. Antar staggered backwards but recovered and came at the redhead and hit him hard in the stomach.

Carl grabbed the pudgy man by the shirt collar and shoved him toward the door. "You need some fresh air," he said through clenched teeth, warding off a jab thrown by the drunk.

The tallest one of the three lunged at Dimitri and tried to land a punch, but the big Russian grabbed the man's fist and pushed him down, forcing him to his knees. "You'll leave my friend alone," he said evenly. The man pushed against him, but Dimitri kept him pinned.

"My hand, my hand," he finally cried. "You'll break it."

"Are you leaving?" Dimitri asked.

"Yes. Yes. Just let go."

Dimitri released the man's hand and the man ran to the door and disappeared outside. Free now, Dimitri returned to Antar and his two attackers. Much larger than either one, Dimitri grabbed the redhead by the back of his shirt collar and dragged him off Antar.

Kyle jerked free and turned on Dimitri. He lunged at him, grabbing him around the waist. Dimitri grabbed Kyle by the hair, brought his head down, and kneed him under the chin, sending him sprawling. Dimitri stood over Kyle. "It's time for you to leave."

Kyle pushed himself up to his feet and ran at Dimitri, who tried to step aside, but the redhead managed a blow to his gut. His face red and his body shaking in anger, Dimitri grabbed the small man and tossed him. Kyle landed on his back and lay gasping for breath. Glaring at his opponent, Kyle struggled to get up.

"No, you don't," Dimitri said, grabbing his hair and bouncing his head against the floor. Finally, Kyle lay still.

Antar was bashing his fist into John's face again and again. Clearly the man was beaten, but Antar continued to pummel him. Dimitri grabbed Antar's arm and pulled him away. "Let him go!"

As if unaware of Dimitri's presence, Antar jerked free and continued beating John. This time Dimitri caught him in a bear hug and pinned his upper arms. "You'll kill him!"

In a rage, Antar broke away from Dimitri, turned on him, and drew back his fist.

"Antar!" Janna grabbed her husband's arm. "Antar! Please! Stop!"

CHAPTER 9

As if awakening from a trance, he looked at his wife and slowly lowered his arms.

Carl set a chair upright. "That fat guy was a handful," he said, brushing his hair back off his forehead. "There has to be a better way to handle disputes." He shook his head and glanced at the inn's owner. "Sorry, Al. This wasn't our idea."

"I know, I saw the whole thing." He gave the two drunks still lying on his floor a disdainful look.

✻ ✻ ✻ ✻ ✻

"Sit down," Tatyana said, pulling a chair away from the kitchen table.

Dimitri did as he was told.

She held a cool washcloth to Dimitri's swollen eye. "Men. It would seem you could think of better ways to settle arguments. You never see women fighting like that."

Dimitri caught hold of Tatyana's wrist. "What choice did we have?"

"You could walk away."

"What about Antar? Were we just supposed to leave him on his own?"

"You could have made him leave."

"No, he wouldn't have." As Tatyana dabbed at a cut on his cheek, Dimitri winced. "And what about our honor?"

"Honor?" Tatyana shook her head. "You could have been badly hurt. Plus, when those men wake up, they will look for you."

"They won't even remember the fight, but they'll know they had one," he said grinning. Then he shook his head. "We shouldn't have taken Antar and Janna with us."

Tatyana planted her hands on her hips. "It was not their fault. They did nothing."

"I don't mean to be harsh, but they don't fit," Dimitri countered, an edge in his voice.

Tatyana began to get angry. "You should remember what it is like not to fit. Once you were an outsider too. How can you be so hard?"

"I remember, but I adjusted. Antar doesn't want to."

"Give him time."

"And as nice as Janna is, she upsets you."

Tatyana folded her arms across her chest. "She is my friend."

"A friend who makes you feel worse about living here." He stared at the floor. "And what was that with you and Antar?"

"It was just a dance. Could I refuse him? He needs people to care."

His voice quiet, Dimitri said, "I didn't like it when I saw you in his arms."

"Dimitri, it was innocent, just a dance."

Dimitri reached for Tatyana and pulled her against him. Resting his cheek against her stomach, he said. "I know. I'm sorry, but I was jealous."

Tatyana caressed his hair. "I am sorry too. I did not know it would hurt you."

Neither of them said anything for a few moments, then Dimitri asked, "And what about Janna?"

Tatyana sighed. "Dimitri, it is not Janna who makes me long for home; it is Russia calling to me. I try to ignore her voice, but I cannot. Every day I pray for contentment, but it does not come. I long for peace. Please try to understand. Please pray for me."

CHAPTER 10

TATYANA LAID YURI IN HIS CRIB
for his morning nap. Looking at his mother, he tried to keep
heavy eyelids open, but they closed, and the infant stuck his
thumb in his mouth and sucked. Tatyana covered him with a
wool blanket. As she gazed at the blonde-haired baby, love
welled up inside her. "Thank you, Father," she said and caressed
her son's soft cheek. She tucked the blanket under his chin. "You
are growing too fast," she said softly, amazed at how quickly the
last seven months had passed.

As she remembered the children who'd died of diphtheria
the last several weeks, sorrow swept over her. The names and
faces of the little ones rolled through her mind. *Why?* she wondered, sick inside at the thought of losing Yuri. *I could never bear
it.*

She glanced out the window. It was the weekend, and children frolicked, throwing snowballs, building snowmen, and sledding. Since the outbreak, quarantine posters had been hung on the doors of stricken houses, keeping people from going in and out. Even healthy households had kept to themselves. There was nothing more they could do to avoid the disease. Tatyana smiled, thankful life was returning to normal.

Someone knocked at the front door, and she hurried to answer it. A small clean-shaven man wearing an oversized coat and carrying a trunk smiled at her. He removed his hat and bowed slightly. "Good morning to you, ma'am."

"Good morning," Tatyana said. The man looked familiar, but she couldn't place him.

"It looks like things are getting better here in town. I didn't see any quarantine signs this morning. Still, you never know, and I figured I'd be doing you a favor by bringing sewing supplies to you." He hefted his black case slightly.

"I usually buy them at the company store," Tatyana hesitated, "but I have not gone lately, and I do need thread."

"I carry only quality wares, and my prices are good."

Tatyana eyed his case. "I suppose . . ."

"Wonderful. I'm sure I've got just what you need." He shook Tatyana's hand. "I'm George Salter. But most folks just call me the threadman. Let me show you what I have," he said, stepping past Tatyana and into the house.

Tatyana stared after him, dumbfounded at his pushiness. He walked confidently across the room, set his case down in front of the sofa, and flipped open the locks.

"I think you'll like what I have here." He looked at Tatyana, who'd barely had time to close the door. Warily she walked toward the sofa.

Opening the lid, Mr. Salter turned the suitcase around so Tatyana could see inside and sat down. Elastic bands held an array of sewing notions in straight rows. There were pins, needles, shoelaces, thread, cards of buttons, hooks and eyes, even scissors. "So, what color thread do you need?" he said smiling.

Tatyana peered inside the case.

"You might be able to see better if you sit down." He patted the cushion beside him.

Tatyana didn't like the invitation, thinking the man forward, but she sat anyway.

Mr. Salter stared at Tatyana. When she didn't say anything, he pressed, "So, what color do you want?"

"I always need white, and my dark blue is nearly gone."

The salesman grinned. "You're not from this country, are you?"

"No," Tatyana said, steeling herself against the contempt that usually came with such statements.

"You from Russia?"

"Yes."

"Thought so. Your accent is still pretty strong. I'd wager you haven't been in this country long."

"A little more than two years."

The man nodded slowly. "You a Communist?"

"No, I am not," Tatyana said, stiffening her back. Why was it people thought all Russians were Communist?

"What are you then?"

"I am a Russian who lives in America," she said curtly.

Mr. Salter reached into a front pocket and took out a pamphlet and handed it to her. "You might want to think about joining the IWW."

Tatyana scanned the paper, but reading English was something she still hadn't mastered. "What is the IWW?"

"The International Workers of the World. It's an organization that helps working-class people. We defend workers' rights."

"What does that mean?"

Mr. Salter leaned back and clasped one knee in his hands. "Well, there are workers and owners. Doesn't it strike you as unfair that it's always the owners who have all the money?" Not expecting an answer, he continued, "If we abolished the wage system, everyone would share the wealth." He glanced around the small house. "I take it your husband works at the mine?"

"Yes."

"He goes down into that mine every day and risks his life. And for what? A pittance. Who makes all the money? The rich mine owners, that's who. They're the ones who make the dough."

Tatyana thought a moment. "But someone must do the work."

"Yeah, but don't you think the ones taking the risk and doing the labor ought to get an equal share of the profits?"

"I guess so."

"That's not how it works in a capitalist society. What happens is the rich get richer and the poor get poorer."

The threadman's words sounded familiar, and Tatyana felt a jab of fear. She looked squarely at the man. "In Russia I heard the same words. The leaders talked of prosperity and equality, but there was only more work, less money, less food. The government said it was for the people, but it imprisoned the citizens, took away our homes, and . . . "

"That's because the Russian government went too far and didn't stick to Karl Marx's plan. A wageless system is good in the right hands." The salesman leaned forward. "I mean, wouldn't it be wonderful if everyone was on equal ground? No rich tycoons telling you what to do and makin' the little guy grovel for a dime."

The idea appealed to Tatyana. Was it possible such a policy could work? "How did you learn about workers' rights?"

"Through the IWW. The IWW has its own newsletter, even a songbook. I'm a member. Do you and your husband want to go to one of the meetings? Usually there's a guest speaker, and we talk about how to make changes in this country. Progress has been slow, but I believe one day we'll be freed from the wage system." He paused and studied Tatyana a moment. "And I think the founders of the IWW were inspired by God."

"God? Why do you think that?"

"At one meeting, the speaker showed us right from the Bible just what he'd been talking about."

"You mean about no wages?"

"No. He spoke about people needing to treat each other fairly and said that no man is better than another."

That is true, Tatyana thought. *God does say we are to be kind to each other, and he loves us all the same. Maybe I should find out more about the IWW.* "I might like to go," she said. "I will ask my husband."

"I'll tell you what, you keep that brochure and read it over. This month's meeting was day before yesterday so it'll be another month before the next one. But I'll be back this way just about that time. We can talk more then, and I can answer any of your questions and take you to the meeting."

"Thank you," Tatyana said as she folded the pamphlet and slid it into her apron pocket.

From his case, he took out a spool of white and one of blue. "Now, then, you need thread; is there anything else?"

"No. That is all. How much does it cost?"

"Five cents for the both of them."

"That is fair," Tatyana said and walked into the kitchen. Taking the money jar from the top cupboard, she opened it and counted out five cents. Returning to the front room, she handed the money to Mr. Salter, and he gave her the thread.

He closed the suitcase. "It was a pleasure doing business with you, ma'am."

Tatyana nodded slightly.

The door opened and Dimitri stepped inside, accompanied by a cold wind. "I didn't know we were having company."

"This is Mr. Salter, the threadman."

Dimitri pulled off his gloves, shifted something under his coat, and held out his hand. "Good morning. I'm Dimitri Broido."

"George Salter," the salesman said, standing and shaking Dimitri's hand. "Nice to meet you. Good little woman you have here."

"He sells sewing supplies." She held up the thread she'd purchased. "I needed two spools."

"I'll be on my way," Mr. Salter said, stepping past Dimitri and outside.

Dimitri shut the door and turned to look at Tatyana. "I have a surprise." He reached inside his coat and took out a box with a Peg-Board back and set it on the table.

"What is it?"

His eyes alight with pleasure, Dimitri turned the mahogany box around so Tatyana could see the front. It was slightly longer than a shoe box and had three large knobs across the front and two smaller ones beneath them.

"A radio?" Tatyana whispered.

"Yep." Dimitri grinned. "It's a tabletop model. Nothing fancy, but I was told it puts out good sound. I thought with so many people sick and everyone having to stay indoors, we could use some cheering up. I've been putting in a lot of hours, and I figure we can afford it."

Tatyana ran her hand over the small wooden cabinet. "How wonderful! We can listen to music and radio programs!" She looked around the room. "Where should we put it?"

Dimitri walked across the room to a small table just under the window, moved a lamp sitting on it to one side, and set the radio in the center. "This will work."

Tatyana followed him. "How do you turn it on?"

"It runs on batteries, so just turn the first dial to the right."

She rotated the knob and it clicked. Static crackled from the radio's small speaker. Dimitri turned another knob, and a man's voice filled the room.

"It works!" Tatyana said jubilantly. "Can we get music?"

Dimitri moved the dial again. Static, then a soup commercial blurted from across the airways.

Tatyana kissed Dimitri. "This is wonderful! Thank you!"

Smiling, Dimitri looked at the receiver. "We'll be able to listen to 'The Amos and Andy Show' and 'Bob Hope,' 'Buck Rogers,' and . . ."

"And 'Big Bands Live,'" Tatyana cut in. "I heard the program at Susie's."

Dimitri sat in an overstuffed chair and threw one leg over the other. "It will be nice to get the news and listen to the president."

"Did it cost a lot?"

"No. I got a good price. Tom had this one on sale." He peered out the window. "It's starting to snow again." He walked to the closet, took off his coat, and hung it up. "Some folks are saying we're going to get a real bad storm. It is getting cold." A man on the radio introduced Benny Goodman's song, "After You've Gone," and the melody filled the small house. Dimitri faced Tatyana. "Would you like to dance?"

Tatyana stepped into his arms. "I would love to."

For a few minutes the couple silently swayed and twirled around the front room. Tatyana laid her cheek against her husband's shoulder. "This is so romantic."

When the music ended, Dimitri continued to hold Tatyana and kissed her. "We'll have to do this more often."

"Mmm," Tatyana said, cuddling close. Neither moved for several moments. Finally, Tatyana stepped back. "Are you hungry? I can make lunch."

Dimitri returned to the chair. "Not yet." Closing his eyes, he rested his head against the chair back. "So, has the threadman been here before? I don't remember seeing him."

"No, but Susie buys from him."

"He sounded like he was on the make. I didn't like him."

"He was a little odd. He gave me this," Tatyana said, taking the pamphlet out of her pocket and handing it to Dimitri. "It's about the IWW, a group that protects workers."

Dimitri studied the leaflet. "I've heard of them. They're against a free market and want a government-controlled society. They're nothing more than Communists." He crumpled the paper.

"I wanted you to read that to me."

"I don't want you to have anything to do with these people."

"But he said the IWW cares about working people."

"That's what they say. But isn't that what Lenin and Stalin said in the beginning? It doesn't work. In the end, it's the government against the people."

"But he seemed to believe so strongly, and what he said made sense."

"I'm sure he believes what he's saying, but he's deceived. Do you want America to be like Russia?"

"Why do you always think Russia is bad? There are many good things about our homeland. Do you not remember anything good?"

"Very little," Dimitri said, his voice hard. "Why do you refuse to look at the truth? I don't understand why you feel loyalty to a country that destroyed your family?"

Tatyana clenched her jaw and struggled to restrain her tongue. After a few moments, she continued, "Mr. Salter said the Russian leaders are the reason it did not work."

Dimitri leaned forward in the chair. "It's a fantasy, Tatyana. There is no society where all the people share the wealth equally. Besides, don't you think it makes sense to reward a man for hard work? It's reasonable for some jobs to pay more than others." He paused. "Remember when I was promoted from hauling lumber to mining? That happened because I worked hard. I was rewarded for my labor. And Carl makes more money than me because he has more responsibility. It's only fair."

"But what about the very rich?"

"Mr. Meyers is rich, and he helped us and my family. If he wasn't wealthy, he wouldn't have been able to give my father a job and my family a place to live." Dimitri stood, walked to Tatyana, and put his hands on her shoulders. "After spending years in school and more years building his business, he should be rewarded. What if it were me, or Yuri? Wouldn't you want us to reap benefits of our hard work?"

"Yes." Tatyana hesitated. "But every day you risk your life when you go to work. If capitalism is fair, you should be paid more."

"I can't complain, I make good money. But the truth about my job is that anyone can do it. Now, not everyone can be like Doc Logan. He is really smart and spent years in school."

"But, I . . ."

"Tatyana, I don't want to hear anymore about this. We're not going to any IWW meetings. And I don't want you even to speak to that man again. You can buy thread at the company store."

Tatyana forced herself to be silent. She knew it would do no good to argue. Dimitri had made up his mind. But she didn't know what to believe.

A rap sounded at the front door.

Dimitri answered it. "Hi Carl. Come on in."

Carl stepped inside. "Hello neighbors."

"Hello," Tatyana said.

"Susie and I were wondering if you two would like to get out and play in the snow. With the epidemic, we've all been cooped up too long."

"Are you sure it is all right now?"

"Doc Logan said there hasn't been a new case in two weeks, and he thinks the crisis is over. Josephine said she'd stay with Evelyn and Yuri."

"Sounds like fun," Dimitri said and looked at Tatyana.

"I would like that, but I will have to make lunch and get Yuri up."

"We'll see you after lunch then," Carl said.

＊ ＊ ＊ ＊ ＊

Susie fell backwards into the snow and gazed at the gray sky. "I love winter." She sat up, grabbed a handful of snow, packed it into a ball, and flung it at Carl. She missed him and quickly gathered up another handful. Carl made his own snowball and threw it at his wife, almost hitting Tatyana.

Laughing, Tatyana jumped aside.

"Sorry," Carl said as he scooped up more snow and bounded toward his wife.

Susie scrambled to her feet and ran as the snowball flew past her face. Laughing, she stopped and pressed snow between gloved hands. "Now you'll get it," she said and threw the icy ball. It splattered against Carl's chest.

"So, that's the way it's going to be," Carl teased, grabbing more snow and chasing her down. When he caught her, he washed her face in the white ice.

Susie squealed and fell to her knees. "Stop! Stop! That's freezing."

He grabbed another handful. "You give?"

"Yes."

Smiling, Carl straightened and held out his hand to his wife.

Still panting, Susie allowed him to pull her to her feet. Unexpectedly, he jerked hard and pulled her against him. A toboggan with two boys astride whooshed past.

"Hey, look out," Carl yelled, watching the toboggan fly down the hill. Then he looked at Susie. "Are you all right?"

"I'm fine," she said, dusting snow from her pants. She pulled her hat down over her ears and stared after the boys. "That looks like fun." Glancing from Tatyana to Dimitri, she asked, "Have you ever gone tobogganing?"

"No. Where I grew up, the land was mostly flat. We used to ride in a sleigh pulled by our horses."

"How about you, Dimitri?" Carl asked.

"A few times. When we lived in New York, we visited friends in the country and did some sledding. But it's been years." Still watching the careless boys, he asked, "Do you know where we can get a toboggan?"

"Yeah, I know a place," Carl said. "Used to be at the top of Lawson road you could get someone to loan you theirs."

"Walk all the way up the hill in the snow?" Susie asked.

"It's not so bad. Come on." Carl took his wife's hand and led the way.

The road was steep and the packed snow slick. Tatyana was cold, and her legs ached. More than once she wanted to return to her warm house, but each time a sledful of squealing, happy children flew past, her enthusiasm was renewed. Besides, she didn't want to appear to give up too easily. Once when they stopped, she panted, "How much further?"

"We're nearly there." Carl smiled. "Believe me, it will be worth the effort." He continued on.

A toboggan piled with four girls headed straight for Carl. "Look out!" one child screamed, and he jumped out of the way as they plowed into the snow bank just beyond where he'd been standing. The girls pitched into the drift.

Giggling, they stumbled to their feet, straightening their coats and hats and brushing snow off their clothing. "That was close," a dark-haired girl said. "I'm sorry, but I'm not too good at steering yet."

"In trade for nearly running us down, why don't you let us take your toboggan down once."

"OK. But, you'll have to haul it back up."

"It's a deal," Carl said, taking the sled. Glancing up the hill he said, "This is a good enough place to start. We're nearly at the top."

Carl pointed the toboggan down the hill, straddled it, and sat in the front. Keeping his heels planted in the snow, he said, "Dimitri, I'll steer. Susie and Tatyana can sit behind me, and you sit in back."

Tatyana looked down the steep hill and then at the toboggan. "Carl, do you know how to steer this?"

"It's been awhile, but I haven't forgotten."

"Come on, it'll be fun," Susie said as she sat behind her husband and wrapped her arms around his waist.

Tatyana climbed on behind Susie.

Dimitri sat behind Tatyana and hugged his wife's waist. "I'm all set."

"I haven't done this since I was a girl," Susie said, her voice eager.

Holding onto the front lip of the toboggan, Carl said, "Here we go. Push with your hands." He put his feet in front of him and pushed off. Gradually the toboggan slid forward.

Closing her eyes, Tatyana tightened her hold on Susie and pressed her cheek against her back. As they picked up speed, white ground whizzed past and cold air lashed Tatyana's face. She felt as if she were flying across an ocean of ice. It was wonderful! When they bounced over a bump, she screamed and laughed as they safely sped on. "I love this!" she shouted. "It is much better than a sleigh ride." Snow drifts piled along the side of the road flew past in a white blur.

"A turn!" Carl called. "Lean to the right and hang on!" The back of the toboggan swung wide as they slid around the corner. For a moment, Tatyana thought they would tip, but the sled straightened and they headed toward another curve.

"Lean the other way," Carl shouted.

This time as they took the bend, the back of the toboggan spun out dizzily, and they flew over a mound of snow. With a hard thump, the toboggan plowed into a drift, tossing everyone off.

Tatyana lay sprawled in the snow. She held still, afraid to move. When she felt no pain, she sat up slowly and shook snow from her hair. Laughing, she said, "That was fun!"

Dimitri wiped a patch of snow off her cheek. "You look beautiful with your cheeks all flushed."

"I feel like a child. I want to do that again."

"Right now?" Carl asked.

"I wish, but no," Tatyana said. "We have to get home. Yuri will be hungry. But another time?"

"You bet," Carl said.

Dimitri stood. "We'd better rescue Josephine."

Carl grabbed the toboggan. "I have to take this back up. I'll see you at home."

"I'll go with you," Susie said and followed her husband. She looked over her shoulder at Tatyana. "Tell Josephine I'll be there soon."

Dimitri laid his arm across Tatyana's shoulders. "That was fun. We'll do it again."

They walked in silence, the snow crunching beneath their boots.

Dimitri stopped abruptly and looked all around, allowing his eyes to rest on the snow-covered rooftops with their blackened smokestacks and then on the white foothills. "This is a good place to live. With good people." He took his wife's gloved hands and faced her. "I wish you would think about becoming an American citizen."

Tatyana's happiness left her, and her eyes filled with tears. "I thought you knew me. I am Russian. That will never change. To become a citizen here would mean betraying who I am." She looked all around. "This is a good country, but it is not my home. And what would I be saying to our son? I want him to be proud of his heritage and to know where he comes from."

"He was born here. He's an American citizen. This is where he comes from."

Tatyana met Dimitri's eyes. "Sometimes I think we will never understand each other. I am not American and will never be." She took a ragged breath. "When the threadman returns, I will go to an IWW meeting with him. I want to know more about their plan." Without another word, she turned and walked away.

CHAPTER *11*

SOMEONE POUNDED ON THE door. "Dimitri," Carl called as he opened the door. "Elise Johnson is missing!"

Tatyana let her sewing fall into her lap. "Elise? Missing? When?"

"When her mother went to get her up this morning, she was gone."

"What about her boyfriend, Michael? Is she with him?"

"No. They talked to him. He didn't know anything."

"Oh, no."

"We're putting together a search team. A group of us are going over to Franklin to check out the mine. Some of the others are combing the woods."

Dimitri grabbed a jacket out of the closet. "I'll help."

"Her mother said she sometimes goes off by herself, but never so early or for this long. Elise has always been fascinated with the mines, and her mother's afraid she might have gone exploring."

Dimitri pulled on his coat. "I hope she has better sense than that."

Tatyana put her sewing in a basket and joined the men at the door. "Is there anything I can do?"

"Pray," Carl said.

Dimitri kissed his wife. "I'll be back as soon as I can."

"Are you sure that jacket is warm enough? It's March and still cool."

"It's fine."

Tatyana laid her hand on his cheek. "Be careful."

Carl stepped outside and glanced at the sky. "We still have several hours till dark."

Tatyana stood in the doorway and watched Carl and Dimitri lope down the path and vault into the back of Dave Hanson's truck. Several others were already seated on the rusting bed. Dave shoved the truck into gear, and his tires spit gravel as he pulled out.

Tatyana prayed, "Father, show them where to look. Please keep Elise safe, and protect the men who are searching." As she closed the door, anxiety pressed down on her. What could have happened to the seventeen-year-old girl? She'd always seemed so responsible. Why would she leave without telling her parents where she'd gone?

Tatyana imagined Elise wandering in a dark mine. Without ventilation, poison gases could build up in the deserted shafts. They could overtake you before you knew what was happening, and it would be too late. Elise could be dead or trapped by a cave-in.

"Oh, Lord," Tatyana said as her anxiety grew. "Anything could have happened to her." Tatyana's heart ached at the possibility. Although her parents had been aloof, Elise had always been friendly. She and Tatyana had chatted often, and Elise loved Yuri.

Tatyana went back to her sewing. Picking up a wool sock she returned to darning, but her mind was on Elise. When she could sit still no longer, she put the mending in her sewing basket, crossed to the front window, and watched the street. Spring grasses bent in the breeze.

Goldy was bawling and Tatyana sighed. "Dimitri must have forgotten to feed her. I am coming." After checking to see if Yuri was still sleeping, she grabbed her jacket from the closet and walked to the back stoop. Sitting on the step, she pulled on her boots and headed for the shed. As she stepped inside, the mingled aroma of hay, oats, and animal greeted her. She liked the smell.

Flipping on a light, she could see the honey-colored calf pushing against the wooden stall, her neck stretched over the gate. Stripping a flake of hay off a bale, Tatyana dropped it in the crib and stroked the calf's forehead. Immediately Goldy buried her face in the feed. With bits of hay sticking out of her mouth and her head nodding, she chewed.

"How are you this afternoon?" Tatyana asked, rubbing the calf's neck. "I wish you could tell me what happened to Elise." Goldy's only response was to grind her teeth as she munched.

She patted the calf one more time and walked outdoors. Heavy clouds were piling up over the Olympic range, and the wind gusted, bending trees. *A storm,* Tatyana thought. *I hope they find her soon. This time of year it could be unbearably cold.*

As she walked back to the house, she could hear Yuri crying and hurried her steps. Stripping off her boots, she washed her hands and went to the baby. Lifting her son out of his bed, she cuddled him close. "Shh. Mama is here." Yuri's crying became a whimper. Tatyana held him at arms length, and with tears still on his cheeks, he grinned at her. "I think you need a change," she said and laid him down again.

After changing and feeding her son, Tatyana placed him on a blanket in his wooden playpen and offered him a Tom Tinker. His eyes alight, he grabbed the beaded doll and waved it back and forth, chortling happily.

Tatyana kept watch at the window, but Dimitri didn't return. "Where is he?" she asked herself out loud.

Trying to pass the time, she dusted and mopped, but still the men didn't return. She turned on the radio, but the music didn't quiet her nerves. She couldn't erase the picture of Elise lying somewhere needing help. Again she stopped at the window and peered out. "Where are they?" she asked, and Yuri squealed his response. Tatyana picked him up. "It is too hard to just wait. I have to do something. What if something awful has happened to Elise?" Holding the baby close, she paced in front of the window.

"The more people looking, the sooner she will be found," she said decisively, carrying Yuri into his room. She grabbed his coat and shoes from the closet, pushed his feet into his soft leather boots, and pulled his jacket on. He smiled, anticipating an outing. After buttoning his coat, she slipped her own on, left a note for Dimitri, and headed for Susie's house.

✱ ✱ ✱ ✱ ✱

"Any word?" Susie asked as she opened the door.

"No, but I could not wait longer," Tatyana said, stepping inside. "I am worried. I want to help look for Elise."

"I've been thinking the same thing, but if she wandered into a mine . . ."

"What if she is just out there somewhere, lost and frightened, or hurt?"

"The men are looking everywhere."

"Did something happen to upset Elise?"

"I guess she had an argument with her parents last night. Something about her and Michael wanting to get married."

"They had a fight?" Tatyana asked, her mind switching gears. "Elise was angry. That is why she left," she said more to herself than Susie. "Do you think she could have left town?"

"They checked the bus station first thing. If she left, it wasn't on the bus."

A memory pricked the edges of Tatyana's mind. Last fall when she'd been picking berries, she'd come across a makeshift shelter inside a large maple stump. Clearly someone had been using it. It was stocked with blankets, pillows, and books. One of the books had been *Jane Eyre*. Until now Tatyana had forgotten about it. And once Elise had hinted that she had a secret place. Was it possible the hideaway belonged to her?

"Would you watch Yuri for me? I have an idea. I might know where she is."

"Sure, I'll watch him, but where do you think Elise is?"

"It is too hard to explain. I should be back within two hours."

"But where are you going?"

"I will take the tracks to Franklin about a quarter mile and follow a trail a little way into the woods."

"Tatyana, maybe you should just wait. It's not safe for you to be traipsing off into the woods by yourself."

"I will be fine. And maybe Elise needs me."

*　*　*　*　*

Tatyana walked as quickly as she could toward the south end of town and the railroad tracks. A gust of wind caught at her hat, and she trapped it beneath her hand, pressing it down more tightly. "I hope I am right," she said as she reached the tracks. She stopped a moment and scanned the pastures lying between the hills leading to Franklin and Lake Fourteen. Ice still clung to the lake's edges. Tatyana tucked her hands into her pockets and shivered.

She caught a glimpse of someone who looked like Mr. Robertson disappearing into the woods beyond Mr. Hanson's pastures. *I wonder if they have looked up here?* "The hiding place was not very far off the road," she said aloud, carefully stepping from one railroad tie to the next.

The woods pressed in on the tracks, and the heavy forest canopy nearly closed out the sunlight, leaving only a green gloom. Tatyana turned and looked back the way she'd come; the street had disappeared. The forest was damp from recent rains, its floor covered with ferns, nettles, and the first white snowdrop flowers of spring. The mingled odors of cedar, fir, moss, and rotting logs permeated the air. Tatyana could feel the cold dampness through her coat.

She kept her eyes on the hillside to her left, watching for the trail she'd taken the previous fall. Once she stopped and called, "Elise. Elise." There was no response, only the wind and the rustle of tree boughs.

Following the tracks, she walked on. A gust of wind swept over the treetops and a branch cracked and broke. It tumbled from limb to limb and dropped at the foot of the tree. Tatyana peered at the top of the lofty fir as it bent in the heavy breeze. *The wind is getting worse,* she thought and hurried on, not wanting to get caught in a spring storm.

A gray squirrel raced across the tracks in front of her and scrambled up a nearby tree. A few moments later it dashed down again, kicking up dead needles as it ran through a cluster of white blossoms hugging the base of the cedar. It disappeared into the undergrowth.

Naked berry bushes trembled, and the snap of a limb cut through the forest hush. Tatyana stopped and watched the underbrush, remembering her encounter with the bear the previous fall. Fear pricked her, and she took a step backward. All of a sudden, a deer leaped over the brambles and stood in a small clearing, its tail flitting as it sniffed the air. The two looked at each other for a moment, then with its tail up like a flag, the deer darted away.

Feeling silly, Tatyana chuckled softly, grateful it hadn't been a bear. Taking a deep breath, she glanced back the way she'd come and reconsidered the wisdom of going into the forest alone. *Maybe I should get someone to help,* she thought but quickly dismissed the idea. *It will take too long.*

When she came to a deer path, she studied it, trying to determine if it was the right trail. It looked like so many others in the woods but seemed about the right distance from the road. Determined, she turned off the tracks and followed the path.

The tracks quickly disappeared, and the trail narrowed, but Tatyana felt compelled to continue. The path was muddy. Mixed in with tiny hoofprints were tracks made from someone's shoes. *She must have come this way,* Tatyana decided, encouraged to keep going.

The mix of pine needles and mud clung to her shoes. She followed the path up an incline so steep she had to grab at brush and tree roots to pull herself along. One moment she was going up the trail, and the next her feet slid out from under her. She grabbed for a branch, but her hand slipped. Lying on her stomach, she slid backwards down the hill. When the ground leveled, she stood and started back up, determined to find Elise. Once on top, she looked down at herself. The front of her coat was caked with mud. She wiped uselessly at dirt, leaves, and pine needles.

Again, tempted to retreat, she looked up through tree branches to the gray sky and prayed, "Father, show me the camp. Please, show me." She closed her eyes and remained quiet. The wind murmuring through the boughs and the chatter of a squirrel greeted her as she waited for God's leading. *Should I go back?* she asked, but sensing no confirmation, she continued on.

A small creek crossed the trail, and Tatyana leaped over it. As she landed, her right foot sank into the mud along the bank. She jerked her foot free, but her shoe remained in the ooze.

Frustrated and balancing on one foot, she bent and grabbed it out of the muck. Then she hopped to a nearby log and sat. She examined the filthy footwear and shook her head in disgust. Using a twig, she scraped away the mud.

She heard a soft laugh. Looking in the direction of the sound, Tatyana saw no one but did see the top of a large stump. *It must be the one,* she thought. "Elise? Is that you?" There was no answer. Tatyana pulled on her shoe and stood. Taking a few steps toward the maple trunk, she repeated, "Elise?" Still no answer. She folded her arms across her chest and said, "Elise, please come out."

A twig cracked, and the bushes parted as the seventeen-year-old stepped out of hiding. The young blonde glanced at Tatyana and then at the ground. "I am sorry I laughed, but you looked very funny."

Tatyana held up her stocking foot and smiled. "I guess I did."

Elise met Tatyana's eyes. "Why are you here?"

"Everyone is looking for you. Your mother and father are very frightened, thinking something awful has happened."

"How did you know where to find me?"

"I found your hideaway last year when I was picking berries."

"Oh."

"We need to let your family know you are safe."

"I didn't mean to cause trouble. I was just upset. This is where I come when I need to be alone to think." Her eyes filled with tears.

Tatyana approached the girl and gently placed an arm over Elise's shoulders. "What is it? Can I help?"

Covering her face with her hands, Elise sobbed and took a step away from Tatyana. "No one can help."

"Please, tell me what is wrong," Tatyana urged. "Sharing burdens makes them lighter."

Chapter *11*

Sniffling, Elise used her shirt sleeve to wipe her eyes and nose. "I don't know what to do." She looked at Tatyana. "Michael and I love each other and want to get married. My parents say we're too young. I know I'm only seventeen, but he's going into the army, and we want to be married before he leaves. He might be sent to Europe, and I've heard there is trouble over there. Something terrible might happen to him." She dabbed at her eyes. "If I don't marry him and something happens . . ." Fresh tears filled her eyes. "I want to be his wife."

"Did you tell me you have known Michael a long time?"

"Yes, ever since we were children." She sniffled. "When we were little, we hated each other. But one day I fell into the creek, and he saved me. After that we were best friends." Elise smiled. "At my sixteenth birthday party last year, everything changed. We saw each other differently." She blushed. "I guess we both finally noticed that we'd grown up. After that, we started seeing each other, going to dances, the movies, and meeting for sodas."

"I know. You were always too busy to baby-sit," Tatyana said with a smile.

"We just wanted to be together all the time. And the next thing we knew, we were in love." Her eyes brimmed with tears again. "I can't stand the thought of him being so far away. What if he finds someone else?"

"Is that why you want to get married?"

Elise thought a moment. "No. I guess I'm not really worried about him falling for another woman. I just want us to belong to each other. That way he'll know I'm here waiting for him." She grabbed Tatyana's hand. "I've seen how you and Dimitri are. You know how it feels to be in love. Sometimes it hurts."

Tatyana smiled and nodded. "I know. It is wonderful and awful. When I see you and Michael together, I can see you are in love."

Elise brightened. "You do?"

"I can see it in the way you look at each other."

"So why can't my parents see it?"

"I am sure they are trying to understand, but they want what is best for you. Have you and Michael talked to them?"

"Yes, but they wouldn't listen."

"Did you?"

A puzzled expression flickered across Elise's face, and she didn't say anything for a moment. "I tried. They said we were too immature to understand what love is. But I do understand." She glanced at the ground and then back at Tatyana. "I'm not a child anymore. I'm a woman."

"I know what it feels like to be in love. I do not know what I would do without Dimitri." She took the young woman's hands in hers. "But Elise, you cannot go against your parents. You and Michael can be committed to each other without being married. If it is love, it will last until he comes home."

Elise moved away. She plucked a piece of grass and twirled it between her fingers. Finally she looked at Tatyana and said, "I was thinking of running away with Michael."

"Please think about it some more. You may regret it the rest of your life. A family is a priceless gift you should cherish. When the time is right, you will be married and leave your home."

"I don't think I can wait. How would you feel to be apart from your husband?"

Tatyana smiled softly. "It would be painful." She looked squarely at Elise. "But being married is sometimes difficult too. And just being married would not change the fact that you will be apart. If you go against your parents, you may not only be separated from Michael but from your family as well. I miss my home and my family." She watched the stream ripple over small rocks and wash through clumps of grass. "I dream of returning to my homeland and family one day." She blinked away tears and said abruptly, "Let us go home. We will talk to your parents."

Elise thought a moment and said sadly, "All right."

✻ ✻ ✻ ✻ ✻

When Tatyana and the young woman turned onto her street, Mrs. Johnson must have been watching out her window because she opened her door and ran to her daughter. Catching the girl in her arms, she held her tightly and wept.

"I'm sorry, Mama. I didn't mean to cause so much trouble."

Mrs. Johnson stepped back and looked at Elise. "I was afraid you might be lost in a mine or lying dead at the bottom of a ravine."

"I didn't mean to frighten you," the girl said earnestly.

"Where have you been?"

"I . . . I was upset and went for a walk along the railroad tracks and took a trail into the woods. I was just thinking and walking."

Just then Josephine pulled up in her truck. She climbed out and joined Tatyana. "I heard you'd found her."

Mr. Johnson climbed out of the back. "You are home!" he said, pulling his daughter into a tight hug. "Where have you been?"

"In the woods thinking." She glanced at Tatyana. "I had decided not to come home."

"Why? Why would you want to leave us?" her father asked.

"I . . . I want to marry Michael. I didn't think I could wait." She looked at Tatyana. "But Tatyana helped me see things differently. I will wait if it's what you want."

Mrs. Johnson smiled. "That sounds like a mature decision for a seventeen-year-old." She draped her arm around Elise's shoulders. "Let's go inside and talk some more." She turned to Tatyana. "Thank you for everything, especially for talking sense into our daughter."

"I did nothing, only listened." She looked at the young woman. "Maybe we can visit again?"

"I'd like that."

Mr. Johnson eyed Tatyana suspiciously. "Well, we'll have to see about that."

"But, Papa . . ."

"You know we've talked about this before, and I've said all I'm going to say for now."

"I don't understand," Elise argued.

"We will not discuss this here." Mr. Johnson took his daughter by the elbow as if to steer her toward home.

Elise didn't budge. "Why?"

Mr. Johnson looked at Tatyana. "I don't mean no offense, young lady, but with you being a foreigner and a Russian, I don't figure you understand our ways. And our daughter won't be needing any immigrant friends. I think you two have been a little too chummy."

Tatyana pressed her lips tightly together and choked back anger. She looked at Elise. "I enjoyed our time together," she said and turned away.

Josephine joined her and draped an arm over her shoulders as they walked.

"Thank you," Mrs. Johnson called, but Tatyana kept walking and didn't look back.

"Don't you worry none about Mr. Johnson. He's always been one to distrust folks," Josephine said. "He's nothing but a narrow-minded man."

Tatyana looked at her friend. "There are many who feel like Mr. Johnson." She struggled to keep from crying. "I do not belong here."

Josephine stepped in front of Tatyana. "Now, you listen to me. The people in this town love you. And everyone will know how you helped Elise, which will only endear you to them more. Mr. Johnson is only one man." She smiled. "There's always gonna be folks who're afraid of anyone who's different from them. But you can't be worryin' about them. This is your home. You're part of this town."

Tatyana smiled and wished she belonged, but she knew differently. Her true home was an ocean away. Like Elise, she wanted to run, not from home but to it.

CHAPTER 12

SIGHING, SASHA LEANED AN elbow on the table and rested her chin in her hand. "Mama, do you think we will have paper soon? I miss drawing."

Tanya continued stirring the soup and looked at her daughter. "I hope so. I've been praying for it too."

"If God doesn't give us some soon, I'll never learn to be an artist like you."

Tanya smiled softly, then tapped the wooden spoon against the edge of the pot and set it on the stove. She walked to the table and took Sasha's face in her hands. "If it is God's will, you will be an artist. Trust him. He is the one who gives us gifts and talents, and he helps us use them." She kissed the little girl's forehead.

"I'll try to be patient," Sasha said as her mother returned to the stove.

Yuri sat in the chair opposite Sasha. "I'll look for some today."

Alexander tousled the little girl's hair. "I will too. There must be drawing paper somewhere in this city."

"Thank you," Sasha said. "But what will I do today? I've done my chores, and I don't have anything to do."

Tanya looked at her daughter. "We need water brought in. Do you think you're strong enough?"

"I'll help her," Elena offered.

Sasha stood. "No. I can do it. And this time I'll be very careful and not spill a drop."

"Are you sure you don't need some help?" Yuri asked.

Sasha ran and picked up the empty wooden bucket sitting beside the doorway. "I can carry it," she said, opening the front door.

Daniel stood on the step, kicking mud off his boots. His expression was bleak as he looked at his daughter.

"Papa, is something wrong?" Sasha asked.

Daniel managed a sad smile. "No. Everything is just fine, little one."

Sasha stared at him. "What is that?" she asked, pointing at a red stain on the front of his coat.

Daniel looked at the stain and shrugged.

Tanya wiped her hands on her apron and joined her husband. Keeping her eyes on his, she said, "Daniel, something has happened. What is it?"

Daniel looked at his daughter. "Sasha, why don't you go out to play. It's a sunny day."

"All right, Papa." She grabbed her coat from the hook beside the door and pulled it on. Looking at her mother, she asked, "Do you think Nadya would have any paper for drawing?"

"Maybe," Tanya said. "Hurry along, now."

With a wave, Sasha jumped off the porch and ran down the street toward her friend's apartment.

Tanya turned her attention on her husband. "Now, what is it?"

The anguish in Daniel's eyes deepened, and his mouth returned to a grim line. "In the forest," he said somberly.

Elena studied him, and her stomach knotted. Something was very wrong. "What about the forest?"

Tanya closed the door and ushered her husband to the table. "Sit. I'll get you some tea."

"First, I need to wash my hands." He followed her into the kitchen, poured some water out of a pitcher, then scrubbed. The water turned pink, then red.

Tanya stared at the crimson water. "Are you hurt?"

"No. I'm fine." He scrubbed, added more water, scrubbed, and rinsed again until the water ran clear. Then he dried his hands and returned to the table.

Tanya filled a cup with pale gold liquid from the kettle and set it in front of him. Sitting beside Daniel and placing her hand over his, she calmly asked, "What has happened? God is bigger than any of our troubles."

Silently, Elena, Yuri, and Alexander sat down at the table.

For a long while, Daniel said nothing. He just held his cup between his hands and studied the tea. He didn't even look up.

"Daniel, if it's that bad, you need to share it," Alexander pressed.

Daniel glanced at the faces around the table and took another sip of tea. His voice sorrowful, he scanned the room. "Where is Valya?"

"Sleeping on our bed," Tanya said.

Taking a deep breath, Daniel began, "I was walking in the woods, looking for firewood, when I heard a gunshot." His hands shaking slightly, he set his cup on the table. "At first I thought it was nothing, but then I heard someone screaming and then another blast, so I hurried toward the sound. While I was running, I heard another shot."

"Soldiers were murdering citizens, weren't they?" Elena asked, a hard edge to her voice. "Their hearts are black."

Daniel shook his head slowly back and forth. "No. When I got there . . ." His eyes brimmed with tears, and he swallowed hard. "A woman held a pistol to her head and fired. I was too late." He gripped his cup. "There were three children—they were all dead beside her. She'd shot them all."

"Oh, dear Lord," Tanya said.

"Who would shoot children?" Yuri asked.

Daniel turned tormented eyes on Yuri. "I think she was their mother."

Tanya closed her eyes—tears squeezed out the sides and rolled down her cheeks. "Dear Jesus."

"How could a mother kill her own children?" Elena whispered.

"A woman gone mad?" Alexander asked.

Elena's eyes flickered with anger, and her voice was hard. "Yes, she was mad. Mad with fear and the agony of watching her children die slowly." She stood and paced the room. "No one knows when it will be his turn. But we know it will come. We just wait and wait." Then she looked at Yuri. "And we all know what happens in prison. If a person isn't executed, he exists in a living hell. It's a miracle Yuri and Alexander lived." She pressed the palms of her hands together. "And everyone is hungry. People are dying of starvation. Why wouldn't a person go mad?" Elena looked at her friends. "That's why we have to leave. All of us."

"Leave? Where will we go?" Tanya asked.

"To America. In America we can make our own life, not wait for it to end."

Tanya looked at her husband. "Should we go?"

Daniel squeezed his wife's hand. "I don't know. Sometimes when I think about you and the girls, all I want to do is get you out of Russia and into some place safe." He shook his head.

"Then I consider what God wants, and I think he's asking us to stay and fight. The battle will not be won if we run from it. We're needed here." He looked at Yuri. "I do not mean to say some shouldn't leave, but I don't believe it's right for me." He gazed at Tanya. "Maybe you and the girls should go."

"I will not go without you. If you stay, then we all stay," Tanya said. "God has always protected us. We will continue to trust him."

Daniel leaned forward and slowly rubbed his palms together. "There is something else," he said soberly. "Alexey was arrested last night." Leveling an even gaze on Yuri, he continued. "There will be no traveling papers for you."

Elena's eyes widened. "What if the police find his forged documents with our names on them?"

Silence settled over the table as the listeners grasped the gravity of Elena's question.

"I don't think Alexey had the papers yet," Alexander said. "I saw him two days ago, and he said nothing to me."

"But what if he did have them? We're all in danger. Every one of us," Yuri said. "You can't stay. You'll be found out. Daniel, your address is on those papers."

Daniel looked at Tanya. "What do you want to do?"

Tanya thought a moment. "I want what God wants."

Daniel stared at his hands, and a shadow crossed his face.

"It's very possible Alexey didn't have any documents yet." Alexander looked squarely at Yuri. "This may be a sign that you should stay. The journey is too dangerous without papers. What will you do when you encounter the authorities?"

"We can travel without documents. It's more dangerous but it can be done. You and I did it. When we traveled from Siberia, we were never stopped. God directed and protected us."

"He doesn't do things the same way every time. You know that. You can't count on it being so easy. What if it is his will that you stay?"

"No!" Elena cried. "I don't want to hear anything about signs from God. This belief in signs is only an illusion you use to make yourself more comfortable with your decisions. It's superstition." She walked to the window and stared at the falling rain. "It's more clear now than ever that we must leave." She turned and looked at Alexander. "I don't want to end up like that woman and her children or . . ." her voice caught, "like Alexey."

"Things are changing," Tanya said. "The government has allowed some people to have their own vegetable gardens, and that is a good thing. Maybe the government will continue to give more freedom and make fewer arrests."

Elena stared at her friend. "I wish I could believe you, but I think it's nothing more than a ploy to gain people's trust. The government will never relinquish its power over us." She looked at her mother's ring, which she'd worn since her parents' arrest, and slowly turned it. With tear-filled eyes, she looked at her friends. "Please do not misunderstand. I love Russia. It is my home. I grew up here in Moscow. For generations my family has lived and died here, but I'm not ready to die. I want to live." Her gaze settled on Yuri. "No matter what you do, I am going, even if I go alone."

Alexander pushed his chair away from the table and crossed to Elena. Placing his hands on her shoulders, he pleaded, "Please, think about what you're doing. We've been safe here. The police know nothing about our activities. God has sheltered us under his wings of protection. Why would he remove his protection now? Both you and Yuri are needed here. I fear that if you try to escape you'll be caught and arrested, or executed."

Elena met Alexander's eyes. "If your God is as powerful as you say, he can watch over us no matter where we are. What I hear, Alexander, is your lack of faith."

Alexander held her gaze. "I have faith he will fulfill his will, but not necessarily ours."

Yuri slammed his fist down on the table. "Enough!" He strode across the room, stopping directly in front of Alexander. "Don't stand in our way! Are you so certain you can hear God's voice more clearly than I?" He took a steadying breath and uncurled his fists. "This is our future, not yours," he said more calmly. "We will leave. There is a way, and God will show us. I know in my heart that Tatyana has a life in America, and I must find her."

Alexander clamped his teeth together, and a muscle twitched in his jaw, but he said no more.

"Yuri, we will do everything we can to help," Daniel said. "I still have names of people who can assist you on your way. You'll have to get a ship out of Leningrad. I don't know how it will happen, but God does. You'll have to leave soon, though. It's a long journey, and it may be difficult to find passage out of the country before winter."

Yuri nodded.

✻ ✻ ✻ ✻ ✻

Tanya handed Yuri a cloth bag that was cinched at the top. "It isn't much, just some hard bread and a little cheese, but it will help. There won't be any berries, it's still too early in the season, but you might find wild plums soon."

"When Alexander and I traveled from Siberia, many people helped us. I'm sure the Lord will provide." Yuri hugged the small woman. "Thank you for all you've done."

"This may help fill your bellies," Daniel said as he handed Yuri a snare. "Rabbits and grouse taste good over an open fire." He rested his hand on Yuri's shoulder. "You're like my brother." He blinked back tears and swallowed hard. "Life will not be the same without you."

Yuri laid his hand over Daniel's. "I will never forget you."

Sasha and Valya sat in Elena's lap and clung to her. Yuri bent and kissed each girl. Valya, her eyes red from crying, looked up at Yuri. "I do not want you to go."

Yuri picked up the child and held her close. "I will miss you, but I must go." He held her a moment longer and then set her back on the couch where she climbed into Elena's lap.

"Yuri," Sasha said quietly. "I understand that you must leave, and I am trying to be strong, but it hurts." She sniffled and wiped her nose.

"Even when you're strong, it's all right to cry. I am hurting too. But I'm already praying we will meet again." He knelt and pulled her close, holding her a moment.

Elena fought tears as she kissed the little ones good-bye. She stood, carefully disengaging Valya. Standing before Tanya, she could no longer keep her emotions in check, and tears brimmed over and onto her cheeks. "I'm going to miss you," she said as she hugged Tanya.

"I will miss our afternoon chats. And when I hear a piano being played, it will remind me of you. Daniel and I and the girls will pray for you. Please know you will never be alone. Each step you take, God will be at your side."

Elena nodded, picked up a knapsack, slung it over her shoulder, and walked to the door.

Only one good-bye was left to be said. Both men had dreaded it, but it could not be avoided any longer. Yuri crossed the room to Alexander and stood before his friend. For a long moment, neither said a word.

Finally, Alexander said, "I was wrong to criticize your decision and try to hold you here. I'm sorry. I have no doubt that you listen to God and that you hear his voice. My love for you clouded my mind. We've been like brothers, and saying good-bye is a grievous wound." He cleared his throat. "I was afraid for you and for me. Anything can happen to you out there. And here I will have to live my life without you."

"You? Afraid?"

Alexander smiled a crooked smile. "Yes. I am no different from you. I struggle like all men. And I know when you go, a part of me goes with you."

Yuri could feel the sting of tears behind his eyes. "Without you I wouldn't have made it. I will never forget you."

The two men embraced; then Yuri stepped back and joined Elena. Looking at his friends, he said, "I will pray for you every day, and I will never forget what you've done for me and who you have been to me. We *will* meet again, if not on this earth, then in heaven."

Daniel handed Yuri a slip of paper. "You'll need this. These are people who can help you. Learn the names and addresses, then burn it." He pointed at one name. "This man, Adolf Joffe, lives in Leningrad, and he might be able to help you get out of the country." He handed Yuri another set of papers. "And these. Take them. They will help sustain you."

Yuri unfolded one paper, and his eyes blurred as he tried to read the familiar words.

Daniel lifted his chin as he quoted the comforting words: "He who dwells in the secret place of the most High shall abide under the shadow of the Almighty. I will say of the LORD, He is my refuge and my fortress: my God; in him I will trust. Surely he shall deliver you from the snare of the fowle, and from the perilous pestilence. He shall cover you with his feathers, and under his wings you shall take refuge: his truth shall be your shield and buckler. You shall not be afraid of the terror by night; nor of the arrow that flies by day; Nor of the pestilence that walks in darkness; nor of the destruction that lays waste at noonday. A thousand may fall at your side, and ten thousand at your right hand; but it shall not come near you. Only with your eyes shall you look and see the reward of the wicked. Because you have made the LORD, who is my refuge, even the most High, your dwelling place; No evil shall befall you, nor shall any plague come near your dwelling. For he shall give his angels charge over you, to keep you in all your ways."

Tears flowing down his face, Yuri opened the door, and he and Elena stepped into the night.

CHAPTER 13

THE DAYS ARE GETTING LONGER,
the nights shorter," Yuri said. "We'll have to hurry if we want
to get out of the city before daylight. If we don't, our knapsacks
will draw attention from the police." He stepped off the porch,
and rain pelted his face. "Maybe the storm will keep the
NKVD indoors."

"Does anything keep them from their duty?"

"We can always hope." Yuri walked into the street. "Stay
close to the buildings," he said, taking rapid, long strides.

Elena struggled to keep up, often lagging behind and having to jog. Finally she stopped, and leaning against a block wall,
gasped for breath. "I need to rest," she called.

Yuri stopped, walked back to Elena, and stood beside her.
Hunkering deep inside his coat, he asked, "Is something
wrong?"

She bent at the waist, rested her arms against her thighs, and sucked down oxygen. Her breath formed a cloud in the cold morning air. "You're walking too fast for me. If you don't slow down, I won't make it." She straightened. "Remember, I'm only five feet two inches tall. You're . . ."

"Six feet," Yuri finished for her. "I'm sorry. All I can think about is getting to the woods before daylight." He wiped moisture from his face. "I feel like a demon is chasing us."

A shaft of light brightened the intersection one block up from them. Elena pressed closer to the building. "Maybe there is." The sound of a car engine rumbled.

"They'll see us here." Yuri scanned the street, searching for a hiding place. He spotted a recessed doorway about ten yards away. "Follow me," he said and ran for it. Just as he and Elena ducked into the shadows, lights stretched across the side of the building, skirting their hideaway.

Elena pushed her back against the wall. "The only cars on the streets this late are the NKVD," she whispered.

Yuri nodded. The sound of the car grew louder. *If only we could blend into the stone,* he thought. Elena squeezed closer to Yuri and deeper into shadow. Their shallow breaths fogged the air, and Yuri prayed the vapor would go unnoticed.

As the dark sedan moved into their vision, it seemed to slow. Motionless, Yuri and Elena held their breath. Two men sat in front. A match flickered, and a cigarette glowed as one man lit up. A spotlight brightened the sidewalk and reflected off puddles. Pressed together against the wall, Yuri and Elena were like one as the light probed their refuge.

The car passed. It did not stop.

The couple blew out their breath. "I was sure they'd see us," Elena said, her voice tight.

"Me too. I don't remember praying so hard. We'd better move on. There are bound to be more patrols." He looked up and down the street. The car was gone. He stepped into the rain.

Elena ran past him, moving away from the direction the car had gone, forcing Yuri to catch up to her. "I thought we were going to take it slower," he said, grabbing her arm and walking alongside her.

"I know, but . . ." Elena glanced back the way they'd come. "I just want to get away from here."

"I understand, but you were right earlier. We have to save our energy. We must trust God. He is with us."

Elena walked on, ignoring his comments. "We can't take a chance of being trapped in the city."

"We'll make it before daylight. God protected us from the police, didn't he?"

Elena didn't respond.

"They should have seen us, but they didn't."

Still, Elena said nothing.

🐾 🐾 🐾 🐾 🐾

The rain continued through the night, drenching Moscow and the fugitives. Nearly free of the city, they found a man lying in a gutter. Yuri stopped and knelt beside him.

"We have to keep going," Elena said. "It's almost daylight."

Yuri pulled off a glove and touched the man's face. It felt ice cold, and when he laid his fingers on the stranger's neck, he felt no pulse. "We can't help him."

"At least he's free of his misery."

🐾 🐾 🐾 🐾 🐾

The sky turned a soft pink as they left the city behind and followed a dirt road that wound up a hill and into the forest. An occasional farm light blinked at them through the early morning gloom. Elena stopped and looked back at the city. She stared for a long time. "It is odd. I know I will probably never see Moscow again, but instead of sadness, I feel relief."

"Maybe because it holds no hope for you."

155

She shrugged, turned, and moved on.

The rain had stopped, and the blanket of clouds thinned. Birds greeted the morning with jubilant song, and breezes rustled young birch leaves. Early spring grasses had emerged but didn't yet provide a protective blanket from the mud, forcing Yuri and Elena to slog through the mire.

Exhausted and cold, they walked on, watching and listening for danger. When a truck approached, they leaped off the road and hid in the brush beyond the ditch. The vehicle moved past, heading toward Moscow, its large tires churning through coffee-brown mud.

"I didn't count on the rain. It took us longer than I thought. We'll have to rest today."

"But shouldn't we put more distance between us and the city?"

Yuri thought a moment. "I remember when Alexander and I were traveling. It's important we don't get too tired, or we might become careless. We can sleep today and travel part of the night."

"It will be more difficult to see unless we have a bright moon."

"True, but it will also be more difficult for anyone to see us."

Elena nodded. "You're right. We'll travel tonight."

"Good. Let's find a place to sleep. I'm tired." Yuri headed into the forest, pushing through a tangle of dwarf birches, cranberry vines, and ferns. He stopped, looked back at Elena, and waited for her to catch up. "Where do we sleep when there is no forest?" she asked.

"We find deep grass or a deserted building."

"If there is one," Elena said wryly.

A large spruce with heavy branches reaching to the ground caught Yuri's eye. "That's what we're looking for," he said, slowly making his way to it. He pulled the boughs apart and stepped beneath the natural shelter.

Elena joined him. "This is perfect. It feels like a refuge."

"We can sleep a while," Yuri said.

Elena sat and rested her back against the trunk. She shivered and pulled her damp coat more tightly about her.

Yuri sat beside her, dug into his bag, took out a piece of bread, and handed it to her.

Elena tore off a large bite. "I'm so hungry." She chewed and leaned her head back and closed her eyes.

Yuri pulled out a blanket. "Take off your coat. It's wet."

Taking another bite, Elena stripped off the coat and hung it from a branch.

Yuri draped the blanket about her shoulders. "This will be warmer." Taking another piece of bread out of the bag, he began eating. Now that he was sitting still, he began to shiver.

Elena pulled the blanket off her shoulders and held it out to Yuri. "You need this. I have my own."

"Thanks," he said, taking the blanket. As Elena had done, he pulled off his coat and hung it from a branch; then he wrapped the cover around his shoulders.

Elena bundled into her own blanket and leaned back once again. "You'll be no help to me if you get ill."

"It's nice to know you care," Yuri said, finishing the last of his bread. He plumped his knapsack as best he could, laid his head on it, and huddled beneath his blanket. Still, he couldn't stop shivering. "This is a good hideout, but I would rather be in the sun."

"Me too," Elena said, lying down.

For several minutes, the two comrades were silent, seeking sleep and trying to control their shaking. Finally, Elena sat up. "I'm never going to get warm like this." She looked at Yuri. "We can help keep each other warm if we sleep together with both blankets over us. There will be more body heat that way," she quickly added.

Yuri sat up. "Uh, I guess that makes sense." *Of course it made sense,* he told himself. *But how can I lie beside the woman I love and not tell her?* He brushed his hair back and stared at the trunk of the spruce, clutching his blanket under his chin.

"Don't look so frightened. I'm not going to bite. This is about surviving, nothing else."

"I'm not frightened." As if to prove his point, Yuri immediately lifted his blanket. "Slide in."

Elena covered his blanket with hers and crawled in beside him. Yuri laid down, his back to Elena. He knew this wasn't what she meant, but he couldn't cuddle with her.

Propping herself up on one elbow, she said, "Yuri." He glanced over his shoulder. She smiled. "If our bodies don't touch, we can't keep each other warm."

"You're right. I know you're right." Yuri rolled over, careful to keep his arms in front of him, which created a little distance between himself and Elena.

She pressed her back against his chest and pulled the blankets tightly over her. "Let's try to sleep."

Yuri closed his eyes, but he was wide awake. Elena's damp hair still smelled of soap, and her body felt soft. He ached to hold her, to tell her he loved her. He tried to think of something else, but his mind wouldn't cooperate. *How can she think I will sleep?*

A few minutes later, Elena whispered, "Yuri, are you still awake?"

"Yes," he mumbled, trying to sound drowsy.

"Do you think we'll get to America?"

"Yes. We'll make it."

She was quiet a moment and then asked, "Do you think when we get there we will be free?"

"Yes."

"I don't think it's possible for anyone to have absolute freedom. Do you?"

"I don't know. Maybe."

"I would like to believe it is," Elena said. "I've heard there are great cities in America. Once I saw a picture of the Empire

State Building, but it looked very plain compared to the palace in Leningrad and the Bolshoi Theater. It was not nearly as grand, and it's supposed to be the tallest building in the world.

"I heard the people in America are rich. They wear fancy clothes and drive cars. Do you think that's true?"

"I don't know." Elena snuggled closer.

Her hair was pressed against his cheek, and Yuri fought the impulse to pull her into his arms and press a kiss against her neck. Struggling to think clearly, he said, "My cousin Lev once told me there are huge farms there that provide grains, fruits, and vegetables for all the people, so no one is hungry."

"It sounds like a beautiful dream," Elena said.

"That may be all it is. We'll know when we get there."

Soon her even, steady breathing told Yuri she slept. He put his arm about her and wished he could tell her of his love. He knew better. She didn't love him. He closed his eyes.

🐜 🐜 🐜 🐜 🐜

The howl of a wolf startled Yuri and Elena awake. They sat up. "What was that?" she whispered.

"I don't know." Yuri listened. The shadows were growing long, and the air felt cooler. They'd slept through the day. Another howl made the hair on Yuri's neck stand up. A few moments later a different wolf answered the first and then a third and fourth. Their calls came from all around. Yuri stood. "We need to go."

"Why?" Elena asked standing up.

"The wolves are closing in on something. And I don't want it to be us," he whispered.

Keeping her hand on Yuri's back, Elena stood. "What can we do?" she asked, her voice panicked.

Yuri held his finger to his lips and cautiously walked to the hanging boughs. Elena stayed close behind him. Cautiously Yuri pulled a branch aside and peered out. He watched the forest for several moments, but there was no sign of wolves.

"Let's go," Yuri whispered. He pulled on his coat and shoved his blanket into his pack. Elena did the same. The two moved as quickly and quietly as they could away from the sound of the wolves. They didn't stop until the howls were far away. Yuri shifted his pack to his right shoulder. "In all the weeks Alexander and I traveled, we never heard them that close."

"Do you think a lot of wild animals are out here?" Elena asked, scanning the forest.

"Yes."

"What kind do you think we'll find between here and Leningrad?"

Yuri smiled. "Wolves."

"Really?" She glanced back the way they'd come. "What else?"

"Oh, fox, deer, wolverine, elk. But if we leave them alone, they'll stay clear of us. You don't have to be afraid."

"I'm not afraid," Elena said, squaring her shoulders. "I just believe in knowing what I have to face and being prepared. Anyway, nothing can be as bad as what we left behind. The animals I worry about carry guns." She headed toward the road. "It will be dark soon."

Yuri followed.

As night settled over the countryside, the temperature dropped. Chilled, Yuri was glad to be moving, even though it was harder to walk in the dark. The ever-present mud sucked at their boots, spilling over the tops, and squishing inside of their shoes.

"I can't stand it any more," Elena said as she sat on a log. "I've got to get out of these." She unlaced a boot and yanked it off. Tipping it upside down, she knocked the heel against the downed tree. Clumps of mud dropped out. "The mud is making my feet hurt."

"I don't think there's any place to wash our feet or boots. And even if we did, they would just get dirty again. We'll have to put up with it."

Elena sighed. "You're right. Do you know how far it is to Leningrad?"

"About seven hundred kilometers."

"Will we have to walk all the way?"

"Probably not. When Alexander and I traveled from Siberia, there were a few people willing to help. A kind farmer might take us part of the way or we could catch a ride on a train. But the police watch the stations closely. We'd be in more danger and would have to get off and on while it's moving. I'd rather ride on a farmer's wagon." He looked at the night sky alight with stars. "We'll keep praying and wait to see what God provides."

"I don't understand your trust in God," Elena said, her voice hard. "He's not kind and compassionate like you and the Belovs say. If that were true, how do you explain all the people who've died? How can a loving God allow a cruel dictator to crush the innocent?" She stared into the darkness. "I remember when life was good, when we laughed and played."

"I remember too," Yuri said sadly. "But, Elena, God isn't to blame for the evil that plagues this country. Satan is the one who spreads darkness. And it will continue until God's people take a stand against him."

"How do people stand against something they can't see?"

Yuri thought a moment. "The only way to battle Satan is to do it God's way."

"And how is that?"

"When men fight they battle against flesh and blood, but this war is spiritual. We fight against dark spiritual forces. Human weapons will not work. God says we must use his armor."

"What is that?"

"First, we need to know his truth so we recognize when Satan is lying to us. And we need to remember we are righteous before God because of Jesus' sacrifice. And we need to be encouraged and strengthened by his peace, knowing there is nothing we cannot do if he is with us. Satan tries to convince us we are lost, but we must never forget that no matter what may befall us, we are forever saved. And finally, we need to know the Word of God, for his word is our strongest weapon—a sword of truth."

"That sounds like foolishness," Elena said, pulling on her boot and lacing it.

Yuri said a silent prayer, asking for wisdom so he could explain in a way Elena would comprehend. "When I was a boy, I remember my mother and father teaching me about spiritual weapons, but I didn't understand. It wasn't until I came face to face with the enemy, Satan, in the work camp that I grasped what they had taught me. I was filled with hatred, and that hatred separated me from the one who had the power. I was too weak to fight. Only after an encounter with God did I know I had to fight his way or die."

"I'm not ready to fight any spiritual battles. Let's go."

A deep croak of a frog fractured the night's quiet. Elena jumped, laughed nervously, and started walking, then stopped. "I wonder if we could catch him. He would be a small meal but still a meal."

"Maybe. If we can catch him." Yuri moved in the direction of the croaking. He stopped and listened. The sound came again. He continued toward it. When the frog stopped his song, Yuri remained motionless. The croaking began, and Yuri dropped to his hands and knees and felt his way over sharp rocks and mud. When he came to a thick patch of grass, the croaking stopped. He knew the frog was close, so he waited, barely breathing. For a long while there was no sound; then the unsuspecting creature croaked, and Yuri lunged at him. He fell flat out on the wet bog but felt no frog beneath his outstretched hands.

"Did you get him?" Elena asked.

"No. There'll be no frog legs for us tonight."

"I never ate them before, but right now I'd try anything."

"Just thinking about having something hot makes me hungry," Yuri said.

"I heard a splash. Is there a pond or lake? I could clean my feet and boots."

"There's water out there, but we should stay away from it. We can't see well enough in the dark and could end up neck deep before we knew what happened."

Elena dug into her sack. "Here. Tanya packed some dried meat." She handed him the venison and took some for herself. Chewing slowly, she said, "It's meat." Taking out the water bottle, she swigged down a mouthful. "I'm really hungry."

"It can get worse."

"Was it worse in prison?"

"Yes. Very bad."

"You never told me what happened there."

"The telling serves no good purpose."

"People should know what happens to Russia's citizens when they are arrested."

"Once I would have said I agreed with you, but now . . ." He took a drink of water, then screwed the lid back on. "I'm afraid it's too late. Russia is probably lost."

"I've never heard hopelessness from you before."

Yuri managed a small smile. "I have not given up. There is always hope, but the evil is very strong here. It has gone too far. We may have stepped off the precipice."

"You're saying the enemy, Satan, has won?"

"No. What is happening here in Russia is only one of the battles. I am saying that maybe he has won this battle, but he will not win the war. God is more powerful. He has a plan. And Satan will lose in the end."

"I don't understand anything you're talking about," Elena said, shoving the water bottle back into her knapsack.

"One day you will. And I hope it won't be too late."

CHAPTER 14

A CLOTHESLINE SAGGING WITH work clothes met Dimitri as he stepped through the front door. Pushing aside a pair of men's overalls, he smiled at Tatyana. "Hello. What do you want me to do with this coat?" He held his arms away from his body. "I'm dripping wet."

While bouncing a crying Yuri on her hip, Tatyana finished folding a man's shirt with one hand. Then she went over to Dimitri. Keeping a safe distance, she kissed him. "You are soaked. Take off your things right here. I will hang the coat on the back porch; you put the clothes in the basket."

Dimitri stripped off his coat and handed it to Tatyana. Holding it at arms length, she headed for the kitchen. "You should shower. You must be freezing."

"A hot shower sounds good," Dimitri said.

As Tatyana returned to the front room, Yuri let out a pathetic wail. She cuddled him against her shoulder. "I'm sorry little one. I know it hurts."

"What's the matter? Why is he crying?"

"He is getting new teeth. After they come in, he will feel better."

"I hope it's soon," Dimitri said, standing in a puddle and shivering. He glanced out the window. "I don't think the rain is ever going to let up. We haven't had a break in over two weeks."

"It will stop." Holding out her free hand, Tatyana said, "Give me your pants. You are making a mess."

Dimitri looked at the floor beneath him where a puddle was forming. "Oops, I'm sorry." He pulled off his boots and then quickly shed his pants and handed them to Tatyana. She carried them to the laundry basket. "The rain better stop soon," Dimitri called after her. "There's already flooding in the valley, and the rivers are still rising. With all the rain plus the snow melt, the folks in Kent and Auburn are in real trouble."

"I heard. It sounds awful."

Dimitri stepped under another clothesline. "Looks like you've been working hard." He frowned. "I wish you wouldn't take in extra laundry. You have enough to do already. We'll get by without your working. You've been looking extra tired lately."

"I am fine. It is just that Yuri has not been feeling good, and with him being up at night . . ." She transferred the baby to her other arm. "I want to help you, and this is something I can do for us and the bachelors in Black Diamond," Tatyana called over her shoulder as she walked into the kitchen. "Dinner is almost ready."

"Do I have time for that shower?"

"Yes."

Pulling off his shirt, Dimitri headed for the bathroom.

Tatyana set her son in his high chair and handed him a cracker. Yuri fingered the food, then pushed it in his mouth and gummed it. Tatyana set out plates, glasses, and silverware. Then she checked the venison roast cooking in the Dutch oven. It looked done. She poked the potatoes and carrots with a fork, and the prongs slid easily through the vegetables. She moved the pot to a cooler place on the stove, then sliced what was left of yesterday's bread and set it on the table.

Rolling up his shirt sleeves, Dimitri stepped into the kitchen. "Smells good. I'm starving." Dimitri pulled Tatyana into his arms and held her close. "Mmm, you smell good too." He kissed her.

"Da da, da da," Yuri jabbered.

"He's talking to me." Dimitri lifted his son out of the chair, and Yuri grabbed his father's hair and hung on. Dimitri carefully opened the little boy's fingers, then holding him out in front of him, he said, "So, you've been a troublemaker today."

Yuri grinned and mashed a sticky hand against his father's cheek.

Tatyana laughed and handed Dimitri a washcloth.

After wiping his face, Dimitri planted a kiss on the baby's cheek and returned him to his chair. Tossing the cloth into the sink, he sat at the table and watched as Tatyana set out the meat and vegetables. "Looks good."

"The potatoes in storage are starting to sprout, and there are only enough left to last about a month. And we need to save some for replanting. We have a lot of carrots left though." Watching the deluge outdoors, she said, "When the rain stops . . ."

"If it stops," Dimitri corrected.

"When it stops, it will feel good to work in the garden again." She cut a portion of potato and a carrot into bite-sized pieces and set them on Yuri's tray.

He picked up a piece of carrot and put it in his mouth.

"He's doing good," Dimitri said with a smile and patted the boy's leg.

Grinning, Yuri flung a piece of potato.

Tatyana picked it up, but he tossed another piece.

"That's enough of that," Dimitri said sternly, grabbing hold of the baby's hand. Yuri pouted a moment and then returned to eating.

Tatyana placed a serving of meat and vegetables on Dimitri's plate. "Did you have a good day at work?"

"It was fine, except that the rumors about the mine closing are still going around. The supervisors haven't said anything to us, but the word is we'll be shutting down and opening another mine here in Black Diamond off Lawson Hill. I hope they start a new operation here; otherwise, I'm out of work."

"I thought there was an awful accident in the mine up there."

"Yeah, but that was years ago. This one would only use the upper levels."

The wind howled as it whipped over the roof and around the eaves, and rain splattered against the window. Dimitri looked at the gathering dusk. "I wish the rain would stop. At work the bosses said that if the flooding continues, some of us are going down to the valley to help sandbag."

"When I was at the store, Mr. Robinson told me about the flooding and how they needed people to help. I would like to, but what can I do?"

"I don't know. I don't think women help with sandbagging. And besides, what would you do with Yuri?"

"Someone would have to watch him for me. I feel badly for those people. I want to do something."

"Well, there's nothing we can do tonight. We'll know more tomorrow." He shook his head. "Every time I go down to the valley, I think how nice it would be to have a farm there. But no more. Carl told me this happens a lot. I'm thankful we're up here in the hills."

✳ ✳ ✳ ✳ ✳

CHAPTER 14

The following morning, Dimitri ate a hurried breakfast and left early, intent on talking to Carl about the flood. He returned a few minutes later. Grabbing his slicker and rubber boots, he said, "The water's still rising in Kent and Auburn, so a bunch of us are going down to help. I guess the Red Cross is looking for volunteers. If you want to come, they could probably use you. Susie said she'd watch Yuri."

"I do want to help." Tatyana looked down at her dress. "But I need to change."

"Hurry up. Carl's waiting."

Untying her apron as she went, Tatyana headed for the bedroom. She tossed the apron on the bed, stepped out of her dress, and pulled on a pair of blue jeans and one of Dimitri's flannel shirts. Cinching her belt, she ran to the back porch and grabbed her boots.

Dimitri stood at the door, Yuri in one arm and a sack in the other. "I've got Yuri and his things ready," he said as Tatyana sat on the sofa and pulled on her boots. She laced them quickly, then grabbed her coat and hat.

"You'll need your slicker. If you have to spend any time outdoors, that wool coat will be soaked in minutes."

Tatyana grabbed her raincoat and threw it over her arm. "I am ready."

Carl headed for the valley. "Yesterday Antar told me that if we went down he wanted to go with us. We'll have to stop and pick him up." As he pulled into the Kamenev's driveway, Carl honked.

Antar immediately appeared on the front porch. Taking the steps two at a time, he dashed to the car. As he opened the door, wind and rain swept in. He slid onto the front seat and pulled the door closed. "Thank you for picking me up." He smiled at Tatyana and Dimitri. "Janna say she is very sorry she cannot come with us, but she is sick."

"Again?" Tatyana asked.

"Yes. She cannot eat. I think she should see doctor, but she does not believe in doctors, so I do not know what to tell her. Maybe you can talk to her?"

"I will, but she will probably be better soon," Tatyana said, knowing Janna thought she might be pregnant. She suppressed a smile. Obviously Janna hadn't told Antar yet. *What a surprise that will be,* she thought.

Antar turned and faced the front of the car. "Is the flood bad?" he asked Carl.

"Yeah. I heard some people have lost homes, barns, and livestock. And the water is still rising."

Tatyana huddled against Dimitri, her stomach quailing. "What do you think it will be like? Will there be people or animals drowned?" she asked, her voice shaky.

"There might be livestock lost, but I haven't heard any reports of people drowning," Carl said, keeping his eyes straight ahead.

As they followed the road that wound into the valley, rain pelted the car. The wipers couldn't keep up with the steady stream of water, and the inside of the windows fogged. Carl turned up the car heater and wiped the windshield with a rag, but he couldn't keep the window clear.

"I will do that." Antar took the cloth and wiped away the moisture.

"Thanks," Carl said, gripping the steering wheel, leaning forward, and peering into the downpour.

As they approached the valley, Tatyana cleared a spot on her window and gazed at the lowlands. What she saw sent a shock through her. "Dear Lord!" she whispered.

The lush farmlands were gone. Instead, a huge lake lay in the bottom of the valley, and there was no sign of the river that usually snaked through the basin. It had washed over its banks and spread across the countryside. In some places, all Tatyana could see of the farms were pitched rooftops. Closer to the edges of the lake, the top of fence posts stuck out of the water, and some homes had been spared.

"I heard Auburn is worse," Carl said.

"What are we going to do? How can we help?" Tatyana asked.

Carl glanced over his shoulder into the back seat. "Downtown Kent is still above the water line. I figure they'll be building a wall with sandbags to protect it. And there are a lot of people without homes who need food, a warm place to sleep, and medical attention. The Red Cross is probably overwhelmed."

Shivering, Tatyana pulled her coat more tightly around her.

※ ※ ※ ※ ※

A huge canvas tent with a bright red cross above the front entrance was set up on the west end of Meeker Street. Carl pulled into a graveled lot already crowded with trucks and cars. "We can start here. Someone should be able to tell us where we're needed." He stepped out of the car, pulled his coat over his head, and ran for the tent.

Tatyana put on her raincoat while Dimitri got out and ran around to open her door. She slid out, and they joined Antar and hurried to the tent. Huddling beneath an overhang, they waited for Carl.

A few moments later, he reappeared. "The man said we're needed on the sandbagging crew. They're working just off Meeker." He headed down the street toward downtown.

"I guess we found our place," Dimitri said, standing in front of Tatyana with his hands on her upper arms. "I probably won't see you for a while. Be careful."

"I will. You too," she said and kissed her husband. Tatyana watched as Dimitri ran to join the others. *Father, keep him safe,* she prayed. Then she turned and walked inside the tent.

Stepping through the doorway, the roar of rain pounding on the canvas roof greeted her. The tent was larger than two or three company houses put together. In the center, a large wood stove radiated much-needed heat. Tatyana pushed her hood off, and water ran down the back of her slicker.

To the left of the entrance, two women dispensed hot soup, bread, and coffee. A long row of cots lined one wall. On one cot, a woman rested her back against the wall, and three children huddled against her. Further down, a baby cried. Someone coughed and choked. One woman sat on the edge of her cot, singing softly and rocking an infant. Most beds had lumps beneath blankets; some had nurses and doctors bending over their occupants.

Tatyana walked over to a heavyset woman serving soup. "I would like to help. Who do I talk to?"

"Are you a nurse?"

"No."

"Oh, dear," she sighed. "I was hoping you were the relief nurse." She scanned the room, removed her apron, and handed it to Tatyana. "I guess the relief will have to be me. We can use you right here, honey." She brushed back short curly hair off her forehead. "We've been praying for help." She smiled. "I'm Imogene Cogmire," she said, holding out a hand.

Tatyana shook it. "I am Tatyana Letinov."

"I'm glad to meet you. Why don't you fill these cups with soup and see if any of these folks are hungry. We can't do much more than give them a warm, dry place to stay and some hot food."

Tatyana took off her coat and hung it on a hook beside several others, tied on the apron, and filled cups with soup. She set them on a tray with slices of bread and approached the woman with the three children. "Would you like soup?"

Her eyes filling with tears, the woman nodded. Tatyana handed a mug to each of the children, who immediately began sipping the hot broth; then she gave one to their mother. "Thank you, thank you. The Lord bless you."

CHAPTER *14*

Tatyana smiled. "I am glad to help." She moved from one cot to the next, handing out soup, bread, coffee, and kind words. Mothers helped children drink the hot liquid and parceled out bread. Children quieted and slept. Over the next several hours, farmers soaked to the skin, mothers with children, old men and their wives, and people looking for family filed into the tent. The volunteers did all they could to help.

Later in the day, Imogene approached Tatyana. "How are you doing?"

"I am fine."

"Be sure to take a break when you can so you don't wear yourself out."

A man wearing a heavy overcoat stepped through the door. Imogene raised a hand and called, "You're just the person I wanted to see." She strode across the tent to confront the newcomer. "George, have you had any luck? We're filling up in here. We need another tent, more volunteers, medical supplies, and food."

"I'm doing everything I can. Right now there just aren't any more supplies. We've got a call in to the army storehouses. We might be able to get some help from them. But it's going to take time."

Antar ran into the tent with a girl in his arms and a hysterical, weeping woman following. "I need doctor! She is not breathing!"

Tatyana ran to him. "What happened?"

"She was in the water. I pull her out."

"We need help!" Tatyana cried, looking for the doctor who had been there earlier. She saw him in the back of the tent. "Doctor! Doctor!"

Imogene was at their side. "What is it?"

"She is not breathing."

"Dr. Sanderson! We need you!"

Already the mustached man with a stethoscope hanging around his neck was running from the back of the tent. "What is it?"

The mother grabbed the doctor's arm. "Please, please help my daughter! She fell into the water!"

The doctor bent over the girl and felt her wrist. "Her heart is still beating." He picked up the teen and laid her facedown on the floor. Straddling the girl, the doctor turned her head to the side and raised her arms above her head. Placing his hands on both sides of her back, just below the rib cage, he pressed upwards. He repeated the movement two more times.

"She's dead! She's dead!" the mother lamented. "Jessica is dead."

The doctor continued. Finally the girl coughed. Then water bubbled from her mouth, and she took a breath. She coughed hard and retched but opened her eyes. The doctor turned the teen onto her side and rubbed her back. Looking at her mother, he said, "She's going to be all right."

The woman kneeled on the floor beside her daughter and placed her hand on the girl's cheek. "You're going to be all right!"

Jessica closed her eyes.

"We need some dry blankets here," Doctor Sanderson said, standing and pressing his hands against the small of his back, then tipping from one side to the other.

Tatyana rushed to get a blanket while Antar carried the girl to a cot. Her mother helped her into dry clothing and covered her with a blanket. Then she sat on a chair beside the bed, holding her daughter's hand. A few minutes later, she wiped the remnants of tears from her cheeks, stood and straightened her coat, then walked across the tent to Antar. Taking his hand, she looked at him, her eyes filled with tears. "Thank you for saving my daughter."

"It was nothing. I did not go far into the water, and the river carried her right to me."

The woman squeezed his hand and returned to her daughter's bedside.

Antar walked toward the doorway.

"Antar," Tatyana said. "You are soaking. Sit a few minutes and have some soup and bread."

"That sounds good," he said with a sigh and sat on a bench.

Tatyana filled a bowl with soup, grabbed a slice of bread, and took them to him. "Would you like coffee?"

"Yes. Thank you." Antar set the food on the bench beside him, braced his elbows on his thighs, and rested his face in his hands.

"I'll get it, Tatyana," Imogene said. "You sit."

Tatyana sat on the bench beside Antar.

He straightened and forced a smile, then taking the soup, sipped it. "This is good." He dipped the bread into the hot liquid and took a bite. "I did not know how hungry I was."

Imogene brought two cups of coffee. One she set on the bench beside Antar, and the other she handed to Tatyana. "Thank you," she said and walked away.

Tatyana took a drink of her coffee. "That was a brave thing you did."

"Anyone would have done it."

Exhausted and close to tears, Tatyana laid her hand on his arm. "Maybe, but I do not think so."

"Tatyana," Dimitri said, his voice cold.

Tatyana snatched her hand back from Antar and looked at her husband. He was angry.

"Dimitri." She stood. "Are . . . are you all right? Can I get you something to eat or some coffee?"

Dimitri clamped his mouth shut, his jaw muscles working. Then he asked, "What were you doing with Antar?"

"I was only giving him something to eat and drink."

"No. It was more than that."

"It was not. He saved a girl. I was thanking him."

Doubt flickered across Dimitri's face, and he looked at Antar who now stood.

"She did nothing." He nodded at the woman and her sleeping daughter. "I helped get her out of water and brought her in."

Dimitri swallowed hard. "I'm sorry. I made a mistake." He looked at Tatyana. "I'm really sorry."

Tatyana was hurt. *How can he believe I would betray him?* But she said nothing, too weary to talk about it.

"I could use a cup of coffee." Dimitri shivered.

"You are cold," Tatyana said. "Take off your coat and I will get you a blanket."

"No. Just some coffee. I have to get back out there. The water is still rising."

Tatyana poured him a cup of coffee. Dimitri took it and sat on the bench with the mug cradled between his hands. He closed his eyes, breathed in the steam, and took a sip. He looked at Tatyana with troubled eyes and took her hand. "I don't know what got into me. I guess I'm tired and . . . when I saw you two, I remembered how you danced that night. I have no excuses, but I'm sorry for jumping to the wrong conclusion."

"I would never disgrace you that way."

"I know. It's just the thought of losing you is more than I can bear. You are part of me." Dimitri kissed her hand and pressed it against his cheek. "I saw two women pulled out of the water today. They were dead." Tears coursed down his cheeks. "I thought of what life would be like without you. I couldn't bear it."

Tatyana took Dimitri's face in her hands. "I am not leaving you. We are one, forever."

CHAPTER 15

TATYANA SET A PLATE OF
pancakes in front of Dimitri and refilled his coffee mug.

"Looks good," Dimitri said as he spread butter on the stack
and drizzled syrup over it. He cut off several pieces and laid
them on Yuri's highchair tray. The little boy grabbed one and
pushed it into his mouth, smearing pancake and syrup on his
face.

A knock came at the back door. Carl opened it and peeked
in. "I hope I'm not disturbing you."

"No. Come in," Tatyana responded. "Would you like some
breakfast?"

Carl eyed the pancakes. "Looks good, but no. Susie already
fed me. I'd like some coffee, though." He dropped onto the chair
opposite Dimitri and leaned his elbows on the table.

"What are you doing up and about so early on a Saturday?" Dimitri asked, taking a bite of pancake.

"Once June arrives, I can't sleep in. I don't know if it's the sunlight or just knowing there's lots to be done. Anyway, I'll be up early every Saturday and Sunday between now and September." Tatyana set a cup of coffee in front of Carl. "Thanks," he said and took a sip.

"Susie and I were thinking it's a perfect day for a trip to the Woodland Park Zoo. There isn't a cloud in the sky, and it's going to be warm. It's hard to believe that only a few weeks ago the rain was coming down in buckets and the valley was flooded."

"It's still not over for the farmers. They've lost some of their crops, and what's left will be late," Dimitri said. "It's a shame. I'm glad we live in the hills."

Carl took another drink of his coffee. "Would you two like to go into Seattle with Susie and me?"

"Do you want to go?" Tatyana asked Dimitri. "Are the roads clear?"

"Oh, yeah," Carl said. "They're fine. After visiting the zoo, we can go on down to the farmer's market. They always have fresh fish and probably some early fruits and vegetables shipped in from down south—maybe even strawberries!" He grinned at Tatyana.

"I would love to go," Tatyana said. "And it will be at least two or three more weeks before our strawberries are ready." She looked at Dimitri with pleading eyes. "I have never been to a zoo. Could we go?"

Dimitri held out another bite of pancake to Yuri who grabbed it off the fork and mashed it between his fingers. "I was planning to work in the garden." He thought a moment and smiled. "But . . . I guess it can wait another day."

Tatyana kissed him. "Thank you, Dimitri. I will help you in the garden tomorrow." She looked at Carl. "What time do you want to leave?"

"As soon as you can get ready. Susie's already making a picnic lunch."

"I've got the animals to tend to, and the garden needs watering, but that's all," Dimitri said.

Tatyana rinsed out a washcloth in the sink. "All I need to do is finish feeding Yuri, clean up the breakfast dishes, and make our lunch. The rest of the house can wait until tomorrow."

"So, about an hour?" Carl asked, draining the last of his coffee and pushing back his chair.

"Tatyana and I will walk down as soon as we're ready."

🐾 🐾 🐾 🐾 🐾

Carl pulled into a graveled parking lot just outside large wrought iron gates with the words Woodland Park Zoo on them. "It has been too long since we've visited," Susie said. "We should come more often. The park is lovely, and I always enjoy seeing the animals." She glanced at Tatyana. "I especially like the bears and lions. They're impressive." Susie flipped her strawberry blonde hair off her shoulder. "This will be fun. I'm glad you came."

Carl and Dimitri stepped out of the car and walked around the front to help the women out with the babies. "I'll get the kids' strollers," Carl said, stepping to the back of the car and opening the trunk.

Large maple and oak trees grew along the edges of the parking lot, their early summer leaves dense and deep green. Well-manicured lawns spread out from beneath them, leading into an open area bordered by huge rhododendrons loaded with pink, white, and red blossoms.

"What a beautiful place," Tatyana said.

"We can picnic here later," Susie said just as a loud screech and howl echoed from beyond the zoo gate.

Tatyana's eyes widened. "What is that?"

Carl unfolded the collapsible strollers. "Probably monkeys or apes. They have both."

"It could be a bird," Susie said. "I remember the exotic birds from the last time we were here. Some of them made unbelievable noises."

A shiver of excitement went through Tatyana as she wondered at all she would see in the zoo. It promised to be new and interesting.

Carl pulled up the hoods of the strollers, locked them in place, then wheeled one to Dimitri. "These strollers are a wonder. Without them we'd be lugging these babies around all day. And Evelyn's getting too big for that."

"Did I tell you she's taken a few steps?" Susie asked.

"Yes, about a hundred times," Dimitri teased.

"A mother should be proud of her children." Susie kissed her little girl. Evelyn's hazel eyes sparkled with mischief as she squirmed and tried to free herself of her mother's arms. "She's ready to take on the world." Susie settled the toddler in her stroller. "Now, you stay put." Then she looked at Tatyana. "She hates to be confined. When she's in her stroller, she's forever trying to climb out."

"We'll help keep an eye on her," Dimitri promised.

Tatyana tucked Yuri's blanket around him. "It is still a little cool." She kissed his cheek, and he beamed. Grabbing the stroller handle, she walked toward the gate, Dimitri beside her. Yuri babbled happily and pointed at a robin hopping across the lawn listening for worms beneath the surface.

"Yuri seems happy, but then he's always good-natured," Carl said.

"Usually, if he is not teething. He does like adventures." Tatyana peered down at her son. "He will be a year old on July thirteenth." She shook her head slowly. "I cannot believe it has been almost a year."

Dimitri circled Tatyana's waist with his arm. "I remember that day. I almost missed his birth."

Susie took Carl's hand. "We nearly lost both of you in that cave-in."

Dimitri smiled. "No, I was actually found. It took looking death in the face to understand what God wanted from me, which was only to accept his gift of eternal life." He looked at his friend. "Thanks to Carl I finally understood." He shook his head. "I can't believe I was so hardheaded that it took a near disaster to open my eyes."

"That's often what it takes for people to see," Carl said. "It would be simpler if we would look to God all the time, not just during times of trouble."

Dimitri nodded. "When I was trapped in the mine, I was wishing I'd paid attention sooner."

They approached a large cage made of iron bars, and a loud screeching filled the air. Tatyana and Susie moved closer. Rotting fruit littered the floor, and an acrid odor filled the air. Tatyana covered her nose. "What is that smell?"

A monkey jumped onto the bars, clinging to them with his feet and tail. "There's your answer," Carl said with a nod at the animal.

Easily swinging from one bar to another, the monkey joined a slightly larger ape. As if being reunited after a long separation, the two clung to each other, then the smaller one climbed toward the onlookers. He stopped directly in front of Tatyana. Small dark eyes staring at her, he blinked, opened his mouth, and screamed. Bouncing against the bars, he reached out to Tatyana with one hand.

Yuri began to cry, and Dimitri picked up the frightened youngster. "I don't think he likes monkeys."

"Why is that one so upset?" Tatyana asked. "What does he want?"

"He probably wants something to eat," Carl said, stepping closer to the cage. "Hey, fella, is that what you want, something to eat?"

The monkey leaped to the ground, jumped up onto a ring that hung from the ceiling, and sat watching the visitors, his eyes moving rapidly from one person to another.

"He looks unhappy," Susie said. The other monkey jumped onto the bars directly in front of Susie and startled her. She stepped back laughing. The animal squealed, leaped to the floor of the cage, then joined his companion in the swing. The two hugged one another. "I wonder what they're thinking."

As Tatyana watched the caged animals, sorrow welled up inside her. She thought she understood what they felt. They'd been forced to leave their homes just like she'd had to leave Russia. Now they lived where they didn't belong. "If they could talk, they would say they want to go home," she said quietly, barely able to hold back her tears. *Stop being silly,* she told herself. *They are animals and do not have feelings like people.* But even as she tried to convince herself of this, she couldn't stop the flood of emotions as she watched the poor animals. She felt angry as she turned the stroller and walked away. "Can we look at something else?"

Dimitri draped an arm around her shoulders and pulled her close as they walked. He said nothing, but Tatyana felt his strength and compassion and leaned against him, grateful for his understanding.

A large bird with long, bouncing tail feathers paraded past. Acting as if he didn't notice the visitors, he stopped and turned toward them. As he did, his feathers quivered and opened into a giant fan of shimmering green and blue with dark rings.

"What a beautiful bird," Dimitri said. "What is it called?"

"It's a peacock," Susie said. "The last time we were here, we saw one do the very same thing. The park attendant told us the males have beautiful plumage and love to show off."

The bird strutted in front of them for a few minutes. Then he folded his display of feathers and walked on. A few moments later, he let out a loud yell that sounded similar to a yowling, disgruntled cat.

"How awful," Tatyana said. "I would think such a beautiful bird would have an elegant voice."

"You would think," Carl chuckled. "He sounds a little like I do when I try to sing in church."

"But you're very handsome," Susie said with a wink.

"Just like the bird. Grand to look at, but watch out when you open your mouth," Dimitri teased.

Carl grinned. "True, true. It's a good thing God didn't say I had to sound good; he only said I'm to make a joyful noise. And I certainly do that."

Susie gave her husband a quick kiss. "I'm sure God appreciates your efforts." Keeping one hand on the stroller, she took her husband's with the other. "Come on, I want to see the lions."

The small group made the rounds of the zoo. The lions were impressive, walking back and forth in their pens and eyeing the onlookers with animosity. After seeing the lions, they visited overfed bears, an aviary, snakes, more monkeys, and elephants. Tatyana was most impressed with the elephants. Astonished at their size, she approached their pen with caution. One of the animals reached its long trunk out to her, but she kept a safe distance. Still, she couldn't completely enjoy watching any of the animals, unable to ignore their caged existence.

The afternoon sun turned hot, and Carl suggested they return to the park to eat. After spreading a blanket beneath a large maple tree, Tatyana and Susie set out a lunch of egg salad, roast beef, cheese, bread, and cookies. Everyone feasted.

"This is the last of our canned apple juice," Tatyana said, draining her glass.

"I don't know if I can wait until fall for more," Dimitri said.

"You did better than we did." Susie pushed herself to her knees and picked up Evelyn. "We were gluttons and used up the last of ours more than a month ago." The baby fussed, kicked her legs straight out, and wriggled free of her mother's arms. She pushed herself to her feet and toddled two steps to her father. Before he could grab her, she tottered and plopped down on her bottom. Shock crossed the child's face, then her mouth turned into a pucker, and she started to cry.

Carl picked her up. "You're all right," he said, patting her bottom. "You certainly couldn't have felt any pain through all this padding. It's about her nap time, isn't it?"

"It is."

Yuri pushed himself onto his hands and knees and rocked back and forth before crawling to his father. "I'm beginning to think Yuri will never walk," Dimitri said. "He's happy enough to crawl. He's pretty fast though." He picked up his son and holding him under the arms, held him straight out. "Yes, you're pretty fast." He set him back on the blanket.

Evelyn whimpered and rubbed her eyes. "It's nap time for you," Carl said.

Tatyana stood. "Yuri too."

Susie took Evelyn and cradled her. "We can let them sleep here in the shade for awhile. Then we'll go down to the market on Pike Street. I've been dying for some fresh ocean fish."

"Do you think they'll sleep?" Carl asked.

"I have no doubt," Dimitri said with a grin and nodded at Yuri who was lying on his stomach, legs pulled up under him, his thumb in his mouth.

"All it will take is a little cuddling time to quiet Evelyn," Susie said as she rocked the baby. The little girl stared at her mother, her eyes heavy.

※ ※ ※ ※ ※

After settling Yuri and Evelyn on an infant blanket and covering them, the adults visited quietly and finished off the last of the cookies. Then they packed up the picnic items. Dimitri folded the large blanket. "We can take a short walk while the kids sleep."

"As long as we keep them in sight," Susie said.

Tatyana and Susie linked arms with their husbands and strolled through the shaded park. "It is beautiful here," Tatyana said. "I know we are in the city, but it does not feel like it. When I was young, my family and I used to visit Moscow, and there was a park like this. One time we went in to see the ballet, but we left early in the morning. It was a lovely day. We picnicked and walked all around to see the sights." Tatyana's chest ached at the memory.

"It sounds like you have good memories of your family," Susie said.

"They were special. Mama and Papa were farmers, but they loved literature and music and their children. And Yuri . . ." Tatyana smiled softly, ". . . he was always into some kind of trouble when he was young. He used to ride his horse as fast as he could across the fields. Mama would scold him for his carelessness. He would act remorseful, but he never changed." She closed her eyes a moment. "And he could sing. He had a beautiful voice. Whenever we had a party, Yuri would sing for us." She glanced at her husband. "Dimitri says I remember only the good, and that is why I still feel so sad. It is true, I remember the special times, but I have not forgotten the hunger and fear and the grief of losing friends and family to Stalin's soldiers." Realizing her tone had turned harsh, she softened her voice and added, "It is better to remember what was beautiful."

A large gray squirrel bounced across the grass in front of them and scampered up a tree. "Oh, look," Susie said. "I love squirrels. They're so cute." She watched the animal a moment and then turned back to Tatyana. "You know, there is a lot to love here too. You've already created many wonderful memories since coming to America. Like today. I'll remember it fondly. Won't you?"

Tatyana smiled softly. "Yes. It is a special day. And I will remember."

✻ ✻ ✻ ✻ ✻

The couples collected their sleeping children and headed for the waterfront. Once there, they tucked the sleeping babies into the strollers and walked to the market with its crowds of people, shouting vendors, loud debates over prices, and unusual smells. In spite of it all, Yuri and Evelyn slept.

They passed bins containing a variety of fruits and vegetables, and although Tatyana was tempted to try something new, she waited until she found a stand with large, red strawberries. She picked up several, checked for ripeness, then smelled the sweet fruit. "How much do you want for your berries?"

"Seven cents a pound."

"That is a lot of money for strawberries."

"The weather hasn't been so good down south. There aren't as many berries this year."

"I still think seven cents is too much," Tatyana argued.

"Take it or leave it." The vendor returned to sorting produce.

Clearly he wasn't going to negotiate on price. Tatyana studied the fruit a moment. *It would be wonderful to have fresh berries for breakfast,* she thought. Finally she said, "I will buy two pounds," and dug into her change purse. The merchant measured berries onto a scale, placed two pounds of fruit in a box, and handed her the berries. She paid him just as Dimitri joined her. Holding up her prize, she said, "We can have some for breakfast tomorrow."

Dimitri smiled and shook his head. "All you had to do was wait a couple more weeks, and we'll have our own."

"I know," Tatyana said, popping a berry in her mouth. "But I did not want to wait."

They wandered through the market, past exotic vegetables and fruits, squid, fish, and imported candies. Each bin had its own unique odor. Some foods smelled sweet, others bitter, and some pungent, but none were exactly unpleasant except for a display of salmon that smelled like they'd been left out far too long. Tatyana confronted the vendor. "The sign says fresh, but I do not think that is true."

The skinny man with a large nose glared at her in annoyance. "Take a look at the harbor. There are boats out there, right?"

Tatyana glanced at the docks. "Yes."

"Well, they stay out and fish for days and then bring their catch to us. I don't know exactly what day they caught them. All I can say is, this fish is as fresh as you're gonna get unless you want to take out your own boat."

"Well, I will not buy fish that is not fresh," Tatyana said and moved on, looking at the dock. Fishing boats, barges, and freighters were tied up. A large, black ship caught her eye. A Soviet flag flew from its mast. Her heart quickened. *It is from Russia! It would be good to talk to someone from home,* she thought and turned to Dimitri. "Could we go to the waterfront?"

"Oh, that sounds like fun," Susie said.

"I guess we can, but why?" Dimitri asked.

"I would like to see the ships up close, maybe talk to someone on a crew."

Dimitri scanned the harbor, his eyes stopping at the Russian freighter. He smiled sadly. "All right. We can go." He turned the stroller and headed away from the market. "We'll get our fish later."

Walking as quickly as she could while pushing the stroller, Tatyana hurried toward the large ship. Being so close to the Russian freighter made her feel closer to her homeland. The ship's deck was so far above the docks that she had to step away from the water and crane her neck to see the activity on board. A man leaned on the railing and looked down.

Tatyana called, "Hello," in Russian, but he walked away. She caught sight of a tall, slender man with brown hair and a boyish face ambling toward the bow, then disappearing. Her heart quickened. Could it be Yuri?

"Yuri!" she called and took several steps back, hoping to see him. "Yuri!" she yelled again. "Yuri!" There was no response.

"What are you doing?" Dimitri asked.

"I think I saw my brother!"

Susie grabbed Tatyana's hand. "Really? Do you think he could be on this ship?"

"Yuri wasn't in the merchant marines," Dimitri said. "He was a farmer." Gently he placed his hands on Tatyana's shoulders and turned her toward him. "Tatyana, I know you want to see your brother, but there is almost no chance that the man you saw was him."

"But what if it was?" Tatyana pulled away from Dimitri and ran toward the catwalk. "I have to know." She stopped at the bottom of the gangplank and waited, counting on a sailor leaving the ship. Before long a short, stocky man with a heavy beard swaggered down the catwalk. "Sir, can you help me?" Tatyana asked in Russian.

"Maybe."

"Do you know if a Yuri Letinov is on your ship? He's my brother, and I've been searching for him."

The man folded his arms over his chest. "No. I know of no one by that name. We have a small crew, and I'm sure I'd know if there was anyone named Yuri Letinov."

Disappointment swept over Tatyana, and she forced herself to keep from asking again. "Thank you," she said softly.

"I'm sorry." He nodded at Dimitri, Carl, and Susie as he stepped onto the dock and walked away.

Dimitri wrapped his arm protectively around his wife. "I wish you'd been right. I'm sorry."

"I knew it was silly to hope," she said sadly, staring after the sailor. "I just miss Yuri so much." Still watching the man, she said, "He looks healthy and happy. Maybe life is better in Russia now. They are trading with America. That must mean something."

"They always trade with us. And the sailor doesn't have to live in Russia; he gets to travel all over the world. He's not like ordinary citizens."

CHAPTER 15

Tatyana stepped away from the catwalk and took her husband's hand. "Dimitri, do you think it will get better in Russia?"

He pulled Tatyana close and caressed her hair. "I wish I could say yes, but I'd be lying. I don't think it will ever really change."

Tatyana pulled away. "Maybe you are wrong," she said, then turned and walked away. She walked fast, not knowing where she was going, only needing to escape. But she couldn't. She was trapped just like the animals at the zoo. She didn't belong in America, and she couldn't return home. *What will I do? Father, please tell me what to do,* she prayed as she walked, putting distance between herself and the ship.

CHAPTER 16

ELBOW DEEP IN SOAP SUDS, Tatyana scrubbed the kettle. Dimitri kissed her neck. "That tickles," Tatyana said, shrinking back.

Holding Yuri in one arm, Dimitri wrapped the other around Tatyana's waist and pulled her against him. The baby grabbed his mother's hair.

"Ouch. Do not pull." Tatyana dried her hands on her apron and gently loosened her son's fingers. Yuri let her hair go, and Tatyana tweaked his nose. "I thought you were already gone," she said to Dimitri.

"Almost. I just wanted a kiss."

Tatyana smiled. Then she kissed her husband and her son. "Besides getting grain and chicken feed, what are you going to do?"

Dimitri grinned. "I told you it's a secret."

With an exaggerated sigh and pout, Tatyana said, "All right, but how long will you be?"

"We'll be back right after lunch. Definitely in time for his nap." Dimitri lifted Yuri slightly. "I've seen how he can be when he's late for naps, and I don't want to deal with that." Dimitri yawned. "I'll be ready for one myself."

"You did not sleep well?"

He rubbed the back of his neck. "I tossed and turned all night."

"Is the move to the Lawson mine bothering you?"

"Actually, I'm looking forward to it. I'll be working closer to home."

"I know you have told me not to worry, but I still do. Anything to do with that mine troubles me. I have heard the stories. It blew up! Some of the men were never found."

Dimitri laid his hand on Tatyana's shoulder. "It was a bad accident, but that was years ago, and this time they're only opening the upper levels." Tatyana nodded, and Dimitri shifted Yuri to his other arm. "What are your plans for the day?"

"House cleaning and gardening and a visit with Janna, if you do not mind," she added, knowing Dimitri didn't like her friendship with the Russian woman. And, although he'd said nothing more about his jealousy over her attentions to Antar during the flood, she wondered if he was still troubled by them.

"I don't mind. But remember, we're supposed to be at Carl and Susie's by 5:30."

"I will not forget. I always enjoy being with them."

"Well then, Yuri and I are off." Dimitri gave Tatyana another kiss and walked out of the room. She heard the front door close as she returned to the dishes.

🌸 🌸 🌸 🌸 🌸

After lunch Tatyana headed for Janna's house. Dimitri and Yuri still hadn't returned, so she left a note telling Dimitri she'd be home by four o'clock. Janna lived on the border between Morganville and Black Diamond, only a fifteen-minute walk.

Today, however, Tatyana walked slowly, savoring the June sunshine and soft breezes. This time of year was her favorite, bringing relief from cold and rain but not too hot yet. The fragrance of freshly mowed grass, wild flowers, and pine were intoxicating. She stopped to study a trillium. Admiring the three-petaled white blossom, she thought, *Lord, your creation is remarkable.*

As an unexpected breeze swept up from the creek bed, her cotton skirt billowed away from her legs, and she straightened, pressing her skirt down with her hands. A heron lifted off Lake Fourteen. Tatyana squinted, shading her eyes to watch as the bird spread its broad wings, circled the lake, then sailed above the trees and disappeared. She wondered what it would feel like to fly. *Wouldn't that be an adventure,* she thought and crossed the street.

A small, honey-colored cow stood along the roadway. She pulled up a tuft of grass and chewed contentedly, her large brown eyes watching the stranger. Tatyana stopped and patted her neck. "I wish Goldy were old enough to give milk," she said and headed down the hill.

She could see Janna's house on the bend, and at the sight of it, could almost smell fresh bread. Janna was always baking. Taking long strides, Tatyana picked up her pace, eager for her visit.

Janna stood on the porch, rug in hand, when Tatyana walked up her drive. "Good afternoon," she said in Russian. "It's good to see you. I'm needing company." She shook the rug over the edge of the porch.

Tatyana climbed the wooden steps. Automatically responding in Russian, she said, "Hello. How are you?"

"Good."

After giving her friend a hug and kiss, she sat in a rocker and folded her hands behind her head. "It's a beautiful day, perfect for being outdoors."

"Where is Yuri?"

"With his father. They went into the valley to buy feed and to do something else that Dimitri wouldn't tell me about. He said it's a surprise." She smiled. "It's my birthday next week; maybe he's buying me something."

Janna grinned. "Maybe. It's nice how Dimitri takes Yuri with him. Not all fathers do that."

Tatyana sighed. "Yes, and Yuri loves his daddy, but my arms feel empty when I'm away from him."

A momentary look of sorrow touched Janna's eyes. Then she folded the throw rug over her arm and said, "Come in. I have tea."

"Is something wrong, Janna?"

"No." Her eyes misted. Taking a slow breath, she said, "It is just that I wish I had a baby. When I thought I was pregnant, I was so happy."

"It will happen," Tatyana said, leaving the chair and placing an arm around her friend. "You and Antar will have children."

"I hope you're right," Janna said and opened the screen door. It squeaked in protest and slammed shut behind them as they stepped inside.

"You have done so much since I was here two weeks ago," Tatyana said. "The couch and chair are new?"

"No. They're used but new to us." Janna laid her hand on the back of the over-stuffed chair draped with a green and yellow afghan. "The upholstery is worn, so I made this to put over it."

"It's lovely. You're crocheting looks perfect." Tatyana fingered the afghan. She crossed to the knick-knack shelf hanging on the wall above the couch. "How wonderful! Matroshka dolls! I have not seen any since I left Russia."

"Those belonged to my grandmother. I was going through my trunk yesterday, and when I found them, I decided it was time to set them out. My grandfather was known for his dolls."

Tatyana picked up one of the wooden eggs. It was hand-painted, had a sweet face with rosy cheeks, and wore a fur hat and white cape. There were four more just like it, each slightly smaller than the next so they could nest inside each other. Tatyana returned it to the shelf. "I would like to have one some day, but I doubt I'll have the chance."

"They are precious to me. I have so little from my grandfather. When I first came here, I didn't put them out because I wanted to keep them safe, but I decided it would be better to enjoy them." Janna walked into the kitchen. "I'll get our tea."

Tatyana sat at a wooden dining table and folded her hands in front of her. House plants were everywhere, on stands, in hangers, and on window sills. "I need more plants in my house," she said. "They add life to a room."

"I don't know what I'd do without my indoor garden," Janna called from the kitchen.

"Dimitri loves plants. He can make anything grow."

"Has he always liked them?" Janna asked, setting cups and saucers on the table and filling them with gold liquid.

"In New York City he had a rooftop garden." Tatyana smiled softly, remembering how much she used to like visiting his garden. It had been her refuge within the city.

Janna handed Tatyana her tea. "When we came to America, we went to New York for a few days. I didn't like it there. I don't think I could live in such a place."

Someone knocked at the door, and Janna answered it. Standing on the porch was George Salter, the threadman. He removed his hat, exposing thinning blonde hair, and bowed slightly. "Good afternoon, Mrs. Kamenev."

"It is good to see you," Janna said, glancing at Tatyana. "But I have visitor, maybe . . ."

"Please, Janna, I do not mind if he comes in," Tatyana said, standing. She smiled at the salesman. "Mr. Salter. How are you?"

A puzzled look crossed the man's face, then understanding. "I remember you." He thought a moment. "Mrs. Broido, isn't it?"

"Yes."

"How good to see you. I was intending to make it back to your house, but I've been busy."

"It is a good thing I am here then," Tatyana said. "I would like to ask you some questions."

Mr. Salter hefted his suitcase. "Wonderful. I can show you both what I have for sale and answer your questions at the same time." Squeezing past Janna, he stepped inside.

Janna closed the door. "Would you like tea, Mr. Salter?"

"Some water would be fine. I'm a bit dry. The sun's warm." He plunked his case on the floor, snapped open the locks, and tipped back the lid. "I've got those buttons you ordered, Mrs. Kamenev," he called after Janna as she walked into the kitchen. He held out a card of large, dark blue, two-holed buttons. Proudly, he said, "I told you I could find them." He grinned at Tatyana. "Anything either of you want, I can find."

"Actually, Mr. Salter, my husband wants me to buy our goods at the company store. He is very loyal to the mining company." She sat on the couch. "But I do have questions about the IWW. What does that mean again?"

"International Workers of the World. I remember we talked about that before. I left you a flyer, didn't I?"

"Yes."

"So, what do you want to know?"

Janna returned with a glass of water and handed it to Mr. Salter.

Tatyana studied her hands a moment, trying to gather her thoughts. She didn't want to offend the man but felt compelled to know more about the organization. She looked at him. "My husband said the IWW is Communist. Is that true?"

Mr. Salter looked at her for a long moment before answering. "There are those who say we're Communists, but they're wrong. Folks are just afraid of new ideas and make decisions without knowing the facts." He leaned forward slightly and gave Tatyana a crooked smile. "This is a democratic country. Do you actually think the government would allow a Communist organization to promote itself?"

"But I thought in this country we could believe whatever we wanted. That is part of being free."

Mr. Salter cleared his throat and sat back. "Yes, well . . ." He didn't finish what he was saying but instead fished out a pair of knitting needles from his case and held them up for Janna. "These are fine needles, the best you'll find anywhere." Janna took the needles. The threadman kept his eyes on them as he said, "We're free, but the United States government still intrudes where it's not wanted. And the IWW is only interested in protecting the rights of working people."

A door slammed and Tatyana jumped. Antar stood just inside the door looking large and angry. "You are lying." He glared at the threadman.

"Antar," Janna said, "Mr. Salter brought my buttons." Wearing a tight smile, she held up the card.

Antar didn't look at them but continued to stare at the salesman.

Sweat beaded up on the threadman's upper lip. He stood. "I beg your pardon, sir, but I am not lying. The IWW is an organization that represents workers around the world."

"You are a liar or a fool."

Mr. Salter's eyes darted from Antar to Tatyana to Janna and back to Antar. "I . . . I am not lying. I have flyers that explain it all, but I don't have any left." He looked at Tatyana. "Tell him about the leaflet I gave you and how it explains the IWW and its work."

Tatyana felt sorry for the man but didn't know if she believed him. She looked at Antar. "He did come to my house about three months ago. We talked about the IWW, and he gave me a paper. I thought what he said made sense, but . . ." She paused. "Dimitri became angry and said the IWW is Communist." She looked at Mr. Salter.

He pushed his hands into his pockets and jingled loose change in them. "There are similarities. But we're definitely our own group."

Antar strode across the room until he stood directly in front of the salesman. "Last time you came you talk about IWW. I say no more talk."

"But she asked me." He nodded at Tatyana.

"You will leave and not come back," Antar said bluntly.

"Suit yourself." Mr. Salter closed the trunk lid and cinched it. His lips pursed, he picked up the heavy case. "You did not pay me for the buttons."

"Oh, I am sorry. How much?" Janna asked.

"Ten cents."

Antar dug into his pocket, counted out the change, slapped it into Mr. Salter's hand, then opened the door and held it for the man. As soon as Mr. Salter had gone, Antar looked at Janna. "You will not buy from him again." He turned and left.

Tatyana sat down at the table. "I've never seen Antar so angry."

Janna sat across from Tatyana. "He hates Communism."

"Do you think the IWW is Communist?"

Janna nodded. "Yes. And I don't want anything to do with something like that." She paused. "After what they did to Russia." Sitting, she sipped her cooled tea and asked softly, "Do you think they could take over here?"

Tatyana's stomach lurched at the unthinkable. "No." She shook her head. "That isn't possible."

"I hope you're right, Tatyana. I think I would want to die if the Communists took over and seized our freedom, forcing us to work for the government, taking our homes, and destroying our lives."

"I thought you loved Russia."

"I do, but not the way it is now."

Tatyana's mind reeled. *Is it possible the Communists could rule America?* Although she'd been unhappy living here, she'd been certain her freedom couldn't be ripped from her. Now, as she considered the possibility, fear welled up. If Communism overpowered democracy in America, she would not only be forced to live far from home but also to endure more tyranny and persecution.

Setting aside thoughts of the IWW, Tatyana and Janna talked about gardening, sewing, baking, and family. Before Tatyana realized it, the afternoon was gone. "Oh, no! What time is it?" She looked at the clock. "Five o'clock! I am supposed to be home getting ready to go to Carl and Susie's. Thank you for a wonderful day. I'm sorry to leave in such a rush." She pushed herself away from the table and hurried to the door. "You must come and visit me next time."

"Good-bye. I'm glad you came," Janna called after Tatyana.

Tatyana walked as fast as she could. *How did I let this happen?* she worried. *Dimitri will be angry.* When she stepped in the front door, he stood in the living room with Yuri in his arms and a scowl on his face. Immediately she began, "I am sorry, Dimitri, but I can explain. Well, no I cannot explain exactly. There is no excuse. Janna and I were talking, and the time passed quickly. I was having such a nice visit. I am very sorry," she ended lamely.

"Yuri and I are ready to leave," Dimitri said evenly.

"It will only take me a few minutes to get ready," Tatyana said, rushing into the bedroom. She pulled off her wrinkled and limp dress, replacing it with a starched cotton frock with pink rosebuds. Letting down her hair, she ran a brush through it and repinned it. Then she splashed cold water on her face, pinched her cheeks, and walked into the front room. "I am ready." She took Yuri and gave him a kiss. Then she looked at her husband. "Are you really angry?"

"I was. But . . . I know how easy it is to forget the time. I've done it myself." He smiled and kissed her forehead. "Come on." Placing his arm around her waist, he steered her toward the door.

When they walked into Susie's home, they were greeted by the aroma of frying chicken. "It smells wonderful," Dimitri said. "It's chicken, right?"

Carl ushered in his guests. "Yes."

"That is my favorite," Tatyana said.

In the front room, Antar stood. "Hello. Nice to see you."

"Hello, Antar," Dimitri said, shaking the man's hand.

Josephine and Susie stepped out of the kitchen. "I also made potato pancakes," Susie said.

"Draniki?"

"That's right." Josephine hugged Tatyana. "And we have strawberries and *pashka*. Is that how you say it?"

"Yes. *Pashka*."

"What is *pashka*?" Josephine asked. "I must say it looks nasty."

"It is sweetened cheese curds with butter and raisins," Tatyana explained. "It is very special. We used to eat it only for Easter." She turned a quizzical look on Susie. "Where did you learn to make it?"

"From me," Janna said, coming from the bedroom with Evelyn in her arms. "I help Susie make this morning before you come." She smiled triumphantly.

Tatyana scanned the faces and then looked at Susie. "Are you having a party? Was I supposed to bring something?"

"We're having a party all right, but you're only supposed to bring yourself," Miranda said, stepping through the kitchen door and wiping her hands on a towel.

"I did not know," Tatyana said, puzzled by all the grinning faces.

"It's your birthday party! Happy birthday!" Susie hugged Tatyana.

"But my birthday is next week."

"I know, but we're celebrating it today," Susie explained. "Carl and I will be gone next week, and I wasn't going to miss it."

Tatyana laughed. "Janna, I just left your house. How did you get here so quickly?"

Janna grinned. "It was not easy. You stay so long I am beginning to worry. I was just about to tell you I was sick so you would go." She laughed.

Tatyana looked at Dimitri. "You tricked me. You pretended to be angry...."

"I wasn't pretending. You were about to be late for your own party." He grinned and pulled her into his arms. Yuri chortled, happy to be cuddled between both parents. "Happy birthday." Dimitri kissed his wife soundly.

"All right, enough of that. I want to eat. I'm starving. We've been slaving in this kitchen all day," Josephine said.

🐜 🐜 🐜 🐜 🐜

Dimitri leaned back in his chair. "That was delicious."

"Would you like coffee?" Susie asked.

"I would," Carl said.

Dimitri rocked forward. "Me too."

"If you make it good and strong, I'll take a cup," Josephine said.

"I don't think it's as strong as yours."

"Well, that's all right. I'll take some anyway."

Susie grabbed three mugs, set them on the table, and filled them with coffee.

"I made something for you," Miranda said, pushing her large frame out of the chair and shuffling to the back porch. A few moments later she reappeared carrying a large sheet cake decorated with white icing and pink candles. *Happy Birthday,*

Comrade was written on the cake in pink. Miranda placed it on the table in front of Tatyana.

Tatyana's throat ached, and tears sprang into her eyes as the word comrade echoed through her mind. She looked at her friends around the table. "Thank you."

"Now, no crying over birthday cakes," Josephine said matter-of-factly and struck a match. She lit the candles and then stood back and began to sing, "Happy birthday to you . . ." The others joined in.

After the last note, Susie said, "Before you blow out the candles, you have to make a wish."

Tatyana swept her hand over her cheeks, wiping them dry. Then she closed her eyes. *Father, you know my wish.* She opened her eyes, a picture of Yuri still in her mind. She smiled and blew out the candles.

"What did you wish for?" Susie asked.

"Don't say," Josephine quickly spoke up. "If you tell anyone, it won't come true."

"It is a very important wish. I will not tell," Tatyana said, knowing such superstition was silly but unwilling to risk losing any chance of a reunion with her brother.

While Josephine cut the cake and Miranda served, Dimitri and Carl slipped out of the room.

Tatyana took a bite of the chocolate cake. "This is delicious, Miranda."

Miranda blushed with pride. "I've always liked to bake."

"Where are Dimitri and Carl?" Tatyana asked.

"They had something to do," Susie said with a playful smile.

A few minutes later, the front door opened and closed, then Dimitri peeked in the kitchen. "Tatyana, will you come into the living room?"

Puzzled, Tatyana took Dimitri's hand and let him lead her into the front room. The others followed.

A cherry wood phonograph with a large red ribbon on top stood just inside the front door. "Oh, my," Tatyana whispered, clapping her hand over her mouth. Slowly she walked to the record player. For a long moment she stared at it. Then she gently ran her hand over the polished wood. "It is mine?"

"From all of us," Dimitri said.

Tatyana's eyes pooled with tears. "But it is so much money. How could you? . . ."

"Because we wanted to," Josephine cut in, crossing to Tatyana and wrapping an arm around her shoulders. "We know how much you love your music. It seemed high time you were able to play it."

"We love you," Miranda said, giving Tatyana a hug.

"I love all of you."

"I have something else for you," Susie said, handing Tatyana a small package wrapped in pale blue paper with a dark blue ribbon.

Careful not to break the ribbon, Tatyana unwrapped the package. It was a book. She turned it over and ran her hand over the imprinted letters. Then she pressed it against her chest. "Oh, Susie. It is wonderful." She hugged her friend.

"Well, what is it?" Josephine asked.

Tatyana held up the book. "*A Twin in the Clouds* by Boris Pasternak." She looked at Susie. "Where did you find it? And in Russian?"

"I have a friend who owns a bookstore in Seattle. When you told me the soldiers took your copy, I asked him if he could get me one. He searched and searched and finally found it."

"Thank you. Thank all of you." Tatyana was crying openly now. Dimitri pulled his wife into his arms and held her. After a few minutes, she looked at her husband and wiped away her tears. "I love you."

"Well, I for one would like to hear some of that fancy Russian music," Josephine said. "I've been hearing about it all day."

Susie brought Tatyana's box of records from her bedroom. "Dimitri carried them over while you were at Janna's."

That night Tatyana introduced her friends to Russian classics. As the music played, the pain she expected to feel wasn't there. Instead, Tatyana felt joy as she listened to the music of her childhood. Everyone laughed, sang, and danced.

Tatyana forgot Mr. Salter's words and her own fears of a Communist America. All she knew was that she was loved by these special friends. Not until this night did she truly comprehend how much they valued her. If she wanted, she knew she could belong to this foreign land. But did she want to? As she snuggled against her husband and he swept her around the room, the thought that maybe she already did belong echoed through her mind. But there was no peace in the idea. For wouldn't that make her disloyal to her country?

CHAPTER 17

Y URI SAT ON THE RAILROAD
track, elbows on his thighs, chin in his hands. "There should be
a train soon." He glanced at the blazing afternoon sun.

"Shouldn't we stay hidden in the woods?" Elena asked. "The
station is just around the bend. Someone might see us."

"It's at least a half mile back. I don't think anyone is going
to wander up this far." He stood. "But you're probably right.
There's no reason to take chances." He ambled to the edge of
the forest and sat beneath a tree. Resting his back against the
trunk, he closed his eyes. "It's nice here in the shade."

Elena sat beside him. "I'm so thirsty. Is there any way we can
get water from the train station?"

His eyes still closed, Yuri shook his head. "Too dangerous. It
may only be a village with a tiny station, but still someone might
see us."

"What are we going to do? I'm really thirsty."

"We'll come across a stream or lake."

"Once we're on the train, even if we see water, we can't stop and get off."

Yuri's mouth and throat were parched too, and he'd thought about sneaking into the station, but soldiers would be on guard, looking for anyone they thought looked suspicious. Without papers, he couldn't take a chance of being stopped. It was too dangerous. He'd been trying to figure out a solution but couldn't think of any way to get water. He smiled at Elena, and trying to allay her fears, said, "We won't be riding that long. And there are other ways of getting liquids." He dug into his knapsack and pulled out two plums. Handing one to Elena, he said, "This will help."

She bit into the fruit and juice dribbled down her chin. She caught the nectar with her finger and licked it off. "We should have stayed on the road. We could have asked a farmer for help."

"You're the one who insisted we take a train. I was fine either way." Yuri bent his legs, leaned forward, and wrapped his arms around his knees. "Besides, we don't even know if a farmer would have helped us. People are suspicious these days."

"I know, but I've changed my mind. I think we have a better chance on the road." She stood, and wiping dirt and leaves from her pants, she looked at the trail leading through the forest and said, "Let's go back."

Yuri snapped his pack closed, yanked it up as he stood, and dropped it over his shoulder. "If that's what you want, but there's no guarantee we'll find a ride or water."

A train whistle sounded, intruding on the quiet, and the rumble of engines vibrated from around the bend. "The train is coming." Yuri ran to the tracks and watched the curve. "We have to make up our minds," he said as he loped back to Elena. "What do you want to do?"

Elena stared at the tracks. "How hard is it to jump a train?"

CHAPTER *17*

"It's not easy, but you can do it."

Elena chewed on a nail. "You're sure I can make it?"

Yuri nodded.

"You have any more plums?"

Yuri grinned and nodded again.

"All right. We'll take the train."

They ducked down in the brush and waited. "We have to wait for the engines to pass before we can go," Yuri said. "We need a boxcar with the door open. If there is one, I'm going to run for it. You stay close behind me. I'll get on first, then help you up."

"But how do I do it?"

"Run alongside, then grab the bar on the door and swing yourself up. Don't let your legs get dragged under the car or you won't make it."

Staying in a crouch and staring at the bend, Elena asked, "So, you have done this before?"

"Yeah. When Alexander and I traveled from Siberia, we got more than one ride on a passing train." He met Elena's eyes. "Don't worry, I know what to do." He turned his gaze back to the tracks. Every nerve strained in readiness, and his muscles tensed. The first engine appeared around the bend, followed by two more. "Three engines. It must be a long train," Yuri said. "That's good." Behind the engines was an open flat car piled with lumber. Next, there were two freight cars with guards standing in the doorway, rifles ready as if looking for game.

Alarm shivered up Yuri's spine as he realized he could very well be the game they searched for. After the soldiers there were cattle cars. Yuri's stomach churned, and he thought he might be sick as he saw what filled those cars. Terrified eyes peered through the slots, and fingers gripped wooden slats. "Prisoners!" he whispered, and his mind filled with images of work camp. His fingers closed over a bush and squeezed. Usually stolypin wagons transported prisoners. Where were they taking these people?

"We can't ride this train," Elena whispered. "There are soldiers and prisoners."

Yuri didn't want to ride it either, but the summer was passing and they needed to get to Leningrad. "Just wait. There might be empty cars toward the back and away from the soldiers. This is a long train. They won't even know we're there."

Following the prisoners was freight. Through open doors Yuri could see farm equipment, concrete blocks, and mortar. There were no more soldiers. "We've got to get one of these cars. Run! Now!" He sprinted out of the forest, across the grassy border along the tracks, and ran alongside a freight car. Elena stayed close behind. The train was picking up speed. Yuri knew that if they didn't get on soon it would be too late. He strained to pump his legs faster, reached for the door handle, grabbed hold, and swung his legs up and rolled onto his stomach. He quickly scanned the car, and grateful it was empty, scrambled inside. Pushing himself to his feet, he turned, then hanging onto the handle, he looked for Elena. She was losing ground.

"Hurry! Faster!"

Elena quickened her pace. She glanced at the ground in front of her, at the train, then at Yuri. Leaning forward, she threw her arm out and grabbed for the door handle but missed and stumbled. Yuri sucked in his breath, thinking she would fall beneath the train. Miraculously she kept her footing. "I . . . I can't make it."

"Yes, you can! Try again!"

Gasping for air, Elena made her legs move faster and held her hand out to Yuri. Straining as far as he thought was safe, Yuri reached for her. "Come on! A little more! You can do it!"

She lunged forward. Her fingers grazed Yuri's, but she couldn't connect. The door handle was so close. She grabbed hold and was yanked off her feet. Suspended above the ground, her body was thrown against the car, then away from it. The ground flew past. She tried to grab the handle with her other hand, but the car's jostling bounced her away.

CHAPTER 17

Yuri reached for Elena's free hand, and, finding it, cried, "I've got you!" Tightening his grip, he pulled hard and swung Elena into the car. Together they tumbled backwards onto the dusty floor.

Panting, they rolled onto their backs and lay side-by-side with their hands still intertwined. Staring at the paint-chipped ceiling, Elena gasped, "I didn't think I was going to make it." She wet her lips, closed her eyes, and smiled.

Yuri disengaged his hand, sat up, and pushed himself to his feet. The train swayed beneath him as he made his way to the door and dragged it closed. He sat back down beside Elena, his legs bent, arms resting on his knees. Grinning, he said, "You scared me."

"You?" Elena sat up. "I'll never do that again. I thought I was going to die. Why didn't you tell me it was so hard?"

"I was afraid that if you knew you'd be too scared to try."

Elena didn't respond.

"You did well. I knew you could do it."

Still breathing hard, Elena only nodded.

Yuri scooted away from the door until his back was resting against the wall. He reached into his bag and took out a plum. "At least we're traveling north and going a lot faster than if we were walking." He held up the sweet fruit. "You want one?"

Elena shook her head no and moved to the side wall of the car.

Yuri bit into the plum, tearing away the skin, then sucking out the soft pulp inside. "Wild plums are small but good. Once again, God has provided."

Elena glowered at him.

After finishing the plum, Yuri pulled out a page of Scripture verses from his pocket. He read Isaiah 65:24. "'It shall come to pass that before they call, I will answer; And while they are still speaking, I will hear.'" Yuri closed his eyes, comforted by the reminder of God's constant and powerful presence. Hungering for more of God's Word, he went on to another verse, in Deuteronomy 7. "'But because the Lord loves you, and because He would keep the oath which He swore to your fathers, the Lord has brought you out with a mighty hand, and redeemed you from the house of bondage, from the hand of Pharaoh king of Egypt. Therefore know that the Lord your God, He is God, the faithful God who keeps covenant and mercy for a thousand generations with those who love him and keep his commandments.' Praise you, Father," Yuri said quietly, folding the paper and returning it to his pocket.

Sitting across from him, Elena stared at Yuri's shirt pocket and then looked into his eyes. "I don't understand how you can believe the Bible is God's Word."

"How can I think otherwise? Its sixty-six books were written by many, many different authors, most who never spoke to each other or even lived in the same time; yet its message never varies. And the prophesies written hundreds of years before they occurred testify that God inspired the Scriptures." He paused. "But more than that, I know the power in his Word. It is real and alive. And with each reading, it speaks to me, and I know God better."

Elena said nothing, only nodded slightly, then closed her eyes.

Father, help her to understand, Yuri prayed.

"I don't remember ever being so tired," Elena said sleepily.

"Well, we walked most of the night, then waited for the train, and getting on would use up anyone's reserves."

Already asleep, Elena didn't respond.

Yuri rested his head against the wall and slept.

The train's rhythm changed, and it slowed. The brakes squealed, and Yuri awoke. His heart hammered. They were stopping! He jumped to his feet as the train slowed, jerked, and stopped. Guards shouted, and doors grated open. He crossed to Elena and shook her. "Wake up! They're inspecting the train! We have to go!"

CHAPTER 17

Elena eyes opened wide, and she sat up.

Yuri held a finger to his lips and crept to the door. All the noise was coming from the front of the train, so he slid the door open just enough to look out. The train was stopped at a water tower. Its spout was being lowered over the tank car. Several cars ahead, a guard stood at the door of a freight car and peered inside. A moment later another soldier jumped down from inside. "It's clear," he said as they moved on to the next car.

"They're coming this way!" Adrenaline pumping through his body and his mind searching for a way out, Yuri grabbed his pack.

Elena shoved her arms through the straps on hers and pulled it on. "How will we get away without being seen?"

Yuri prayed, *Father, we need your help. Show us a way.* He peered out the door again. The same soldier watched while the other climbed inside the next car. Cautiously, Yuri slid the door open further. It grated slightly, but the guard didn't seem to hear. "We have to go now," he whispered, "or they'll find us. They're inspecting every car. Follow me and do as I do."

Elena's face had turned ashen. She clutched her pack's straps tightly and nodded in agreement.

Yuri watched the soldier standing guard. Instead of paying attention to what was going on around the train, he stared inside the car. If Yuri and Elena hurried, they might get out without being seen. "Now!" Yuri jumped out of the car, landing softly on his feet, and dove beneath the train. Elena vaulted out and scrambled after him.

Lying on his stomach, Yuri glanced over his shoulder at Elena. "You all right?"

"Yes," she said in a tremulous whisper.

Yuri could see polished black boots, two sets on each side of the train. The ones on their right were moving toward the front, while the ones on their left continued working their way back from car to car. *If we crawl forward, they'll be at the rear of the train when we're up front. We might have enough time to escape into the forest,* Yuri thought.

"What do we do now?" Elena asked.

"We crawl forward, then at the right moment we run for the woods."

"We're not going to make it, are we?"

For a moment Elena's despair fed Yuri's fear. Then he remembered Peter and how he'd walked on water until unbelief caused him to sink. Yuri closed his eyes. "Father, I know you're with us. Help us be strong and to have faith in you," he prayed quietly. Glancing back at Elena, he said emphatically, "We'll make it. Now follow me."

Staying flat, Yuri inched forward. Rocks cut into his arms and legs, and the ties pressed against his ribs, but he kept moving. He stopped when the guards were only one car ahead of him. The two sets of boots on the other side of the train had disappeared. Yuri pressed his cheek against the cool gravel and lay perfectly still, barely breathing. He knew Elena was doing the same.

The guards moved to the car above Yuri. He heard the door slide open. Two polished pairs of boots stopped only inches from his face. "So, who do you think they're looking for?" one of the guards asked.

"Don't know. I just follow orders." The guard grunted as he pulled himself up into the car. Yuri could hear his footfalls overhead. Sweat ran into his eyes, but he didn't dare brush it away.

"There's going to be a card game tonight," said the guard standing alongside the car. "You want to join us?"

"Will there be vodka?"

"It wouldn't be a game without vodka."

Yuri heard the strike of a match. Then he smelled cigarette smoke.

"I'll be there." The soldier jumped from the car and stumbled, falling to one knee and tearing his trousers. He swore loudly. His hand was so close that Yuri could have reached out and touched it. Yuri held his breath. The guard pushed himself upright. "I'll be glad to dump these prisoners. They're getting on my nerves, and they're starting to stink." He slammed the door, and a lock fell into place. The boots moved on.

Yuri looked for other sets of boots but saw none. He continued forward, pulling with his arms and pushing with his legs. He could hear Elena also dragging herself through the gravel. When he thought they'd gone as far as they dared, he turned and glanced back. The guards were nearly at the end of the train. They'd be done soon. The prisoners above plaintively cried for food and water. "We must be under one of the prisoners' cars." Taking one more quick look front and back, he said, "We have to go! Run for the woods!" He scrambled out from under the car, Elena right behind him.

Feeling as if a demon of death pursued them, Yuri and Elena ran. They didn't look back. The words, *Help us, Father. Help us, Father,* echoed through Yuri's mind with each footfall. He could hear Elena's puffing and the scatter of rocks as she followed. At any moment he expected to hear shouts and gunfire, but neither came. When he reached the forest, he dove into the underbrush, and staying flat, crawled forward, finally lying absolutely still, sheltered in greenery. Elena laid beside him.

They still heard no sounds of pursuit. Yuri cautiously turned to watch the train. The two soldiers marched back up the row of cars. As they passed a prisoners' car, one of them poked his stick between two slats and ran it back and forth across knuckles. "You Zeks get back! Get back!"

Yuri felt sick. He knew what the men and women were feeling—the humiliation, anger, and overpowering fear.

The whistle blew, and the train's engines picked up momentum. The soldiers climbed into a car at the front, disappearing inside. The last of the water was loaded, and steam hissed, fogging the air as the train prepared to leave. The wheels turned once, and the train jerked forward. Yuri's eyes were rooted on the hands and faces visible through the slats. Deep within, sorrow and a silent groaning filled him. He knew he had to do something. Without thought he ran toward the train.

He heard Elena's desperate whisper, "Yuri!"

He kept running and pulled Scriptures from his pocket. When he reached the closest car, he pressed the paper through the slats. Hands received it. "It is God's Word. Read it. He wants to talk to you." He shoved another page through. Eager hands grasped the gift.

The train picked up speed, and Yuri had to run to keep up as he stuffed more pages inside. For just a moment, his gaze met hopeless, fear-filled eyes. He touched a prisoner's hand. "You're not alone. God is with you. Let him help you. He loves you!" No longer able to keep up, Yuri had to stop, and the train sped past.

"Yuri, come back!" Elena called.

Yuri turned and saw the caboose quickly approaching. He had to get away before he was seen! He fled back into the protective cover of the forest.

Gulping for air, he leaned against a birch. He couldn't stop his tears. Yuri turned and faced the tree. Pressing his face against the cool bark, he sobbed. Years of torment roiled up from deep inside.

He felt Elena's hand on his shoulder.

"I can't help them. I can't help them," Yuri anguished.

"You did."

He looked at Elena. "I pray God will help them."

"You gave them something to hang on to." She watched the train move away. "I wouldn't have done it," she said sadly. "But then, I've never done anything brave."

Wiping his eyes and nose with his shirt sleeve, Yuri walked back to the tracks. The train was gone. He stood, his shoulders hunched, his arms hanging loosely at his sides, and stared at the empty tracks for a long time. Wiping his nose again, he glanced at the water tower. Water still dripped from the pipe. A soft smile touched his face. "You said you were thirsty. Do you think that's enough water?"

Elena grinned. "More than enough."

Yuri draped his arm over Elena's shoulders. She wrapped an arm about his waist, and the two walked toward the tower. "This God of yours sometimes surprises me," Elena said.

CHAPTER 18

Y URI KNOCKED ON THE cottage door and waited. No sound came from inside, and no one answered. He knocked again. This time a quaking voice asked, "Who is it?"

"Yuri Letinov and Elena Oleinik. We're friends of Daniel Belov." Yuri didn't know how much he should say. What could he reveal and still remain safe? When the door didn't open, he continued. "I'm from Moscow. Daniel said you sometimes help travelers."

The door opened a crack, and gray-blue eyes set in a face that looked like old parchment peered out. "Sometimes I help pilgrims who wander the earth."

Yuri wondered if the man was referring to the pilgrims in the Bible who were Christians. He said, "We are pilgrims."

The man opened the door wider and studied Yuri a long while, then shifted his gaze to Elena. "And what kind of help do you need?"

"We've been traveling many weeks and are hungry and tired," Yuri explained. Then taking a chance, he added, "We're believers."

The man smiled, revealing a missing front tooth. "I am Paul Miliukov, a believer also. Please, come in." He stepped back, making room for Yuri and Elena to enter. They squeezed past the man's rounded belly. With a quick look outside, he closed the door. "So, you've been traveling a long while?"

"Yes, many days. And most of the miles have passed beneath our feet." Yuri lifted his right foot, sole up, and revealed a hole.

"People just don't trust strangers any more." The old man shook his head. "It's sad, very sad." He looked at Elena. "You both must be exhausted. Please, sit. I'll get you some tea." Yuri and Elena sat on a threadbare sofa, and Paul shuffled to the kitchen. He filled a kettle with water and placed it on the stove. "It will only take a few minutes to boil," he said, returning to the front room and slowly lowering himself onto a straight-backed chair. The room fell silent, the ticking of a clock the only sound. It chimed three times, and all eyes looked at the wooden mantle clock. "That belonged to my mother," Paul explained. "She used to say the chimes reminded her of the church bells that once called her to prayers."

"It's lovely," Elena said. "And that doll is beautiful." She nodded toward a cabinet on the far wall where an elegant porcelain doll with blonde hair and a red satin gown was on display. "Did it belong to your mother also?"

"No. No. My Gusta used to collect dolls." He pushed himself out of the chair and hobbled to the cabinet. His hand shaking slightly, he picked up the doll and studied it. Then he caressed its hair. "My wife was very proud of her dolls." He placed it back on the shelf. "This is the only one I have left. The others went to our two daughters after she died. But I kept this one. It was her favorite."

"I'm sorry about your wife," Elena said.

"She's happier now. Her last months were difficult," he sighed. "I miss her." The kettle whistled. "Ah, it's ready," he said, limping back to the kitchen. "I try to remember that Gusta is standing before God now, singing praises. I sometimes think about how we will be together again and wonder if she's getting impatient for me." He filled a small silver ball with tea leaves and dropped it in the kettle. "That will just take a few minutes," he said, returning to his chair. "So, where are you traveling to?"

"Leningrad," Yuri said.

"It is a beautiful city. I have not been there for a very long time. Maybe before I die, I will visit. Have you visited Leningrad before?"

"No," Yuri said.

"Then you are in for a treat." Paul smiled and looked at Elena. "And you? Have you visited the grandest city in all of Russia?"

"Yes," Elena said but didn't elaborate.

Paul nodded, and the room turned quiet again. Finally, he asked, "Do you have family in Leningrad?"

Yuri glanced at Elena, then said, "No. No one."

"Will you be spending much time in the city?"

"We will only be there as long as it takes for us to get a ship."

"Ah, so you're leaving the country?" Paul held up his hand. "Never mind. I ask too many questions. The tea should be ready." He started to rise.

"Please, may I get it?" Elena asked.

"Oh, yes. That would be wonderful. My joints complain loudly these days. Thank you."

Elena walked into the kitchen.

Paul settled back. "The cups are in the cupboard to your left."

Elena took down three cups and filled each with tea.

Pointing at the counter, Paul said, "There's a bit of apple there. I'll take a slice in my tea."

"Tanya used to do that," Elena said, locating a knife and slicing the apple. "It sweetens the tea." She put a slice in each cup, and after giving Paul and Yuri their drinks, got her own and returned to the sofa.

Paul took a sip. "It is perfect. Thank you."

Yuri leaned forward. "Mr. Miliukov, do you know Daniel Belov?"

"I don't actually know him, but some, uh, travelers who knew him have stayed with me. I've heard he's a good man."

"A very good man," Yuri agreed. "I'll miss him."

"So, where are you going?" He raised his hand. "Oh, I'm sorry, I didn't mean to intrude."

"No, that's fine. We're going to America."

Paul raised his eyebrows. "That will be a very big change."

"My sister lives there, in New York City. I must find her," Yuri explained. "When she left, I told her I would join her, and that was three years ago."

"It is good to live close to family. My daughters are gone, they and their husbands. Where, I do not know." His eyes teared, and he blinked hard. "Now I live alone and make room in my house for God's pilgrims. It's all I can do." He cleared his throat and said jovially, "You must be hungry. I have some stew and bread. And my stomach is feeling hollow."

"I must admit to being hungry," Yuri said.

The old man pushed himself out of the chair and hobbled to the kitchen.

"Can I help?" Elena asked.

"No. No. All I have to do is warm up some stew and slice the bread. Rest your feet."

Elena snuggled back against the sofa and sipped her tea. "It feels good to sit on something soft and to have a roof over my head. I almost forgot what it feels like to be in a home."

"I'm glad I can help," Paul said, sawing through a half loaf of bread. "So, it's been a long time since you've slept in a bed. Why don't you take mine. I'll sleep out here."

"Oh, we're not married," Yuri said, feeling his face heat up. He glanced at Elena. "We'll be fine out here. Elena can have the sofa, and I'll take the floor. And we'll be on our way first thing in the morning."

Paul smiled. "The chickens are laying more eggs than I can eat. I'd like you to stay and share breakfast with me."

"All right. Eggs sound good," Yuri said with a smile.

Paul took three bowls out of the cupboard. "There is church tonight. Would you like to go? I'll understand if you're too tired."

Elena stared at the floor, but Yuri immediately replied, "Yes, we'd love it!"

🐜 🐜 🐜 🐜 🐜

After their meal, the three set off on foot to the home of one of Paul's neighbors. Wishing she'd stayed home, Elena followed the two men. They turned up a driveway leading to a small cottage, and Paul knocked on the back door twice in rapid succession. Then he waited a moment and knocked once more. He glanced at Yuri and Elena. "We have to be careful of the NKVD," he said as the door opened.

"Come in, come in," a tiny woman with dark curly hair said. "Paul, how good to see you. How are you feeling?"

"I'm fine, just a little stiff as usual. I've brought friends. Yuri Letinov and Elena Oleinik, I would like you to meet Praskovya Ivanovna."

Wearing a warm smile, she took Elena's hands in hers. "Welcome. Welcome."

Elena managed to smile in return but still wished she were home sleeping. She was exhausted, and church was the last thing she wanted to do.

Their hostess looked at Yuri. "It is good to have you with us."

"We're happy to be here."

"Please, join us," Praskovya said as she walked through the kitchen and into the living room.

The front room glowed with candlelight. Candles flickered before religious icons of saints and one of Mary, the mother of Jesus, plus dozens reflected from prisms in a candelabrum sitting in the center of a table. The smell of incense was strong, and Elena was reminded of the church she'd attended with her family as a child. She'd never liked it much.

"We practice Orthodoxy here," Paul said. "This house is not as elegant as a cathedral, but it's the beauty in the hearts of believers that matters to God."

"I was always taught church isn't a building, but God's people," Yuri agreed.

"Exactly." Paul placed his hand on Yuri's arm. "I would like you to meet our priest, Father Rublev." Leaning on Yuri, he hobbled across the room to a tall thin man wearing a long black robe.

Elena followed reluctantly.

"Father Rublev," Mr. Miliukov said, "I'd like you to meet my friends, Yuri Letinov and Elena Oleinik."

The priest gently took Elena's hand and bowed slightly. "It is a pleasure to meet you and an honor to have guests."

Elena didn't know how to respond. She felt uneasy but managed to say, "It is good to meet you, Father."

The priest turned to Yuri. "It is always a fine day when I get to meet another brother."

"I am honored to meet you," Yuri said, surprised at the man's warm and friendly demeanor. The few Orthodox priests he'd met had been more reserved.

As if on cue, the people quieted, and Father Rublev walked to the front of the room. Yuri and Elena stood quietly with the others as the priest led the group in worship. Some of the songs were familiar, but many Yuri had never heard, so he simply closed his eyes and listened to the words of redemption and hope, reveling in God's promises. After that, the priest cited the litany as he dangled his censer from a cord and incense filled the air. Chants and prayers followed, and finally, some who had gathered offered words of testimony.

When the service ended, Elena stepped outside and sat on a large rock in the backyard. She looked up at the stars and wondered if God truly existed. So many of her friends and the people tonight seemed to know God. He was real to them. For her he'd always seemed imagined, and at best, distant.

Yuri stepped out the front door. "So here you are. I was wondering where you went."

She stood. "Can we go?"

"I'll get Paul," Yuri said with disappointment in his voice.

✹ ✹ ✹ ✹ ✹

Elena lay on the sofa that night listening to the ticking clock and Yuri's quiet breathing. She felt unsettled. Over the years, she'd sat through many religious services and still didn't know God. What was it that she didn't understand that Christians did? What made them different from her? Pulling her blanket up under her chin, she asked, "Yuri, are you still awake?"

"Uh huh," Yuri said sleepily.

"I'm confused. When I was a child, we practiced Orthodoxy, but I don't remember it being like tonight."

"A child's mind sees things differently than adults do. And I think tonight's service was less formal than at the church."

"But it was not like our church in Moscow."

"Churches may be different, but there is still only one God and one Savior. Our ways of worshiping may vary, but what binds us together is our belief in Jesus Christ and his sacrifice."

"I think I liked church at the Trofernoff's in Moscow better. It felt comfortable."

"Me too, but the spirit of God is working here and in Moscow." He paused, then asked, "I thought you didn't care."

Elena hated the question. She didn't want to care, but inside something was happening; a longing to know more pulled at her. She wanted to know God. "I don't care," she said. "I was just used to the other way."

✳ ✳ ✳ ✳ ✳

After a breakfast of eggs and toast, Yuri and Elena continued their journey, taking Mr. Miliukov's blessings as well as fresh water and food with them. He'd been more than generous, and Yuri worried the old man had left himself lacking.

They walked all day, careful to stay off the road. The going was easier now that the weather had warmed and the mud had dried. That night they stopped and camped in the woods. Yuri trapped a rabbit while Elena picked berries. As Yuri turned the rabbit on a spit, hot juices dripped and sizzled in the flames. His mouth watered in anticipation, and his stomach grumbled with hunger.

Elena sat with her legs folded beneath her and poked at the fire with a stick. "Your stomach is rumbling louder than mine," she said with a smile.

"The smell of this makes me extra hungry." He tore off a chunk of meat and tasted it. "It's ready." Carefully he cut away a leg and handed it to Elena. "It's hot."

Holding the meat between the tips of her fingers, Elena blew on it and then tore off a small bite with her teeth. "It tastes wonderful." She took another bite. "Do you think there are rabbits in America?"

"I don't know. I guess so. It seems like there are rabbits everywhere."

"But an ocean separates the two countries."

224

Yuri shrugged. "I guess we'll have to wait and see. But I hope so," he added, taking a bite and chewing with relish. "Rabbit has always been one of my favorites." Using his teeth, he stripped off the last piece of meat. "When I was in camp, I would have given almost anything for something this good."

Elena leaned forward. "What did you eat?"

"You don't want to know."

"Yes I do."

"The camp gave us trash soup. It was bad. Sometimes we would get a piece of fish, but usually there were only bones and scales. We'd find pieces of grass and leaves, but we never knew exactly what was in it. Still, we were thankful for something hot. Other than that, they handed out moldy bread twice a day. We were always hungry and ate berries and mushrooms if we could find them. When we couldn't get that, there were slugs and rats."

Elena grimaced. "I could never do that."

"I didn't think I could either, but I got hungry enough." He finished off his bread.

"What was it like in prison?"

Yuri poked a stick into the fire. He didn't want anyone to know how loathsome he'd been, especially Elena. *But maybe she needs to know,* he thought. Staring at the fire, he said quietly, "I've never told anyone what happened to me there. I'm not proud of who I was." He took a drink of water, still uncertain he wanted her to know the full truth. "All I thought about was myself and how I could survive. I was filled with fear and rage. I raged at the government and the men who beat me and the man who turned me in, but mostly I raged at God."

Elena was silent.

"Bitterness ate at me, destroying me from inside like a poison." He smiled as he remembered Alexander. "But Alexander was right there with me at the work camp. He never gave up on me and kept talking about God and God's love. For a long time I wouldn't listen, not until I was thrown into the isolator for trying to kill a man. The guards left me there to die."

"What's an isolator?"

"A deep pit cut out of the frozen ground."

"I can't believe you'd try to kill anyone."

Yuri tossed a stick into the fire. "I was a different man then. I'm ashamed of who I was." He glanced at Elena.

She met his gaze. "There are many of us who don't like who we are," she said softly.

"God redeems us no matter how we feel about ourselves or what we've done. At the moment when I least deserved his love, he reached out to me."

The light of the fire illuminated the anguish on Elena's face. "Aren't there some sins that are too bad to forgive?"

"No. God forgives every evil thing we do. He loves us so much he sacrificed his own Son. When Jesus died, he took all our sins upon himself so we don't have to carry them. He forgives every sin, if only we'll believe in him and trust him. When we place our lives in his hands, we become pure, without blemish."

Yuri studied Elena. For so long he'd known something tormented her, but he'd never probed, believing she'd tell him when she was ready. Now it was time for her to be free of it. "Elena, what torments you?" he asked gently. "From the first time I saw you standing in the back of that truck, I saw your anguish."

Elena stared into the dying flames, saying nothing for a long while. "I've never told anyone." She looked at Yuri. "You think you know me, but you don't. You've called me comrade, but you've never known what a coward I am."

Yuri prayed for God's wisdom as he waited for Elena to continue.

"I deserted my family," she blurted. "The soldiers came, and I did nothing." She pulled her knees up to her chest, and hugging them, rocked back and forth.

"Tell me what happened," Yuri encouraged.

Taking a ragged breath, Elena said quietly, "My family was wealthy. There was nothing I didn't have. We were bourgeois and became enemies of the state." Her hand shaking, she wiped wetness from her cheeks. "Our friends were disappearing. We didn't know what was happening, but we knew that it was bad and might happen to us." She stopped and took a deep breath. "One night the soldiers came. They dragged away my mother, father, and baby sister. I hid in a closet and listened to my sister scream and my mother cry and beg for mercy. I could hear the soldiers' shouts and the blows as they beat my family. And I did nothing." Tears spilled from her eyes. "I heard my father shouting, then a soldier threatening to kill him, and my mother begging them to stop and please spare my father's life. I . . . I wanted to do something, but I didn't. I just stayed in the closet. And then they were gone."

Yuri's own tears spilled over as he stepped around the fire and sat beside Elena. Wrapping his arms about her, he pulled her against him. For a while, they cried together, then Elena looked at Yuri. "I want to be brave, but I'm not. I always hide or run. When you gave the Scripture verses to the prisoners on the train, I wanted to be like you, but I hid because I'm a coward." She pushed herself away from him. "You should hate me! I do!"

"I can't hate you. I love you." He quickly added, "We're comrades. And God loves you. You've done nothing wrong; you've only tried to survive. You couldn't have helped your family. If you'd tried, you would have been taken too."

"Even if it meant dying, I should have done something. You would have."

"I just told you what a coward I've been, that I was hateful and afraid. I still am sometimes. None of us can do it right all the time. But even so, God never leaves us." He gripped her upper arms and shook her gently. "Elena, hear me. God loves you. He wants you to spend eternity with him. That's why he sent his Son. All he wants is for you to trust him. It's his love that makes us brave."

Elena shook her head as more tears spilled. She pressed her fists against her eyes. "I . . . I want to believe you. I want to be brave like you and the Belovs—to find peace. I'll never have peace. Every moment I'm afraid, and I know I deserve to be hated."

Yuri pulled her close again and said softly, "Elena, God wants to take all the fear, all the hatred, and give you peace. Please trust him, trust his Son. Jesus loves you."

"It's so hard to believe he loves someone like me."

"He does."

A sob escaped as Elena asked, "He really loves me? Even though he knows how awful I am?"

"Yes. He loves you."

She buried her face against Yuri's chest. "I want to believe. Please help me to know God." She cried hard as Yuri caressed her hair and rocked gently back and forth. For the first time, Elena opened her heart in prayer and felt the flood of an extraordinary love she knew came from God.

CHAPTER 19

TATYANA SWIRLED FROSTING over the bottom layer of cake while Yuri banged an aluminum lid against the floor at her feet. She stopped and watched him. *I should be happy,* she thought. *Today, Yuri turns one.*

Instead, Tatyana was troubled. Her son's first year had passed, and there was still no hope of returning to Russia. She feared he would grow up and never know his homeland.

Yuri tossed the lid and then clung to the cabinet as he stood. Babbling happily, he pulled on his mother's dress. Taking a swipe of frosting on her finger, Tatyana offered it to the little boy who smiled his appreciation before dropping back onto his bottom. She wiped sweat from her brow with the edge of her apron, remembering how miserable she'd been the previous July when Yuri was due. Glancing at her son, she said, "I am happy I am not in that condition again in this heat." Carefully removing the

229

second layer of cake from a metal rack, she placed it on top of the frosted layer and secured it with toothpicks.

The back door opened, and Dimitri stepped inside. "Hi."

"Hello," Tatyana said.

Dimitri picked up Yuri and held him up over his head. "Happy birthday, son."

The little boy laughed and chanted, "Da, da, da." He grabbed his father's cap and snatched it off his head.

"Oh, no, you don't," Dimitri said as he retrieved the cap. Giving Yuri a quick kiss, he set him back on the floor, and then peered over Tatyana's shoulder. "Mm, chocolate." He kissed her cheek. "I love chocolate."

"Your son is like you. He loves it too." She glanced at the wall clock. "I am late. I did not think this cake would take so long. Carl and Susie will be here any minute."

"Don't worry. They won't mind waiting. Besides, I'm late too. I need to shower and get some of this garden dirt off me." He looked at his filthy overalls and hands and immediately headed for the bathroom. Using the cupboard for leverage, Yuri pushed himself to his feet and toddled after his father.

Tatyana watched the little boy and called to Dimitri. "Your son is following you."

"That's okay. He can shower too. We'll take one together."

Tatyana smiled as she considered what a good father Dimitri was. She returned to frosting the cake, and after she'd finished, placed a single candle in the middle. For a few moments she stared at it. Since her first birthday party in this country, she'd liked the American tradition of celebrating with cake and candles, but now that it was her son's celebration she felt uneasy, wishing he were learning the ways of his homeland instead.

With a sigh, she set the cake on top of the refrigerator. Peeking under the Dutch oven lid, she poked the roast with a fork. It was tender, so she turned the heat off and set a pot of peeled potatoes on the stove to cook. Dumping a jar of corn into a pan, she put it on to heat and then turned her attention to setting the table.

A knock came at the front door, but before Tatyana could answer it, Susie stepped inside and called, "We're here!"

Tatyana met Susie, Carl, and Evelyn in the front room. "Hello. How are you?"

"We're wonderful," Susie said, handing Tatyana a brightly decorated gift box. "For Yuri."

"Thank you, but you did not have to bring a present." She set the box on top of the phonograph.

"He'll probably be more thrilled with the paper than the gift," Carl said. "Evelyn was." He looked around the room. "Where is the birthday boy?"

"He is in the shower with Dimitri. Would you like some iced tea or lemonade?"

"Lemonade sounds great," Carl said, sitting Evelyn on the floor. The little girl tottered to Yuri's toy box.

"I think I'd like tea." Susie watched her daughter. "She certainly knows where to find the toys."

His face flushed and hair still wet from the shower, Dimitri walked out of the bathroom, a naked Yuri cuddled against him. "We'll be right back. He needs a diaper." Dimitri disappeared into the boy's bedroom. A few minutes later he reappeared with Yuri wearing a short-sleeved shirt with cotton creepers. Smiling, he said, "Now he's ready for a party."

Dimitri set Yuri on the floor, and the little boy scrambled toward Evelyn. Reaching the toy box, he hung on to the edge and pulled himself up. Facing the little girl, he grabbed the block she had, but Evelyn refused to give it up. Raising her voice to a high-pitched scream, she tugged until Yuri let go. Seemingly unperturbed, Yuri simply picked another block out of the box.

"Well, we can see who's going to be the boss of those two," Carl said with a laugh. "I hate to think what Yuri's life will be like if they end up married."

"Some men need a little extra help now and then," Susie quipped.

Carl eyed his wife. "Even if they don't want it?"

"Even so."

Dimitri scooped Yuri up. "I'm ready to eat. What do you say about having dinner?" Yuri wrapped his arms about his father's neck, and Dimitri looked at Tatyana. "Is it ready?"

"Yes. I just have to mash the potatoes."

* * * * *

After dinner Tatyana set the birthday cake on the table in front of Yuri's highchair. She lit the candle, and his eyes brightened as he watched the flame. Everyone sang "Happy Birthday" while the little boy grabbed for the candle. Dimitri deflected his hand, and when the song ended, he blew it out for him. Everyone clapped, and Yuri grabbed a fistful of cake, shoving it in his mouth.

Tatyana cut and handed out pieces of cake, Yuri first. When the little boy was finished, she wiped his face and hands and gave him a wooden truck she and Dimitri had purchased at the company store. "See, the wheels turn," Dimitri said, spinning the wooden tires. Yuri grabbed the toy, fingering the cab and wheels, then banged it against his tray. "No, not like that." Dimitri rolled the truck back and forth. Doing his best to imitate his father, Yuri pushed the truck, but it fell to the floor.

Susie replaced it with her gift. "I got this out of the Sears catalog. I think he'll like it." She helped Yuri remove the paper and open the box. She took out a small plastic cow, a horse, and a pig. Yuri picked up the pig and chewed on it.

"That's what he does with everything," Dimitri said.

"He'll learn how to play with them soon enough," Carl said.

Although Tatyana smiled and laughed at all the right times, her melancholy lingered. She wanted more for Yuri than candles and gifts. She wanted the bonds of family, the old traditional

232

songs played on the balalaika or mandolin, and folk dances handed down from generation to generation. She wanted him to know his heritage. Here he had American traditions, and as he grew up, he would be American. He might even hate Russia, like his father. An ache settled in her chest.

"Tatyana, are you all right?" Susie asked.

Tatyana didn't know how to answer; she thought she'd managed to disguise her mood. "I am fine," she finally replied.

"You seem far away and sad."

Tatyana hadn't intended to share her sorrow but heard herself say, "I am, a little." She swept a lock of hair off her son's forehead. "I worry about Yuri. How will he learn about his heritage? He is so far from home. If he lives here in America, how will he ever know what it means to be Russian?"

Dimitri slammed his cup down on the table. "He's not Russian. He's American. He was born in America."

Tatyana fought tears. Why couldn't Dimitri understand? She met his angry stare. "That is not who he is. You and I are Russian. He is Russian."

"He's Yuri Broido, American, just like his father."

Carl cleared his throat. "Uh, maybe we should go."

Susie picked up Evelyn. "I think that's a good idea. It's late and Evelyn needs to get to bed. Thank you for a wonderful meal," she said to Tatyana. "We had a good time."

"You do not have to go," Tatyana said.

Carl stood. "Yes, we do," he said with a smile.

＊ ＊ ＊ ＊ ＊

After Carl and Susie left, Dimitri walked into the living room. He flipped on the radio, sat in his chair, and began reading a book of short stories. Tatyana washed Yuri and put him to bed. Then she cleared away the dishes. Angry, she slammed them into the sink. *Why can't he understand? He's forgotten he's Russian. And I do not want to raise my son as an American.* After she furiously scrubbed and dried the dishes, she slapped the towel over the back of a chair and left the kitchen. As she walked past Dimitri, she said sharply, "I am going to bed."

Dimitri didn't even look up. Tatyana blinked back tears, gritted her teeth, and stormed into the bedroom. Quickly undressing, she pulled on her nightgown and dragged a brush through her hair. On her way to the bathroom, she glanced at Dimitri. He still sat in his chair, staring at his book. Tatyana had to say something. She marched across the room, and with arms folded over her chest, stood directly in front of her husband. "How can you read when there is so much we need to talk about?"

Very calmly Dimitri looked at her and laid the book in his lap. "What do you want to discuss? We've already talked about Yuri's future. It's been settled. He's an American and will be raised as such."

Her hands balled into fists, Tatyana asked, "How is it you do not understand? It is important for Yuri to know who he is and where he comes from. He needs to know Russia, its people, and its culture."

"He can know all that. You can teach him."

"It is not the same. . . ." Tatyana hesitated, knowing her next statement would only anger Dimitri more. "He must live in his homeland to know it. I cannot show him a life. There is too much to learn and understand."

Bristling, Dimitri stood to his feet. "How can you even suggest placing our son in such danger? Are you so deceived you don't know the hazards, or are you just foolish?"

Tatyana felt like she'd been slapped. Dimitri had never spoken to her so harshly.

"Russia is a place where people die." Dimitri tossed his book onto the coffee table. "He's never going to Russia. Never."

Frustration, hurt, and anger flooded Tatyana. "Janna asked me to go with her when she visits her aunt and uncle in Seattle tomorrow. I am going and taking Yuri with me."

Dimitri clenched his teeth, and his jaw muscles twitched as he stared at his wife. Abruptly, he turned and walked out of the house.

✳ ✳ ✳ ✳ ✳

"I'm so glad you decided to come," Janna said in Russian as she scooted across the bus seat to allow room for Tatyana and Yuri. "You'll like my aunt and uncle. They used to live in Moscow but moved here nearly ten years ago."

Tatyana nodded and forced a smile, her mind a jumble of confused thoughts. *I shouldn't be here. I should be with my husband.*

As the bus pulled out of the station, she thought about her morning. Breakfast had been torture. Dimitri ate his eggs in silence, and she couldn't get down her toast. When Dimitri left for work, he didn't even say good-bye. "Maybe I should not go," she muttered.

"What?" Janna asked.

Stores and homes moved past her window as they left Black Diamond behind. Tatyana knew it was too late to change her mind. "Nothing," she said and leaned back in her seat, cuddling Yuri against her.

Seattle, as always, was congested with cars, buses, and people. The smell of cigar smoke, gasoline, and spicy food greeted Tatyana as she stepped off the bus at the terminal. A short squat man standing in front of her puffed on a cigar. He glanced at her, grabbed his bag, and walked off. Tatyana took a deep, cleansing breath, thankful his cigar had gone with him.

"Your hands are full with Yuri. I'll get our bags," Janna said, picking up their luggage. "My aunt and uncle only live a couple blocks from here." She smiled at Yuri and kissed his cheek. "You have been such a good boy, not giving your mother any trouble."

"You were very good," Tatyana said, giving him a squeeze. Grateful for cooler weather and partial cloudiness, she fell into step beside her friend. The roar of buses and cars, the honking of horns, and the bustle of foot traffic was a little overwhelming. She was used to the slower, quieter pace of Black Diamond, and for a moment, longed for the more peaceful surroundings.

They stopped in front of a six-story apartment building. "This is it. They live on the second floor," Janna said. She opened the door and stepped into a cool lobby. It was clean but simple with a well-worn red carpet.

Tatyana followed Janna up a flight of stairs. With Yuri in her arms, she was thankful Janna's aunt and uncle didn't live on the sixth floor. They walked down a narrow, dimly lit hallway and stopped at apartment 212. Janna knocked and flashed a smile at Tatyana.

The door opened and a tall, gaunt man with bright blue eyes smiled out at them. "Janna! How good to see you!" he said in Russian. "We didn't know what time to expect you." He pulled the young woman into his arms and kissed her on each cheek. Finally releasing her, he said, "Please, come in."

The visitors stepped into the small apartment. "Uncle Vladimir, I would like you to meet my friend, Tatyana Broido, and her son, Yuri. Tatyana, this is Uncle Vladimir Voznesensky."

"It is very nice to meet you," Tatyana said.

Vladimir took her hand. "I am so happy to meet a friend of Janna's. She has told us about you." He patted Yuri's leg.

Tatyana instantly liked the friendly man and hoped she'd be able to return for more visits.

"So, Janna said you are from Moscow," Vladimir said.

"I used to live on a farm outside Moscow. But that was a long time ago."

"Is that you, Janna?" a woman asked from another room.

"Yes, Aunt."

A plump woman with dark brown hair and eyes and wearing a flour-dusted apron stepped into the front room. "How wonderful to see you! It is so good of you to come!"

Janna hugged the woman. "It is good to be here. You know I love to visit. I miss you both so much. I wish you lived closer."

The woman stepped back and smiled at Tatyana. "And did I hear your friend is from Moscow?"

"Yes, Aunt Masha. This is Tatyana Broido. She lives in Black Diamond too. Tatyana, I'd like you to meet my aunt Masha."

The woman's eyes sparkled with delight as she hugged Tatyana. "I've been baking all day just for you two. Janna, I made your favorite—apple strudel."

Janna took a deep whiff of cinnamon and apples. "I thought maybe you had. It smells wonderful in here." She shook her head slowly. "I wish I could make strudel like you."

🦋 🦋 🦋 🦋 🦋

That evening Tatyana felt as if she'd gone home to Russia. The Voznesenskys were warm, straightforward people full of tales about their homeland. And their apartment was filled with bits and pieces of their lives. Russian Orthodox icons hung on their walls, and the shelves and cabinets were decorated with Russian ornaments and momentos. One shelf held a Matroshka doll and Russian Easter eggs as well. An angel, painted in bright colors and shimmering beneath a glossy finish, smiled at them from behind a glass cabinet door. Tatyana remembered seeing one just like it on one of her trips to Moscow.

After a meal of thick chicken stew, fresh bread, and the sweet treat of apple strudel, Vladimir brought out his harp organ. "I try to play every day. It reminds us of home and the good times there." He sat at the dining table and played Russian folk songs while Masha, Janna, and Tatyana, with Yuri in her arms, sang, danced, and laughed. Tatyana's heart was warmed as her son experienced the music of their homeland. She was reminded of the many celebrations she and her family had shared and could almost hear Yuri's beautiful tenor voice. He'd always been asked to sing when they had gathered.

In a quiet moment, Tatyana sat at the table with the others and sipped tea. She asked Masha, "Do you miss your home?"

"Yes. Sometimes. But as you can see, we brought much of it with us." She smiled. "We never forget how blessed we were to grow up in Russia, but we also know we are lucky to live here in America. In Russia life is very difficult. Now we have a good life and our freedom, and we are thankful for that."

Tatyana felt a little surprised. They seemed so Russian. She wondered how they had been able to make the transition she still struggled with.

Masha reached out and laid her hand over Tatyana's. "I can see in your eyes that you miss your home."

Tatyana nodded. "I can't seem to leave it behind."

"You don't have to leave it. Remember and cherish it, but don't forget you also have a life now. God moves us from place to place, but each new location can be home. You must make it so."

"Sometimes it's not easy living here," Vladimir said. "It's more and more difficult to keep a job or to find a new one. And with the depression . . ."

"Yes, Vladimir, but even with hard times, life here is better than in Russia," Masha said with a smile. She swept her arm out in front of her. "Is there anything we need that we are living without?"

"No. We have all we need," Vladimir agreed, planting a kiss on his wife's mouth.

Masha held his face a moment and returned the kiss.

"Have you heard from Andrei?" Janna asked.

"Yes. We received a letter. It was so good to hear from him, to know that he is alive. It's a miracle, really, to get a letter from Russia." Masha hesitated. "I said nothing because I'm not certain you want to hear what he has to say."

"It is that bad?"

"Yes. But we knew that," Vladimir said sadly.

Masha reached out and laid her hand on her husband's. "One day we'll see our son again."

The old man nodded.

"I've been writing and writing to my brother," Tatyana said. "But I never hear from him. Do you think he gets my letters?"

Masha was quiet for a long moment, then with a sigh, said, "I cannot say, but I know that very little gets in or out of Russia."

"Could you read the letter to me, Masha?" Janna asked gently.

"You're sure you want to hear?"

"Yes. I love cousin Andrei and his wife Yudina, and Michael and Svetlana. I need to know how they are."

Masha pushed herself up out of the chair and shuffled across the room to a wooden cabinet. "The postmark is four months old," she said as she sat down. Tenderly, she removed the letter from its envelope and unfolded it. Placing her glasses on her nose, she read, "My dear Mama and Papa, I will have to keep this letter short, for there is little time now for writing. I have not heard from you in a very long while, but I'm certain you must have sent letters. I know you will do all you can to stay in touch. I pray this letter will make it to you.

"I'm sorry to have to tell you my sweet Yudina is gone. She died of a fever. With so little to eat, she was too weak to fight the infection. As you know, it's sometimes difficult to keep fighting. Without Yudina my life feels empty, but the children need me, and so I push on. We are no longer living on the farm. It belongs to the government now. We've been moved to a *collective*. There was no other way."

Masha nudged her glasses up and dabbed at her eyes with a handkerchief. Then she gave a bereft Janna a half smile and continued.

"Life here is not so bad. There is food and a house. We work and live and thank God for all he gives. I try not to think of the days on our own farm and our old way of life, but I must admit I often find myself thinking of it. When I do, peace seems illusive. Please pray for me and the children.

"You were right to leave, and I pray one day we'll be free and will join you in America. Oh, what a joyous reunion that will be. You can show us all around that great country where God is glorified.

"I know God will bless us and we will know freedom, either in this life or the next. He is our hope. Please pray for Michael and little Svetlana who misses her mama so much. With all our love, Andrei Voznesensky."

Masha mopped at her tears as she tucked the letter back into its envelope.

"I'm so sorry," Janna said, wiping away her own tears. "Yudina was a kind woman." She looked around the room. "Sometimes I feel sad that I do not live in Russia, but when I'm reminded of what has happened there, I'm thankful I am here."

Memories flooded Tatyana. She'd been so foolish. She'd buried the reality of Russia and had created a fanciful dream to replace it. Yes, there had been beauty, but a hideous evil had been substituted. She'd forgotten.

She could now feel the hunger and fear, actually taste the dust stirred up by the truck that had taken her parents, and she felt the emptiness planted within her as they had disappeared. Cries of the tortured echoed through her mind—so many lives destroyed. The faces of loved ones filled her thoughts. Their courage is what she should have remembered, not fraudulent memories.

Tears of sorrow and anger came. *Father, forgive me. I've been so ungrateful. I've been so blind.* She felt a comforting hand on her shoulder and thoughts of Dimitri flooded her. He'd been right. She needed to tell him. She needed his arms around her.

Her vision blurred by tears, she looked at Janna. "I need to go home—home to Dimitri and to Black Diamond."

CHAPTER 20

Tatyana dried the last plate, set it on the stack of dishes, then wiped down the counter. The front door opened and closed. She heard Dimitri say, "Have a seat." His boots echoed against the hardwood floor. Wearing a mischievous smile, he stepped into the kitchen. "Hi. I'm back."

"Who is with you?"

"Elise."

"Elise? But her parents do not want her here."

Dimitri raised his hand. "I know. But I asked her to watch Yuri, and her mother said it would be all right."

Tatyana draped the towel over the refrigerator handle. "Why would she need to stay with Yuri?"

Dimitri glanced out the window and then looked at Tatyana.

"What is it?" She placed her hand on Dimitri's arm. "What are you up to?"

"Nothing. It's just that I . . ." He took a deep breath. "It's just that . . . Well, I have something I want to show you." Taking her hand, he led her out of the kitchen.

"What is it?"

"You'll see."

As they stepped into the front room, Elise, who'd been sitting on the sofa, stood. "It is good to see you."

Tatyana gave the young woman a hug. "How are you?"

"Very good. But I miss Michael. You know he went into the army and is stationed in Europe." She smiled prettily. "We plan to get married when he returns on leave in January. He writes me almost every day."

"I am happy for you," Tatyana said.

"I'll send you an invitation to the wedding."

"We will be there."

"We wouldn't miss it," Dimitri said. "And thanks for staying with Yuri."

"He just went down for a nap and should sleep," Tatyana said.

"We better hurry. I'm working the swing shift tonight."

Tatyana folded her arms over her chest and eyed Dimitri ambiguously. "Where are we going?"

"It's a surprise," he said, taking her hand and leading her out the front door.

"Good-bye," Elise called after them.

Dimitri, with Tatyana in tow, walked down the front path, onto the street, and headed north. The afternoon sun was high in the sky, and with no clouds to block its rays, it felt hot. Tatyana had to walk fast to keep up. As a car swept past kicking up dust, she yanked on her husband's hand. "Slow down. You act like you are in a race."

Dimitri threw her a contrite grin and slowed his steps. "I'm sorry. Sometimes I forget my legs are a lot longer than yours."

"It is not only that. You are walking very fast. Why? What is going on?"

"I don't want to tell you. I want to show you."

After walking at least a mile, the town of Black Diamond behind them, Tatyana wrenched her hand out of Dimitri's and stopped. "This is far enough. I am not taking another step until you tell me where we are going."

Dimitri stopped, and for a moment, he acted as if he might tell her, but instead he said, "We're almost there. Just a few more minutes."

With an exaggerated sigh of resignation, she caught hold of his hand, and they continued. Tatyana's mind clamored for an explanation for his behavior. There was nothing but trees and fields here and an occasional farmhouse. They had no friends living in the area. And if he were simply going to show her a new duck hunting pond or swimming hole or berry-picking patch, he wouldn't act so secretively. *What could he possibly want to show me?* Tatyana hurried her steps, impatient to solve the mystery.

Finally Dimitri turned off the main road and onto a narrow dirt lane. They walked another quarter mile before he stopped and faced an open field bordered by forest. Holding out his arms, he said, "This is it."

Tatyana gazed at green and yellow grasses intermingled with pink thistles, purple chicory, and bright red paintbrush. It was lovely, but she'd seen many such fields. What was so special about this one? She looked at Dimitri. "This is what? Why are we here?"

Dimitri took a deep breath. "These eleven acres are for sale. A man at the mine owns it. He said we could have it for a good price. It's perfect for us," he added, his voice animated.

As understanding settled over Tatyana, her mouth dropped open, and her eyes swept the property again. "You want to buy it?"

"It's a nice piece. Even this late in July there's a lot of green grass, which means good pasture for livestock. And over there in the southwest corner, there's a pond. That'll make our job of watering easier."

A mosquito landed on Tatyana's arm, and she slapped, it then flicked it away. "It is a good place to grow mosquitoes," she said sarcastically.

Dimitri ignored her caustic tone and continued, "There's a couple acres in timber that we can use to build a house and barn. I figured one acre would be enough for our home and any outbuildings, which leaves six for a pasture and two for a big garden. We should have extra vegetables we can sell."

Dimitri's excitement was matched by Tatyana's panic. How would they pay for it? And buying property meant permanence. If you owned a place, you didn't just pick up and leave. They would build and stay. After her visit to Janna's aunt and uncle's, she'd been happier and had even considered Black Diamond home, but this . . . she didn't know if she was ready for this.

"We might even be able to build a house for Mama and Papa. That way my brother and sister could live in the country like they've always wanted. Samuel could have a cow, and Ella could grow her flower garden. If they came, it would mean a lot of extra hands in the garden."

He rested an arm around Tatyana's shoulders and pointed toward the southeast corner of the property. "I thought we'd build the house back there and the barn up this way a little," he said, pointing at a grove of fir trees. "Can you see it? We could be happy here in our own place."

Tatyana didn't want to hurt Dimitri, but sorrow settled over her at the thought of forever closing the door to returning to Russia. Taking a step away from him, she said softly, "Dimitri, I do not know if I want to buy property yet. It . . . it is so permanent."

"I thought you said you were happy and wanted to stay in Black Diamond."

"I am happy, and I do want this to be home, but buying land so soon . . ." She shook her head slowly back and forth. "I . . . I am not ready yet."

Dimitri clamped his mouth shut and stared at the tree line, then he looked at Tatyana. "You're still thinking about returning to Russia, aren't you?"

"No. I . . ."

"I cannot believe this!" He swept off his cap and slapped it against his thigh. "After what you said when you returned from Seattle? You told me you understood it was impossible to return. That you wanted to make Black Diamond your home."

"I do want to stay, and this is home, but I . . . I feel . . ." She hugged her waist and turned her back to Dimitri. "I cannot explain how I feel, but it is just too soon to plant such strong roots." Angrily, she wiped away tears.

Dimitri stuck his cap back on his head and kicked at a rock. "Just because we buy land doesn't mean we will never move. We won't be chained to this place." He eyes roamed the property.

Guilt swept over Tatyana. She knew he must be thinking about all the plans he'd made for them and now realized they might not happen.

Dimitri stepped around Tatyana and faced her. "I thought you'd like this place. It's right for us." Gently he took her hands in his. "Just think, our own house. And there is room for children to run and play. We can put up a swing set for Yuri, and that big maple over there would be perfect for summer picnics. We could even get a pony for him. And I'll plant hundreds of strawberry plants just for you."

Tatyana loved the images Dimitri was painting. She wanted to be caught up in his dream, but to do that she would have to put to death her own dream. A knot tightened in her stomach.

"We'll have to come up with a down payment," Dimitri said. "He wants two thousand dollars for the land but will take ten percent down and we can make payments on the rest. All we need is two hundred dollars, and it will be ours. I thought I might get a second job."

Tatyana remembered the savings jar. Dimitri knew nothing about it. She'd been stashing extra money since arriving in Black Diamond, hoping one day to have enough for passage home.

"Tatyana, please think about this before you make up your mind. I believe it's what God wants for us."

As Tatyana gazed out over the acreage, a breeze blew her hair into her eyes and she brushed it back. The smell of warm grass, wild flowers, and cedar floated on the wind. She closed her eyes and breathed deeply. For a moment, she could see a small house with a broad front porch tucked within the trees, but the indescribable sorrow wrenched it away. "Dimitri, your dream is a good one, but . . ." She searched for words to express her feelings. "I know that I cannot return to Russia, but in my heart it is still home. To buy this land and build a new home makes me feel . . . I feel like a traitor to my family and to my homeland." Tatyana touched Dimitri's arm. "I . . . I cannot think about it right now. I am sorry." She turned and started for home.

Dimitri remained where he was and watched her go.

✷ ✷ ✷ ✷ ✷

Tatyana returned home. She thought about the land and about Dimitri's excitement. The property was lovely and would make a nice little farm. She allowed Dimitri's dream to wander through her thoughts. *It would be nice to live on a real farm again. It has been so long.* She remembered working the fields with her father and Yuri, and the vegetable garden she and her mother planted and tended each year.

She placed a Tchaikovsky record on the phonograph. The calming music washed over her, bringing her homeland close. But instead of the familiar longing to return, she felt a sad joy at the life she'd had there. It was part of who she'd once been, not who she was now. And she realized she no longer belonged there.

That night after putting Yuri to bed, Tatyana took down the money jar from the cupboard. She knew it wouldn't be enough for the down payment they needed, but it would help.

First she counted the paper money, and to her surprise, it totaled thirty-one dollars. Next she added the coins, which came to five dollars and twenty-three cents. She stared at the savings, and realizing how foolish she'd been to hang on to hopes of returning to Russia, finally abandoned the dream. Now it was time to help her husband.

Tatyana placed the money in an envelope. She'd give it to Dimitri when he returned from work. Licking the seal, she pressed it closed, then slipped it into her apron pocket. "It is time I was free."

Feeling lighthearted, Tatyana returned to the front room and placed another record on the phonograph. She folded the clothes on the sofa and looked around the tiny house. It had been a good home. She'd learned a lot since becoming Dimitri's wife. Now, together, they would not only build a new home, but new memories as well. She smiled softly.

The floor beneath her jolted, and the phonograph needle scraped across the record. Tatyana stood completely still. "What was that?" she asked aloud, her mind going to Dimitri. Had something happened at the mine? She'd heard about bumps that shook the earth and brought down tunnels. Sometimes they could be felt miles away. Is that what had happened?

Tatyana walked to the window and looked out. Everything seemed normal. She remembered how Dimitri and Carl had been trapped and nearly killed in the cave-in last year. What if something had happened again? "No," she told herself. "If something were wrong, the siren would have sounded, and the emergency crews would be heading to the mine."

She rubbed her bare arms and paced in front of the window. Although common sense told her all was well, uneasiness clung to her. She needed to see Dimitri. She felt the envelope in her pocket and decided she couldn't wait to tell him about her decision and the money. He needed to know.

Her mind made up, she walked to the closet, took out a sweater, and pulled it on. Then she ran to Elise's.

When Elise answered the door, Tatyana asked, "Could you stay with Yuri for a little while?"

"Is everything all right? You look upset."

"I am fine. I just need to speak to Dimitri."

Elise turned and asked, "Daddy, is it all right if I go to the Broido's? Tatyana wants me to watch Yuri."

Tatyana could see Mr. Johnson sitting in a chair, a paper lying on his lap. He looked at Tatyana and managed a half smile. "I suppose it won't hurt to go over for a while."

"Thanks," Elise said and followed Tatyana. Once they were outside, she asked, "Did you feel the earthquake?"

"Is that what it was?"

"I think so. It was a small one though."

Tatyana was even more certain nothing had happened at the mine. "Yuri is asleep," she told Elise. "I will not be gone long."

Elise looked at the sky. "It will be dark soon."

"I will take a lantern," Tatyana said with a reassuring smile. "And it is not far if I follow the tracks."

When they got to the house, Tatyana grabbed the lantern off the back porch. "You be careful," Elise said.

"Do not worry." Tatyana headed for the mine. She walked fast, driven by her need to share her newfound dream with her husband and hoping to make it before dark. The forest quickly closed in, and the dusk deepened. The closer she got to the mine, the more foolish she felt. She'd had no reason to run out here. The shaking she'd felt had been a harmless earthquake, and her change of heart could have waited until Dimitri finished his shift. She stopped, turned around, and took several steps toward home, then abruptly turned and continued toward the mine. She wanted to talk with Dimitri now.

When she arrived at the mine, everything was as it should be. Darkness had settled over the buildings, and the lights were on, making the plant look surreal. The machinery was indistinct, looked larger than normal, and deep shadows hung between the equipment. Tatyana headed toward the hoist house where the drone of engines filled the air. She stepped inside.

A large man looked up in surprise but smiled and tipped his hat. "Can I help you?"

"I am looking for Dimitri Broido."

"He won't be up until the end of his shift, but I can send someone down to get him. Is it an emergency?"

"No. But it is important."

"All right then. We'll get him for you."

She pushed the door part way open. "I will wait outside," she said, then stepped out and let the door close behind her. Tatyana wandered around the yard for a few minutes, then sat on an overturned barrel. She let her hands rest in her lap, stuck her toes into the graveled yard, and rocked slowly back and forth. The air had turned cool, and the moon was rising above the trees. She breathed deeply and closed her eyes, feeling contentment. She relished the sensation. For so long discontent had plagued her, making true peace inaccessible.

A man trip rumbled up the tracks and stopped. Dimitri climbed out, his eyes searching the yard until they stopped at Tatyana. She stood and waved, and Dimitri hurried to her. "What's wrong? Is it Yuri?"

"No. He is fine." Tatyana laughed. "Actually, I am being silly. The house shook and . . ."

"I know, we felt it. Just a small earthquake."

"Anyway, I was worried about you and decided I needed to tell you something that could not wait. It is about this afternoon."

"I've been thinking too, and I understand about that."

"No, you do not. I feel very bad. You were so happy and thinking about our future and I . . . well, I was confused and sad."

"I shouldn't have sprung it on you so quickly. I'm always jumping into things without thinking. . . ."

Tatyana pressed a finger to Dimitri's lips. "I am not confused anymore. Sometimes change is painful, even when it is good. I was trapped into a way of thinking that made no sense, and it was hard to let go, but now I have." She took the envelope out of her pocket and pressed it into Dimitri's hand.

"What's this?"

"Open it."

He tore open the envelope and stared at the contents. "It's money. Where did you get it?"

"I have been saving. I want you to have it for our land."

Dimitri's eyes shimmered in the moonlight, and he took Tatyana's hands and pressed them against his chest. "How could you save so much money—and why?"

"If I tell you, you must promise not to get angry."

"I promise."

"I thought maybe if I could save enough we could go to Russia." Quickly she added, "I know now I was not thinking right. I just missed my home so much." She was crying now. "I was wrong. You have been a good husband and father, and I deceived you. You've worked so hard to make a home for us here. I'm sorry, so sorry."

Dimitri kissed Tatyana's forehead and pulled her close. "I'm sorry for all you've been through. I never wanted to make your life more painful. I only wanted you to be happy."

"I know." She pressed her hand against his cheek. "I have been foolish and blind. This is my home. I am thankful for the life I had in Russia and my family there, but it is time to say good-bye and to begin building a life here."

Dimitri smiled. "You can't imagine how long I've wanted to hear you say that." He pulled Tatyana into his arms and kissed her. "I love you."

"I love you. And I want you to buy the land. It is a good place to raise our family." Tatyana smiled.

CHAPTER 21

"L ENINGRAD!" ELENA SAID, holding her arms away from her body and turning in a circle. Her oversized wool coat hung straight down from her arms, and her long wool skirt flared slightly. "I love this place. It has been years since I've been here." Smiling, she sat on the ground, stretched her legs straight out in front of her, and ran her hands through the grass.

Yuri smiled at Elena. "You've changed. I don't think I've ever seen you so carefree."

"Well, I'm a new creation, remember?"

"I can see that." He cleared his throat and glanced about. "And I'm glad you're happy, but you'll have to contain yourself a little. We don't want to attract attention."

"Oh, I'm sorry. It's just that I'm truly elated. I didn't think we would make it this far. I thought we'd either die or be arrested before we got to Leningrad."

Yuri stared across the Neva River at the Winter Palace. The enormous building perched on the opposite bank of the Neva. Its white pillars, countless arching windows framed in gold, and immense size made Yuri feel provincial. His mind flashed on the opulent life he'd once imagined for himself, and he smiled at the childish foolishness. Then he quickly dismissed the empty fantasies. "I've never seen anything like it. Have you been there?"

"At the palace?"

Yuri nodded.

"Yes, with my family."

Yuri sat beside Elena and rested his arms on his knees. "It's beautiful."

"Oh, even more so inside. There are great marble halls and a magnificent cathedral. Incredible paintings hang on the walls, and statues stand guard in the many rooms and hallways. Even they seem small beneath the high-domed ceilings. It is unlike anything I've seen."

"Even from here, it's magnificent." A boat moved up the river, making a wake as it passed. "Did you and your family visit Leningrad often?"

"We were here many times on holiday. When I think about it now, that part of my life feels like a fantasy. It was an unbe-lievable time." Her eyes misted. "I would call it charmed. We visited palaces and magnificent gardens, and in the evenings we attended ballets and operas." She closed her eyes and took a deep breath. "I had no idea it would end so horribly."

Yuri rested his hand on her arm. "Memories are precious gifts."

Elena met Yuri's eyes. "I know."

A tall, pretty woman with three young girls parading in front of her walked along a path. The children skipped ahead and circled back. The youngest one took her mother's hand and smiled sweetly as she walked past Yuri and Elena.

Yuri waved and the girl ducked behind her mother's skirt. Then he said, "Watching families picnicking and frolicking in this park makes the life we left behind seem so unreal—almost as if it couldn't exist alongside goodness."

"But it does. On the surface Leningrad is beautiful, but the same evil that has spread across and reached into the heart of our country is here."

"You sound cynical."

Elena turned an astonished look on Yuri. "No. It's truth. The enemy has overrun Russia. His evil prowls through the country, enveloping all of the Soviet Union."

Yuri nodded. "You're right. You sound like me. You were listening," he added with a smile and plucked a blade of grass. "We need to find Adolf Joffe. Daniel said he would be at the Joffe Watch Repair Shop."

"That seems simple enough. I'll ask someone," Elena said, pushing herself to her feet. She walked across the grass to a nearby vendor.

As Yuri watched, he smiled. Since placing her life in Christ's hands, her step had been lighter, her smile brighter. The haunted look in her eyes had been replaced with hope. She was animated as she talked to the vendor. When he shook his head no, Elena approached an old woman. She didn't know where the shop was either.

When Elena returned, she said, "No one knows anything about a Joffe Watch Repair Shop."

"It's a big city. We'll just keep asking."

A man hobbling along on a cane approached. "I'll ask him," Elena said, walking up to the man. The stranger smiled and pointed toward the city as he talked. A few minutes later, Elena returned. "It's not too far," she said with a triumphant smile. Taking Yuri's hand and pulling, she said, "Come on, no more resting. We need to go."

Yuri pushed himself to his feet. "I'm coming, I'm coming." He grinned. "So, you know the way?"

"I do," Elena said, walking toward the foot path. Yuri followed.

The old gentleman had given clear directions, and it wasn't difficult to find the shop. It was far from the elegant part of town, tucked between old stone buildings on a narrow, cobblestone alley. Many businesses along the street had boarded-up windows; some were abandoned. One had a line of clothes hanging out its window. Evidently the owner lived above the shop.

"So this is the real Leningrad, nothing like the palace," Yuri said as he stopped in front of a battered wooden door. Joffe Watch Repair Shop was painted on a placard hanging alongside the entrance. He turned the knob and stepped inside with Elena close behind.

An old man sat behind a scarred counter and was working on a disassembled watch. Creasing his eyebrows into a furry peak, he peered at Yuri over small round glasses. "May I help you?"

"My name is Yuri Letinov, and I'm looking for Adolf Joffe."

The old man studied Yuri and Elena, his lined face creasing into a frown. "I will tell him you were here." He returned to the watch.

"He isn't here?"

"My son does as he wishes. I have nothing to do with his affairs."

Steps sounded on a wooden staircase just beyond the counter, and a moment later, a burly man with a heavy, black beard appeared. "Ah, we have customers," he said with a smile. "My name is Adolf Joffe. May I help you?"

"I am Yuri Letinov, and this is Elena Oleinik."

Remaining at the window, Elena nodded and then returned to peering outside.

"We are friends of Daniel Belov," Yuri explained.

Without looking up, the old man muttered something under his breath.

"I know Daniel." Adolf pulled out two wooden chairs. "Please, sit."

Yuri took one chair, but Elena stayed at the window. Adolf sat on a rickety bench resting against the front of the counter. He looked from Yuri to Elena. "Daniel is a good man. Did he send you?"

The old man stood, and leaving the watch on the counter, walked out of the room and up the stairway.

"Daniel said you might help us," Yuri pressed, hoping he wouldn't have to give away his purpose for coming unless Adolf made it clear he already knew. It wasn't easy to trust.

"I have helped some of Daniel's friends. How is he?"

"He's well."

"And Tanya and the children? The last time I saw Daniel, his son, Nikolai, was growing like a weed."

"They are good," Elena said caustically. "But there is no son named Nikolai." Facing Adolf and folding her arms over her chest, she asked, "Why did you say they have a son?"

Adolf smiled. "Just my way of making certain you really know the Belovs. Forgive me, but I must be cautious."

"We need to know if you will help us," Elena pressed.

Adolf leaned forward, resting his arms on his legs. "What is it you need?"

"When we left Moscow, we were given your name and the name of this shop and told you could help us get out of Russia," Yuri said. "It is dangerous for us to stay here now. We want to go to America." Meeting Adolf's eyes, Yuri added. "My sister is there. I need to find her."

"I'll do what I can. Right now, there's a ship in the harbor that will be sailing for America. But we may not have much time." He straightened and leaned his back against the counter. "It won't be easy. Do you have papers?"

"We have no traveling or work papers. Our identification papers are false, and we hesitate to use them. The problem is, the man who was preparing our traveling papers was arrested. We don't know if the authorities confiscated any forged documents. They may have our names."

Adolf stood. "Do you have a place to stay?"

"No. We know no one here," Yuri explained.

"You can stay with a family I know here in Leningrad. You can trust them."

"Do you think we can sail on the ship that's docked now?" Elena asked.

"I don't know. I'll have to see what I can do. It will take some time to get papers, plus we'll need a photograph of each of you. I'll contact you when all is ready."

* * * * *

Eight days later, Adolf came early in the morning. He'd acquired the necessary papers. Yuri quickly scanned them. They looked authentic.

"These should get you on board," Adolf said. "The ship leaves this morning, and they need a couple to work in the mess hall." He grinned. "It seems the couple who was working had to make a change of plans at the last minute."

"How did you do that?" Yuri asked.

"I can't tell you." He placed a hand on Yuri's shoulder. "Now, get ready. There's no time for contemplation." He turned to leave, then stopped. "Oh, and learn your new names, Mr. and Mrs. Yuri Dobrynin."

Yuri and Elena's eyes opened wide, and they looked at each other.

"There was no other way," Adolf explained.

Elena chuckled. "This will be very interesting."

"The name will take some time to get used to, but I don't really mind our being married," Yuri teased.

Elena blushed but said nothing.

"All right. Get your things," Adolf said. "The ship won't wait. If you miss this one, it could be a very long while before there's another."

When they reached the pier, Adolf pointed to a small wooden shack. "You need to get past the guard inside. He's the one who'll decide if you're who you say you are. After him, you're on your way."

"Thank you for your help," Yuri said.

Grasping Yuri's forearm, Adolf asked, "You're certain you can't stay and help us here? We need more people to join the battle."

Yuri took a deep breath. "No. I can't. I believe in the cause, but God has called me elsewhere."

Adolf looked at Elena.

"We are comrades, and we stay together," she said.

Adolf straightened. "All right then. From this point on, you'll be on your own. Once you step on board that ship," he nodded at a freighter moored at the pier, "you'll begin a new life. I wish you both good luck. And may God be with you." He tipped his hat, then turned and walked away.

Yuri and Elena looked at each other. Yuri took a deep breath and tried to quiet the butterflies in his stomach. "Here we go. There's no turning back now."

Elena had gone pale, and she grabbed Yuri's arm. "I'm scared."

Yuri placed his hand over hers. "We're not alone, Elena. We have each other, and God walks this path with us. He won't desert us."

Elena managed a small smile, threw her shoulders back, and headed toward the shack with the dreaded official who would accept or reject their papers. Yuri walked beside her, praying fervently for God's favor and protection.

The door creaked as Yuri pushed it open. He held it for Elena, then followed her inside. The two stepped up to a gaunt-looking guard who was bent over paperwork. He didn't bother to look up for several moments. With a quickly scribbled signature on the bottom of a document, he pushed the paper across his desk, leaned back, and looked at the two young Russians. He said nothing but studied Yuri and Elena, his gray eyes suspicious.

It seemed to Yuri that everyone in Russia was suspicious.

"What do you want?"

"My wife and I are assigned to work on the ship that is leaving this morning."

"Your papers?"

Yuri handed him their documents and continued to pray while the man studied them. He glanced at Elena and noticed her legs were shaking and asked the Lord to give her peace, or at the very least, to hide her nervousness.

Pen in hand, the official set one document down and carefully examined the other. Finally setting the papers on the desk, he rocked back in his chair, and using the end of his pen, pushed his hat further back on his head. "Why do you want to work on a freighter? There are few comforts, and the seas can be rough; plus there's nowhere to go on a ship. It seems an odd place for a young couple."

"It's because we're young, sir, that we want to work on a ship. There is no place to spend our money, so we can save it. We would like to have a family." Yuri took Elena's hand. "Plus, we are loyal to our country and the mariners who serve it. We feel this is a way to be of help." Yuri hoped he'd been believable.

Elena only nodded in agreement.

Chewing on the pen, the man eyed them both closely and then leaned forward, planting the front legs of his chair back on the floor. He stamped the papers and handed them to Yuri. "Good luck to you."

"Thank you." Yuri picked up his knapsack and followed Elena out the door. They'd made it! He wanted to run and shout. Instead, he forced his legs to move slowly, took Elena's arm, and headed for the ship. "That was easier than I thought."

"Maybe for you. I thought I was going to be sick, and I couldn't keep my legs from shaking."

"Well, we're one step closer," Yuri said with a broad smile. Then he looked heavenward and said, "Thank you, Father."

They walked up the gangplank and approached the first crewman they met. "We're with the galley crew," Yuri said.

"Your names?"

"Yuri and Elena Let . . . Dobrynin." Yuri couldn't believe he'd nearly said his real name.

The man consulted a list. "You're in cabin 314." He pointed toward the front of the ship. "The berthing compartments are in the bow. Take the first staircase, go down two flights, then take the corridor leading toward the front of the ship. After you stow your gear, report to the cook. He'll tell you what to do."

Yuri tipped his hat, and still holding Elena's arm, headed for the bow. The third doorway opened onto a small landing, and a narrow, metal stairway led down into the ship's lower compartments. Only a single dim bulb lighted the stairway.

Yuri took two steps, but Elena didn't follow. "Wait," she said, staring into the dim passageway. "I don't like this, Yuri. I feel like a rat trapped in a cage. Once we leave the dock, we're stranded on this tiny island."

Yuri glanced back down the stairway and at the door they'd just stepped through. "I know it's a little close and feels strange, but we don't have a choice. This is our only way to freedom." He took her hand and added gently, "You're strong, Elena. You can do this."

"No. I'm not. I'm scared to death."

"Have you forgotten how you faced the firing squad and did what you had to do to escape? And when we helped Daniel and Tanya with the typhus outbreak in Klin, you stayed and worked even though your own life was threatened. You've always done what you had to, and you will now."

Elena tipped her chin up a notch, swallowed hard, nodded, then took the first step.

Yuri turned and walked down, doing his best to ignore the confining steel walls. The silence and closeness reminded him of prison. He swallowed his own rising panic as he descended deeper into the ship.

When they reached the third landing, Yuri gave Elena a reassuring smile before walking down a narrow passageway. The odors of sweat and oil mingled in the stale air.

There were numbers above each doorway, and Yuri kept walking until he found 314. "This is ours," he said and opened the door. He held it for Elena. "After you, Mrs. Dobrynin." He smiled and bowed slightly, hoping a bit of humor would ease the tension.

Elena lifted an eyebrow and stepped past him. "Thank you, husband."

Although it was done playfully, in his heart Yuri wished it were true. He wanted to be holding the door for Elena, his wife. For just a moment their eyes met and held, then Yuri followed her inside and surveyed the room. It was cramped with two bunks on one wall, a cabinet with a sink and mirror opposite, and a porthole on the outside wall.

Elena sat on the bottom bunk, tested the softness, and said, "This one is mine." She stripped off her pack and set it on the foot of the bed. "It won't be so bad."

Yuri tossed his bag on the floor and rested his hand on the top bunk. "I guess this one is mine."

Elena laid down and put her hands behind her head. "How should we act?"

"What do you mean?"

"Well, we're supposed to be married."

"How do other married people act?" Yuri bent and planted a kiss on Elena's cheek. "Like they love each other?" he asked, his voice tender.

"That won't be difficult," Elena said, averting her eyes and slowly sitting up.

Yuri's heart caught. Did she love him?

"I mean, we've watched Daniel and Tanya for months. We'll just have to think about them and do what they do."

Yuri cleared his throat and straightened. "Yeah," he said, zipping open his pack and taking out his heavy coat. He hung it on a hook beside the door and opened the small cupboard beneath the sink. "There are two shelves. I'll take the bottom one."

As he placed his underclothes, one extra pair of pants, and a shirt in the cupboard, he tried to concentrate on what might be ahead of them, but his mind was on Elena. All he could think about was how he wanted to tell her he loved her and that they should spend their lives together. But what if she didn't feel the same? He glanced at Elena and discovered her beautiful dark eyes were watching him. Was it possible she cared for him too? He stood and opened the mirror that camouflaged a medicine cabinet where soap, toothpaste, toothbrushes, and a razor had been supplied. "Looks like they take care of their sailors." He looked out the porthole. "I think the hardest part of our journey is behind us."

"There's a lot of ocean between us and America," Elena said dryly, joining him at the window.

She stood so close that Yuri could smell the soap she'd used to bathe with that morning. His mind reeled as he fought the impulse to take her in his arms. "Could you sound more hopeful?"

"I know God is watching over us, but I won't relax until I'm standing on American soil."

"God brought us this far, and I don't believe he will abandon us now."

A sharp rap came at the door. "You're needed up top. The cook wants to see you," a man called from the other side.

Elena and Yuri both turned and stared at the door. "And so we begin," Elena said. "May God grant us his favor."

CHAPTER 22

W HEN ARE WE SUPPOSED TO
sail?" Elena asked, scrubbing the bottom of a large skillet.

"Late this afternoon is what I heard," Yuri said.

Elena scanned the cramped galley. It would be a chore to
keep clean. There were two large coal stoves along one wall,
scores of cabinets above, and large flour and sugar bins below on
the opposite wall. Hanging above a broad porcelain counter
were countless pots, pans, and ladles. She could almost hear the
clamor they would set off during rough seas. She returned to
scouring and scrubbed so hard the metal pad cut into her skin,
but still the burned potato remnants wouldn't budge. "I won't
feel at ease until we're at sea." She held up the pot. "I can't get
this clean."

Yuri stopped swabbing the floor, and leaning on the mop
handle, said, "Just keep at it."

Elena held out irritated, red hands. "Soon I won't have any skin left."

Yuri rested the mop against the wall. "Let me try." He crossed the room, rolled up his sleeves, and took the scouring pad from Elena. "All it takes is muscle," he said with a grin as he scrubbed. After he finished scrubbing, he dipped the pot into hot rinse water and held it up. "Clean." Handing it back to Elena, he said, "You just need a little more strength in those arms."

"But I am strong. I can't help it if I'm small. You told me that God created us. So, if I'm small, he must have wanted me to be." She smiled smugly and dried the pot.

Yuri leaned on the counter and looked at her. "You're right. God definitely knew what he was doing when he created you."

Elena felt her face heat up. She turned abruptly and placed the clean pot on a shelf. "You better get back to work. You wouldn't want to get a reputation as a loafer."

Returning to his mop, Yuri dunked it, squeezed out the excess water, and ran it over the filthy floor. "By the time we get to America, I'll have more miles on this mop than this ship has under its hull."

"It could be worse," Elena said.

"I've known the worst."

The plump cook, Mr. Vissarion Gerasimov, lumbered into the kitchen. His fat face creased with worry and suspicion, he folded his arms over his chest and said, "The NKVD is on board."

Elena's stomach lurched. *They know about us! They're here to arrest us!*

The cook continued, "They're looking for someone. You wouldn't know who, would you?" He stared at Yuri, then at Elena. "You two are the newest crew members. We had no trouble before."

Yuri met the man's eyes and said calmly, "There's no reason they would be looking for us. It must be someone else."

As if trying to decide whether to trust Yuri or not, the cook studied him a moment longer. Sweat had beaded up on his forehead and dripped down his cheeks. "Good," he finally said. "I'm responsible for the people working in my kitchen, and I don't believe in breaking the law. Everyone who works for me serves Mother Russia. I expect absolute loyalty."

Elena stepped forward. "Mr. Gerasimov, we are both loyal Russians and would do nothing against you or our government."

"I'm glad to hear that." He looked at the half-finished dishes and the floor. "Get back to work." He clumped out.

As soon as the cook was out of earshot, Elena crossed to Yuri and gripped his arm. "What are we going to do? They must be looking for us."

"We don't know who they're searching for," Yuri said evenly. "There are a lot of people on this ship. It could be anyone." He dunked his mop into the bucket and wrung it out. "We'll keep doing our jobs and pray we're not their target. The NKVD does routine sweep searches hoping to dislodge some poor soul. We only need to stay calm and not give them reason to suspect us."

Elena took a deep breath. "I'm sure you're right. If the NKVD hasn't come aboard before, it's just been luck." She returned to the dishes and tried to remain calm, but as she waited for the police, her anxiety grew and her hands shook. *I should pray,* she finally decided. She let the pan in her hands rest in the soapy water and closed her eyes. *Father, I'm a new follower. I don't know anything about trusting you. I need your help. Please, watch over and protect us.* Feeling slightly better, she opened her eyes and returned to her work.

As she considered the possibility of Yuri's being arrested, her heart ached. It would be horrible for him to go through that again. *Father, if anyone is arrested, let it be me,* she prayed. Even as she made the request, she felt shock. She'd never been willing to sacrifice her life for someone else's. She glanced at Yuri. *I love him.*

The last dish had been done, and the sink and counter glistened when the officers came to the galley. Yuri was scrubbing a stove top and turned to face them. Elena stood beside him, folding and refolding a towel. He placed a steadying hand over hers, and she quieted.

A tall soldier with a square jaw and high cheek bones cast a disapproving eye on Yuri. He walked through the kitchen keeping his back straight and arms stiff. His shining boots clicked against the floor. He stopped in front of Yuri. "Your papers."

Yuri dug into his front pocket, removed the documents, and handed them to the officer. "They are in order."

"That is for me to determine," the man said coldly as he began to study the documents.

Elena's insides felt as if they were spiraling. Her legs shook, and she was having trouble breathing. *He's going to see they're forgeries! I have to do something!* Taking a deep breath, she stepped forward. "Sir, we are Russian citizens doing our jobs, nothing more."

The man's nostrils flared slightly as he shifted his cool gaze to Elena.

Elena's anger flamed. How many times had she seen that look of arrogance. He knew nothing about her. Yet, he had decided that like dirt under his nails, she deserved no respect. She struggled to control her rage, swallowing years of anger. She forced a smile.

"Your papers," he said, his voice edged with steel.

Keeping her tone calm and courteous, she said, "My husband and I work on this ship to help our country. As he said, our papers are in order. We have done nothing. Why do you treat us like criminals?" She knew she was hurdling down a dangerous path, but she needed to distract the man and knew no other way. "We are hardworking citizens and love our country. We would not break the laws Stalin has put into place. We understand he will bring about a better Russia."

Wearing a sardonic smile, he said evenly, "Nevertheless, I must see your papers."

Elena handed him the documents. Her heart pounded, her stomach churned, and her mouth was so dry she couldn't collect enough spit to wet her lips.

The soldier carefully read her papers and again looked at Yuri's. Seeming disappointed, he returned the documents. Meeting Elena's eyes, he said, "Everything seems in order." A smile played around his lips. "I wish you luck in your efforts to serve our country."

Elena nodded slightly. The strength had gone out of her, and she felt weak and dizzy. *Father, hold me up,* she prayed.

The officer scanned the kitchen, ran his finger over the top of the stove, and examined it for dirt. "Good work," he said, turning and marching out, the other policemen following.

Struggling to remain upright, Elena listened to their footfalls, only letting out her breath when she could no longer hear them. She drooped against the counter. "I thought I would die from fright."

Yuri pulled her into an embrace. "You were wonderful!"

"I was stupid. I should have said nothing. But I was afraid they'd discover the documents were false. I probably put us in more danger by speaking."

Yuri pulled her closer. "I have to admit, for a few moments I was afraid for you and wanted to tell you to be still." He smiled. "But I'm proud of you. For someone who believes herself to be a coward, you're very brave."

"I'm not brave. I was scared to death. My legs are like noodles, and I feel sick."

"Having courage does not mean you aren't afraid; it's doing what you must in spite of fear. You did what you thought you had to. When he was looking over my papers, I was beginning to worry he might find something to use against us. Your distraction may have saved our lives." Giving her a quick squeeze, he added, "And I think he liked your spirit."

"It's a good thing. If he'd hated it, we'd be on our way to prison right now." Elena liked the feel of Yuri's arms around her and allowed herself to lean against him. "I'm sorry for putting you in danger. I couldn't bear it if you went back to prison."

Yuri's eyes turned serious. "I couldn't endure being separated from you again." He took a steadying breath. "There is something I've wanted to say for a long time. And now I'm going to say it." He paused. "I love you." He searched her eyes and pressed his lips to hers.

Elena returned the kiss then wrapped her arms about him and rested her cheek against his chest. She felt safe in his arms. "Yuri, we've been friends so long, and you've never . . . you've never done anything like that. Why didn't you tell me your feelings?"

"I wanted to. But . . . I was afraid. I've loved you for a long time—I think since the very first when I saw you in the back of the truck after we were arrested. I knew you had to be scared, but you acted so bravely. I wanted to know you even then."

Elena stepped back. "I never knew. I thought maybe, but when you came back from the work camp, you were so distant."

Yuri caressed her hair and kissed the top of her head. "In camp I thought about you all the time. And I wished I'd told you how I felt before I was imprisoned. But you'd always made it clear you didn't want that kind of relationship, so I said nothing."

"I was afraid of love. And I tried hard not to love you."

"I dreamed of the day we would be reunited and planned how I would hold you and tell you that you were my life. But when I came home, you looked at me with revulsion."

"No. That's not true." Elena looked up into Yuri's eyes. "I will admit I was shocked at your appearance. You didn't look like the Yuri I'd known. Prison had taken so much from you, but I still cherished you. And I wanted you to love me, but I couldn't tell you. I thought you didn't care for me that way, so how could I share my feelings?" Elena reached up and caressed Yuri's cheek. "But now, I'm telling you, I love you." She smiled. "There was a time I thought I'd never be able to say those words. For years I was angry and too afraid to care for anyone. I thought that if I didn't love or admit to myself that I did, then I couldn't be hurt. But it hurts more not to love."

Yuri chuckled. "We were such fools, allowing pride and fear to rob us of the precious time we've been given."

Elena hugged Yuri. "I'm not afraid anymore."

He buried his face in her dark hair and breathed deeply. "You smell so good." He laughed again. "I love you. I love you." He lifted her until her face was even with his and whispered, "I love you."

Elena wrapped her arms around his neck and hugged him.

Yuri kissed her again. This time he allowed the kiss to linger. "All these weeks I've wanted to do that." Gently holding her hands, he turned them palm up. "Elena, after we get to America and I find my sister, will you marry me?"

She looked into Yuri's eyes and knew she loved him. "Yes. Yes, I'll marry you. I want us to be together forever." She cuddled closer. "Our lives may change or end in a moment, but whatever time the Lord gives us, I want to spend it with you."

Yuri caressed her hair. "No one knows the number of days God has given him to walk the earth. But we have eternity. Imagine, eternity together," he said with a smile.

🐾 🐾 🐾 🐾 🐾

After the NKVD left the ship without prisoners, Yuri and Elena went up on deck to say farewell to Russia. As they stood at the rail, the ship's horn blasted, and the heavy ropes holding the freighter were loosed and thrown on board. Slowly they moved into the harbor and toward their new home. Yuri kept his arm around Elena, and she leaned against him as the dock merged with the shoreline and the city of Leningrad grew smaller. Sunlight glinted off windows, and the water sparkled.

Elena closed her eyes as a cool breeze cut across the bay and swept over the ship. Opening them, she gazed at the extraordinary city. The sky, like a pale blue backdrop, made it glow with warmth while wispy white clouds settled overhead like a gossamer crown. "It is beautiful," she said, her sadness growing with the distance.

"Are you all right?"

"Yes. But now that I'm leaving, I grieve. This is my home. Once I had so much here."

The wind whipped Yuri's hair across his face, and he brushed it back. "I feel the sorrow too, but even so, I know we're doing the right thing."

Clinging to Yuri, Elena said, "We'll never see Russia again, will we?"

"Probably not, but we have a new life ahead of us. One, I pray, that will hold less fear."

Elena sighed. "I'm tired of fighting to survive. It will be so good not to have to battle just to live."

"Our battle will continue, but now it will be different. As Christians we can't escape the struggle that has been going on since the beginning between God and Satan. And although we'll be an ocean away from Russia, the enemy will still be on the prowl. He knows no boundaries."

Elena felt a shiver of fear run through her. "Your words frighten me."

"We don't have to be afraid. God lives in you and me. And there is no one greater than the one who dwells within us."

"I feel his presence, and know I'm not the same. I'm stronger and less afraid." Resting against Yuri, she asked, "Why did it take me so long to understand?"

"What matters is that now you do." Yuri gazed out at the open sea, and his eyes teared in the cold wind. "I wonder what Tatyana is doing, what her life is like. Sometimes when I try to remember her I can't see her clearly. It's been too long." He looked down at Elena. "You'll like her, and she'll like you."

"I can't wait to meet her." Elena caught a furtive movement just out of her vision and turned to look. A tall man quickly disappeared through a doorway. "I think someone was watching us. What if he overheard? He'll turn us in, and we'll be arrested and sent back to Moscow at the next port."

Yuri craned his head around to look. "I don't see anyone. Are you sure he was there?"

"Yes, I saw him. A tall man."

"Well, he's gone now. There's nothing we can do. We just need to be more careful."

Elena turned and watched as Leningrad disappeared into the mist. Doing all she could to draw on her faith in God her protector, she tried to believe freedom was only weeks away.

CHAPTER 23

Yuri sprinkled brown sugar over his mush. "We'll be in New York tomorrow."

Elena took a small bite of cereal and grimaced. "I have never liked porridge. It's always been a little hard to take first thing in the morning." She sprinkled a second teaspoon of sugar over her cereal, poured milk into the bowl, and stirred. Taking another bite and washing it down with coffee, she said, "I know I shouldn't complain. This is much better than some of the things you've been forced to eat. But a plate of eggs would taste good."

"Maybe when we get to America we can have eggs."

Leaning forward, Elena asked quietly, "What is our plan? How are we going to get off the boat tomorrow?"

"I haven't figured it out completely. We'll just have to wait for the right opportunity, I guess. But I do know that once we're ashore we'll find Tatyana before we do anything else. I pray she's still living at the address on the letter."

"And if she's not?"

"I . . . I don't know. I guess we'll just have to find her." Smiling, he continued, "Then I'll look for work, and we'll get our own place." He reached across the table and placed his hand over hers. "Then we can get married."

Elena smiled. "I like the last part of the plan, but the rest sounds a little shaky."

"God will show us what to do."

Elena straightened, her eyes glued to something behind Yuri. "That man is here again," she whispered. "He's trying to act like he's not interested in us, but he keeps looking our way. What do you think he wants? Could he be with the NKVD?"

Yuri quickly glanced over his shoulder. "I doubt it. They're usually more up front about things," he said sardonically.

"Then who is he?"

"If he's the man we saw on deck our first night, he may have overheard us talking and is still trying to get more information so he can turn us in. Some people believe it's a good way to gain approval from the government." Yuri stirred his cereal but didn't take a bite.

"If he were going to turn us in, wouldn't he have already done it?"

"I don't know. Probably." Yuri lowered his voice to a whisper. "All I do know is that tomorrow we need to get off this ship without being seen."

"But how?"

He picked up his cup of coffee and took a sip. "I was thinking that we could . . . "

"Maybe I can help," a man's voice broke in.

Yuri jumped, splashing coffee. He looked into the deep brown eyes of the man who'd been observing them.

Chapter 23

He had a mug of steaming coffee cradled in his left hand. Removing his hat and exposing graying hair, the stranger bowed slightly and said, "I'm Lavr Kornilov."

Yuri nodded and answered, "Yuri Dobrynin." Although he maintained a calm demeanor, his mind searched frantically for a defense in case Mr. Kornilov had decided to turn them in. He extended his hand toward Elena. "My wife, Elena." She gave him a slow nod, her eyes suspicious.

"May I sit?" Mr. Kornilov asked.

"Certainly," Yuri said.

Taking the chair at the end of the table, Mr. Kornilov set his coffee in front of him and warmed his hands on the cup. He looked at Elena, then Yuri. Keeping his voice low, he said, "I know you are not who you say you are."

Yuri's stomach lurched, and he straightened his back. Elena's eyes widened in fear. "Why would you say such a thing? Of course I am who I say I am," Yuri declared in a pronounced whisper.

"Please, I do not mean to alarm or offend. And I wish you no harm." The man smiled kindly. "I want to help."

Yuri didn't know how to respond to this stranger. How could he trust him?

"You've been watching us. Why?" Elena asked.

"It is my job."

"Are you with the NKVD?"

"No. I'm sorry, but I can't tell you who I work with, only that I help Russians who are defecting."

The word stunned Yuri. Only traitors defected. He'd never connected the word with what he was doing.

"You two aren't married. I was told there would be a man and woman on board posing as a husband and wife. When I overheard your conversation the first night, I knew it must be you."

Yuri looked at the stranger and said pointedly, "We still don't know who you are."

277

"I can tell you only that I have compassion for those who must escape the Russian authorities and that you can trust me." He paused. "If I wanted to turn you in, I would have done it already." He took a drink of coffee. "Do you want my help?"

"We've done nothing wrong," Elena said.

"You lied about being married."

"It isn't easy to find work, and the ship needed a couple. We needed the job, and that is all."

"There is work for all Russian citizens, except those without papers or in trouble with the authorities," Lavr said bluntly. Elena's face reddened.

"You've broken the law. If you're caught, you'll be arrested." He drained his cup, set it on the table, and calmly folded his hands in front of him. "Are you defecting?" he asked, meeting Yuri's eyes.

Yuri cast a questioning look at Elena before he looked back at Lavr. "I need to know who you are."

"I've already told you, my name is . . ."

Yuri held up his hand. "No. I don't want to know your name. I want to know why you're talking to us."

Lavr leaned forward and said in a hushed voice. "I received word from a certain watch repairman. I can say no more." He stood. "If you do not want my help, then there is nothing I can do."

Yuri studied the man. *He must be trustworthy, he knows Adolf Joffe. And even if he isn't telling the truth, we're lost. He knows too much already.* "How can you help us?"

Lavr relaxed and sat back down. "You need a way off the ship. I can help you. I work as a supervisor in the cargo hold. When we dock, the ship won't stop at Ellis Island; there are no passengers to let off, freight only. We're scheduled to stay only one day in port, so the cargo will be unloaded immediately." He glanced around the empty cafeteria. "There are people always watching for defectors."

"Please, could you not use that word?" Yuri asked.

"Sorry."

"Then how do we get off?" Elena asked, struggling to keep hysteria out of her voice.

His gaze settled on the young woman. "You'll be part of the cargo." Turning to Yuri, he said, "And you'll be part of the crew that unloads freight. In half an hour, I'll walk by your room, knock once on your door, and drop a uniform on the floor. I'll make it look like an accident in case anyone sees me, but you must retrieve the clothing right away." He looked at Elena. "Tomorrow morning at eight o'clock I'll come for you."

Yuri folded the napkin in front of him and then unfolded it. "What time does the ship dock?"

"We're scheduled for nine o'clock." Lavr tipped his empty cup on edge and stared at the bottom. "Until then, behave as normally as possible."

"Why did you wait so long to tell us who you are?" Elena asked.

"I didn't need to say anything until today. To do otherwise would only place us all in greater jeopardy."

Pushing her cereal bowl away, Elena asked, "Why are you helping us?"

He took a deep breath. "I help because God has asked me to. It is my part of the battle." He stood.

Yuri shook Lavr's hand. "Thank you."

Wearing a half smile, he nodded. "Go to your cabin and wait for my knock. I'll be there in thirty minutes." He turned and walked out of the cafeteria.

Not wanting to appear like they'd had a meeting with Lavr, Yuri and Elena waited a few minutes. Yuri took Elena's hands. "Relax. You look tense. Your shoulders are all bunched up." He grinned and raised his shoulders in an exaggerated way.

Elena chuckled, took a deep breath, and forced her muscles to relax, dropping her shoulders. "Is this better?"

Yuri nodded. Standing, he picked up their cups and bowls and set them on the counter as they walked toward the cafeteria door.

"Yuri. Elena," the cook called. "I need your help. Boris is sick and can't work this morning."

Yuri tried to think of an excuse but couldn't come up with one that would be acceptable. He simply said, "We need to get something from our room. We'll be back soon."

"No. I need help now. After you're finished here, you can go to your cabin."

"It will only take a few minutes."

The cook was holding a towel, and in an instant, he whipped it around his arm. His voice tight and controlled, he said, "You'll clear the tables and wash the dishes, now. Do you understand?"

"Yes, sir," Yuri said.

"Good." The cook turned and walked out.

"Now what do we do?" Elena whispered as they stepped into the galley. She nearly gasped at the pile of dishes in the sink. "These will take too long. We'll never get back to our room in time. If someone sees the clothes, how will we explain?"

"Maybe I can sneak down."

"If you're not here when Vissarion comes back . . ."

"I'll see where he is." Yuri grabbed a washcloth and small tub and walked back into the cafeteria. He nonchalantly placed dishes, cups, and saucers in the tub and washed a table while searching for the cook. Vissarion sat at the back of the room, eating and reading a book. He seemed unaware of Yuri.

It will only take him ten minutes to finish his meal. That's not enough time for me get to the cabin, wait for Lavr, and get back here, Yuri calculated. But if he keeps reading, I'll have more time.

He looked at the clock on the wall. It had only been ten minutes since Lavr left. *If I wait another ten minutes, it should be pretty close.* He returned to the kitchen. "Vissarion is eating, but he's also reading. I'm counting on the book to keep him occupied. I'll work ten more minutes and then go to our cabin."

"What will I say if he comes in and you're gone?"

"Just tell him I went to the toilet."

"And if he goes looking for you?"

Yuri raised an eyebrow. "It would be unlikely. He has no reason to suspect us of anything." He kissed her cheek. "Just act like you always do. He won't notice anything except how beautiful you are."

Elena smiled. "All right. I'll do my best." She returned to cleaning plates while Yuri collected dishes and washed tables. The cook ate and read. Ten minutes later, Yuri casually carried a tub of dishes into the kitchen and set it on the counter. "I'll be back as quickly as I can." He hurried to the corridor and down the stairs. As he approached his cabin, he could see there was no clothing yet, so he ducked inside and waited.

He paced the small room. Several minutes passed. "Come on, come on," he muttered. His mind went over the conversation they'd had with Lavr, and worry set in. What if it had been a trap? Maybe he should go back to work. "No," he told himself. "Wait another five minutes. It will make no difference anyway. If he's turning us in, there's nothing I can do."

He stared out the porthole and thought of Elena in the kitchen. If Vissarion had discovered he'd gone, he might be looking for him. *Father, blind him to my absence,* he prayed just as one short rap sounded at the door.

Immediately Yuri crossed to the door and opened it, catching only a brief glimpse of Lavr as he turned down a nearby corridor. Taking a quick look up the hallway and seeing no one, he gathered up a brown pair of slacks, a matching long-sleeved shirt, and a pair of black work boots. Stepping back inside, he closed the door and shoved the clothes beneath the bottom bunk. Then he hurried back to the galley. His heart nearly stopped when he found the cook overseeing Elena's work.

Vissarion glared at Yuri. "Where have you been?"

"The toilet," Yuri said as he picked up his pan and wash-cloth. "I'm nearly finished here, sir."

With no more than a nod, the cook walked out of the room.

* * * * *

Lying on her back, Elena folded her hands behind her head and stared at the bunk above her. She couldn't sleep. Only a few hours separated her from either prison or freedom. She closed her eyes and took a slow, deep breath. *Freedom.* The word played through her mind like music. *Father, please help us. Make us strong and wise.*

The steady vibration of engines and gentle roll of the sea felt comforting. Moonlight shimmered through the porthole like a bright reminder of God's presence. She understood her life was about to change forever and wished she knew what life held for them. The bunk overhead squeaked. "Yuri, are you awake?"

"Uh huh. Can't sleep. All I can think about is what's ahead. At this time tomorrow, we'll be free. I don't know what that's like. And if all goes well, before the day is through, I'll see Tatyana. It's hard to believe she's so close."

"I pray you'll find each other."

"I'm almost afraid to hope," Yuri said softly as he climbed down and knelt beside Elena's bunk. "I want you to know, if it doesn't go well, I'm still grateful for the weeks we've had together." He took her hand and pressed his lips to her fingers. "I thank God for you."

Elena smiled softly, her love for Yuri swelling. "We've been comrades a long time." She searched his face. It was a good and handsome face. And although the harshness of life had stolen the innocence from his eyes, they still held tenderness, hope, and love. "Yuri, anything could happen tomorrow. And we might not be together any more."

He took a deep breath. "No matter what comes, I will never stop loving you. Even if I die tomorrow, I wouldn't change anything." He smiled. "We've come a long way from that pit outside Moscow. I'm grateful God allowed me to know you."

＊ ＊ ＊ ＊ ＊

Gray morning light filtered into the cabin, and Elena blinked her eyes, surprised she'd slept. "Are you awake?"

"Yes," Yuri said, jumping from the top bunk. "I was just about to wake you." He stretched his arms over his head and bent from side to side. "It's still early. Let's go up on deck and take a look. I'll wait out here," he said, stepping into the corridor.

Elena washed her face in cold water and ran a brush through her hair. She looked at her reflection. Her eyes looked darker than usual. A shiver of fear coursed through her at the realization of what lay ahead. Taking a deep breath, she said, "I can do this."

As they made their way to the deck, Elena wondered what she would find. She'd heard stories of an enormous city and a statue of a lady standing guard over the harbor. Yuri was just ahead of her, and as he opened the door to the deck, she could smell the salty scent of the ocean. She followed him into the cool, moist air. Bundling deeper into her coat, Elena shivered, more from tension than the chilly temperatures.

The ship steamed into an enormous harbor bordered by skyscrapers, looking like giant spruce and reaching from earth to sky. A statue of a woman stood watch, a torch in her uplifted hand. A flood of emotions swept over Elena, and she felt the ache in the hollow of her throat as tears filled her eyes. She took Yuri's hand. "It's true. There is a lady. She's beautiful."

"The torch represents the light that leads newcomers into a land of freedom." Yuri's voice caught.

"It reminds me of how God is a light to the lost," Elena whispered, gazing at the statue. Her eyes took in the imposing city and moved across the water to a huge compound of red brick buildings with ornate towers, before wandering back to the statue. "America," she whispered.

"We'll be free," Yuri said with conviction. "We'll find Tatyana and begin a new life."

"Impressive, isn't it?" Lavr said, placing his hand on Yuri's shoulder. The couple turned and looked at their benefactor. "I thought I might find you out here this morning," he said with a smile. "Are you ready?"

"Yes," Yuri said.

"Follow me," he said as he headed for the stairwell and led them down into the cargo hold. They passed wooden crates, bales of Russian tea, and furniture. Lavr stopped in front of a wardrobe. Unlocking the cabinet and opening the door, he said, "Elena, this is your hiding place."

She stared at the wardrobe. "I'll be locked inside?" Her voice trembled.

"Yes. I know this isn't easy for you, but you'll be fine." He offered her an encouraging smile. "There's no other way."

"All right." Elena climbed inside and folded her legs up close to her chest.

"Yuri, you'll have the key." Lavr held it up. "You'll have to be the one to let her out. No one else will know she's in there. I'll be staying with the ship."

"You're going back?" Yuri asked.

"Yes. Maybe one day I'll join you and the others who've made America home, but right now I must do God's work in Russia." He looked at Elena. "Are you all right?"

"Yes," she said with a tremulous smile.

Yuri kissed her. "I'll get you out as quickly as I can."

"I'll be waiting for you."

"It won't be too long. The tugs will have us at the docks in no time." Lavr shook Elena's hand. "Good luck to you."

"Thank you. May God bless you," Elena said.

"He already has." Resolutely, Lavr closed the door and locked it. He handed the key to Yuri. "As soon as we dock, we'll begin unloading. You better get your work clothes on. I'll be here and will put you to work."

His heart beating wildly, Yuri hurried back to the cabin, praying he wouldn't meet the cook. He and Elena were supposed to be working that morning, and he didn't have an acceptable excuse. He put on the pants and shirt, then the boots. He quickly laced them, and hoped Lavr was right that they would unload immediately. It wouldn't take long for him and Elena to be missed.

He opened the door, peered out, then stepped into the corridor. Fighting the temptation to run, he walked at a normal pace. Another crewman approached. Yuri didn't recognize him and gave an inner sigh of relief. As they passed each other, Yuri nodded but said nothing. When he stepped into the cargo hold, he didn't see Lavr. He hurried up and down aisles of cargo, searching. When he came across the cabinet, he rapped on the side and whispered, "Elena."

"Yes."

"Are you all right?"

"Yes. I'm fine."

"It won't be long now. Just hang on for a little while longer."

The thrum of the freighter's engines stopped, and a few minutes later Yuri felt a slight bump and shudder as they came to a stop. Excitement and fear swept over him. He tapped on the wardrobe and whispered, "This is it." A group of men led by Lavr appeared and began untying and shifting crates. "I have to go," Yuri said. "I'll see you soon." He joined the men.

When Lavr spotted him, he pointed at Yuri. "You, I need you over here."

Immediately Yuri joined the crew preparing bundles of Russian tea for transport. One man stared at him a moment, and

Yuri worried he might recognize him from the galley, but the man simply nodded and returned to work. Yuri glanced back at the cabinet that held Elena. There was a lot to be unloaded before they reached her. *Father, help her endure,* he prayed.

After unloading tea and several other pieces of furniture, they finally prepared the wardrobe to be moved. It was placed with another that was nearly identical, and they were carefully packed with cushions and lifted out of the hold. Yuri watched the swaying cabinets and wondered what was going through Elena's mind. She must be frightened. *Lord, remind her of your presence.*

Again, Lavr pointed at Yuri and two other men and shouted, "You, you, and you. I need you in the warehouse. They're in a hurry to get this cargo out of the crates. You two," he looked at the other men, "get the tea ready for delivery, and you," he looked at Yuri, "I need you to help with the furniture." He filled out a form and handed one to each man. "Show this to the Master at Arms. He'll let you off."

＊ ＊ ＊ ＊ ＊

After receiving permission to join the warehouse crew, Yuri walked down the gangplank confidently. As he set foot on American soil, he wanted to shout his joy. Instead, he marched to the warehouse, intent on rescuing Elena. He glanced at Lavr who was watching from the deck. Gratitudes welled, and he longed to yell his thanks, but simply nodded, and Lavr smiled. *Bless him, Father,* Yuri prayed as he stepped through the doors of the massive warehouse. He grabbed the cabinet key out of his pocket, the coolness of the metal bolstering his confidence. Now all he needed to do was release Elena from her hiding place.

CHAPTER 24

W HERE IS SHE?" YURI ASKED, dwarfed by rows of bundles, boxes, and crates in the cavernous warehouse. Trying to look as if he belonged, he walked the aisles but found no wardrobe. He hurried his steps. She'd been locked inside a long time. Did she have enough oxygen? He knew that at the very least her muscles and joints were strained and cramped. Memories of trips he'd made crammed inside a locker in police vans occupied his mind, and his concern grew.

He searched the aisles again but still didn't find her. *Maybe this is the wrong warehouse. Maybe I misunderstood.* Taking long, fast strides, he returned to the entrance, looked about to make certain no one was watching, then stepped out the door and studied the wharf and building. The warehouse took up nearly an entire block. It had to be the right one.

He retraced his steps, heart pounding, and mind racing. *Could I have missed the wardrobe? If it isn't here, where is it?* His panic grew and he prayed, *Father, help me find her.* Was it possible they'd found her and she'd been returned to the ship? He couldn't lose her now. They'd crossed hundreds of kilometers from Moscow to Leningrad, made it past the guards at the Leningrad port, sailed across an entire ocean, and now that they were so close, it was incomprehensible that they'd fail.

As he worked his way through the warehouse again, Elena's name echoed over and over through his mind. Starting at the front, he walked the long rows. After covering three aisles, he turned and began down the next when he spotted a door he'd missed. *That must be it!* he thought, forcing himself not to run as he headed for the room.

He opened the door and stepped inside. Furniture crowded the space. Some was stacked haphazardly, nearly to the ceiling. If the cabinet with Elena in it had been placed so high, Yuri didn't know how he would release her. He hurried past tables, chairs, sofas, and wooden cabinets but found no wardrobes. *She must be in here somewhere.* He glanced around. He was alone, so he called, "Elena. Elena, do you hear me?" He listened, wishing his heart and breathing would quiet.

A muffled "I'm here" came from the back of the room.

"Keep talking to me," he said and walked in the direction of the sound.

"Please, please hurry."

"I'm coming." He ran down the aisle and turned a corner.

"I'm here," he heard again, and there it was, tucked between a cabinet and another sideboard. The door had been turned toward the wall. He'd have to pull it out. "Elena, I'm here."

"Please, get me out!"

"I have to pull it away from the wall. Brace yourself." Yuri hauled on the cabinet but couldn't get a good grip. He changed his grip to the bottom lip. Careful not to tip it, he pulled until there was room enough for him to squeeze between it and the wall. He quickly stepped behind the wardrobe, inserted the key, and opened the door. Elena spilled out and into his arms.

For a moment she clung to him. "My legs fell asleep," she said. "I don't know if I can stand."

Lifting her, Yuri held her close and cradled her a moment; then he carried her into the aisle.

"It took so long; I was so scared. The air was hard to breathe, and my body hurt all over. It will take a while to straighten out the kinks," she added with a smile.

Yuri kissed her. "I prayed and prayed, but I couldn't find you." He tightened his hold. "Thank God you're safe. Do you think you can stand now?"

Elena nodded.

Yuri carefully set her on her feet. Taking her hand, he said, "Come on. We need to get out of here and away from the ship before someone sees us." Elena's legs were still weak, so they walked slowly.

When they reached the entrance, Yuri peeked outside. Longshoremen were stacking and hauling crates in and out of the warehouse. No one looked familiar. "They must be Americans," he whispered. "When we don't show up for work, Vissarion will report us missing. They'll be looking for us." He scanned the docks. Everything appeared normal. "We need to get away from here."

Staying in the shadows, they stepped outside. Yuri could see Soviet uniforms on board the ship but none on the pier. "Let's go. Don't look at the ship, and walk normally. We don't want to attract any attention." Pulling his cap further down on his forehead, he took Elena's arm, and the two walked down the wharf, controlling the urge to run.

The dock was alive with foot traffic. Yuri and Elena weaved their way through sailors and laborers, strolled past ships, small shops, and taverns. People chattered in languages they'd never heard, and the smell of fish, crude oil, and fried food permeated the air.

As they stepped away from the quay and joined the pedestrians on the street, Yuri breathed a sigh of relief, and he and Elena smiled at each other. They'd made it. Now it would be easy to lose themselves in the crowds. Buses, automobiles, and taxis clogged the streets, honking horns and revving engines revealing the commuters' impatience.

The smells changed, and Yuri's mouth watered as the aroma of sausages and sweet breads penetrated his focus to keep moving. Until now, he hadn't realized how hungry he was. They walked several more blocks before he stopped. Sitting on the steps of a dilapidated tenement, he said, "I'm hungry and thirsty."

"Me too," Elena said, sitting beside him. She leaned her elbows on her legs and rested her chin in her hands. Looking up and down the street, she asked, "But what do we eat? And how do we pay for it?"

"I have a little money." Yuri dug into his pants pocket. "It's not much," he said, holding out a handful of change.

"I wonder what we can get with that?"

Yuri stood. "We'll find out."

Elena rose, took a deep breath, and looked up at the buildings on both sides of the streets. She had to crane her neck to see the tops. "This is a very tall city. I wonder how big it really is? Do you think it's very far to the countryside?"

Yuri shrugged. "Don't know, but we can find out." He smiled broadly and gazed up and down the street. "We're in America now. We can go wherever we please." His eyes stopped on a vendor. "First let's get something to eat." He nodded at the merchant. "We'll see what he has," he said and stepped off the porch. Walking up to the man, Yuri said, "We are very hungry and would like to buy something to eat."

The man gave him a quizzical look. Then he said something in English and shrugged his shoulders. Realizing the vendor couldn't understand him, Yuri pointed at his stomach and said slowly, "Food. Hungry." He took out his coins and pointed at some strange-looking sausages.

The vendor held up a hand and shook his head. "No. No. Need American money."

Yuri didn't understand the words, but he understood the shaking head. He looked at his coins and asked, "Why won't you take my money? It is good."

Again, the man said very slowly, "American . . . money . . . only." He closed the lid on the roaster and looked the other way.

Elena frowned. "He does not want our money. Maybe Russian money isn't good here."

Yuri pulled the envelope with Tatyana's address on it out of his jacket pocket. "We need to find my sister. Our empty stomachs will have to stay empty a while longer." Showing the man the envelope and pointing at the address, he asked slowly, "Can you tell me where this is?"

The man squinted as he read the address, then pointed up the street as he spoke. Yuri didn't understand what he was saying but said, "Thank you," and tucked the envelope back in his pocket. Looking at Elena, he said, "We'll go that way and ask someone else."

They headed up the street in the direction the man had pointed. Yuri looked at the numbers on the envelope and tried to match them with the numbers on the doors of businesses, but they were nothing alike. It would be more difficult to find Tatyana than he'd thought.

After asking several people for help and making little headway, the smells of a bakery lured Yuri inside. "Maybe someone in here can help."

"We'll find her," Elena reassured Yuri.

The smell of donuts and cake made Yuri's hunger pangs worse, and his mouth watered. He felt the change in his pocket and wondered if they would take his money here. A man with a long, thin mustache worked behind the counter. "Please, sir, I do not speak English, but I need to find this address." Yuri dug out the envelope once more and held it up.

The man grinned broadly. "You are from the Soviet Union?" he asked in perfect Russian.

"Yes," Yuri said, hope and relief washing over him.

"So am I." He reached across the counter and shook Yuri's hand. "Domensko Rykov."

Thank you, Father, Yuri quickly prayed. Then he said, "How good it is to meet another Russian! My name is Yuri Letinov, and this is Elena Oleinik. We just arrived and are looking for my sister. She lives at this address, but we cannot find it."

The man examined the envelope. "It is not too far from here. Yet, it's a world away. Only the very rich live in this neighborhood."

"My sister works for a man named Reynold Meyers," Yuri explained.

The baker nodded. "I will get my son. He can show you the way. Please sit. Are you hungry? Or thirsty?"

"Yes," Elena answered. "Very. And the vendor wouldn't take our money."

"You still have Russian currency? They should have exchanged it for you before you left Ellis Island."

"Oh, uh, I forgot," Yuri fumbled, afraid to tell the man they'd sneaked into the country.

"Well, here, it is no charge." Mr. Rykov took several donuts and pastries out of the display window and arranged them on a plate.

Yuri dropped into a chair at a small round table.

Elena stood and stared out the window. "This America is an incredible place. There are so many people, and they are all dressed in such fine clothing, and there are so many cars. Everyone must be rich."

Mr. Rykov chuckled as he placed the baked goods on the table. "No. Most Americans aren't rich, but some are. These are hard times, and many people are struggling. Still, it's a good life here." He returned to the kitchen, brought back two mugs and a pot of coffee, and filled both mugs. "You enjoy. I'll get my son," he said and disappeared up a flight of stairs just beyond the counter.

Elena sat beside Yuri and took a pastry. Biting into it, sweet red filling squeezed out. She caught the drippings with her finger and said, "This is wonderful. Try it." She offered Yuri a bite.

As he chewed, a smile appeared on his face. "I think I will like living in America." He gulped down a mouthful of coffee and took a donut. "I can hardly believe I'm about to see my sister."

"It has been a long time since she wrote that letter, Yuri. She might not be there anymore."

"If not, we'll look until we find her."

Mr. Rykov returned. "My son will be down in a few minutes. He's finishing some chores." He grabbed a chair from another table and joined them. "So, you just came to this country?"

"Yes, today."

"How did you like the trip through Ellis Island?" The man shuddered. "I hated that."

"Does everyone come through Ellis Island?"

"Yes. That's where you're checked by the doctors and your traveling papers are cleared . . ." Mr. Rykov stared at Yuri. "You didn't come in that way, did you?"

Yuri looked at his coffee, then he met the man's eyes. "No. We were on a freighter."

The man continued to stare and asked, "So, you do not have immigration papers?"

"I thought in America everyone was free and didn't need papers," Elena said, her voice shrill.

"You are free, but all people coming into the country must go through immigration."

"What happens there?"

"Doctors examine you. If you're sick you aren't allowed in right away, and for some conditions people are sent back. After that, officials ask you questions and fill out forms, then your foreign money is exchanged for American dollars."

Yuri took the last bite of donut. "What happens when an immigrant doesn't go through that?"

"You may not be able to find a job. You're breaking the law and could get sent back." Mr. Rykov folded his hands on the table in front of him and looked directly at Yuri. "Did you defect?"

Again, the word grated on Yuri. He looked at Elena, weighing whether or not it was safe to tell the truth. With a sigh, he finally said, "Yes. We worked on a freighter to get here. Then we escaped. We're looking for my sister."

"Will they send us back?" Elena asked.

"Maybe. This is a good country and welcomes immigrants, but right now it's in financial trouble and some people believe immigrants are taking jobs from Americans. So the government arms aren't as wide open as they used to be. But no matter what, you must be cleared to live here. If you report to immigration on your own, your chances of staying should be good. But if you're caught . . ." He shook his head.

"Oh, Yuri," Elena said. "What are we going to do?"

"We'll do the right thing." Yuri took her hand. "Trust God." Shifting his gaze to Mr. Rykov, he said, "First, I must find my sister."

A young boy appeared at the bottom of the stairs and said something to Mr. Rykov in English. "This is my son," the man said. "Andre, I'd like you to meet Yuri Letinov and Elena Oleinik."

The boy nodded and smiled. "It is good to meet you," he said in stumbling Russian.

"We are happy to meet you," Yuri said.

"Andre, I need you to help them find an address."

Yuri handed him the envelope. "This is it," he said, pointing to the return address.

"Oh, Fifth Avenue. I can show you. It's not too far." The boy crossed to the door. "Are you ready?"

Yuri drained his cup and stood. "Yes." He shook Mr. Rykov's hand. "Thank you."

"I'm glad to help. Come back and visit."

Elena ate the last of her second donut. "Thank you. We will." She followed Yuri and the boy out to the street.

Andre walked just ahead of Yuri and Elena. He proudly showed off the neighborhood park and the new shoe store that had just gone in where he planned on shining shoes to make a little extra money. As they turned onto Fifth Avenue, he said, "This is the rich part of town. I don't come here often. Is your sister rich?"

Yuri laughed. "No. She works for someone who is."

Checking the address on the envelope against the addresses of houses, the boy finally stopped and pointed at an enormous home with a tiny yard. Roses grew along a white picket fence, and a red brick walkway led up to a broad front porch. "This is it," he said. "Good luck to you." He tipped his cap a little to one side and smiled broadly. Then, with a wave, he walked back the way they'd come.

Yuri and Elena stood at the gate, uncertain just what to do. Yuri didn't know if it was proper to walk up to the front door of such a fine mansion. Did people do that in America? "If Tatyana is still working here, the only way to find out is to ask," he finally said and unlatched the gate. Pushing it open, he stood to one side while Elena walked through. *This is it,* he thought and followed Elena up the walkway. *Please be here.*

295

A broad staircase led to the front door. Yuri stopped at the bottom and stared up at the top floor of the huge home. A tiny window looked down on the yard and street. "In Tatyana's letter, she said she would sit at her window on the third floor and watch the world go by," Yuri said. "I wonder if that's where she sat when she wrote this."

Taking a deep breath, he grabbed Elena's hand and walked up the staircase. At the large mahogany door, he grabbed the knocker and tapped it against the wood. His heart pummeled and his stomach flip-flopped. He waited. There was no response, so he knocked again, the rap sounding hollow.

Quick, sharp steps sounded from the other side of the door, the knob turned, and the door opened. A tall, thin woman with gray hair pulled into a tight bun and a stern expression stood in the entryway. She looked at Yuri and Elena, then said something in English.

"I am Yuri Letinov. I am looking for my sister. Do you know if she is here?"

The woman stared at Yuri, a quizzical expression on her face. She said something else.

Yuri didn't understand and repeated slowly, "I am Yuri Letinov. I am looking . . ."

The woman held up one hand, rattled off a string of unfamiliar words, then closed the door.

Yuri stared at the knocker. How could he make these people understand?

"Maybe we should get the man at the bakery to help us," Elena suggested.

"He'd probably help if we asked, but he's already done so much. I hate to ask him."

The door opened again, and this time a small woman with brown hair and a smile stood beside the tall, stern woman. "Hello, may I help you?"

"I don't speak English," Yuri said.

"Ah, you are Russian? Mrs. Wikstrom thought so. That's why she called me," the woman said in Russian.

Yuri smiled. "Yes. I am."

"My name is Augusta Broido. It is good to meet you. This is Mrs. Wikstrom. Is there something we can do for you?"

"Yes. I think so. My name is Yuri Letinov, and I'm looking for my sister, Tatyana."

Mrs. Broido's mouth dropped open, and she covered it with one hand. "Yuri! You're alive!" She squeezed her eyes shut and cried, "Praise Jesus!"

"You know about me? Then you must know Tatyana?"

Wearing a bright smile, Augusta said, "Yes. Yes. I know her very well. She married my son."

"She's married?" Joy flooded Yuri. "Is Tatyana here?"

Augusta's smile disappeared. "I'm so sorry, but she moved away. She's lives in Washington State now."

"Washington State? Is that far away?"

"Yes. I'm sorry, but it is."

"How far is it?"

"About two thousand miles, maybe more. I don't know for sure."

Yuri's joy was swept away. He thought he'd found her. How could he travel so far? He had no money.

He felt Elena's hand on his shoulder. "You'll be reunited. God will see to it," she said softly.

CHAPTER 25

YURI LOOKED UP FROM THE postcard and watched Mrs. Wikstrom as she dipped pancake batter out of a bowl and dropped it onto a griddle. He could hear it sizzle and smelled the sweet aroma.

He looked back at the card. What should he say to Tatyana? It had been so long since he'd seen her, and there was so much to say, but the postcard provided little space. His eyes moved across the table, and he found Elena watching him. "I don't know what to tell her."

"Just say we're coming. And that you love her. After we get there, you can talk all you want."

Yuri returned to the card, "My dear Tatyana, I am here in America and will be coming to Washington. Our train leaves the second day of September. I love you and cannot wait until we

299

are reunited. Your brother, Yuri Letinov." His eyes blurred with tears at the thought of seeing her again.

Flora, Augusta's sister, set plates of pancakes and eggs in front of Yuri and Elena. "Mrs. Wikstrom is a wonderful cook. And she made her special pancakes just for you."

"They look good," Elena said, taking a bite. "They taste wonderful. Please tell Mrs. Wikstrom thank you."

"I keep hearing my name," the housekeeper said, "but with all of you speaking Russian, I can't understand a thing you're saying." With a grin, she added, "I think that's a little unfair."

"I said you're a good cook," Flora explained. "And Elena wanted to thank you for the delicious food."

Mrs. Wikstrom smiled. "Thank you, Flora." She looked at Elena. "And you're very welcome. It's good to have you here." She dried her hands on a towel and looked at Flora. "I have beds to strip. I'll leave the dishes for you and Augusta."

Yuri swallowed a bite of egg. "We thank you for your graciousness and the good food. I'm sorry we were late for breakfast."

"Yuri thanks you for your kindness and also for your cooking, and he apologizes for being late to breakfast," Augusta translated.

Mrs. Wikstrom smiled. "Thank you. I'm glad to do it." She walked out of the room.

"You don't need to apologize for being late," Augusta said. "After all you told me last night, you've been through an ordeal and must be exhausted. In fact, I'm concerned about your traveling again so soon. You've been on that ship for weeks, plus all you went through before. It would be good if you could rest a while before taking on another long journey. Mr. Meyers has more than enough room, and he's made it clear you're welcome to stay as long as you want."

Yuri looked at the kind woman. "I know you're probably right, but I can't wait longer. I must see my sister."

Flora filled their glasses with milk and then sat beside Elena. "Yuri, I met Tatyana on the ship when we traveled from Russia. We became friends immediately. She's a dear. When I first saw her, she was so frightened but tried to be brave." She reached across and patted his hand. "She's missed you terribly."

"I feel awful when I think about how scared she must have been making the journey alone and then discovering our uncle was dead. . . ." He straightened slightly. "But I'm still glad I sent her. It would have been horrible if she'd stayed."

"She's a strong girl and held up well," Flora said. "And if I remember correctly, young Dimitri was more than happy to watch over her." She chuckled. "They've been married nearly two years. It's hard to believe."

Yuri shook his head. "My little sister a wife and mother. It seems so strange." He poked the last of his egg, swirled it in yolk remnants, and ate it. "And because of Mr. Meyers's generosity, I'll be able to see her soon."

"He must be a very kind man," Elena said. "It costs a great deal of money for train tickets."

"He is kind, but I remember when he wasn't," Augusta said. "It's amazing what the Lord can do once we give him our life."

"I know." Elena took a drink of milk. "Only a few weeks ago I gave my life to God. He's blessed me in so many ways, and I feel like a different person. It's like putting on glasses and being able to see clearly. For so long I looked at life through my anger and fear."

"The power of God is beyond all comprehension," Augusta said. "The Mr. Meyers we first knew would never have opened his home to us when our apartment building burned, or given Pavel a job, or helped an immigrant couple." She tucked a loose hair in place. "I'm ashamed to say I had judged him harshly. God was much bigger than my small mind." She looked at the young couple and then patted Yuri's cheek. "God does all kinds of miracles. You two are in the midst of one. Yuri, Tatyana

301

thought you were dead. She'd write letters to you every week, trying to believe you were alive, but she was afraid her hopes were only fantasies. Sometimes she'd cry." Augusta's eyes misted. "She will be so happy to get your postcard."

"Could you address it for me?" Yuri asked and handed her the card.

"I will, and I'll drop it in the mailbox for you." She smiled, and her eyes sparkled with joy. "I wish I could be there when she reads it."

Reynold Meyers stepped into the kitchen. He nodded and smiled at his guests. "Augusta, could you tell them I've made an appointment at the immigration office? They'll need to be legal before they can leave for Washington."

Augusta translated, and Yuri asked, "What will happen there? They won't send us back, will they?"

"I don't see why there should be any problem," Mr. Meyers said. "The government is accepting immigrants, and if I understand you correctly, you'll be arrested and probably executed if you return. If that's the case, I'm sure you'll be accepted. And if there's any trouble, I'll just have to pull a few strings." He pushed his fingers into a glove. "You'll have to fill out papers and have a physical examination." He looked from Elena to Yuri. "You are healthy, aren't you?"

Augusta told Yuri and Elena what Mr. Meyers had said, and they both assured him they were healthy.

Flora smiled. "But a little skinny. We'll have to fatten you up a bit before you go roaming across the countryside."

Elena stood and faced Mr. Meyers. "Thank you, sir, for all your help. You have been generous and kind. I'm very grateful."

After Augusta told Mr. Meyers what Elena had said, he nodded and smiled. "I'm glad to help."

Yuri stood and shook their host's hand. "Thank you. We will never forget your generosity."

Again Augusta translated.

CHAPTER 25

"Actually, I owe you," Mr. Meyers said. "It was your sister who helped me find Christ. I can never repay that." He grinned. "Plus, I spent so many years being a scoundrel, I rather enjoy helping people now. It makes me feel good." Turning to leave, he said, "I'll meet you out front."

✵ ✵ ✵ ✵ ✵

Wesley Boseman, the Black Diamond postmaster, pushed his glasses up on his nose and smothered a sneeze. "Blast this dust." He stuffed another envelope into a mail slot, grabbed a handkerchief out of his pocket, and blew his nose. Replacing the handkerchief, he sighed. He was tired of working in this dusty little post office. He'd been a postman for forty years, and nothing ever happened except griping customers, lost mail, and more dust.

He grabbed another stack of mail and began poking envelopes into boxes. When he came across a postcard addressed to Tatyana Broido, he stopped and examined it. He'd always been careful with her mail, knowing it was important to keep an eye out for a possible Communist conspiracy. A person could never be careful enough.

His heart quickened as he looked at the writing. The note was written in a foreign language. *Probably Russian,* he decided. Slicking back the last few remaining hairs on his bald head, he licked his lips and glanced at the outer office, not wanting anyone to discover him reading someone's mail. The lobby was empty. He turned the card over. A picture of the Empire State Building was on the front. He flipped it back over. Tatyana's address was clearly written in English, but the message was foreign. "Why would anyone who can write English compose a message in another language? The person must be hiding something." He stared at the note, trying to decipher the words. "Hmm. This could be something important." Again, he glanced around to make sure he was alone and slipped the postcard into the top desk drawer. He'd make sure the postal inspector got a look at it. He smiled. There might even be a reward involved.

✵ ✵ ✵ ✵ ✵

Yuri watched the countryside flash by the train window. America was bigger than he'd expected. After traveling for four days, they had one more long night left before reaching Washington. He was tired of sitting and staring at parched plains. The miles of dust and dried-up farms reminded him that hardship visited all men. Sorrow settled over him as he considered Russia and the people he'd left behind. *Father, watch over them,* he prayed, wondering what Daniel and Alexander were doing and hoping they were well.

It seemed strange that for so long he'd thought about Tatyana and prayed for her, never knowing her fate, and now after crossing an ocean and a continent, he prayed for his friends on the opposite shore of the Atlantic. *If only I could be close to both,* he thought, but for now he was content just to see his sister. Anticipation swept over him, and his weariness dissolved. He tried to imagine their meeting, but no matter how hard he tried, he couldn't capture the reality of their reunion.

"What are you thinking?" Elena asked. "You look so far away."

He blinked at Elena, trying to bring himself back to the present. "I was far away, thinking about our friends in Russia and about Tatyana."

"I miss Daniel and Tanya. I wish they had joined us."

"Me too. But I wonder what God has for us here. I know he brought me here for more than just Tatyana. He has a plan, but everything feels so unfamiliar; I can't imagine what I'll be doing."

Elena brushed a strand of dark hair off her face. Staring out the window, she continued, "I think now I understand why they stayed."

"I wish they hadn't. I know they're doing God's will, but selfishly I wish they were here with us." He braced his foot on the seat across from him. "I would love to share all of this with them. America is an extraordinary place. And I wish they knew I'd found Tatyana and that I am about to see her." He grinned. "I must admit I'm having trouble remaining calm. I'm very impatient."

Elena smiled. "That's understandable. I'm eager myself, and I've never met her."

"When I was in the work camp and prison, memories of my family were like a fairy tale. As time passed I became confused and sometimes didn't know what had been real and what was a dream." He took a deep breath. "I depended on those memories and the hope of seeing the people I loved again to help see me through those days." He squeezed Elena's hand. "I'm so glad I found you. Here we are in America, traveling on this remarkable train, and I'm about to be reunited with my sister. It's hard to comprehend." He raised Elena's hand to his lips and kissed her fingers. "I have so much to thank God for."

"Me too," Elena said softly.

Yuri sat back, held Elena's hand against his chest, and took a deep breath. "Freedom feels good. When I'd try to think about how it would be, I couldn't imagine. We don't have to carry identification or traveling papers, and we don't have to worry we'll be stopped and questioned, maybe arrested. We can travel wherever we want, work where we want, and live where we want." He smiled. "It's a wonderful thing."

Elena flashed Yuri an embarrassed smile. "For so long I've wanted to be free, but now that there are no obstacles, no constraints, I feel a little lost. I know it sounds crazy, but I'm used to being forced into decisions and now . . . well, I have to make my own choices. It feels peculiar. I'm not used to it."

"I understand," he assured her.

"Aren't you afraid at all?"

Yuri gazed out the window. "Yes. I'm afraid we'll get to Washington and Tatyana won't be there."

*   *   *   *   *

Tatyana set the laundry basket on the ground and rested her hands against the small of her back. Crickets chirped as evening approached. The days were growing shorter, and fall would soon return. She looked at the sky. Wispy clouds stretched across a pale blue background. It was lovely. Smiling, she was reminded of the day they'd gone huckleberry picking the previous year. It had been a wonderful day in the mountains. She looked forward to returning to the meadows filled with flowers and berries. So much had happened. Before, it hadn't felt like home, but now she belonged and wanted to look at the place with her new perspective. She could take in the beauty and know it was hers to enjoy as long as she lived here.

A sudden breeze caught at the clothes on the line. *I better stop daydreaming. I still have to get dinner on,* she thought and unhooked the clothespins holding a flannel shirt. She pressed the soft material to her face and breathed deeply. She liked the fragrance of clean clothes and fresh air. She folded it and placed it in the basket. Next, she unfastened Dimitri's work jeans. They were stiff and unyielding as she folded them.

"Tatyana," she heard in a familiar voice.

With the jeans draped over her arm, she looked up, but saw no one. *I must be imagining things.*

"Tatyana," she heard again.

She whirled around and faced her brother. At first she thought her eyes were lying to her, and she blinked. He was still there. No more than twenty feet from her, Yuri stood smiling at her. A wave of emotions surged through Tatyana, and she felt dizzy. "Yuri?" she asked, her voice barely more than a whisper.

"Yes. I'm here."

"Yuri!"

CHAPTER 25

"I told you I would come."

Dropping the jeans, Tatyana ran to her brother, throwing her arms around him. Clinging to one another, tears of joy coursed down their cheeks, and they repeated each other's names again and again.

Her hands shook as she wiped the wetness from her face, then his. She took a tiny step back. "It's a miracle! How did you get here?"

"I sent you a postcard. Didn't you get it?"

"No."

"I wanted you to know I was coming." He gazed at her. "You've grown up. It's hard to believe the woman I see here is the same little sister I said good-bye to three-and-a-half years ago."

"And you, big brother, have become a man." Tatyana hugged him again. "My dear, dear brother. I can't believe you're here. I thought you were gone forever."

Baby Yuri toddled across the grass and grabbed the hem of his mother's dress. Tatyana picked him up. "This is my son."

Yuri took the little boy's hand. "Hello, there."

"His name is Yuri. When I was little I wanted to be like you, bold and fun-loving. Maybe he will be like you." She held the baby out to her brother. "Yuri, meet your uncle."

Taking the little boy in his arms, Yuri said with a grin, "He's handsome just like me." He turned and looked at Elena and Dimitri, who stood quietly, watching the reunion, tears in their eyes. Carrying the baby, he crossed the yard to Elena and hugged her with one arm. "Now my life is as it should be. Tatyana, this is Elena. We've been comrades since the day I was taken from the farm. We're going to be married."

Tatyana hugged the small woman. "I'm so happy to meet you."

"I feel like I already know you," Elena said. "Yuri has told me so much."

Tatyana linked arms with Dimitri. "This is my husband, Dimitri. He's been watching over me since the first day I arrived in America."

"Your mother told me," Yuri said, extending his hand. "I'm Yuri Letinov, and I'm honored to meet you."

Dimitri patted Yuri on the back. "Just as Elena has said, I feel I know you," he said in imperfect Russian. "Ever since I met Tatyana, she has talked about the brother she left and how one day they would be reunited."

✱ ✱ ✱ ✱ ✱

That night after a meal of roast beef, boiled potatoes, and corn, brother and sister excused themselves from the group and wandered out to the yard. The moon was full, the air cool. It smelled like overripe blackberries and fresh-cut hay. They sat on the damp grass and watched as the first stars appeared.

Tatyana pulled her knees to her chest. "I used to look up at the night sky and wonder if you were looking at it too. I'd try to imagine you staring at the exact same star I was. I knew I was being silly, but it made you seem closer."

"I did gaze at those stars." Yuri plucked a piece of grass. "There was a time when I felt God had forsaken you and I, but a good friend reminded me God was watching over both of us, and I was assured he knew we needed each other."

"Is there no one else left? Mama and Papa never returned?"

"No. And Uncle Alexander was killed just after you left. We were both arrested. He was shot. That's when I met Elena." He took a deep breath. "And the others—I don't know what happened to them, except for Lev and Olga. I heard they were moved to a collective. Everyone else was gone when I last visited the farm."

Yuri reached over and brushed a strand of blonde hair off Tatyana's shoulders. "I'd forgotten how beautiful your hair was.

Mama always thought you were too vain about it, and I remember thinking you were just plain vain." He laughed.

Tatyana leaned against her brother. "I was." She looked up at the moon. "Yuri, are we safe here?"

"Yes. God says no one can snatch us out of his hands." He met his sister's eyes. "He's greater than anything in this world. And we've seen how he watches over us and cares for us. We don't need to be afraid."

Tatyana sighed. "For a long time I yearned for Russia and wanted to return, even though I knew it was dangerous. I felt out of place here, and Russia was my home. Only recently I've come to understand that this is where God planted me and it's where I belong. He knew you would join me," she said with a smile and patted Yuri's arm.

"Tatyana, we're home wherever God places us. Here on earth we're pilgrims, but we will never be homeless as long as we understand our true home is in the heart of Christ."

Tatyana sighed. "Now I understand that I'm home. I have always been; I just didn't know it."